WITHOUT REASON

Kobzar Lizardhands

<u>PROLOGUE: A Warm Night in a Cold World</u>

Friday, 12 February, 2021

There are far too many senseless deaths in this world. A man can go to a bar, get drunk and say something unwise, and next thing you know, murdered. The quick flash of neon on steel, a splash of red, and... well... and that's all I suppose. And those who watch their tongues are no safer, all it takes is a nervous mugger with a weapon or coming home during a robbery. Heck, even looking askance at some unstable moron tweaking on something heavy can set him on a murderous rampage. And wasn't that exactly what they were talking about on the news last night? What a bleak future fortune holds for this world.

When did we become so desensitized to each other—so numb to life itself—that this kind of aberration became tolerated, even expected? Why do people still bother locking eyes with their neighbours when all that can be seen is a coloured ring around empty black. When did we stop looking into *each other's eyes. Far more honest are those whose shifty gazes slide this way and that, never quite catching your own. Or those so nervous their eyes barely leave the ground. The meek truly are worthy of some kind of inheritance for that integrity alone—though certainly not on this Earth. This cold Earth.*

Yes, neighbours make small talk, friends go to dinners, and even complete strangers will often greet one another on the street, but it's all empty. The neighbours are glad to be away, glad to be back in the comfort of their side of the fence, taking refuge behind their own walls.

The friends may truly care, but pointless fears of conducting oneself in an appropriate manner arbitrarily defined as 'normal' far too often prevent any real connection. Time after time, a once-meaningful friendship is reduced to token phone calls and symbolic outings; nothing more than representative visits paying respects to a friendship long-since dead. And all the involved parties are too afraid to move on. Too afraid that this carcass of human connection is the closest they'll ever come to a real human intimacy again.

And the strangers are no better. Sure, fleeting connections are sometimes made, more often in silence than in greeting: just the meeting of two sets of lonely eyes and the strained grasping of two desperate souls reaching for what they know to be a suitable counterpart for human intimacy, any kind of intimacy, only to be gruffly dismissed by a mind too fearful to act on instinct. More often than not, acknowledging nods or words are offered out of fear alone. Eyes meet and smiles flash like the

6

baring of fangs: I'm here and you're here and let's not hurt one another—but no, let us not be friends either, for I could never trust one who brashly bears fangs and leers at me so. And just never mind that I'm doing it right back.

Yes, it is a cold, cold world indeed. Even families, the hallmark of intimacy, are nothing today as they once were. Fathers too nervous flashing fangs with the neighbour, mothers too busy visiting friendships in hospitals, and by the time any kind of parent realizes the wrongs they have committed on their poor children, they're already grown. They are already flashing fangs and paying respects just the same. Of course, should their kids have kids and the now-grandparents try to become involved, such intervention is resisted as fiercely as the grandparents had resisted their own parents' help. And so the cycle is endless.

No wonder there are so, so many pointless deaths in this world. In this world where we each think we walk alone. But reasons are not excuses. And senseless murders just make everything a little colder.

A bleak, cold world indeed.

It was a very noble thing then that Steven Yung, so very tired of shivering, did what he could to make his own part of the world just a little bit warmer. Yes, this murder was far from senseless.

It had been a true friendship—a relationship really—with genuine smiles and real eye contact. He had seen deep within her eyes during their time together. How he loved her eyes. He had continued to look into them until the very end, his sad smile mirrored by her own—still beautiful in its drug-slackened state—even as he opened a matching red grin a few inches below those scarlet lips. He had truly loved her.

Love is what it takes for a murder to mean something. To really mean something.

And that it really had meant something was proven repeatedly as he continued to weep while he painted the sigils around her body. His two fingers busy brushes, dipping in the wound then scraping on the floor. Wound to floor, wound to floor. And the weeping only got worse as he moved on to the walls. This was no graceful shedding of a single tear, nor a poignant stream of them tracking down his cheek, these were ugly, wracking sobs, and his artistry suffered for it. Tears mixed with the blood causing it to run here, his shaking hand obscuring the mark there. To his own critical eye, it was truly a mess. But it was raw, it was real, and that was what mattered. The symbols were, after all, nothing more than symbols, the true meaning came in what they represented.

Returning to the body of his beloved, Steven calmed himself for the final markings he would make. He retrieved his knife from where he had left it next to Vanessa's head, just beyond the blood-painted knotwork that now encircled it. He cut open her blouse from the bottom, going no higher than modesty would allow—he was a gentleman after all—and began carving into her stomach. A nine-pointed star with her navel at its centre. He thought it a far more symmetrical rendering than its counterparts painted on the walls.

Seemingly unable to cry anymore, or perhaps at peace already with the nobility of his mission, he started humming to himself as he moved on to finish the markings on her palms and forearms, her shins and the soles of her feet.

After several minutes, with his preparations finally complete, he knelt at the feet of his lover to pray.

'For love and for peace I have offered this sacrifice. For intimacy and humanity this blood is Yours. All friendships pale before the One True Friend; all loves lie at the feet of the First Love. My Friend, my Lover, my Companion.'

He then dipped the first two fingers of his right hand in the blood pooled at his victim's feet, and on his own forehead traced a nine-pointed star, accentuating each line with a phrase. 'My eyes. My ears. My lips. My touch. My heart. All are with You. All are for You. All are Yours to take. What's mine is your own.' He marked a circle where the nine points met, closing his prayer with the words, 'together we are one.'

It was nearly midnight by the time he was finished. He took off his garbage-bag vest, the clothes underneath, and his gloves, throwing them all unceremoniously into a corner of the room. He dug a set of what would pass as janitorial clothing from his duffle and quickly changed. He then threw the duffle into the corner with the rest of his discarded clothes, took one last look around, and made for the door.

As he switched off the lights in the auditorium, the projection of rotating constellations became visible once more. It was breathtaking in its beauty. *Oh how my Nessie loved to sleep under the stars!* He opened the door and blew her a kiss as he stepped out into the corridor where his custodial cart awaited. The automatic lights took a moment to flicker on, comforting him with the promise of the building's emptiness.

'Goodnight, my sweet Nessie,' Steven whispered as he closed the door gently behind him, blowing one last kiss just before it shut.

Steven stopped in a bathroom to wash off the blood from his arms and face. He departed without worrying about the stains left on the mirror and in the sink. He noted with a slight amusement that it was the women's washroom—*that might stump the authorities for a bit.* There was still plenty of blood caked into his hair, some had stained his sleeves in washing, and he was certain the tone of his hands had not been that ruddy before, but it was dark out and he did not expect to see many people on his way home. And if he did, well, the Friend would protect him. So with a sigh Steven left the bathroom, took the elevator down to the first floor —abandoning the custodial cart inside and sending it back up to the fourth floor as he left—and set out across the university campus towards home.

Outside all was silent but for the wind and Steven's jovial whistling. Peculiar for a university campus barely a month into the term. Just a quiet Friday night where so many students had suddenly found themselves feeling like staying in.

Such was the power of his god.

And how beautiful the stars above are shining, seemingly impervious to the city's light pollution on this particular night. Is this the Friend's personal thanks for my devotion? A display of Your awesome power to reaffirm my faith? Or is it the stars themselves, whose alignment tonight is so special. Lust and Comfort, Honesty, Fidelity, Empathy, Devotion, Generosity, Gratitude, and Cooperation, the nine virtues of friendship as embodied by the Friend's constellation. A nexus of stars wherein it is said my god sits, as if atop a celestial throne. Each of those stars now equidistant from the central star representing Love.

Or rather, a central cluster of stars, as Vanessa had shown him earlier in that auditorium. He knew some of his brothers and sisters would not be happy to learn that, but the symbolism was nothing more than empty images to make devotion easier for the weak of faith. Besides, he had always thought their nine-pointed star constellation looked more like a wheel anyway.

Nine spokes of equal support round a central hub representing nothing less than the greatest virtue of all: love. Sure a star shines bright, and light is perhaps representative enough for disciples of weaker gods, but a wheel rolls over obstructions in its path. And my god is no small wheel.

But for all the power of that god, his walk home was not completely uneventful. At the very edge of campus, as he whistled his way past a large building, its well-lit interior making it possible to see into the tinted windows, Steven Yung noticed two young girls. Seeing them running about and waving frantically, his breath caught for a moment, thinking they had seen him and noticed the blood from afar. As he got closer however, squinting to see through the partially obstructed windows, he saw that they were not waving at him, but were dancing.

The campus's actual janitors, apparently: two young women, one mopping the floor, the other wiping tables, and both dancing as if without a care for the security cameras or possible passers-by. Steven could hear the music and their laughter faintly from outside the windowed wall, and though he attempted to pass the building unnoticed, it was evidently bright enough outside for them to see him as well. At catching sight of him the two girls froze and looked to each other, mouths open in surprise. Steven turned away and kept walking, a nervous sweat beginning to warm his forehead.

Both girls then broke into convulsions of laughter and, apparently unaware the man they looked at was covered in blood, offered him a friendly wave. Muttering a silent thanks to his god, Steven returned the wave with a smile and continued on his way.

Friend embrace me! Did you see it in their gazes? When they looked at each other before resuming their hysterics? There was warmth in that look. A life to it. Yes, my god sends me a sign. Intimacy is returning! Humanity can be saved!

It is a warm night indeed!

And with a new spring in his step, Steven Yung smiled the whole way home, fangs bared and glistening eyes leering at every shadow that moved.

PART I: Rivers Will Rise

Verse is a wave:
Rising, cresting, falling,
Troughing

Forget iamb and rhyme
Verse is only about time
The rise, the fall, the rhythm.

So drag those sibilant syllables.
Long and slow.
And feel the rhythm.

There is nothing but time:
Just the fall and the rise,
The rise, the fall, the rhythm.

Take in the hypnotic sound,
The waves breaking on shore,
And drift off with the rhythm

And let this be your song.
Let it be your siren call.
That life is nothing but rhythm.

And then shake your head—
Shake it violently—
Break!
The rhythm!
And wake up!
Angrily!

Because verse is governed by no laws
Verse is about choice.
Life is choice
So fear not the consequences
Of looking life's laws in the eyes
And spitting!

Verse is a Wave
\- Roman Kalichka

CHAPTER ONE: Darko Feels Tired

Monday, 15 February 2021

Darko Richovsky awoke with a start. Seated, arms crossed, and alone in the now-empty lecture hall where his class had finished half an hour before, it took a moment for the young student to orient himself. Collecting the papers on the small table in front of him, covered more in doodles than actual notes, he was amazed, and more than a little concerned, that he had somehow slept through not only most of the class, but everyone leaving it as well. His sleeping had been all over the place since his return from the Christmas break, but lately it was getting out of hand.

With a sigh, he stood up and stretched. Before he even reached the apex of the stretch, his vision blurred and he braced himself for the oncoming dizzy spell. His single free hand placed on a chair in the row below was not enough this time and, mind moving too slowly to react, his legs gave out beneath him. The rapid shift in weight pitched him forward and sideways, his books left his other hand as instinct had him reaching to the floor to absorb the impact. Too slow.

To his benefit, the tight quarters of the aisle slowed his fall as his backpack caught on one of the tables, but his strengthless hands did little more than slap the tiles before his head cracked against the floor.

Though never actually losing consciousness, his thoughts were distorted during these head rushes. Distant, yet somehow sharper, more intense. Seemingly trapped with a focus on whatever wayward strand of thought crossed his mind at that precise moment. And for no logical reason he could determine, this particular head rush had filled his mind with an image of the Clearwater River.

The edges of the image were a blurred, swirling distortion, but the centre was sharp, vivid as a dream. Three faces, female, beautiful. They lay just beneath the surface of the water, the current rushing past in a thin film, unbroken by the features of those faces. Their eyes were open and Darko felt as if he was somehow only millimetres from each face simultaneously. The moving water made no sound, the banks of the river were nowhere to be seen, but these details went unnoticed. Somehow Darko knew the river, knew the precise location— not far from the footbridge he took when walking to and from the University. As one, the three women opened their mouths and spoke in perfect unison. Their voices were silent, yet Darko heard what they said in his own internal voice, as if talking to himself.

'Rivers will rise,' he said.

And suddenly he was slipping back to his present state, his awareness expanding to take in the fact that he had fallen, hit his head. A moment later the pain came, almost comically slow, first the sting of his hand that had slapped the floor, then his head. *Crap, that hurts!*

A side-effect of his sleep-deprivation—one of several and none healthy—Darko had dealt with the increasing dangers of these head rushes as he did all his problems: by ignoring them. If he refused to acknowledge these concerns, they could not trouble him. He had a list the length of his arm of things not troubling him: sleep deprivation, a worsening cough, a building student debt, an undeclared major despite being nearly halfway through his second year—and never mind those steadily-dropping grades—the list could go on… if he let it. And so he did not let it, did not even think about letting it.

Darko felt for blood, afraid to move. His hand felt no wetness, only a bump large enough to displace some hair. He got up once more, slowly this time and, as he collected his things, his phone started vibrating. He glanced at the caller ID: RANDY BAUER. He started out for the Student Union Building as he answered.

'Hey, what's up?'

'Hello Darko. Where are you? We said we were going to meet at one o'clock and it's already nearly half-past. Maria is already here with myself and we have been waiting for a while. We were just wondering if you are still coming to meet us for lunch.'

Randy always sounded so formal on the phone, the disconnect from his in-person parlance rather amusing to those who knew him well. As soon as Randy stopped to wait for an answer, Darko could hear a girl's laughter in the background. *No doubt Maria laughing at Randy's strange affectation of phone-speech.* A laughter Darko repeated internally.

'Yeah, sorry. On my way now.' The clarity of Darko's speech seemed to diminish of its own accord, as if to make up for the formality of Randy's, careful to maintain the natural balance of conversations that took place in person.

'Just got caught up talking to some classmates.' The lie came easily to Darko. He did not want to worry his friends any more about his sleep deprivation. He should never have told them about it in the first place. And they would have no way of knowing that he had barely spoken to a single classmate all semester. In fact, his list of friends was quickly shortening to include only these two childhood companions. And he feared if he was not careful, he would lose them as well.

'Well, please do not tarry overlong, we are eager to discuss the weekend's tragedy with you. We were hoping your brother might have heard tell of what happened through his police friends.'

Darko could not keep his laughter inside this time. '*Tarry overlong,*' '*heard tell?*' *Sometimes you have to be pretending!* Maria's laughter rang again through the other end of the phone.

Darko had reached the SU building, 'I hate to disappoint you, but I haven't heard a thing.

'Anyways, like I said, I'm on my way to you now, so we'll talk in a bit.' He hung up without waiting for a response.

As Darko made his way up the stairs to the food court, he noticed he had four unread messages. One from Maria and Randy each, sent half an hour ago asking where he was, one from his sister asking him if she should bring anything when she came over to dinner tomorrow, and one very weird message from his brother.

Even getting a message from Demir was something of a rarity; the man had never really progressed to the text-messaging era. It was just something he was not comfortable with. If he wanted something he would call, unless very specific circumstances restricted him from doing so. If getting a text from Demir was not odd enough, the contents of the message certainly were: **Darko. I need you and Ana to come to dinner on Wednesday. We have a lot to talk about.**

Jeez! If any kind of text needed a phone call this was it! Now I'm gonna be worried about you for the next two days, Demir, you ass.

As troubling as the message was, Darko's habit of ignoring his troubles seemed to take over true to practiced form, pushing thoughts of the text away the moment he spotted his friends at their usual table by the corner windows. Darko had truly not meant to push this particular worry aside, his family, after all, was one of the few things he did not need to struggle to feel passionate about. But habits have a way of gaining control, and so thoughts of the text were hurriedly buried away.

Seeing him from afar, Maria and Randy began waving, their warm smiles eliciting his own goofy grin.

'Darko! How's your day going? We hope you don't mind, but we sort of decided for you,' Maria said, gesturing to the large pizza and three drinks already on the table.

'Thanks guys. The day's been great, but better now. I mean, you can never go wrong with pizza.' Sitting down in the seat they had saved for him, Darko reached for the drink Randy pushed his way, still beaming like a fool, and was surprised to taste Root Beer. A taste of their childhood friendship. Sharing Root Beers while their parents enjoyed the non-root form of the drink out in his father's fields after an afternoon of hard work. *A simpler time. A nicer one too.*

The three of them enjoyed their lunch with a bit of small talk and a pointless, if entertaining, discussion of what a land-squid might look like. Once the pizza had been polished off and the land-squid issue back-burnered, Maria settled deep into her chair, planted her chin in her hands and her elbows on her knees, and looked to Darko with an expectant, 'So…?'

He sighed heavily. *Tell me again why you wanted to major in criminology? No, on second thought, if I have to sit through another telling of the case of ten year-old Detective Maria foiling a kidnapping, I'll puke this pizza right back up on this table. You do know criminology deals with crimes that have already been committed, right? You won't be able to ride the high of saving some girl's life forever.*

As bleak and unfair as he knew his own outlook to be, Darko could not shake the belief that a major in criminology would lead to a wholly unsatisfying life—not that he had come up with the nerve to declare his own major yet.

With a fresh sigh, Darko pulled out his laptop and settled a little deeper into his own seat, preparing for a long conversation.

'Like I said, I haven't *heard* anything. But I did happen to catch a glimpse of something in Derek's notepad when I was visiting my brother on the weekend.' Darko clicked on a sketching programme and waited for it to open.

'Sorry, which one's Derek again, is he the giant, or his little runt of a partner?' Randy had met both of Demir's police friends several times, but never seemed capable of keeping their identities straight.

'Derek Woods would be the giant. And Donald Philips is still five-four, and could kick your ass,' Darko responded with a laugh.

'I remember like this: Officer Woods is tall, like trees, and Philips is short, like... I don't know, a screwdriver?' Maria blushed slightly as both boys laughed at her analogy. Having loaded the desired programme, Darko set his laptop on the table and turned it to face his friends.

'Ok, so this is what I saw. Derek pulled out his notepad to mark some reference book titles my brother was giving him, and this was on the open page with "cultic" and a question mark written at the top. I was standing behind him and could see it clearly. He even stopped and looked like he was about to show Demir for a second before he flipped to a new page. I only saw it for maybe ten seconds, but I remember it pretty well, and drew up a sketch to try to find something online.'

On the screen was a nine-pointed star with a central dot from which the nine lines extended. It was rendered in the centre of a palm, and on the wrist and forearm snaked some lines of artistic knotwork. There was nothing overly remarkable about the knotwork, it was just two intertwining lines that seemed to start in loops at the base of the wrist and snake upwards along the forearm beyond the page.

'Hang on,' said Maria. 'How do you even know this is related to the murder?'

'Didn't you hear the news? They said the body and the room had been all marked up with cultic symbols. *Cultic,* Maria!' Randy was getting excited as he always did when they discussed crime —sometimes alarmingly so. But Darko had known Randy since before he had started preschool, and he knew Randy was more terrified of crime than he was interested in it. He hated to even leave his house after dark. Which made him a bit of a shut-in during these winter months. But Randy put on a bravado for his friends that had just been accepted as a natural human response. There had been no calling him out on it, no questioning his motive, or offering to exclude him. It had simply been accepted as one aspect of their group dynamic.

'Ok, ok, fair enough, but it's not like that's their only case, and who's to say some other case didn't involve cultic symbols? Or maybe it's some gang graffiti which they entertained as possibly being cultic. All I'm saying, is that we can't be sure it's related to this case.'

'Maria's right,' said Darko. 'But at this point it's all we've got. And I've got to say, I found nothing online that really corresponds. There's plenty about nine-pointed stars across several religious and cultic groups, but nothing really rendered like this, as simple lines from a circle. And nothing with the knotwork as well. So I guess until we find something else, this is it for now.'

The other two sighed; Maria out of a resignation that patience would be required, and Randy out of a relief that he had temporarily been saved from being plunged into another amateur criminal investigation. As Darko packed away his laptop, and their conversation once more fell to the topic of the land-squid, which by this point had somehow become a giant land-squid capable of wearing combat boots, Darko could feel a sleepiness settling in again. He decided that, given his episode this morning, he would skip his afternoon classes and try to get some rest at home.

The time neared 3:00 and the three friends said their goodbyes. Darko made sure to stand up as slowly as possible, keeping his head down and pretending to be looking in his bag for something. If he had another collapsing dizzy spell in front of his friends, they would make him seek medical help. He only swayed a little, his mind flashing briefly to the river again and the same three faces, before the dizziness subsided and he was able to stand completely.

After making plans to meet for lunch again on Friday, the three friends departed. Maria left for the Business Building, where they were hosting the classes traditionally held in the Sciences Centre. The SC was entirely closed off to the public as a result of the ongoing police investigation. Randy made his way alongside her for an actual Business class in the same building.

Making as if for the Humanities Building for his General History course, Darko ducked outside along the way, out of sight of his friends. Feet set on his home, and mind set on his bed, Darko left the campus.

Darko's walk home was usually about 45 minutes, the majority of it spent among the beauty of the the river valley, a large stretch of protected nature that cut through the centre of the city. Darko had always revelled in this walk. Though the bus could get him home in twenty minutes, he much preferred this extended route.

The small woods on either side of the river, and the intertwining, unpaved paths reminded him of his childhood. Before his dad had died, the man would take Darko and his two siblings for walks in the woods on the family farm. The faint smell of pine sap, the crunching of slightly frozen leaves and other forest debris, the whisper of the wind rattling branches and causing old trees to creak and groan, it all took him back to a time gone too soon. A happier, carefree time. Or at least a time when what cares there were had been trivial.

As he mused on his childhood, trying to remember a particular walk when his father had taken them to one of the many branches of this same river, Darko began to stray from his usual route. He turned left far earlier than normal, moving off the main path down one of the many thinner, lesser-used paths. This one likely made by animals, or those more exploratory walkers. Off to his left he spotted a few tents—homeless people often set up little camps in the valley as it was technically under Park Ranger rather than City Police jurisdiction, and the former were more empathetic to their plight. He idly turned away from those tents, mind wandering as carelessly as his feet, continuing down the valley for some time.

With a start, Darko stopped himself only a couple paces short of a sharp bank that would have taken him right into the river. High above and to the left, he could see the street bridge that spanned the valley, the sounds of traffic echoing loudly on the water. More immediately to his right, through a copse of trees that leaned over the embankment, he could see the footbridge only a few minutes' walk away. And directly before him, along the dark loam that made up the steep embankment, Darko noted with a concerned curiosity a bed of flowers, their bright orange petals a stark contrast to the bare grey earth from which they had sprung.

Since when do flowers grow in February? Sure the February thaw has been warmer than usual this year, but everything will freeze again in less than a month. There's still snow on the ground!

Looking up towards the river, Darko recognised this location as the setting of his head-rush-induced vision. His breath suddenly catching in his chest, Darko noticed three young women, roughly his age, sitting on the opposite bank—which was also covered in little orange flowers—watching him.

Their faces matched those from his vision. Their long, summer dresses, each with a variant floral pattern, extended to their ankles and there the hem floated in the water above their bare feet which rested in river. They should have been freezing, even with the full-length sleeves of their dresses, yet they looked absolutely comfortable where they sat. The middle one, her golden hair shimmering as if slightly damp, suddenly called his name.

'Darko.'

The word rang out in a sing-song voice, flowing smoother than the course of the river below, her Slavic accent as comforting as the voice of his deceased father, and, for a moment, Darko thought to swim across that cold river to the three lovely women and their sure-to-be welcoming embrace. Quickly regaining his senses, Darko recognized them from stories told by his father in his childhood, and read from dusty books in his youth: rusalky.

River spirits in Slavic folk belief, similar to the mermaids of Western European lore, but less… fishy. Rusalky were supposedly responsible for the fertility of both the land and its inhabitants. It was a common form for the departed souls of unmarried girls to take, particularly those who had suffered violent deaths. Darko had never seen one in person, indeed had doubted their very existence, and had expected them, if real after all, to appear far more ethereal.

Though Romanticism and the jumbling of various beliefs under the appropriation of Folk Studies had left rusalky associated with the kidnapping and drowning of young boys, Darko's father had explained that the creatures were primarily concerned with crop growth and helping women to bear children. He had told Darko that a rusalka would normally only ever kill one man in her lifetime, one who would then become her husband in his afterlife.

'*A chance to wed in the afterlife as recompense for dying so young,*' his father had explained, thinking the whole thing rather romantic.

'*Still a murder,*' Darko had insisted. *And an awful lot to bank on 'normally.'*

Looking directly at the one who had spoken, Darko smiled and said, 'You can save your heart for another. I'll wait for a warmer day before taking a swim.'

To his confusion the three smiling faces across the river changed to expressions of shock. The one on the right spoke, 'How is it that you can see us? Or hear us? Our calls should be audible to your subconscious alone.'

Darko had no answer, and as the three women lowered themselves gracefully into the water he grew uncomfortable, taking a few steps back from the riverbank and hanging on to a sturdy tree just in case they tried something. They disappeared beneath the water across from him, and the river was too deep, too murky to see anything. Darko considered leaving, but before he could reach a decision, three faces emerged from the water immediately below, and three forms rose in tandem until they appeared to stand on the water itself, their heads now level with the top of the embankment. Their dresses were completely dry.

'This one has power,' spoke one.

'Our kind of power,' said another, seeming to emphasize that first word.

'Yet this is not the one we seek,' the first again.

'The other is far more powerful,' said the third.

'But not of *our* power,' emphasized the second again.

Darko was completely lost. He had no idea what they were speaking of. He knew his family was unlike other families—at least his father's side. His father had shown many times his ability to control that local branch of the Clearwater in the woods on their farm, changing its course to water the crops and livestock or diverting the flow during floods. He had explained to Darko and his siblings that even their name, Richovsky, was one given by peers of their ancestors who had recognized the abilities of their family, and their power with rivers. Though his father had died not long after those lessons, Demir had tried to carry on their father's explanations of the world. Demir's lessons had always seemed far closer to fairy-tales than the reality that they had lived before their father's passing.

Maybe I have some of the power that Tato had. Though Darko had never displayed any ability to control water as a child, he had always thought the potential for such power was innate.

Looking down at the three faces below him— and weren't they beautiful faces—words seemed to rise to his lips on their own, interrupting the golden-haired rusalka as she began to speak once more.

'Rivers will rise.' He was not sure why he said that. Or why he now looked down at the three expectantly, as if he had just imparted some great wisdom. But to his surprise, it seemed he had.

'This one is right.'

'This one is wise.'

'Perhaps this one should be sought over the Newcomer.'

Darko made to interject, to ask for an explanation, but as he opened his mouth the golden-haired one—clearly some kind of leader of the three—cut him off with a raised hand. 'No. You are right, you have convinced us. We shall not seek the Other just yet. But be warned, Riverspawn, you are still weak, and far less appealing to us than the Newcomer. We will not wait long.'

With that, the three began to descend simultaneously into the water once more, and Darko did not think they would resurface this time. Still not knowing what she spoke of, but unexplainably fiercely jealous that this so-called Newcomer was potentially more appealing to the women than he was, Darko blurted out the first thing to come to mind. He grasped for any scrap of knowledge on rusalky he had, and for some kind of defensive remark to save face in light of how the conversation was ending. He recalled of an old Slavic tale about a musician who had encountered a rusalka princess: 'Well you're no Volkhova yourself.'

The golden-haired rusalka looked up at him once more and simply smiled; her two dark-haired counterparts fixed him with frowns. Somehow all three looks were offensive.

As they slipped beneath the surface with hardly a ripple, Darko suddenly had a dozen burning questions for his brother who, by virtue of being older, would surely remember more of their dad's knowledge of otherworldly beings.

Darko jogged the rest of the way home, pausing only briefly on the footbridge to look once more at the river. It was enough to bring on a sudden and intense longing for those beautiful faces.

CHAPTER TWO: Ana Rides the Bus

Tuesday, 16 February 2021

With a sigh she buried her head in her locker, hoping Stephanie would leave her be. Alas, the older girl pressed through the throng of students crowding the hallway eager to be on their way home. Stephanie continued her prying as if their conversation had not been interrupted by the hundreds of kids separating them since the bell rang. She shouted to be heard.

'But you were there weren't you, Snizhana? On Friday night? You were working when it happened, right?' Stephanie Horowitz was annoyingly energetic, even for 3:00 on a school-day afternoon. And Snizhana Richovsky had endured the girl's pestering questions during every quiet moment for the past eighty minutes. Her patience had come to an end.

'It's *Ana*!' Snizhana managed to growl back without a physical retaliation. She hated her full name. There was a reason hundred-year-old names remained hundreds of years old—*it's because nobody likes them!*

Only her parents had insisted on not using the shortened form of her name. Even for all her indignation, from a very young age, her father would just laugh, calling her Ana a few times before forgetting and reverting back to her full name. Him she understood, he had picked the name after all, so he had probably liked it—though why her mother had assented she would never know. But there was absolutely no reason for anyone else, especially Stephanie, not to use Ana. *She probably just wants to remind everyone, for the hundredth time, that she's fluent in three languages and knows how to pronounce a foreign name.*

Luckily for Stephanie's loud and as-yet unbruised mouth, Milana stepped in.

'Yeah we were working. But we don't normally clean in the Sciences Centre. We actually don't even know the other janitors, really. Just our boss, but he only does groundskeeping stuff. Outside and during the day mostly. So, hate to disappoint, but we didn't see or hear a thing.' Ana locked eyes with Milana for the briefest of moments in a silent thank you, and smiled at Stephanie as a small peace offering. She actually kind of liked Stephanie, but she hated her own name more than she valued that tenuous friendship.

The three of them took the same bus into the city five days a week and, as much as Stephanie could annoy her from time to time, Ana would rather not have another thirty-minute bus ride squished between Milana and Stephanie in icy silence. *Though… come to think of it, the last time that happened had been Stephanie's fault too.*

Stephanie was talkative. And positive. The exact combination that, when making herself the topic of conversation, made every other person in earshot feel inadequate in every way. In reality, Stephanie had just been lucky. Unnaturally so. Now isn't that a childish thought. Stephanie had been recruited as the Marketing Vice President in some fancy up-and-coming company out of a buffet line last fall. One of those seemingly ordinary and completely unpredictable happenstances that could change someone's life forever.

The three girls left their school behind. They were, predictably, the only students to board the Acton-bound city bus and filed to their usual spot at the very back.

Fine, Stephanie, you can have your unnatural luck and vice presidency, and I'll take my painful self-awareness of what a bitter person I am, and we'll all be fine so long as we both keep our mouths shut about it.

'So,' Milana asked as the three of them settled into their seats, graciously bringing Ana out of a state of self-pity before it began, 'any more crazy stories from your job, Steph?' Ana could not help but smile at Milana's question. Stephanie hated being called Steph.

It was a comforting thought to Ana that her best friend was willing to sink to new lows just to have her back. Of course, being the perfect person that she was, Stephanie simply ignored the use of her hated nickname as if anything that pointedly rude simply could not have happened.

'Nothing nearly as crazy as that New Year's scavenger hunt, but for Valentines' Day we've started doing this "friendship" thing where we were all assigned a supposed virtue of friendship and we have to find out who has the same virtue without letting them know. The winner of every pair apparently gets to be their loser's direct supervisor for a year! It seemed like fun at first, but the stakes are way too high. Everyone wants to beat their opponent, so no one is letting anyone else know what virtue they've got. It's a bit ridiculous to be honest, at this rate it'll be next Valentine's Day before we find out, and by then it'll be too late to boss anyone around.'

She finished the sentence with a laugh, but a certain gleam in Stephanie's eyes prompted Ana to pry, 'Oh? And who would you like to boss around?' Stephanie had talked about the hunks at her work plenty of times since starting her job back in November, and her answering smile confirmed Ana's guess.

Ana couldn't help but smile herself, maybe even out of genuine happiness for Stephanie. Though, more likely, she decided, at a sense that even Stephanie, under her crown of perfection, shared the same adolescent weakness for crushes as the rest of them. *It's a little bit adorable.*

'So, what virtue did you get?' Milana continued prying.

Stephanie hesitated at Milana's question and, after a moment, stumbled over her answer, 'Umm, well... Actually... Okay, this is going to seem weird, but I really want to win, and—it's not that I don't trust you guys—its just that, what if someone else on the bus knows someone from work, or you say it somewhere by accident and someone finds out and—'

Milana saved Stephanie from further rambling—and from turning any more red. 'Hey, it's okay. I was just curious. You really don't have to tell us.' For all her comforting gestures and friendliness, Milana shot Ana the kind of look that could only be interpreted as a thoroughly astounded, *what the hell?!*

As put-together as Stephanie seemed, she could be inordinately fragile sometimes. Ana had always taken Stephanie's occasional fragility as just some act to get the attention of boys, but the more she got to know Stephanie on these bus rides, the more human the girl actually seemed.

Strange how that happens when you get to know someone. Ana couldn't help but laugh internally at her own sarcasm. She never thought she would be one to display the "frenemy" behaviour she so despised seeing in others. *Even that word is like a rusty nail in the temple!*

A buzzing from her backpack reminded Ana that she hadn't checked her messages since lunch. Figuring there was a lull in conversation anyway, she decided it would not be rude to read her texts. There were three from Milana: a comical picture and two messages continuing their ongoing conversation about plans for the upcoming weekend.

One message was from her work saying not to come in this week as police investigations were underway—her boss had already called to tell her as much on Monday morning. Instead of the usual school-judo-work schedule for Tuesdays and Thursdays that made every day in between an experiment in how well one could hide the symptoms of exhaustion from one's overly-concerned—and frankly overly-nosy—teachers, this week's work-days were going to be replaced with a dinner with her brother tonight, and one with Stephanie and her relatives on Thursday.

The last message was from her brother, Darko, replying to confirm their dinner plans for later tonight. As she scrolled, she paused on the strange message she had gotten from Demir the day before.

Ana. I need you and Darko to come to dinner on Wednesday. We have a lot to talk about.

She had meant to call Demir yesterday and ask about it, but calculus homework had kept her up past midnight. She considered calling him from the bus, but no, she wouldn't be able to hear him over the noise of the bus anyway.

Stephanie closed up after her weird outburst and though some conversation was exchanged over the next twenty minutes it took to get to her stop, it was stilted and shallow, the kind where you forget what you said the moment the words leave your mouth. *So much for avoiding another awkward bus ride.* Not that Ana really felt like talking either. Though she tried, she couldn't imagine what Demir's message might be about, but the more she thought about it, the more it worried her.

Even after they said their goodbyes to Stephanie, Ana and Milana remained locked in their respective introspective fugues, not saying a word. Both got off the bus a little dazed, and neither moved for some time.

Standing at their stop watching the bus roll away, Ana finally roused herself back to life.

'Hey, Milana, wake up, look around you, dummy. We're here!' If the shouting didn't help, the shaking certainly did.

'Did you just call me dummy?' There was a playful, yet threatening edge to the question.

Ana just offered a coy smile, followed by a deft side-stepping of the punch that swung for her arm.

They began making their way to the Faculty Services building to look at the courses that had already been announced for next year. Neither of them had been accepted yet of course, and they weren't even sure if there would be an opportunity for electives in their first year, as they had already spent hours tailoring their course loads in preparation for vet school, but even dreaming of the possibilities was exciting. And Ana looked forward to being able to flaunt her knowledge of university courses her brother had doubtlessly never heard of as an added bonus.

Ana had been walking a full arms-length away from her friend, just in case the girl got any ideas about retrying that punch. She let her guard down as she held open the door to Faculty Services and was rewarded with a thank-you jab to the arm. The edge of Milana's fist hit an older bruise, its lingering sting a reminder to Ana that she should probably stop saying things that led to Milana hitting her.

Milana opened the second door for Ana, offering her arm for a reciprocal punch as well, one Ana declined with a smile. *It's nice to be the moral superior once in a while.*

'I was thinking,' Milana began, as they made their way up the stairs to FS-41, the room with a full course catalogue posted along the walls. 'Since we're here anyway, we could probably squeeze in a class between judo and heading to your brother's.'

That is truly a tempting offer.

Ana and Milana had decided over the Summer, when they got their jobs as night janitors at the University, to sit in on as many classes as possible in preparation for the following year. Any question of immorality in doing so—as Stephanie had been quick to point out when they offered to bring her to one such class—was greatly eclipsed by the lies on their resumes that had gotten them the jobs in the first place, and was therefore deemed negligible.

'You know we can't, Milana. You've seen how out of it Darko can be. We're going as much to make sure he isn't starving as to visit him.' They both laughed at that as they arrived at FS-41, where they were quickly awed to silence by the sight of the room.

Though Darko had described it to them, neither had been fully expecting what lay before them. Apparently some past project of the Faculty of Design, one updated constantly by the current students, the empty lecture theatre was a battlefield of colours, shapes, and—*is that a piano hanging from the ceiling?!*

42

From FINE ARTS, scrawled in a bright green cursive above the door they came in, to COMPUTER SCIENCES in a black, digital font on the floor where rows of seats should have been, the entire room was covered in the school's course catalogue. Ana could not believe they had never been here before. The details of the MUSIC department hung from the ceiling next to the piano in cardboard cut-outs, and would have been impossible to read without binoculars or a very tall ladder—both of which were offered beneath a small legend framed just under the room's clock.

Though it was certainly a stunning sight, the room's information was scattered in the sort of pandemonious chaos only an art student could have conceived—let alone thought would be useful for any individual with an actual interest in learning something from the information in the room. The handful of kids down in the corner by EAST ASIAN STUDIES looked like they might have entered the room hours ago—not that they could even tell, with the room's only clock painted over in details about the required courses for double majoring in Engineering and Business.

Ana had a feeling they were going to be late for judo.

CHAPTER THREE: Darko Wakes from a Nap

Tuesday, 16 February 2021

Who sleeps till three in the afternoon? You've gotta be kidding me!

Adding to his sleep problems over the past month and a half, Darko occasionally had compensatory sleeps—like the 22-hour one he had woken from not an hour earlier. This was the fourth such sleep, and the longest so far. They seemed to come out of nowhere and, worst of all, he never felt particularly better-rested after such a sleep. If anything, Darko felt groggier than normal. At least, that's the rationalization he made for himself for having left home without his phone or backpack.

They were both right there! I just texted Ana and grabbed them, and left.

Except... I didn't grab them.

How could I not have grabbed them?

He had rushed out the door to the bus stop, hoping that by taking the bus he might catch the tail-end of his last class but, realizing on the ride that he had forgotten his backpack, he decided it simply wasn't worth going. Not that he had a habit of taking notes in Philosophy anyway, but the absence of the backpack was enough to convince

44

himself he would not gain anything by going. The thought that his loss of interest in the class—once his favourite of the semester—might be a symptom of a larger problem was quickly pushed down along with the absence of his backpack and phone as Darko looked for something to occupy his time before heading home to prepare supper for his sister and her friend.

Crap, I'll need to buy groceries too.

Deciding he'd better start heading home right away to be able to grab groceries and find a recipe suitable for impressing his sister, or at least for keeping her off his back, Darko made his way back toward the bus stop.

On his way he thought he might have seen his sister entering the FS building. *But no, that couldn't be her, she doesn't even work today. She's only in the city for judo tonight isn't she? Jeez, I've got to pay more attention when she tells me her plans.*

He decided it wasn't worth potentially harassing some stranger just to say hi, but during his internal debate, the bus he had meant to take pulled away. It would take about the same amount of time waiting for the next bus as walking so, thinking the walk might help wake him up a little, Darko headed for the river.

It was just off of campus, as Darko left the paved walkway onto one of the many packed-earth paths spidering through the river valley, when he realized he was being followed. Though it made Darko uneasy, it was not exactly a matter of concern, even with man muttering to himself and the half-empty bottle's drops of something-darker-than-water pitting what was left of the snowbank to the side of the path. Who was he to judge some homeless guy for being drunk this early in the afternoon—he had only just woken up after all.

Though the river valley was a beauteous, peaceful reprieve from the stark artificiality of the city surrounding it, its tranquility was occasionally marred by some of its squatters. Setting up camps in the forested areas allowed the city's homeless to evade harassment by local police by virtue of the valley being under the jurisdiction of national park authorities. Authorities who had their hands full preventing idiotic tourists from feeding themselves to the bears, and therefore had little care for a few people with tents just trying to make ends meet. And aside from the occasional violent incident, the only complaints were from the Council concerning so-called *visual pollution* of the valley.

On principal alone, Darko had been in full support of the river valley's homeless camps. That was until Maria showed him that the so-called *occasional* incidents of physical and sexual assault were literally taking place on a daily basis—all thought to be caused by no more than a dozen or so of the valley's denizens.

Darko turned abruptly down one path, then another, sweat began to bead beneath the brim of his toque, as the man continued following him after each unpredictable turn. Not one to jump to conclusions—*there are several reasons a scruffy-looking man might be muttering to himself half-drunk, and walking uncomfortably close behind a stranger on a secluded river valley path, right?—* Darko kept on walking, forcing himself to remain calm.

The man was practically stepping on his heels now, and though he couldn't make out a single word, Darko was sure the muttering was angry, and possibly even directed at him. Darko stopped trail-hopping, sticking only to the main path in hopes of coming across another person, someone to dissuade the muttering maniac from trying anything violent. Darko did not fear being mugged—he had been mugged twice before—but he was afraid to find out what the already-angry man might do upon discovering Darko had no wallet on him. No phone either, not even so much as a watch. In fact, the coat he was wearing was the most expensive thing on him, and he was not about to give that up—*it's supposed to drop to twenty below on the weekend.*

Before he knew it, the footbridge was before him. The river was frozen solid along the banks, with disks of pancake ice floating downstream in the quickened current of the river's narrowed flow.

Suddenly forgetting all about the angry man on his heels, Darko came to an abrupt halt. *Wasn't the river completely unfrozen yesterday? Did I* actually *see rusalky here?!*

I must have dreamt it in that involuntary coma-nap. But no, they're there now…

In a dreamlike haze, the image of three faces just beneath a thin surface of water rose before him. But they were not in the river, he could see the river flowing before him, not a rusalka to be seen. They rose before him, a perfect mirroring of his head rush-induced vision from the day before. They took up his entire field of view, obscuring his vision, and leaving him suddenly weak in the knees.

Those weak knees buckled.

The faces loomed, increasing in opacity, blocking out all other stimuli. The voices of the women rang out in unison even though their mouths remained unmoving.

Rivers.

The voices stroked like silk, yet struck like steel. From some place far away, Darko sensed himself laying sprawled on the ground. He had the faintest sensation of his foot being kicked by the scruffy, muttering man. A man whose presence went completely out of Darko's mind as the rusalky continued speaking.

Will.

The voices were overwhelming, not out of volume, but out of some kind of oppressive weight. The edges of his vision, which moments before held firm to the scene that actually lay before him, were now filled with shadows. The shadows raced around like arcs of electricity threatening to bring on a migraine that would bring Darko to his knees had he not already been sprawled like a corpse at the edge of the footbridge.

RISE!

Darko felt his hands rise to grip his hair, pressing hard against his ears, as that last syllable continued to ring, deafening. Crushing.

Darko was faintly aware of the bottle falling from the man's hand, like a green spear slicing through the vision of the three women which rippled in its passing. The spear lanced down in slow motion, its wake obscuring Darko's vision and replacing it, not with clarity, but with pain. A wounded voice cried out in audible imitation of what Darko felt in his head, and he was not even sure if it was his own.

The shadows on the edges of Darko's vision closed in, obscuring the still-rippling faces of the two flanking women, leaving only that of not-

Volkhova, whose eyes were painfully burning a hole in his skull—specifically above his right eye where, somewhere, some part of him was aware of green glass breaking on impact.

As glass and beer splashed across his face and chest, Darko came to, the arcing shadows taking over his vision completely, a coruscating play of darkness and light.

Ever so slowly, the darkness dissipated into a watery version of his surroundings. Darko sat up, wiping beer from his eyes and brushing shattered glass from his jacket. The maybe-homeless drunk who had been kicking at his foot a moment ago was nowhere to be seen.

What was to be seen, was far more shocking.

Stark naked before Darko stood a man beaming with possibly the most genuinely inviting smile Darko had ever seen. Alarmed, and not entirely sure this wasn't another one of his dizziness-induced episodes, Darko clambered to his feet, backing several steps away from the man as he did so, and offered shakily with an unbidden blush, 'Can I help you?'

Smiling even deeper—if such a thing were even possible—the man made his way closer to Darko in a walk that could only be described as...
pendulous.

'Hello, Friend.' His voice was warm and surprisingly deep for a man as lean and short as he was. Darko could not help but smile in response as the man continued, 'Good to see you up and about. But come, your head is bleeding. We must take you to get it bandaged. It looks like a small enough cut, but head wounds are nothing to take lightly.'

Still somewhat suspicious at the sudden presence of the naked man—though such suspicion was surely unfairly prejudiced on his state of undress—yet not wanting to seem rude, Darko took the man's outstretched hand, but did not advance when the man began moving.

'I think I'll be fine on my own. Thank you, Sir.' Even as he said those words, Darko did not completely believe them. This man was obviously so concerned over Darko, that he came to help without even bothering to dress first. And refusing the help of a man so concerned as to risk frostbite in normally-unfrostbitten places would simply be too rude.

Besides, who could say no to such a kind smile?

Before Darko could take back his refusal, the mysterious naked man took matters into his own hands.

'Nonsense.' The man moved closer, and though Darko was sure he should feel embarrassed, or at least uncomfortable with the arm suddenly around his waist, and…other parts… swinging dangerously close, Darko hardly took notice of it. 'We must make sure you are taken to safety.'

And as the man tried once more to depart, this time his waist-entangled arm pushing Darko along firmly, something stopped Darko from moving. Some thought or voice rang in his head, just beyond grasping. So he stood firmly in place, trying to focus on that one slippery idea in his mind. Trying to not let it escape.

He did not notice the man's warm smile turn to a glare, did not notice as the man's naked human form seemed to shimmer in and out of perceptibility, becoming ethereal, then material once more. So intent was Darko on retrieving his lost thought, that he did not even notice his own stolid resistance as the strange man moved behind Darko and with grunting effort tried to force him into motion with two hands. The man then took to trying to drive Darko forward with a shoulder, using his entire bodyweight. Still he did not budge.

The faint wind in the air seemed to have more of a physical impact on Darko than all this man's considerable efforts.

At last, Darko gripped that elusive thought. Or scene rather, as something that complex had to be more than a single thought. *Rivers will rise* he told himself as the image of a beautiful, water-covered face filled his mind, two similar faces flanking it, somewhat obscured by his inability to concentrate.

Didn't I just have a recurrence of that scene moments ago? Isn't there a missing homeless man who caused it? And shouldn't his unexplained absence concern me? Moreover, shouldn't the sudden appearance and extreme closeness of this naked man concern me? Naked?!

'WHAT THE F—' Darko cut off his own question as he spun, fist leading, to face the strange man.

The naked one was quick though, and he had been prepared for a retaliation, knowing from the first moment of Darko's hesitation that there might be trouble. Most of the race of folk would have obeyed him with nary a second thought. Clearly this boy was no ordinary human.

The naked man, who was not a man at all, ducked the blow even as he veered into his true form. Shadows coalesced where he had once stood. A thickly textured cloud of darkness, it almost seemed a palpable form. Yet Darko's strike was much faster than the beast had anticipated. Faster, even, than the creature's transformation, and Darko's swinging fist connected with the edge of the its jaw less than a heartbeat before it dissipated into shadow.

The shadowy cloud hung stunned in the air for a moment, another fist striking harmlessly through it, before it dispersed into invisibility. Its many tendrils snaked into the surrounding natural shadows, jumping from one to another, back up the path and away from the footbridge.

A rather stunned Darko shakily took a few steps onto the bridge before steadying himself against the handrail, mind reeling.

Not far away, deeper into small woods along the edge of the river and out of sight of Darko, the man that was not a man began to gather himself. From tendrils of shadow hiding in the shade of a rock here and a tree there, a darkness began to take shape. This time the creature sembled into a roughly-humanoid figure, its lower half seeming to bleed into the natural shadows on the ground. Four matching forms sembled before him, and if anger could be discerned by the wreathing of darkness like flames upon the brows of these beings, then those four were enraged.

Through hisses, clicks, and a sound like that of crackling leaves, the four older wraiths made their displeasure at the youngest's failure plain. The drunk man's soul had been safe enough to devour —there had been little resistance left in the man's mind whether he was drunk or not—but the four others knew their limits.

As soon as the boy had started to wake, Shiloksa's brother's had fled. They had yet to make their bid to the Newcomer, and could not risk being caught feeding in grounds that probably belonged to the Newcomer—or would soon enough. But Shiloksa was young, eager to prove himself, and now he had proven himself foolish. That he had been so easily resisted meant that the five of them had just made a powerful enemy and, as it would put them in a weak bargaining position with the Newcomer, it was an enemy they could ill afford.

Darko's breathing had only just returned to a normal rate, his mind only just stopped questioning its own sanity, and his legs only just regained their strength beneath him, when shadows began to fill the edges of his vision once more. This time they were not accompanied by any psychedelic vision and, though they were far darker and raced far more furiously than the last instance, they were accompanied by no dizziness, no threat of migraine. In a rare moment of perfect clarity, Darko made the connection to the naked man and his shadow-self.

Bracing for the man's return, Darko stepped back off the bridge and began searching among the nearby trees and undergrowth for a stick, a large piece of that broken bottle, any sort of weapon he could use.

There. Not far from the foot of the bridge, along the river's edge was a long stick of driftwood, roughly the length of a broom handle. He slid down the steep bank, and onto the frozen edges of the river. One foot punched through ice and into frigid water as he did so.

Damn! It's gonna be a cold walk home.

Looking back up to the path, just above the steep embankment, Darko saw not one shadowy form coalesce, but five.

And none were naked.

Had he imagined that part?

Their forms seemed somewhere between shadow and physical. His eyes struggled to focus on them, sliding off toward the surrounding shadows whenever he tried to concentrate on any single form. Half-panicking, Darko wondered if he would even be able to harm them in their current manifestations. He stooped to quickly pick up the driftwood, he would brandish it as a staff and hit anything that came close. He would not let these things take him easily.

As he lifted the driftwood from the ground, the dried and cracked stick simply snapped in half.

Fuck!

Five vaguely humanoid bodies of shadowy darkness began to approach the lip of the bank above, cutting off his route to the bridge as angry hisses and clicks sounded between them, darting from one to another. They loomed at least seven-feet tall and every shadow in sight seemed to sway, as if pulled by some magnetism, toward these creatures. Darko backed as close to the river as the frozen section would allow, debating whether to run for it or to try swimming away. Hadn't he once read that wraiths were not able to cross running water? *If these even are wraiths. Or maybe that's vampires I'm thinking of...*

The five figures converged at the ridge of the embankment, their torsos and heads looming forward over the edge toward him. Darko stepped back, his foot plunging into the cold river once again. But somehow rather than responding with alarm, that icy wetness seemed to calm him.

The cold did not seem to matter so much this time. After all, it was a cold day, and the water was really not that different from the air.

And that air is actually more bracing than cold, come to think of it.

And as his next deep inhale brought a lungful of resolve close to his heart, it brought with it a faintly floral scent as comforting as the current swirling round his legs. The sound of the water too, brought a tranquility, and that steady, soft flow of the river now seemed to be roaring in his skull, waves rolling furiously like the firing of synapses in his mind—he could think his way out of this. He took another step back so both legs were firmly shin-deep in the river, and faced the five wraiths with a newfound courage.

He knew, instinctively, that he would not be able to outrun these living shadows, and he was unsure if he could physically harm them—unless they took the shape of naked men, and *surely* he had only imagined that part. But he knew he had been able to repel one by simply resisting him—punching him aside—so perhaps, if he didn't collapse in some weird vision again, he could repel them all with his mind alone.

Go away. I command you to be gone.

The five shapes seemed to hesitate.

Darko was not really sure what to think. As he stood his ground in the river, he imagined punching the shades, their shadowy limbs exploding on impact. He pictured them dissolving into shadowy puddles to be stepped on and squished back into darkened, unmoving reflections of the world around them. And, unbidden, Darko imagined the faces of not-Volkhova and her two friends. *Such beautiful faces.*

The five shapes moved forward. *Ok, maybe they're not hesitating.*

Like a wave, the five forms seemed to flow down the embankment. And suddenly they were within arms reach. And not stopping.

Darko should have been screaming. He should have been diving away into the river and swimming frantically to the other side. Or he should have taken notice that the lower halves of the shades which had before been one with shadows on the ground, now formed human-like legs in this unshaded area of the shore. He knew his mind should have been thinking of something else—anything else. But the only image in his mind was that of those three pretty faces of not-Volkhova and her friends. He smiled.

Their words rose in his head like a song, *rivers will rise,* pulsing in time with the blood rushing in his ears. To his right, the edge of his vision began to ripple and writhe in blue and white, like a giant, frosty wave was about to crash down across his sight.

The shades suddenly halted, outstretched arms of shadow remained hanging in the air. Clawed, tenebrous hands, hanging menacingly mid-swing above Darko's head. They did not retreat, but they appeared panicked. Their clicking and hissing began again, sounding frantic.

The large wave that had been building at the edge of Darko's vision now seemed to hang, ready to crash down. Yet it waited. And suddenly Darko realized those shadowy heads were no longer pointing in his direction, but off to his right.

Risking a quick glance, Darko looked to see another form standing in the river—three forms in fact. He did not have to turn completely to know that it must be not-Volkhova and her friends. After all, in the kind of day where he was accosted by a drunk, a naked man, and five shadow-things, how could it *not* be those rusalky?

Darko could not decide whether or not he should be happy to see them. Of course he would be more than happy to look at them—if these pesky shadow-people would just leave him alone long enough to steal a glance. But a not-insignificant part of him still feared those women might drag him under the river to murder him. And for all the hesitation they had caused in the wraiths, they did not seem to be getting involved any further. It would not take long for the wraiths to realize that.

Chancing a second look at the girls, this one long enough to see not-Volkhova with her arms crossed and looking directly at him with that beautiful smi—*is she frowning? Why is she frowning? What did I do?* This time he turned his head far enough to see a swirling waterspout just behind his right shoulder.

Jumping in surprise, Darko nearly lost his footing as the loose river rocks rolled about underfoot. He knew instinctively that the wave in his vision was a representation of that same water spout and, though he could not say how, he knew he had created it.

He considered willing it forward, to make that wave in his vision fall upon the shades before him and send those shadows retreating back into the dark forest behind them. But, not entirely sure how he had created it, Darko doubted he would be able to control it well enough to hit anything. And the more he thought about that towering spout of water just over his shoulder, the more he feared he might accidentally release it too early and knock himself face-first onto the shore to get a mouthful of ice, rock, and sand.

Maybe he would use his mind to get rid of these wraiths after all.

Turning his full attention to those towering shadows once more—using all his concentration not to let his gaze slide to the right where a far more appealing sight might be found—he was shocked at his own lack of fear now in facing these creatures. Their outstretched arms and clawing hands had retracted, and were now reserved for frantic gesturing as the five hissed and clicked among themselves in argument, heads swivelling from Darko, to the rusalky, to each other.

Darko cleared his throat pointedly but still the senseless chatter continued.

'Hey!' Darko shouted and then almost wilted as those five shadowy, heads turned to regard him with their eyeless gazes. Almost.

'Mark my words, Wraiths—' he sure hoped they were wraiths after calling them that— 'rivers will rise.' He was completely winging this, he did not even have a clue what that phrase meant, but it seemed to be a theme over the past couple days, so he was hoping it would work again. He faked a stern confidence in his words that no doubt helped create an impression on the wraiths. He just wished he actually felt some of that confidence himself.

'This will be your only warning. Don't make my friends get involved.' He gestured with his head toward the three rusalky, nearly breaking his resolve not to look at them in the process. 'If you think of terrorizing anyone along this river again, I will not be as merciful.' He gestured with his eyes up over his shoulder and to his surprise the wraiths physically reeled, as if they had only now become aware of that towering cyclone of water. They scrambled back up to the crest of the embankment with none of the deadly grace that had so marked their menacing descent. *How did they not see it? That spout is like ten feet high.*

The smallest of the forms, apparently regaining some of its lost courage, turned and began a slow advance to the crest, looming over its edge toward Darko once again. The other four clicked and hissed furiously behind him. Just as the one looked as though he were about to drop down the embankment and charge for Darko once more, a sharp hiss from one wraith silenced them all, and four sets of dark, ethereal arms clawed the fifth form away from the edge. All five dissipated then, their shadowy tendrils dispersing in a retreat that left all trace of them gone in a heartbeat.

Darko turned, unable to keep the grin from his face, to face the rusalky. He was careful to step back onto the shore as he did so. *Maybe they only kill one man in their lifetime, but why take a chance that that man isn't me?*

The three rusalky had waded closer and now stood less than ten paces away, the river level up to their waists. Beneath the surface of the river, their summer dresses were magnified by refracting light, their floral prints swaying about with the current. Above the water, those dresses seemed bone-dry. The three continued to approach Darko slowly, hips swaying sinuously just beneath the water, hands dragging this way and that across the surface, seeming to direct the river's currents as they did so.

Darko did not say a word. After how confusingly their conversation had gone yesterday, he decided he would let them do most of the talking.

Between Darko and the rusalky his water spout still towered, water surging as it swirled violently, threatening to rain destruction on any who dared cross him. He was not exactly sure how to make it go away.

The three women came to a stop in line with that water spout. Not-Volkhova looked to it, then to him, raising an eyebrow. 'Now you would threaten us? With… water?'

Darko's cheeks grew hot as the other two rusalky began snickering. He had to regain some kind of control in this conversation before it derailed completely.

'It worked on the wraiths. You don't seem that much scarier to me.'

Not-Volkhova frowned. 'I thought you had called them wraiths. Those were not wraiths, Riverspawn, they were impa shilup.

'A common enough misconception I suppose, but wraiths are dead shadows of the once-living; impa shilup have never died. They are souls corrupted into immortality by cruelty and darkness. And an intelligent being would have killed them.'

'I didn't see you stepping up to help out' Darko retorted defensively. He could barely keep up with what she was saying. He had never even heard of an impa shimpa before—*that is what she called them, isn't it?* He desperately needed to ask Demir about all of this.

'Do not be upset Darko,' the rusalka closer to the still-raging water spout spoke, 'we told you we will not declare for the Newcomer.'

'Yet.' Added not-Volkhova, unimpressed.

'As agreed,' said the third, 'We will wait.'

'We will wait,' repeated not-Volkhova.

And as mysteriously as they had arrived, suddenly all three were slipping back beneath the surface of the water. The colours of their floral dresses continued swirling beneath the surface for a few moments more before they too disappeared, and all trace of them was gone.

Standing alone, with the water-spout towering over him, Darko suddenly felt much colder. That conversation had not gone as he had hoped.

At least they didn't realize I have no control over this water tornado.

As he turned to make his way up the embankment once more, the water spout came crashing down. The force of the water shot him forward, splayed up against that steep embankment, before clawing him roughly back across the rocky shore, the thin strip of ice, and into the gelid waters of the Clearwater River.

Gasping for air, Darko clawed his way back onto the shore. Soaked clothes weighing him down heavily. A fire began burning hot in Darko's chest.

Who the hell are these impa shimpa—or whatever the hell they're called?! Why the hell was that one naked?! Those damned rusalky had better stop following me! Or else just drown me already!

I should've stayed in bed.

Darko did not exactly have a clear plan in his head. His clothes were soaked through, the wind was picking up on a day that was already far from warm, and there was only about another hour of sunlight left on this February afternoon. Yet, consumed as he was by a sudden, indignant anger, Darko was not phased by these minor setbacks. After clawing his way up the embankment, slick with a fresh layer of water that was fast turning to frozen mud, he began scouring every shadow for signs of the impa shilup.

He could not be sure if it was just in his own messed-up vision, or if it was actually visible, but Darko noticed that some of the surrounding shadows seemed to *bleed.* Like water flowing down a channel, the shadows seemed to drip, leaving clear signs of the winding path the impa shilup had taken away from the bridge. There was no way of discerning the five separate shadow-trails that the creatures had left, but all seemed to be moving in the same direction.

So it was with a measure of difficulty that Darko followed the trail up, out of the valley. Here there was a clear split in paths with four tracks of bleeding shadows turning right and a single trail breaking off to the left. Reasoning that one would be easier to confront than four, Darko gave pursuit, across the street, through an alley, and down an unfamiliar road.

CHAPTER FOUR: Brother Darko and Sister Ana Have Supper

Tuesday, 16 February 2021

Ana and Milana got off the bus only a block from Darko's apartment shortly before 7:00. They were early. So engrossed had they been in the university's famous course-catalogue room, that they had completely missed judo practice and decided to head straight over instead.

Ana's brother lived in one of rougher neighbourhoods of the city, so the two girls sacrificed the speed of the back alley for the safety of the main road. The lack of painted lines on the road and the burnt-out streetlamp overhead might have marked the street as abandoned in other cities, but Acton was not exactly known for its up-kept infrastructure. Despite the darkness of the street and the shady group of men lounging outside one of the run-down duplexes on the block, Ana did not feel particularly unsafe making her way to Darko's. It was only one block after all. Besides, she had always sort of wanted to apply her judo in a real-world setting. Just… hopefully a not-too-dangerous one.

Keeping an eye on her surroundings—at the very least she should be looking out for Milana—

Ana began idly speculating what Darko might have planned for supper.

What if he has no food. Should we have brought something? Maybe some snacks at least. Or some kind of side dish?

Greybrick House was an aptly-named building. Well, other than the house part. It was a squat, three-story apartment block, each floor housing four apartments except for the top floor, where a fire years before and the resulting partially-collapsed roof had closed the northeast unit permanently. Darko lived directly beneath that unit, and on more than one occasion when visiting, Ana could have sworn she heard footsteps coming from the supposedly-abandoned room above.

As they approached the steps leading up to the main landing, Milana moved in close and gripped Ana's arm hard. Turning her head to see the cause of her friend's alarm, Ana heard the scrape of feet on pavement before she saw anything. The group of men who had been lounging around outside one of the duplexes had begun moving toward them. Though there was still a good hundred metres between them, it was clear that the two girls, or at least the building they stood in front of, marked their destination.

Ana decided she did not want to try applying what she had learnt in judo after all. She jammed the buzzer for Darko's apartment and began rummaging through her backpack for that spare key Darko had given her a year before, just in case.

'Hurry,' Milana whispered loudly in her ear.

Flinching from the tickling of Milana's hot breath in her ear, Ana's fingers touched something cold and metallic. Glancing back over her shoulder as she pulled out the key, Ana saw the group of men crossing the street toward them.

There were five of them, looking rather thick in what seemed like far too many layers of coats, hats, and scarves, and they strode with a singular purpose toward the two girls.

Milana snatched the key from Ana's hands and quickly unlocked the apartment door. Pulling Ana in after her, she turned around and shut the door to ensure it locked behind them, and continued dragging Ana towards the stairwell.

Resisting her friend's pulling, Ana stood her ground at the edge of the stairwell, crouching down and zipping her bag shut as she watched the four men approach the door. They did not appear to be speaking to one another, but each was sporting an almost comical grin, shining teeth a brilliant contrast to their darkly-stubbled faces. One cupped his hands to the glass door, peering into the building, eyes locking on Ana's. Another tried the door and, finding it locked, began knocking gently.

'Let's go, Ana.' There was an edge of fear in her friend's voice, '*Please!*'

Ana felt affronted that these men should be harassing them so. She had had her fair share with rougher types growing up in Oak Creek but Milana, though she too had grown up in the same town, was a far gentler person. And Ana would not let anyone —*not anyone*—make her friend feel uncomfortable. Part of her wished those men would come in, so she could beat some common courtesy into them.

Her own violent thoughts were alarming. After all, Milana would not feel any safer if those men came inside. She was not sure where the fire within had come from, but she pushed it down with more rational thinking.

We're inside, we're safe. Let's go see Darko.

She stood up, ready to head up the stairs with Milana, when one of the four tried the door again and, with a soft *click*, it opened for him.

Spinning hurriedly, Ana grabbed her friend's arm and dragged her bounding up the steps. Milana pulled Ana to the side just in time to avoid colliding with an elderly man coming down the stairs. Ana had not even noticed him.

He gave the two girls a warm smile despite the fact that they had nearly trampled him and continued his slow, purposeful descent to the landing. The man was about Ana's height, but looked far shorter for his sunken shoulders and bent frame. The frosty wisps covering on his pate seemed to dance in the air above his head, as if a static was drawing them to the ceiling far overhead.

Something about his presence immediately calmed Ana. The man looked infinitely at home as he descended the last stair onto the landing, as if he had spent every one of his considerable years in this building. And Ana found herself following the man down the stairs, Milana's resisting pull keeping her a few steps behind.

Coming around the edge of the stairs into the entryway, Ana saw the five men, halfway to the stairs, suddenly halt mid-step and hesitate uneasily before the old man.

'You are not welcome in this building.' His voice was stern, threatening even, yet somehow impossibly friendly all the same.

For all their menace in chasing the girls here, the hard features of the five men he confronted somehow seemed to melt then. Severe jaws receded into softness, patchy stubble gave way to handsome shadows, and all at once the five men seemed possessed of some preternatural charm, their leering smiles now enchanting

'Good evening, Sir.' The tallest of the five men took a step forward as he greeted the man, marking himself as some kind of leader of the group. 'I promise we won't be long. We're new in town and just here to visit a friend.'

Ana knew she should not believe them, knew that they almost certainly had some nefarious designs on getting to herself and Milana. And yet, she started to doubt her readiness to jump to conclusions regarding their desires. After all, could they not just be here to meet a friend? Who was she to judge? *Can there truly be deception behind such kind eyes?*

Milana too stepped down next to Ana and seemed to be second-guessing herself as she watched the exchange unfold between these five handsome gentlemen and the old man.

'I will not repeat myself. Leave.' The elderly man seemed unperturbed by the transformation of the five, their suddenly gentle eyes and kind demeanours. And for a moment, Ana felt a twinge of sadness for the man's rejection of them. The scene seemed frozen, the men before them unmoving, matched in a battle of wills: homely warmth against charming kindness.

It was a short battle.

The elderly man took a single step forward and the wills of the five before him seemed to evaporate as, in terror, they scrambled over one another out the door and down the street beyond.

Ana's doubts over their intentions disappeared with the first of them out the door, and she was suddenly very grateful for, and not the least bit frightened by, the old man's intervention.

'Th-thank you.' Milana managed to squeak out, echoing Ana's own internal sentiment.

'Not a problem, my dears. Now, you'd best be on your way, your brother's company will not keep themselves.' And with that, the man opened the evidently-unlocked door of the nearest apartment, and stepped within. The door shut, followed by audible clicking and scraping as it locked behind him.

I've never met him before, have I? Darko must have told him we were coming. Maybe Darko saw us from the window and sent the man to help. But how was that old guy supposed to be more help than Darko?!

Ana could not fathom what it was about the little old man that had frightened away the younger and tougher men with nothing but a few threatening words and a single step forward. Her suspicious thoughts were interrupted.

'You didn't mention Maria and Randy were coming.' Milana half-asked about the company the old man had mentioned as the two began their ascent up the stairs for the second time. This ascent far more relaxed.

'I honestly didn't know.' Ana responded. She thought it was weird that Maria didn't text her, the older girl was usually elated to see her and Milana. *But who else could it be? It's not like Darko has made any new friends since he got to university. At least none close enough to bring home or tell anyone about.*

Milana stopped by the door, rapped on it sharply, and offered Ana the key back.

'We let ourselves into the building, we might as well let ourselves in here.' Ana took her key back and opened the door to her brother's apartment. She took a deep whiff as she swung that door open, testing the air for whatever excuse for supper her brother had whipped up. But rather than the smell of cooking food, she was met with a pleasantly floral scent.

Kinda feminine, but at least this place doesn't stink like garbage and man-sweat.

Swinging the door open fully, Ana was shocked to see not Randy and Maria but, rather, two strikingly-beautiful women in summer dresses. One was leaning casually against the kitchen counter, flipping through a binder of Darko's school notes—which Ana could see from here were made up more of sketches than actual notes. The other lounged in Darko's armchair, engrossed in one of her brother's textbooks. She looked up at

Ana and Milana frozen in the doorway and raised a single questioning eyebrow.

'Why hello,' The one from the counter offered, her voice as soft as the features of her face and as friendly as those wide, disarming eyes. The faintly-Slavic accent was comforting to Ana, reminding her of her father.

'We're friends of Darko's,' the stranger continued, walking to the door, and gesturing for the girls to come inside. 'I'm Rosalia, and this is my sister Omelja. Please, join us.'

Ana stood in stunned silence until a gentle push from Milana rocked her into motion. Stepping into the room, she shook Rosalia's offered hand and, feeling skin that was somehow softer than that silken voice, Ana found herself short of breath, her attempted introduction coming out as nothing more than a sigh and pitchy squeak.

Milana took over introductions as Ana just stood and stared. Suspicion at strangers in her brother's home or at her brother's absence did not even cross her mind. In fact, staring as she was in her slack-jawed silence, very little did. There was one powerful, incredulous thought however, one that repeated over and over. *Why the hell are you friends with my brother?!*

He had followed the trail of bleeding shadows back through the river valley paths, up to the university campus, across the city's main bridge to the north side of the Clearwater, and deep into the city's downtown core. As the sun dipped lower and the shadows grew longer, the trail became increasingly harder to read. Darko lost it there in the heart of the city, where the shadows of three towering business complexes darkened every street for several blocks on every side.

He did not know if the impa shilup's destination was somewhere near that area or if the creature had discovered its pursuit and sought to lose Darko among the shadows of narrow alleys and towering skyscrapers. He had followed the trail at a half-jog for more than an hour, his determination allowing to go unnoticed that, in place of a hypothermic chill, his soaked clothes had turned warm, keeping him comfortable and energetic in his pursuit. Now, with the trail vanished and the adrenaline of indignation sapped away by the fruitlessness of his hunt, Darko suddenly felt exhausted.

Dissatisfied, grumpy, and once more beginning to question his sanity, Darko began making his way home when it dawned on him that he had completely forgotten about his sister coming for supper. It was nearly seven, and the closest grocery store was a fifteen minute walk away, his home another fifteen from there.

It was in that grocery store, freezing his hands as he grabbed whatever fast-cooking items he could from the freezer aisle, where Darko began to suspect that the hunter had become the hunted. A figure peered from the edges of every aisle, floated behind the checkout line, and made his way, unburdened by any purchases out the doors and down the sidewalk after Darko.

The figure was wrapped up in a heavy winter coat, hood pinned up and obscuring his face. The ski-pants and oversized gloves reminded Darko of some baba over-prepared for winter. Though his eyes did linger enviously on those gloves for a moment.

To his pursuer's credit, the movements were just natural enough, the path just coincidental enough, that it took Darko until the end of the next street before he was convinced he was indeed being followed—and by that time, he was beginning to panic.

The figure seemed too short to be an impa shilup in human form—not to mention overdressed—and though Darko thought he could surely outrun his pursuer, dressed as he was in thick winter clothing, to do so would mean leaving the groceries behind. He was already going to be late to meet his sister, and he was not about to show up empty-handed on top of that.

So, rounding the corner only two-blocks from home, Darko suddenly broke into a run across the street. Disobeying the traffic lights, he zipped perfectly through a break in honking vehicles, and began walking up the street, away from his home. The squealing of tires and a fresh chorus of angry honking from behind marked the continued pursuit.

He spotted a middle-aged couple emerging from a parked car and walking up to one of the nearby apartment buildings. Slowing down to prevent arousing suspicion, he tucked his bags into one hand and opened the first door for the couple, offering a friendly smile as they walked by. He followed them into the entrance and, stepping ahead of them once more he pulled his keys out of his pocket, pretending to fumble with them.

'Sure is cold out there today, I think my milk froze on the way home.' His light-hearted laughter seemed to disarm the couple who, until now, had been regarding him somewhat cautiously.

Continuing his charade with the keys, he pretended the bulk of his groceries caused him to drop them clumsily. Just as he stooped to retrieve them, he let one of the bags slip through his fingers. 'Whoops! Sorry about that, I'll have this door opened for you in just a sec.'

'Don't worry about it, dear, we'll get that for you.' The woman pulled out her own keys and opened the door for him, allowing Darko to enter first. The man's frowning stare seemed unconvinced by Darko's clumsiness but he made no move to stop the boy.

'Thank you so much. I guess my stomach's bigger than my muscles ha ha.' Darko grabbed his things and moved into the apartment's lobby with another smile. The wife offered a friendly laugh in response and Darko felt his face growing warm as the husband stood his ground in the entrance, frown deepening.

A little sorry for tricking them, but not wanting to wait around long enough for them to change their minds, Darko made for the two corridors flanking the elevator. He moved down the one marked with a sign for the garbage room and breathed a sigh of relief as he heard the click of the door locking shut behind the couple.

The hallway forked, Darko darted left, hoping for the best. Just then he heard a loud, incessant pounding from back the way he had come, followed by a man's booming voice, 'we can't let every stray in! Leave that one to grab his own keys and go find the boy!' The knocking grew louder as Darko reached a back door, opening it to a dark alley just as a great crashing of glass came up the hall behind him.

He did not wait to find out if his follower would discern the route he took or if the couple was now giving chase as well. Orienting himself in the alleyway, Darko set off at a run and, despite his burdening groceries, he sustained the pace for the full two blocks home.

Ensuring the door locked behind him and risking one last look into the dark and empty street, Darko allowed himself a moment to catch his breath. He glanced at his watch and, seeing that it was already after seven, rushed up the stairs to his apartment.

As he rounded the first flight he nearly sent an old man flying. The man was also climbing the stairs and, apparently struggling with arthritis or some other age-induced frailty, was taking his sweet time about it.

'Oh please, go around me son.' Despite the friendly offer, the man continued gripping both the hand rails and did not make any effort to provide room for Darko to pass.

With a sigh, Darko struggled to contain his frustrations. It was not the old man's fault he was late, after all.

He managed to keep the frustration from his voice—mostly. 'No, no, that's fine. Go ahead. Please.'

Darko hardly knew the faces of the other tenants, let alone their names, yet he was fairly confident he had never seen this man before. He was on the short side to begin with, and the stooping posture put the two almost at a height despite Darko being a step below him. Wispy strands of snowy hair sporadically dotted the man's otherwise-bald head. Those ghostly filaments stood erect, seeming to flicker like candlelight in some imperceptible wind, straining for the ceiling high above.

He used the time waiting for the man to ascend the flight to fully recover his breath and wipe some of the sweat from his face. As impatient as he was to make it to his apartment and get to making supper before his sister arrived, Darko could not help but feel a pang of sympathy for the man's plight, living as he was on an upper floor of an old apartment building with no elevators. He thought to ask after the man's name, but, self-conscious of his still-unsteady breathing, Darko held his tongue.

After what seemed like two full minutes, the man had ascended the flight and, as he rounded the corner to continue his way to the top floor, Darko rushed past him to his own apartment.

He stepped in to an unexpected and, quite frankly, panic-inducing scene. Four women sat at his kitchen table, so deep in conversation they had not noticed him opening the door. His sister and her friend's early arrival he could understand, but the two women in summer dresses, he could not. A faint but pleasant floral scent reached him, and he knew who they were without needing to see their faces.

'Uh…hello?' Was the most eloquent greeting he could manage, and he felt his ears grow hot as four pairs of eyes turned to regard him. He walked to the kitchen and began to unload his bags to avoid those piercing gazes.

'You're late,' one of the rusalky accused.

'And too reckless,' the other added, her tone equally hard.

'And I'm hungry,' Milana added, jokingly.

'And you brought food!' His sister's joyous tone was enough for Darko's heart to slow a little, his ears cool from volcanic to merely scorching.

'Yes I brought food. And I have enough for everyone.' He turned on the oven and unpackaged the frozen pizzas he had bought.

Do they even eat food? I would have home-cooked something for Ana's sake if these rusalky hadn't been here. But, given the circumstances I'm sure she'll understand. That is, if I ever get a chance to fill her in on the circumstances without these damned river bitches stalking me.

Darko was about to offer drinks to everyone when the door opened. He turned to see the overly-winterized figure who had been following him. One sleeve of that winter coat was torn away, the arm underneath soaked in blood.

'You!' he shouted, grabbing a kitchen knife and positioning himself between the man and the table where his sister sat.

Liquid laughter flowed from within the darkness of that hood. A woman's laughter, serene and completely disarming. She lowered the hood to reveal herself as not-Volkhova, her blonde hair spilling out over her collar and shoulders like rapids breaking around rocks in the Clearwater.

'We must talk, Riverspawn. Your recklessness will be your undoing. You stumbled blindly in the wake of shadows and so, predictably, they eluded you. But in all your stomping around you made your presence—and your power—known to more sinister things. One does not need to be behind to follow you.'

'What are you talking about?' Darko demanded. 'Why are you here? And what happened to your arm?'

'I am talking about that couple you encountered in the apartment building. They've been stalking you since you left downtown. Did you not see the hunger in their eyes. They were no humans—not anymore. They were wechuge, and they would have devoured you had I not stopped them.'

Darko swallowed hard. 'Stopped... them?'

'Yes, you fragile infant. They are dead and you are alive and you are welcome. But I did not come to scold you. I came to discuss with you.' She had begun unzipping her oversized jacket when her eyes fell, for the first time, on Ana and Milana behind him.

'Ah,' she halted, 'Another time then. I am sorry for intruding on your company. Come sisters, we shall leave him to his guests for tonight. We have other business to see to, and—'

She stopped abruptly, striding several steps toward Darko, eyes fixed over his shoulder.

'Well, a little Riverspawn. This is unexpected.'

'There is also a big Riverspawn,' another of the rusalky added from behind Darko, 'East of the city.'

'We have chosen wisely,' the third finished, suddenly at his ear. He made to step aside, when the second came from the table to flank him.

'We have not chosen anything yet,' the third reminded.

Darko stood completely still, the three impossibly-beautiful women forming a triangle around him, uncomfortably close and, yet, painfully not close enough. Not-Volkhova's face was centimetres from his own, and she turned those depthless eyes to look directly into his. His breathing came raggedly, as if he had forgotten how his lungs worked.

'Perhaps…' not-Volkhova hesitated. He could feel the warmth of her breath on his face, taste its sweetness on his tongue. He was sure the whole room must be able to hear his heart pounding.

'Perhaps the choice was never ours to make.' She turned away looking…*embarrassed? Impossible!* 'Now, let's be on our way.'

She strode away then, right out of his apartment, the other two following in her wake. As not-Volkhova stopped to close the door behind them, she turned to address him once more.

'And Darko,' a coy smile breaking on her face, 'I don't know if you're as clumsy inside your kitchen as you are outdoors, but do try not to soak yourself again.' Laughter from the other two drifted in from the hallway as she shut the door behind her.

Darko remained motionless in the middle of his apartment, mouth slightly agape, heart still pounding, and kitchen knife still held loosely at his side. His head felt thick, almost fuzzy.

'Uh…Darko?' his sister called from behind him. Her voice seemed distant.

Damn! They did see my disaster with the water spout.

Darko.'

The scraping of a chair behind him marked Ana's impatient rise, he heard her approaching, felt her take the knife from his hand to put on the counter. His eyes stayed glued on the closed door as Ana started waving her hand in front of his face.

How am I so inept around her. Damn her and her soggy sisters.

'Darkoooo.'

A dumb grin tightened Darko's slackened jaw. *At least she finally smiled.*

CHAPTER FIVE: Morning at the Richovsky Farm

Wednesday, 17 February 2021

The sound of a crying baby made its way out of the long, single-story house and drifted to the ears of the man in a thick coat, trudging his way down the well-worn path between that house and the barn. With fewer chores to take care of in the Winter months, Demir Richovsky's morning routine consisted of little more than checking in on the cattle before returning to the house to start the day with his main job.

For the second year in a row, one of the four cows who still bore milk had failed to fall pregnant the year before and Demir feared what it would mean for this year's production. The cow in question, Beth, had been lethargic for more than a week now. Though she was only six, Demir was beginning to think this season might be her last. There had been no milk this morning from her.

Though it was still early, the sun seemed to rise sooner out here away from the city. That orb was already almost entirely visible above the distant line of trees marking the edge of the Richovsky farm two kilometres eastward.

Hearing a barking that seemed to punctuate the crying infant, Demir shielded his eyes and surveyed the snow-covered fields. He caught sight of the family's three dogs, bounding their way homeward from a couple hundred metres away. Even now, with their second child almost a year old, the dogs never failed to respond to even the most innocuous cries.

Demir reached the door only moments before the dogs who, after leaping to greet him with slobbery kisses, pushed their way through ahead of him.

'Stop.' Alexander Richovsky demanded of the dogs from just inside the door. For a four-year-old, Demir's son was remarkably responsible. He grabbed a nearby towel to wipe down the paws of the dogs. To their own credit, the behaviour of the dogs was just as impressive. They stood with infinite patience, lifting one paw at a time, as the small boy wiped them dry.

'Thanks for doing that, buddy. *De Mama*?' Demir had always valued the bilingual home he had grown up in, and though he would no longer consider himself fluent in his mother tongue, he did his best to instil all the Ukrainian he remembered into his son.

'N*a kukhni, z Klara*'

'*Z Klaroyu*,' Demir corrected. His son had a tendency of forgetting to decline names.

Alexander waited for Demir to take off his boots, then grabbed his dad's hand tightly and led him toward the kitchen where his mother and sister waited. Three dogs padded their way after the duo, much calmer now that they were inside.

In the kitchen, Klara was in Morgan's arms, her bawling slowed to snivelling. Morgan was bouncing the child in one arm and holding an open book in the other. The two girls swung their heads to regard Demir as he entered the room. Both girls had been asleep when he left to complete his morning chores an hour ago. He had hoped he could return in time to take care of Klara and give his wife a bit of extra sleep.

Alas, there's never enough time for anything on the farm. Words his father had once said. Words he repeated now to his own son, only half-recognizing the wisdom in them.

'Say hi to Daddy,' his wife's cheery voice was comforting. Despite growing up on a farm where early mornings were a lifelong necessity, Demir had always hated waking up early. His wife, on the other hand, who had slept most of her youth beyond noon whenever possible, took to mornings like that first ray of sunshine over the horizon. *My ray of sunshine.*

At seeing her dad, Klara's snivelling turned to a smile, and she reached for him, cooing.

'Come on, baby. Let's let mama eat, and you can come work with tato.' Demir gave his wife a kiss and poured himself a cup of coffee.

'*Ty yiv?*' Demir asked his son.

Alexander shook his head even as he pulled out a chair to join his mother at the table for breakfast.

'Enjoy your breakfast,' Demir offered as he left the room with Klara.

Demir took his daughter to his makeshift study. The room had been his growing up, and after he married, Demir had replaced his old bed with a desk. When Alex was born, the room had then been changed into a kind of play room, so Demir could keep an eye on the boy while he worked. Since Klara had come along, the only changes had been an updated computer and the gluing of soft foam all around the desk. Since she had started crawling, his daughter had hurt herself more often than Alex in his entire four years of life.

'You're gonna be a handful aren't you?' Demir poked at Klara's nose before setting her down next to her stuffed moose. He sat deeply in his chair with a sigh, and woke his computer out of sleep mode.

Labelled a Computer Scientist by the alumni association that had not stopped hounding him for donations since the day he graduated, and a Coding Machine by his boss, when he was not tending to the steadily-declining family farm, Demir worked in web and application development. He had been working for a promising Acton startup, Sightliner, since the last year of his degree, and their steady growth allowed him to live and work comfortably here on the family homestead, just outside of Oak Creek.

By the time Demir made it through a handful of the company's latest emails, emptying half his coffee in the process, Alex had finished with breakfast and joined Klara on the floor. He pulled out the set of foam blocks Klara loved so much and began erecting towers for his sister to gleefully knock down.

One email after another was read, mentally noted, and deleted. Demir slurped at his coffee, opening another.

Announcement. We are installing a new, larger fridge in the break room. Please ensure that, by next Monday, all your...

Delete.

Memo. Client *Finster and Gable Inc.* has defaulted on their payments. All work on their web development is to stop immediately. Report to me for new projects. -David.

Delete.

I told him that was a bad contract. The minute they tried to get out of paying the graphic designer,

I knew they'd be trouble. This is what you get, David. Over fifty working hours down the drain.

One of the perks of having worked for Sightliner for so long, was that Demir was able to pick and choose which projects he worked on. And, though pushed by his boss to help out on the Finster and Gable project, he had refused. Rightly so it would seem.

Holiday Update. Due to a violent altercation over the Valentine's Friendship team-building exercise, the contest is hereby terminated. Any found to be participating will be immediately suspended.

It's this kind of office bullshit that makes people want to work from home. I do not envy you, David.

The ringing of the doorbell brought Demir's nose out of his monitor as he listened for who might be at the door. He frowned at his now-empty cup of coffee.

His wife's cheery voice drifted down the hall, followed by a man's muffled response. Though distant, Demir had no trouble recognizing the voice of his grandfather, Nathaniel Bennett.

Not now, Papa Nate! Demir blinked away the water that came unbidden to his eyes. He rubbed hard at his bearded cheeks, bracing himself for confronting his grandfather.

After Demir's mother had died, her father had stepped in to help wherever he could. Though the man was inept as a farmer, he had been there almost constantly to watch Demir and his siblings while their father worked the land. And when his Demir's father passed as well, only a few years later, Papa Nate had been there to save Demir the countless crushing burdens all descending at once. He had saved Demir from the funeral preparations, bills and utility payments, had saved Demir from the insurmountable task of raising his siblings alone. He had even moved into the family home, had made sure they never needed to even consider selling it. He had paid for Demir's college, ensuring he did not once have to worry about making ends meet.

Other relatives had helped as well of course— his father's brother, Vasyl, his uncle and aunt on his mother's side, Joseph and Caroline—but none had been as devoted as his grandfather. And it seemed a cruel joke now that such a kind man, such a selfless man, had been diagnosed with bone cancer.

Caught late, metastasized, multiple tumours. Get your affairs in order. Could be two days, two weeks, or two months.

'Fuck,' he breathed, ignoring Alexander's worried glance.

The news had been crushing to Demir. Nathaniel admitted that he had been diagnosed on the third, and had hoped he would not need to tell anyone, but in a desperate phone call on Friday afternoon, in an attack of weakness that left him too feeble to even drive to his appointment, Nathaniel had told Demir everything.

After driving him to the doctor, Demir had spent the weekend taking his grandfather to get a second, and third opinion. He had researched for hours on alternative treatments, he even spent two nights at his grandfather's house, so he could be there for him, and hired an in-home nurse for when he could not.

It was then on Sunday afternoon, after a weekend of being driven around the city by Demir, that Nathaniel confided he was not going to seek treatment.

He had begged Demir not to tell anyone, had said he only wanted some help to take care of funeral arrangements and the executing of his will. He even tried to guilt Demir into compliance, saying that he had done so much for Demir, the least Dermir could do would be to honour his wishes.

That had hurt. Demir had gone home Sunday afternoon to a full house. His two best friends and Darko had all come to visit and for hours Demir hid every worry, every emotion from them. For the first time in decades, he had lied to Darko's face.

It was not until evening, when everyone had finally left, that Demir spilt his every soul-bursting doubt and worry onto his ever-patient wife, and spent most of the night shivering on the roof of the barn, pondering life and death. Up there on his childhood perch of solitude, Demir had come to a decision. *The man's wishes be damned, Darko and Snizhana deserve to know.* Though he could not deny that he would probably attempt the same in Nathaniel's situation, he had the selfish privilege of not being in that situation, and so he would tell his siblings. Tonight, at dinner.

His grandfather had no doubt come this morning to talk him out of it. With a sigh, Demir rose from his desk.

'Keep an eye on your sister.' Wincing as his voice broke, Demir cleared his throat, nodded to Alex, and went to meet his grandfather.

Nathaniel Bennet stood on the shoe-mat in the doorway. Frederic, his in-home nurse—and now, apparently, driver—stood quietly behind, hands folded over his belt buckle.

Demir greeted his grandfather with a wordless hug. The weak response to his own tight embrace incited cascading mental images of veiny tumours marring marrowless bones. The purple-black blight filled his mind, globular night webbing across bone, swallowing all trace of white.

He knew bone cancer looked nothing like that. He had spent more hours in the past few days researching it than he had sleeping. Still, it was the nightmarish images rather than technical sketches that filled his consciousness.

'Easy there, Demir, or you'll crack the only cancer-free bones bones I've left.' His grandfather's easy laughter used to ease his mind. Now all he could focus on was permanently committing that sound to heart. One last, sweet memory of laughter.

His wife's laughter from behind echoed with the ring of betrayal. *Don't encourage his morbid humour. Don't encourage death's cruelty.*

Demir reluctantly eased his grip. 'Sorry, Papa Nate.' He took a step back and levelled a sombre gaze Nathaniel's way. 'I know why you're here, Papa, but I won't cancel the dinner. Darko and Ana deserve to know. I know I'm not the best at goodbyes—' Demir looked away, blinking moisture from his eyes. 'Dammit, Papa! They deserve to deal with it in whatever way they want!'

Morgan stepped forward and squeezed his arm; not out of sympathy, he knew, but to chastise him for speaking so harshly to his grandfather.

His grandfather's disarming smile relaxed Demir's mood a little. Either the cancer or the pain management meds were wreaking havoc on Nathaniel's body. The man's crooked-toothed grin was now marked by holes of black where teeth had fallen out in recent days.

Another rush of images. Tumours enveloping white bone.

'Demir. I went to see your mother this morning. Saints Peter and Paul Cemetery always looks so nice in the morning. Crystals of ice, like a morning dew, crenellated the granite headstone. White and silver crowning black, like the edge of the Milky Way in the blackest of skies…'

Nathaniel's gaze slipped from Demir to someplace in the distance and he grew quiet, contemplative. His voice trailed off. With a jerk, his mind seemed to return to the present and his eyes locked on Demir with a resuming *hmm!*

'Well, Demir, I stood for a long time at that grave, looking from your mother's stone to your father's and asking myself what your parents would have said. How they would have treated the matter. And, well, I think you have grown into the perfect combination of both of them.'

He took a step forward and patted Demir on the shoulder. 'I'm not here to convince you to break up your little dinner party, Demir. Hell of a theme for it though, eh? But if you're spilling the beans to your siblings, at least let those beans be on the table to do a little explaining of their own.'

Demir offered a weak smile in response. He had never been talented at disingenuous expressions, and Nathaniel's frown told him his smile was fooling no one. Still, he was grateful for his grandfather's efforts at compromise.

His wife spoke up from behind, ever the better of the two of them when it came to assuaging anxieties. 'Well, Nate, none of us has ever labelled you beans. Nuts, definitely, but never beans.'

Demir's wife and grandfather laughed easily at the lighthearted jest. Even Frederic was laughing as he excused himself and departed with promises of returning to pick up Nathaniel after supper. Demir just sighed. *How can you all laugh when death looms in the doorway? How can you joke? How can you do anything but rail and rage against the injustice of it?!*

His wife's hand settled on his arm again. This time it was a comforting gesture, as if she could hear the hopelessness of Demir's thoughts. And he was not convinced she could not. She was a most uncanny woman.

'Have you eaten, Papa?' This time Demir's voice was pleasant, rather than accusatory, his soft smile a genuine, welcoming one. He would not thank his grandfather, not for this compromise, for he knew it was not for his sake that Nathaniel had relented, but for Darko and Ana's. He would not apologize either, for he had only been upholding the family values taught to him by this very man, in insisting on this confessional dinner. But he would offer that smallest of tokens given by hosts to guests since the dawn of civilization—food.

Nathaniel accepted the offer with a smile, the missing teeth in that grin not seeming to deter the man's appetites in the slightest.

Demir led the way into the kitchen with his wife, Nathaniel only steps behind.

Morgan took the reins in the kitchen, using her hips to guide Demir gently out of her way as she set about preparing a small breakfast for their guest. 'Go get the little ones, Dear. I'm sure they'll be happy to see Papa.'

'Oh yes,' Nathaniel chimed in from the table as Demir helped guide him into a seat, 'and Papa would be delighted to see them!'

Demir returned to the study-playroom to find Klara contentedly beating on a foam block with both hands. Alexander was sitting in Demir's computer chair swinging his feet lazily. Both looked up at their father as he entered the room. Klara offered a gleeful *ahhh-aaa!* in greeting. Alexander looked up at his father curiously— somehow before the boy put voice to thoughts, Demir knew exactly what was coming—and asked 'is Papa going to die?'

Fuck.

Papa's gonna have to wait. You and I are gonna have a long chat.

'Come sit with Tato on the floor, Alex. Let's talk about Papa.'

CHAPTER SIX: Friendship Underground
Wednesday, 17 February 2021

Steven Yung, in present company known only as Honesty, watched another of the nine Major Virtues —his so-called peers—pull the trigger on his SIG Sauer to plant a bullet deep in the skull of the drugged and incoherent teenager. Though he grimaced at the barbarity of it, Steven spoke the words of the sacrificial prayer alongside the other eight Major Virtues.

'For love and for peace we have offered this sacrifice.' The deep chorus of nine voices speaking in perfect unison was echoed by the slightly-mistimed repetition of the eighteen Minor Virtues crowded in a rough circle behind them.

'For intimacy and humanity this blood is Yours. All friendships pale before the One True Friend; all loves lie at the feet of the First Love.' His mouth spoke the words, but Steven's heart was not in this prayer. *In this room, a gathering of the 27 highest-ranked and most holy servants of the Friend. And we meet underground. What a fucking cliché!*

'My Friend, my Lover, my Companion.' Steven stepped forward with the others to place a hand on the still-warm corpse to finish the prayer.

'My eyes. My ears. My lips. My touch. My heart. All are with You. All are for You. All are Yours to take. What's mine is your own.' He then stretched out his two hands to join them with sixteen others hovering over the body of their sacrifice, closing their prayer with the words, 'Together we are one.'

Together we are one—in a mouldy basement. Holding back sneezes and trying desperately not to touch the damp walls. We might as well have met in a cave for all the sanctity of this place. My brothers and sisters, you shame me!

The nine Major Virtues stepped to the side, allowing the Minor Virtues to carve the corpse with symbols of their faith. Steven noted with a twinge of irritation that there was no feeling to their actions, no devotion to their craft beyond precise cuts with keen blades. It might look prettier than his own handiwork at the university, but the power of the sacrifice suffered for it.

What sacrifice? I see only a slaying here. This offering was not carefully chosen, it was a killing of convenience. An OD-ing teenager thrown into a van, given a dose of naloxone to delay the inevitable, and quickly finished off with a bullet to the brain before the dirty heroin could finish its handiwork. Where is the art in that? Where is the sacrifice?! *We have given nothing to the Friend in*

*this offering save for barely ten minutes of our
time. Hardly a worthy gift to our god.*

Steven looked away from the spectacle with an inward sigh, turning instead to regard his fellow Major Virtues. He took a deep look at each of them: measuring, appraising, and in that moment judging their worth as servants of the Friend.

Comfort. It was you who chose the victim of this sacrifice, was it not? Finding the most convenient offering for the least effort. You misinterpret your role, Sister. You are not meant to find your own comfort through laziness, but to provide comfort and reassurance to others through your unshakable faith. You are not worthy of the Friend's gifts.

Fidelity, ever at the side of your fellow Virtues, never doubting, never naysaying. The blindness with which you serve discredits the sincerity of your loyalties. Do you not realize that our teachings promote elitism? What kind of friendship would it be if it was offered to every stranger met. If you could but learn to offer your fidelity discriminately, you would truly embody the virtue you claim to represent. Still, I'll count you an asset yet—till you prove otherwise.

Generosity, Devotion, Cooperation. Snivelling, grovelling sycophants without a single leadership instinct in your frail, bloodless hearts. You are not welcome here. Leastways not by me. The Friend sees through the skeletal masks of your hollow loyalty.

Though it was strictly never supposed to occur, Steven knew two of his fellow Major Virtues by name. Ljuba Kowalchuk lived across the hall in Steven's apartment and represented one of the defining friendships that had incited his devotion to the Friend. *Ljuba, Major Virtue of Lust. I wonder if there's a measure of nominative determinism in that...*

Ljuba seemed to feel the weight of Steven's gaze and looked his way with a wink and coy smile. Of all the virtues the Friend embodied, it had taken Steven the longest to fully understand the significance of lust. True friendship, he now realized, was not restricted by social boundaries of conduct determined to be proper, or seemly. True friendship took all involved parties to the very limits of their love for one another. *After all, all friendships revolve around love—the central virtue of the Friend's teaching—and love has no physical boundaries.* In Steven and Ljuba's case, their friendship involved a most unbridled lust in each other's beds, the stairwells of their apartment, the rooftop—anywhere Ljuba's husband would not catch them in the act.

She may not adequately represent the virtue of lust in all its forms, but she certainly knows true friendship, the foundation for any real faith in the

Friend. I have no doubts in you, Sister. His eyes lingered on her a moment longer, dropping to drink in the athleticism of her body. *I do hope to meet you in the stairwell back home…*

With an effort, Steven dragged his gaze past Ljuba to Carl Fischer. Carl was a coworker at the finance firm where Steven worked and the two had partnered on many a difficult account.

Fischer, virtue of Gratitude. I taught you to fish by bringing you the Friend's light. Hah! There's something biblical in that. I've no doubts in your devotion, Brother.

Steven turned his eyes to the last of the Major Virtues: Empathy. She was a quiet girl, and the youngest of them. Steven figured she could not be older than 21. Despite the transparency of her demeanour, she remained unreadable to him. She seemed to drink in the personality of whoever she was standing closest to, at one moment seeming a perfect complement to Carl, the next to Ljuba. Steven forced down images of the young woman wrapped up in Ljuba's long legs.

Whatever doubts or anxieties one was feeling, Empathy had the perfect response. Not to erase those worries, but to make them feel understood. And often she didn't even need to say word. She lifted her gaze to match Steven's own, and in those brown eyes he knew she understood him. Not his thoughts, not his beliefs, but his every emotion.

She's doing it right now! You're good, I'll give you that.

Empathy: the dimmest of the stars in the Friend's constellation, the quietest of our Major Virtues. Quiet, but no less integral. The Friend named you well, Sister.

Comfort, Fidelity, Generosity, Devotion, Cooperation, Lust, Gratitude, Empathy, and me, Honesty, nine Major Virtues yet only five of us actually virtuous. It will be a no small effort to manifest the Friend here in our company weighed down as we are by the others. But fear not, Friend, I shall not rest until You are born as a corporeal being, Your power no longer limited by Your lack of physicality. And under Your wing, we shall restore love to this cruel world.

It was a silent prayer, his own to make up for the pitiful sacrifice his peers had offered. He knew the Friend heard not intent, only action. And he had much to do this day in the name of his god.

Steven waited until the Minor Virtues were finished with their part of the sacrifice. As titleless acolytes filed into the room to clean up the mess, the Minor Virtues dispersed, two to a Major Virtue. The assignments of the Minor Virtues had been given in a deep and powerful prayer—one of the most meaningful experiences in Steven's life. In the midst of that prayer, he could feel the power of his god coursing through him. He had been

106

connected in that ceremony to the Minor Virtues of Grace and Forthrightness.

He did not wait for the two to find him in the crowd. Steven strode from the room, up, out of the dingy basement, and into the light of the midmorning sun pouring through the kitchen windows. He could feel his companion Minor Virtues behind him, slowly making their way up the steps even as he left Generosity's house to await his companions in his car.

'My asshole itches,' Forthrightness stated flatly a minute later as he opened the rear passenger door. He took his seat awkwardly, rubbing his buttocks back and forth on the upholstery. 'Ahh, better.'

'Good to see you too, Fort. Try to filter a little when we get to Nessie's parent's house, will you?'

'Fuck you,' Fort answered, already tugging on his ear as he did whenever in a car.

Grace was far more… graceful in her entry to the vehicle. She took a seat next to Steven, offering a friendly hello with a smile as she buckled.

'Grace,' Steven nodded. He looked over his shoulder, 'seatbelt please, Fort.'

'I don't care if I die. The Friend will have me.' Despite his protests, Fort obeyed and went back to tugging his ear quietly.

Behind her friendly smile, Grace was hiding a growing unease. The nine Major Virtues of the Friend had not been selected on any sort of merit, they had simply been the first to conduct an organized meeting away from the safety of their internet forum.

Eating the organs of a stillborn calf and conducting some strange carving ritual on the burnt bones and suddenly you're the Friend's own cardinals. Sanctimonious sons of bitches! Hypocritical hierophants! Every single one of you! Well... except Empathy. She alone might save the rest of them...

No, no!

Distraction ill suits a member of the faithful. Where was I?

Right, Steven Yung, Honesty. I admire your ambition, offering your own unauthorized sacrifices and taking your devotion to the Friend to the next level. But Honesty is no Major Virtue of friendship. Friends must lie to one another for the sake of their feelings. You and Forthrightness can continue conducting your renegade rituals right up until you're thrown out of the church. And Grace shall take your place. A new title for that misnamed star in the constellation.

Speaking of churches, it's about time we moved out of that rickety basement and into someplace beautiful. Someplace worthy of the Friend's love.

Someplace with windows and shiny, golden
candlesticks. And psalms of devotion. And
splendid, heart-melting paintings. And glorious,
bone-shaking organs. And, and, and....

Fort was watching Grace's growing smile in the side mirror. He knew his own face would be too dark behind the tinted window for her to see his reflection, knew he could stare at her pretty nose the entire drive without her noticing.

'Aspergers. I am bereft of these Aspergers,' he thought to himself. 'People with Aspergers haven't the slightest clue of any sort of filter.' He tugged harder at his ear, eyes still locked on Grace's nose. 'They exhibit repetitive behaviour, they exhibit social problems, they speak in strange and idiosyncratic ways—a blue flamingo in the same pond eating the same shrimp, but developing unique pigmentation.'

He stopped his ear-tugging, reflecting on the deepness of his metaphor. 'I'm not a fucking flamingo. I'm Fort. And Fort is a blender. I blend in. I blend things. Blend ideas. Blend patterns to make new patterns.'

The tugging resumed. 'Like the Friend, always blending. Epsilon Boötis, binary star. Two blended to one.

'Arrogant of us to think we found Her first, our bright and beautiful star. Izar, Mizar, Mirak, Mintek al Aoua, Cingulum Latratoris, Gěng Hé yī, a thousand names for the Friend. Pulcherrima, the Loveliest. Love, the Friend. Two celestial bodies: HD 129989, stellar classification K0 II-III, hydrogen core burnt out, expanded to more than thirty times the Sun's radius, with four times its mass in binary revolution with HD 129988, stellar classification A2 V at an angular separation of 2.852 ± 0.014 arcseconds and a position angle of $342.°9 \pm 0.°3$. Two lovers, entangled for life in the infinite vastness of Space. Wow!'

'That's right, Fort,' Honesty called from the front as he parked the car along the sidewalk outside of the home of Terence and Julia Herald, parents of Vanessa Herald. 'Wow, indeed!'

Forthrightness gasped with a start. 'Honesty read my thoughts again! He is truly wise. The Friend has blessed him with such wisdom. Such power! I shall follow Honesty to my death.'

'I'll bet you know as much about our sacred little constellation as Nessie did.' There was a sadness in Steven's tone, despite the smile on his lips. It made Fort uneasy.

'I miss Nessie,' was all he could think to say.

'Me too, Fort. Me too.'

Grace jerked forward in her seat suddenly, peering into the side mirror. 'Ugh! Stop staring at me you creep!'

Fort reeled back, moving his hand from his ear to his seatbelt and writhing against its fast restraint. 'Shit! Caught again! Such a pretty, pretty nose! I want to shove my nipple up those tiny nostrils!'

'I'm gonna puke!' Grace shouted back.

'Woah. *Woah!* Let's all relax a little. We've got to be on our best behaviour for the Heralds. This is a great opportunity to express our devotion to the Friend through the development and enrichment of new friendships. So let's remember we're all friends here and try our best to get along inside.' Steven's mild, kind tone, soothed his companions and the three exited the car in relative peace, making their way up the sidewalk to ring the doorbell of the Heralds.

In seconds, the door opened to reveal Terence, Julia, and Wendy Herald, the grieving family of Nessie. At seeing their dead daughter's fiancé, the three broke down into tears. Frantically, they gestured for Steven to enter, enveloping him in the kind of hug that told Steven he would always be welcome in their home.

'Got 'em!' Fort said from still outside the door, eliciting a sharp elbow in the ribs from Grace.

After a moment of raw emotion, Julia, Nessie's mom, peeled herself away from the group hug, levelled a meaningful gaze at Steven and breathed a sigh of relief. 'We were so worried! Thank God you're okay!'

CHAPTER SEVEN: A Friendly Police Visit

Wednesday, 17 February 2021

Constables Donald Philips and Derek Woods had arrived just before lunch time and, although Demir knew they had come to discuss business, the pleasantries shared between the longtime friends seemed to drag on and on. None of the three had the heart to cut short this rare opportunity of spending some time with each other. Of course, Morgan putting on that large pot of stew hadn't helped in the least. Now, as the three sat with full bowls, eager spoons, and freshly made, aromatic bread, Demir was only just allowing himself to forget the worries of his troubled mind when the doorbell rang.

He rose with a start, cursing himself internally for letting his guard down. Morgan was occupied helping Alex to find a seat at the table and Papa Nate, having eaten earlier, was off *watching* Klara as the two napped with full bellies in front of a curling match. Demir was already on his feet and out of the room by the time Morgan looked up.

Family dying, friends too busy to come by more than once every few months except on business, and now some ambitious, corporate-greed fuelled salesman comes preying on the struggling farmer.

The gods'll give you what's yours, I promise you that. In this life or the next.

He answered the door, grim and gloomy, a curse-filled sendoff poised to leap off his tongue when his eyes settled on the newcomer and, with a nearly-audible *click,* recognition set in. Tongue slower at adapting to the unexpected than his mind, his greeting spilled forth in a confused jumble.

'Fuck—hey bud! Good you t'see ya!'

'Well a friendly fuck-hello to you too, Demir,' the other man replied.

Despite being neighbours, Joel Johnson and Demir ever seemed incapable of finding the time to see one another. Lately, the only time Demir had managed to meet Joel had been in Acton at the veterinary clinic he owned. He couldn't quite figure how, but nearly a year had passed since the last such visit.

'I hope you don't mind me popping by, but I saw the cruiser out front and figured there might be a couple gents I know in here.'

Demir was already smiling and gesturing for Joel to join them inside when Derek called from the other room.

'Is that Dr. Johnson? Tell him to get his ass in he—Whoops! Sorry Mrs. Richovsky—tell him to get his butt in here!'

Demir led Joel cheerily to the kitchen, filling a bowl and plate for the man as he found himself a seat at the table.

Being the only official trainer of police dogs for several communities in the area, the doctor knew most of the force quite well, and he fell easily into the conversation at the table. Demir felt himself relaxing again. Immediately guilty over the feeling, he sat up straighter and glanced worriedly at his wife with each lull in conversation. Eternally patient and understanding, she ignored his worried glances utterly—other than to offer small, reassuring smiles. Demir could practically read her thoughts.

You'll give yourself an ulcer with all your worrying! Just sit back and enjoy the moment. Forget about work today, forget about Papa Nate for now, don't worry about Alex and me. Enjoy the moment. Life is worth nothing if you don't actually live it. He knew she was fine. He knew she would ask for help with Alex if she needed. Still, he could not shake the guilt that came with a lowered guard, could not convince himself that things would be okay if he stopped worrying.

So worry he did. He ate robotically, his eyes shifting their guarded gaze from his friends, to Morgan and Alex, to the open door into the living room where Papa Nate and Klara slept, back to the conversation unfolding at the table. And his ears went from focussing on that conversation—'I shit you not, a litter of fourteen pups! One stillborn, but the others all remarkably healthy'—to his son —'Are you sure this is *barabolja*, Mama?'—to the gentle snoring in the other room. And on, and on that cycle continued until his spoon scraped the bottom of his bowl enough times for Morgan to shoot him a look.

It was not long after, with a measure of expectance—and admittedly a degree of relief— that Demir settled back into his chair, listening intently when Joel asked the officers how their work was going. *This is where reality comes barrelling back to the table…*

Derek and Donald breathed a collective sigh between the two of them. They looked to each other with a surrendering weariness, then addressed the table.

'I suppose sooner or later it was bound to come up,' Donald began. 'It's not like we came here for lunch—though we do appreciate it!' he hastily added, patting his stomach for good measure. 'We came for you, Demir.'

Morgan, who had until now been politely pretending not to hear anything of the conversation sat up straighter, leaning protectively closer to her husband. Her eyes met Demir's for the briefest of moments, and in that fleeting connection her soul poured into his.

The effect was visceral. Demir's spine found the back of his chair and though his eyes were now back on the two police officers, patiently waiting for them to go on, his mind was reeling. Sadness, worry, anger, a wish that he protect himself—no, a threat—empathy and sympathy, pride and pity, more feelings than he could put a name to washed over him, pouring deep within him and taking root in his heart. There was but a single word that could identify it all. *Love.*

My dear, how could I betray such a love? Of course I'll be careful. I'm sure they only want a bit of information. And, even if they offer for me to join them on a ride-along, I won't go this time. Not ever again. One bullet grazing my temple is enough for a lifetime, I should think.

His hand brushed that old scar subconsciously. Beneath his mop of dark hair that bald streak lay hidden, just above his ear, the faint ridge of scar a permanent reminder that there is evil and danger in the world, even today. *Even sixteen year olds can be so full of hate as to want nothing more than to destroy all trace of happiness and hope in the world. And even a grown man, accustomed to tragedy, can piss his pants behind an office desk and weep in terror as his world comes collapsing in around him.*

Demir swallowed hard, letting the painful memory wash over him, and then out of him, past him into some unknowable place that allowed him a measure of peace. He met Derek's serious gaze as the taller officer continued.

'Like Donald was saying, we're here for your brain, buddy. Nothing to do with computers or coding or electronic security this time. We just need to borrow your memory and maybe a book or two if you've got the time. Don't worry, Morgan, we won't be taking him anywhere this time.'

Though no one dared speak of the disaster that had taken place the last time his two friends had involved Demir in a case, the tension at the table seemed to crackle with invisible arcs of lightning between them. Dr. Johnson excused himself to find a bathroom and even little Alex was perceptive enough to decide that now was a good time to run off and play somewhere else. Demir feared his wife might say something that would drive his friends from the table, but to his surprise she said nothing. She had said enough in the look they shared. She would not care how the police conducted themselves now, only in how Demir would respond.

He was the first to break the silence. 'I'm happy to help. Show me what you've got for me.'

With that simple offer, the pressure released and an ordinary calm returned to the kitchen. Morgan helped Demir in clearing off the table as the two officers dug through their case files to present what they needed Demir to have a look at. Dr. Johnson's laughter drifted in from the other room where he had been talked into playing a game by Alexander.

It was not, strictly speaking, Demir's knowledge his friends sought this time, but that of his father. The boys had all grown up together in Oak Creek, and the two officers well remembered Pan Danylo Richovsky entertaining them with tales of the fantastic. The three of them would entertain themselves long into the night pouring over his hand-drawn journals of all the extraordinary creatures and people he had claimed to study.

'I'm sure I don't have to remind you that anything you hear or see today is in the strictest confidentiality. It's this latest murder that brings us here,' Donald stepped back from his careful arrangement of files and photographs. 'I'm sure you've heard on the news about the cultic connections and symbols and, while we're not willing to rule it out, the truth is that there's no precedence for anything like that in Acton. Our first thought was to dig through old case files since symbols like the ones this killer left are usually a calling card of some kind, but they turned up nothing.'

Demir abandoned his effort on the dishes to lean over the table, peering intently at the bloody symbols carved into various body parts. The crime scene photographer had been careful, sterile, in capturing an anonymity in the photos. The angular framing, the fact that not a single photo included more than only a single part of the body—leastways none on the table. It did not simply detach Demir from the victim's identity, it severed him from the victim's very humanity. He was sure it was having an effect opposite that intended, for he felt sick to his stomach. A taloned, grip took hold of his abdomen and bile rose in his throat.

Unaware of Demir's discomfort, Donald went on. 'Even in past cases where the immediate assumption was *satanic,* in the end it was never anything more than a guy, or a bunch of guys, hoping to cause a scare among the more religious of Acton's citizenry. But we've got a feeling, Derek and I, that this is different. I'm not saying it *is* satanic, just that it's different.'

As if they had rehearsed, Derek took over, not a beat missed between them. 'That's right. The depth of the marks, their precision, their... dare I say, artistry.' A morbid excitement overtaking him, Derek started pacing short lanes in the space between the table and the kitchen counter, pausing only to gesture dramatically with his hands or to point out a detail in one of the photographs.

'It's... raw. It's... beautiful. It's fucking passionate!'

'It's fucking murder.' Demir reminded Derek, his dry tone betraying the roiling disgust within.

Derek seemed unfazed by the remark. 'Yes, a murder with passion! The victim knew the killer, that much is clear. It seems there was a certain amount of... complicity in her death. I can't give anymore details at the moment, but in this one case, whoever the killer was, we think these symbols meant something, really *meant* something to him.'

Derek's excitement seemed to wear off in a moment of silence, and when he spoke again it was with that professional matter-of-factness that all officers seemed to adopt. He was Derek no longer, but Constable Woods. 'Now we turn it over to you. What do you make of these symbols, Demir? I have this sketch as well. It's less... bloody. I meant to show you on the weekend, but I never did find the right moment. As far as we can tell, the knotwork is purely ornamental. It's the central symbol we're interested in. On the victim's forehead. *There.*' He pointed. 'Looks a bit like a wheel, or some kind of nine-pointed star. It doesn't check out with any of the more... conventional religions, but we're ready to hear your take.'

Demir took his time studying the symbol, looking from the photograph of the victim's forehead to the sketch in Derek's notepad. He let the image fill his mind, imagining a hundred different iterations of the symbol, possible land features that it might reflect, medieval and ancient civilizations who might have made use of such a thing, contemporary digital designers it might belong to, and for all his mind delved, he found nothing.

Slowly, he shook his head. 'I'm sorry guys, I have no idea what that might be. I've got a couple of my dad's old books stacked away in a bedroom closet somewhere that you're welcome to take a look at. But I know those books well, I don't think you'll find anything like this in their pages. Plenty of nine-pointed stars, sure, and plenty of wheels, but nothing depicted quite like this. And certainly nothing that might be readily associated with murder.'

Both of the officers were crestfallen. Demir had seen them working enough of their cases over the years to know that they had hit a dead end. They likely had only this one lead to go off of, and this one contact outside the station they could turn to. And he had let them down. He sighed quietly. *They're like insulted puppies. Can't I give them something.*

It took him nearly the full two minutes of his friends clearing the table of their array of gruesome images for Demir to realize he might be able to help yet. The two officers were ready to say their goodbyes and depart when Demir interrupted them.

'Hang on a moment, guys. I might not know anything off hand, but I studied this stuff in university. I've got the contact information of a couple experts on folklore and its material culture. If I can't find something, I'm sure one of them will be able to. Give me two or three days. I'll send out some emails and let you know what I come up with.'

'That's great! Thanks, Demir!' Donald said.

'And Demir,' Derek added, 'depending on the outcome, we may be able to get you a small paycheque out of this. Consultation fees, and all that,' he explained with a wink.

While her husband and the officers had their official little discussion, Morgan had found her way into the children's room where Alex had sat Dr. Johnson down and was *reading* the man one of his picture books. Joel laughed freely as Alex narrated his observations of the pictures in a mixed jumble of English and Ukrainian.

Once the story had finished, Morgan had her own brief conversation with Joel. They talked of Dem's grandfather dying, conventional treatment options and experimental approaches, which led into the subject of Joel's work, his dog training next door and his clinic in the city. She was surprised to hear that Joel's clinic had had a police visit only the day before when an innocent holiday-themed activity had resulted in attempted murder charges between a receptionist and a nurse.

Didn't I hear something similar on the news? About some Acton finance company? Morgan struggled to place the faint memory. She was sure she had only been half-listening at the time. *Maybe an accounting firm?* She shrugged internally, not really caring except for the fact that it might give them something to talk about. *Well, I suppose I can look it up later.*

A few minutes of stilted conversation later, Morgan was bidding their three visitors farewell at the door. She had been planning to return to the living room to check on Papa Nate and Klara, both of whom should be waking from their naps soon if they were hoping to sleep at a reasonable hour tonight, but those plans were delayed when she saw the glint of sunlight off of something metallic about thirty metres up the long driveway.

She went out barefoot to collect what she assumed was a carelessly-tossed piece of garbage, walking quickly across the thin layer of snow. Curses tumbled in her head with threats of what she would say or do if the garbage turned out to be from one of the two cars which had just left their property. She had just been settling on the perfect combination of creative threat and abominable accusation when she stopped short of the curious metallic sliver at the edge of her driveway.

Not any wayward scrap of garbage, but a sword lay there, it's shining edge making the surrounding snow seem soiled and dull by comparison. She bent to retrieve the object, questions burning, when something rocketed into her from behind. The blue and white of the sky overhead was a sickening blur as her whiplashed head was rocked back. Then, as it rocked forward to come slamming down, chin hitting chest hard enough for Morgan to bite clean through the tip of her tongue and all the fluid in her head seeming to break in single, terrible wave against the front of her skull, all turned to black.

CHAPTER EIGHT: In Honesty's Absence

Wednesday, 17 February 2021

In the absence of honesty, lips and tongues cannot be held accountable for mind's ruinous machinations. Even the most docile and timid of personalities can say the most unexpected things. In honesty's absence, entire relationships can be built and destroyed, the worst of enemies cast in love, the best of friends rent apart. In honesty's absence, moderation, self-control, and seemliness fall away, surrendering to the authority of lies mistaken for truth.

In Honesty's absence, a secret council of Generosity, Devotion, Cooperation, and their new confidante, Fidelity, sat in Generosity's kitchen sipping lemonade, awaiting the direction of their leader.

Lust stood while the others sat, a small, symbolic gesture to remind them that they were nothing without her. That without her, they were hardly virtues at all, but husks of faith without direction. They believed without feeling, prayed without devoting, Lust hated them all.

But you have your uses.

'So how do we do it?' Devotion asked, eager to put their plan to action.

'He will aim to be home for six o'clock.' *He always does. It gives us one perfect, blissful, rushed hour together before my husband returns. Ahh, that thrill in the last few minutes from when Stig texts he's pulling in until he gets upstairs. Those last few seconds of skin against naked skin. The rushed dressing, Steven's dash to his own apartment across the hall, my effort to slow my breathing even as Stig comes in the door, eyeing the sweat on my brow, the dark pool of it between my breasts dampening my blouse. He looks me up and down but never says a word, never voices his questions. To proud to say what he suspects*

'He always drops off Forthrightness and Grace first. His route will take him through the underpass beneath Koo-Koo-Sint Highway and that's where you'll do it. Pray to the Friend for accuracy, and throw the concrete blocks. All four of you, because we cannot make a mistake in this.' She could feel her chest flushing, her breathing speeding up. There was a perverse pleasure in planning the death of a man. She would revel in it with her husband this night.

I will miss you, Honesty, there's no doubt of that. Miss your hands, your lips, your biting teeth. I'll miss the kindness in your eyes, that patient stare even when, inside, you're fuming over your own infidelity. But honestly, Honesty, you don't know the first thing about the virtue you claim to represent. Committing your own secret sacrifices in the name of our shared god, shutting out the rest of us, where is the honesty in that?

Your own fiancée, that was cruel. Clever, but cruel. I could feel *the power when you killed her. Across the river, in the comfort of my living room, on the couch deep in the throws of lovemaking. And that sacrifice broke through it all. If you were not already the Friend's favoured disciple, you are now. And I can't have that.*

Your admission of the deed was honest enough, but to truly embody your named virtue you would have remained honest to the cause and honest to your peers. You would never have betrayed us in trying to buy your own power with solitary sacrifices.

But it's too late for that isn't it? So you leave us no choice but to take that power now. To stop your rise and replace you before you destroy our church with your divisive, independent action. Church? No, even I am too skeptical for that. We are a cult plain and simple. But like a church we have structure, we have rules and hierarchy, and I will not let you dictate what those are. If we are to give the Friend a right hand, then I mean to be that appendage.

Though the four at the table had returned to talking among themselves, Fidelity was eyeing her askance. Lust's chest and cheeks had started burning with her thoughts of leading this sorry cult into glory under the guidance of the Friend and, though Fidelity's gaze seemed innocent enough,

Lust felt a suspicion there. She could not have that either.

'Change of plans. Generosity, you, Devotion, and Cooperation will travel together. You'll operate the overpass together. Fidelity, come with me, darling, we'll make sure the deed's done from the main road. But there's plenty of time before we'll be needed and it's time we got to know one another. Won't you come to the mall with me?'

Lust almost laughed at the other woman's excited smile. *I'm not surprised, darling, you seem like one of those pretty little girls bitter at her mother. No doubt you've scorned every other female influence in your life and now you blame early puberty and lifelong jealousy for your inability to make friends with women.*

After quick farewells, Ljuba Kowalchuk led the woman out of Generosity's house into her car. 'What do you think, the mall first? Some shopping, manicures, maybe massages if there's time, then we can grab lunch to go and see to all this ugly business with Honesty?'

'Oh that sounds wonderful. This was a great idea, Lust, I sure could use a break from the dark of that basement and the crass stupidity of some of those other Virtues. Not that I don't respect them,' she carefully added, 'it's just that they don't quite understand our gentler dispositions do they? Not all virtues are equal is what I suppose I'm trying to say.'

'Oh, I know exactly what you mean, dear. Buckle up, love, I'll just put my purse in the trunk and we'll be on our way.'

Ljuba walked around to the open trunk and checked on its contents. Two cell phones sat on the floor of the trunk, each her only point of contact with the two Minor Virtues that had been assigned to her. She had yet to share more than a handful of words with either of them. They would have to earn their place before she accepted them into her graces. She unzipped her first aid kit tucked away behind the phones, withdrew the handgun that was hidden there, and placed it in her purse. She closed her eyes slowly, taking a few deep breaths.

Oh, Fidelity, how laughably disloyal you are. I don't know if you plan on betraying our little secret council, but I'm not about to let you try. The sacrifice of one Major Virtue is bound to be numbingly powerful on its own. But just imagine! Two Major Virtues, sacrificed within minutes of each other: it just might be enough to manifest the Friend this very night. And then your sacrifice will be truly honoured, Fidelity, and your faith respected more in your death than it ever has been in your lifetime. You are correct in thinking the Major Virtues are unequal, but woefully off the mark in where you place your own value.

With one final, calming breath, Ljuba grabbed her purse, slammed the trunk shut, and returned to the driver's seat, tucking her purse behind it.

'Guess I'll be needing it at the mall anyway, better to have it handy.' she said with a smile.

'Good thinking,' Fidelity smiled back.

And the two continued flashing their fake smiles and sharing meaningless conversation as they made their way down the road toward the mall, not an honest word or gesture between them.

Weightlessness.

Morgan's thoughts and feelings were suspended in a kind of super-sensory fugue. It was as if everything and nothing occupied her awareness. Or, more accurately, as if everything occupied her awareness without any attached meaning. It was a pleasant sensation.

It did not last.

The taste of iron.

Slowly, infinitely slowly, some faculties seemed to return, starting with that sweet taste that enveloped her being. Thick, iron. Embracing. Cloying.

Pain!

Suddenly the sense of weightlessness evaporated, as if her suspended body came slamming down in that field of darkness. She could not see, could not hear, nor sense her surroundings, but she knew she was crying out. The vibrating of vocal chords, the rush of air pushing past her teeth and blood-soaked lips. She spat out that blood, with a coughing wail, *felt* it land, splashing against some surface.

A new presence.

Ah... sorry about that. I was so excited to reach out to you, that I fear I may have shared the experience of my own death with you.

'Wha-?' Morgan thought the question more than asked it, but it seemed enough.

You can understand, it's in your blood after all. Lured by the gleam of metal where metal should not be found. Of course, in my case, rumours of King John's treasure spurred my curiosity. True what mum said, then: curiosity kills.

Though the other had a strange manner of speech that barely seemed English, and her accent confounded even the simplest of syllables, Morgan had no trouble understanding her. It was as if they spoke in thoughts, shared emotions and impulses, rather than through the words they traded.

Though in your case, the presence continued, *there are no fens around to drown you. If you keep lying there, mind you, you'll melt enough snow to drown yourself anyway. Come.*

At once the blackness was gone. Morgan found herself under a blue sky in the middle of a farmer's field. The sun shone warm on her back and from someplace far off, the faint peeling of a police siren could be heard.

'Where are we?'

The Fens, dear. About eight miles east and five north of Wisbech. Before you lies the vastness of the Fens before the Wash.

What does any of that mean? Fens? Wash? All I see are more farms.'

Anglia, dear. We're in Anglia. At the sight of my death.

Morgan looked instinctively to her feet. And was surprised to see a slippered pair not her own. Examining the body she seemed to be inhabiting, it was both familiar and strange. The longer she concentrated on any particular feature, the more corporeal it became, but if her eyes or concentration strayed in the slightest, the features dissipated into ghostly ethereality, wisps of memory fading.

Beneath those ghostly legs that were both her own and someone else's, the earth did the same thing. Concentration caused the farm to fall away, the land to flatten and sink as water came to soak the earth. Here, beneath her, long ago had been the Fens.

'Why are we here?'

Accidentally. I think. I suppose I brought you here. Not intentionally, mind you. It's just that I know this spot rather well. Better than any other in the world, in fact. My body was never found, you

*see, and I was reluctant to stray from it. My son
nearly found me once. He stood right over me, the
pressure of his feet pushing down on the soft earth
to force my corpse deeper into the fen. The body's
probably long gone now though, pushed a half-
dozen paces deeper, or gone entirely, washed away
with the draining of the land.*

*Oh, but I'm boring you. I did not approach you
to sadden you with tales of my death, or to
entertain you with stories of the haunted Wayland
Wood. I came to help you.*

Morgan felt her hands plant on her hips and
chest protrude proudly. Defiantly.

'Help me? I don't need any help. Who are you
anyway?'

Who am I? The presence was both offended and
surprised. *Oh dear! Why, I am Jane, of course!
And you, you are my daughter. Well, separated by
some generations, naturally. And I'm here to
protect you.*

'Protect me from what?'

*Are you senseless, daughter? Can you not feel
how close we are?*

The Anglian farmland floated outward and away
and Morgan found herself once again surrounded
by blackness. In the blackness Morgan lay on her
side, hands pressed tight to her mouth. Above her
stood a middle-aged woman, her appearance

134

familiar and comforting. She could see traces of herself in that face. The slight upturn to her lips on the left side, the peculiar epicanthic tilt that had incited countless questions of her heritage in gradeschool, even the slight misalignment of shoulders—something Morgan had always assumed to be environmental—was a match between them.

Jane reached down to place a comforting hand on Morgan's shoulder. Morgan could feel the warmth of that hand through her clothes.

See. We are so close you can feel me. Me, a spirit. I have been following you for fourteen days, and not once have you felt my touch, nor heard my voice. But today when I reached out, I nearly killed you. There is a power gathering here, in your city of Acton. A god is being made. And I am not the only being receiving power from its proximity.

Those words hardly seemed to explain a thing, but with the shared emotions and that warm touch on her shoulder, Morgan knew the thoughts of this woman. Knew the truth she spoke. Knew her confidence and her doubts. One of those doubts rose in her, and Morgan could not hold back the question.

'Why you? You can't be the oldest of my ancestors, nor the closest. Why you? And why do you follow me?'

I don't know. Perhaps I simply care the most. I never could find satisfaction after my death. I spent years waiting for someone, anyone, to discover my body. To bring peace to my husband and children. No such peace ever came, and eventually I wandered from my body. Wandered from my beloved Norfolk, from the folk I knew and loved. By this time four generations had died since my passing. I chose one descendent at random and clung tight, following family after family for generations.

I've seen six countries. I've witnessed such tragedy you could not possibly believe, watched growth immeasurable, and felt the crushing loss of entire lines being brought to a horrific end in a single, devastating accident. Sometimes it's a fire, sometimes a flood, or a virulent sickness. Most recently it was a car crash. Now, too few branches of my progeny remain, and none in my beloved Anglia. I found you quite by accident recently and found my smile in your own. So I've followed you since.

Morgan could feel the love Jane had for her family in her recollection. Love for them all. Some children had made her proud, others had devastated her in the shameful lives they had led, but Jane loved them regardless. And now all that love, generations upon generations of love, was focussed on Morgan and her family.

'MORGAN!' Out of the darkness bloomed colour. A white sky and the white snow-covered earth. And red.

Covering her hands and dripping in runnels between her fingers blood stained, pooling in the melting snow beneath her head. The vision of Jane was gone, replaced by the harshness of the scene surrounding Morgan, but the woman's presence was still close, crowding the back of Morgan's mind.

Mandrivnyk, the youngest of their dogs stood protectively over Morgan, nose sniffing warmly at her neck.

Behind her the sprinting footsteps of Demir came crashing closer and his comforting voice dulled the pain in her mouth. 'Oh, my Morgan. My love, what happened?'

Large, gentle hands, lifted her head gingerly, probing her face for signs of injury. As her head was lifted she could see the tip of her tongue lying there in the snow. She feebly reached for it, feeling a desperate sense of loss, but Demir's gentle strength brought her arm back down.

From far off she could hear Jane's voice again. *Don't worry, my daughter. Your husband and I will take care of you.*

In the basement of Generosity's house, fourteen of the Minor Virtues stood around the sacrificial altar atop which Empathy stood, advocating the supreme goodness of each of them.

'Minor Virtues?' she was saying, 'there is nothing *minor* about you! It's nothing more than an unfortunate appellation distinguishing you from those eight of our brothers and sisters who think themselves somehow holier than you. No one is more devout than you! None of those eight humbles themselves before the Friend the way we do. They seek to use the Friend to their own means and, whatever happens, we cannot allow that. Say it with me!'

And say it with her they did: 'We. Can. Not. Allow. That!'

'That's right, brothers and sisters! We are not less than them because we came later. What of those followers who came after you? They receive no title, no invitation to our sacrifices. Does that make them less than us?'

'NO!' they answered as one.

'No it does not. It matters not what those eight do now. We'll let them practice their arcane alchemy and stargazing until the moment the Friend arrives physically. And then we make this the Friend's temple! We shall purge those who need purging. Cleanse the selfish and unfaithful among us, for only the most pure, most devout can serve the Friend. And we shall be the first among that hallowed following!'

The roar of support rocked Empathy back. Though she drank it in, it frightened her. It terrified her how easily fanatics could be made of almost anyone. *Say the right words, feel the right feelings, and they are agitated clay for shaping, angered potential energy eager for kinetic release.*

Oh, how I shall release you. Not upon the Major Virtues, but in effort to surpass them. You will be released upon this world with the flame of faith. The most ardent of flames. And with its ardour, you will burn a new era into this world. An age of severity, of higher highs and lower lows, an age of empathy and compassion: the Age of Friendship. And on the Friend's divine winds, I shall soar as your Queen.

CHAPTER NINE: The Children of Danylo Richovsky

Wednesday, 17 February 2021

Having missed most of the week's classes through a mix of unpredictable sleep and unavoidable apathy, Darko figured missing another day's worth would not be so bad—*there's that apathy again.* Unable to sleep, he had spent most of the night online, refamiliarizing himself with everything his father had once shared about folklore. And after several hours of everything from PhD dissertations to fan-fiction, he had given up.

What good would it do anyway? It's all the same. Every culture on Earth has their own so-called unique cultural beliefs and lore, but they're all identical. The exact. Fucking. Same. The details may differ, the creatures and the stories, but they share universal ideas: love, hatred, betrayal, life, death, afterlife. Gods and heroes, benevolent spirits and wicked, treacherous fay, some of it's probably real, but most of it? Theories, stories. Even with my exposure to the supposed supernatural *in my younger days, I'm still waiting to wake up and find out I've just been dreaming the past few days.*

That seemed highly unlikely, for the little sleep he had gotten had been fitful and filled with frightening dreams of its own. Darko had found himself looking down on the body of the old man from the stairs. He was sprawled in the lobby of Greybrick House, his throat slashed, his hands cut off and missing. And as Darko stared down in horror at the grisly scene, he noticed a dripping of bright blood falling slowly onto the man's face. Following that stream of drops, Darko lifted his gaze to a gleaming, blood-soaked knife held fast in his own hand.

The rest of the dreams were remembered only in slivers. A fragment of staggering emotion here, a splash of vibrant colour there, a glimpse of himself standing in the abandoned, burnt-out shell of a room above his own. The room seemed suspended in time. Light poured in through cracks in the boards covering the windows, catching the black dust of crumbled cinders suspended across the room—dust that seemed to have been immobile for centuries. That dust swirled behind him as Darko walked from the door, across the charred floor, eyes sweeping over blackened, fire-scarred furniture to arrive on the room's sole occupant. That old, wispy-haired man sat calmly in the room's darkest corner, fingers tented above his flat stomach. The rest of the scene eluded Darko's memory. There was just the eerie creak of the rocking chair and the man's low chuckle as Darko drew nearer.

Unable to sleep more, but weighted by exhaustion, Darko had decided to head to Demir's early rather than go to school but, as he had turned into the driveway, he noted a police cruiser and another, unfamiliar vehicle with German shepherd stickers on the rear window where others displayed caricatures of their families. Though he knew Maria would never forgive him for not barging in and demanding to know more details about the university murder, Darko decided not to disturb them. There were enough ignored problems in his life already, and Darko decided he could do without another.

He left the driveway then, instead driving a kilometre and a half farther up the road to park in a small outlet of the highway. There, he slipped between the strings of barbed wire that made up the fence and took a moment to drink in his surroundings.

He came to visit Demir often enough, but all too rarely did he visit the land itself, his family's homestead, the sliver of Richovsky that his father had carved out of Canada's rough landscape to call his own. Darko's gaze passed over the snow-covered fields. From the house at the northeast corner of the property to the west where the woods began, darkening Richovsky land in a rough triangle making the wheat fields which would turn from white to golden with the summer appear deceptively small. In those woods, the Richovsky land extended another full parcel to the west where their small herd of bison roamed free year-round.

Darko let his gaze drop to where he stood, ankle deep in snow. His shoes were just slightly too low and he knew his socks would likely be soaked by the time he was done in these fields, but he also knew he could not turn back. Not now. It had been far too long since he had stood here.

I know this place. I've walked every corner of this land in my youth. I know its every fold and crease, the gentle decline of the wheat field into the woods, and the twin valleys within those woods connected only by the wending river Tato claimed that he had guided—Hah! I always figured you meant with pick and spade, Dad—out from the main flow of the Clearwater and into Richovsky land.

I know this place. I remember the smell of this soil, the taste of the dust settled beneath the towering wheat. I've bled into the earth here, slept on it, trampled it, and worked it into life. And it remembers me. Even the frozen ground softens beneath my feet, recognizing me after all these years, under all this snow, to call me back. To welcome me home.

It had been a whirlwind of an afternoon. After racing Morgan to the hospital to get stitches—he still hadn't gotten a clear answer about what had happened—leaving Papa Nate behind to watch the children, Demir had returned home to once more find a police cruiser in his driveway, and none other than Constables Woods and Philips, and Doctor Johnson sitting in his living room, talking with Papa Nate and playing with the kids.

Demir helped Morgan into bed. She was not one for sitting still and, even with the pain meds that had practically knocked her out, it was a struggle getting her to stay there.

'You need rest, Morgan. You'll be up shortly enough, I'm sure. So give yourself a break, at least for now.'

After a half-hour of gentle encouragement, Demir left his sleeping wife in their bed to see what had prompted the return of his friends. They met him in the kitchen, grim-faced and without any of the carefree humour that had accompanied their earlier visit. Demir knew whatever tidings they brought would not be good.

'What happened?' he asked, bracing himself for the answer.

'It's Doctor Johnson,' Derek began, looking nervously to the vet, 'We had barely returned to the station before he gave us a call. We thought it was all a sick joke at first, but a call's a call, so we had to check it out.' He grew quiet, his voice just above a whisper. 'It was a bloodbath. Triple homicide, and one of the dogs as well. Looked like they were all slashed to death with scalpels.' He shook his head and took a few steps away to sit at the table, as if he could physically distance himself from the violent memory.

Donald took over for his partner, moving protectively close to Joel as he elaborated. 'Someone had written "In the name of love" on one of the walls with blood. Based on the staffing roster for the day, Joel says there's a nurse unaccounted for. He thinks she was taken hostage, but my money's on her for the murder. It's why we pulled Joel out of there. We've got to ask you a favour now. There's no official reason for him to be under any kind of protection, but I'm not about to trust his life with some young, love-crazed nurse murderer out there. Can he stay with you—unofficially of course—just for the next little while until we can sort this out a little more?'

Demir was reeling, struggling to process all that the police were saying, but instinct took over and he found himself distantly accepting a request he was still having trouble contemplating. 'Of course. You can stay in my old room, it's sort of an office now, but there's a futon in the closet we can put together for you. You can stay as long as you need.'

And before he knew it, whirlwind continuing, Derek and Donald were heading out the door, leaving Demir and Joel alone in the kitchen.

Finally shaking off the shock of the news, Demir turned to Joel—who by this point had grown tired or bored enough to seat himself at the table.

'Fuck, man…' Demir breathed. 'I'm glad you're alright. I can't beli— I can't say… Holy crap, that's rough.' He shared a long look with Joel then, unable to stop himself from thinking of the man's death, lying murdered in that same veterinary office.

Unbidden, that thought then turned to his grandfather's looming death. Not a death of sickness, but an image of Papa Nate cut apart brutally and laying beneath a blood-written banner espousing some bullshit about love being the spark for whatever burning hatred could lead to so savage a murder.

He shook his head hard, banishing the dark thoughts. *Focus on Joel, focus on the living. He's here now, he's your friend, and he probably almost died today.* 'You want some tea?'

Ana always felt a little odd going back home. She still considered the family farm to be her home despite the fact that she had spent the school months since Grade Eleven living with Milana at her aunt's house. It was just more convenient. Without a vehicle of her own, and with Demir working and Morgan always with the babies, it had been the only reliable way of making it to school everyday. But during Summer Vacation and on the occasional long weekend, Ana returned home.

Home to her old room. Home to all those memories, the vibrant and visceral memories of days spent playing with her brothers, with Papa Nate and Milana. It was home to ghostly memories too. The whisper of a barely-remembered motherly voice calling Ana from her room to come and eat, the ethereal form of her father, impressively tall darkening the doorway as he came in smelling of wheat, dust, and sweat after a day spent in the fields.

Her eyes kept straying to the surrounding countryside even as Milana tried to engage her in conversation, the passing scenery a conduit for wandering thoughts. She could name the family who lived on almost every farm between Oak Creek and Demir's place. This area was mostly filled with Ukrainian immigrants, some families in the country for four or more generations and still living as if they were back in Ukraine more than a hundred years before. A hundred thirty years before when no recognized country of Ukraine existed, when it was no more than an idea, a concept—hardly universal—used to unite diverse peoples from the shores of the Black Sea to the swampy forests of Polissia, from the Carpathians to the *dyke pole* where Soledar stood alone to tame the Donets.

Of course, most families in this region were from northeastern Ruthenia, which would make their homes now part of Poland, but that didn't stop them from speaking their unique form of Ukrainian and wearing *vyshyvanky* to the area's sole Ukrainian church every Sunday. A Catholic church, a relic of the Uniate movement that so briefly flourished in their homeland.

It's all like a sad memory. Like the ghosts of mom and dad. They celebrate something that no longer exists, that hasn't existed for over a hundred years and was never nearly as strong as they imagine it to have been.

Her father had come from the city of Brody in 1989, they thought they would fit right in with the rest of the Ukrainians. But they were from too far East and their language had been too Russified for them to really belong. So her father had kept mostly to himself, and in school Ana had insisted on the shortened form of her name, not daring to mention her heritage lest some overzealous nationalist, for a nation he or she had never stepped foot in, decide to step up and chastise her for letting the Soviet Union corrupt her tongue and culture.

'So what do you think Demir's big, scary text message was all about?' Milana asked.

Ana had shared the message with her earlier that day, and asked her to tag along for moral support for whatever awaited them at supper.

Ana realized that this was now Milana's fourth attempt to start a conversation. *Shake it off, Ana, you're being anti-social, locked in some internal reverie reflecting on things that stopped being a part of your life since you met Milana!*

Since their friendship had begun three years earlier, Ana no longer let those people or their views affect her. *People like Stephanie Horowitz and her perfect job at that perfect tech startup.* She shook away thoughts of Stephanie, *Don't let them get to you!* And turned to face her friend.

'I have no idea, but I have a feeling whatever it is, I'm blowing it out of proportion. I'm sure it won't be that bad.'

The self-reassuring smile she gave Milana was hollow. Ana knew it and Milana knew it, and the latter had enough care not to say anything about it.

'I'm sure you're right.' Milana responded. 'At the very least, there's no sense worrying about anything until we know there's something to worry about.'

Ana's smile deepened with that wisdom and when she looked out the window again, she thought not of ghosts, but of the stark beauty of the countryside in the deep of Winter, the only ghosts worth noting the *snow ghosts* of white-blanketed trees.

Welcomed so warmly by the land he had abandoned to attend meaningless classes in the city, in that grand conceit labeled education, Darko decided to walk the fenceline. It was a fondly-remembered tradition. Before he had passed away, Danylo Richovsky would take his family weekly on an expedition around the perimeter of their farm. 'It's important to know your land' he had said each time, and those words came floating back to Darko then out of a long-forgotten memory to guide him in his journey around the fenceline.

He meandered along the Northwestern corner of the fenceline, following the slow decline of the field, until reaching the secondary, internal fence. Unlike the simple thrice-stringed barbed wire, the inner fence was made up of tall wooden pylons connected by an intersecting latticework of branches. Darko had spent long hours with his siblings lacing those smaller branches through the larger ones. He felt he had left a part of himself in that fence. It was, in a word, formidable.

Still not enough to stop a determined bison—not even close—though, I suppose it's visible enough to deter most would-be escape attempts. And isn't

*that a damn profound metaphor? How many walls
in our lives are flimsy, brittle things that could be
shattered with a lowered head and a running start?
And yet we keep our heads high, and we walk at a
relaxed, cool pace, not wanting to risk making
others uncomfortable.*

Rather than being built inside the older, more
permanent barbed-wire fence, the Bison Wall—as
Ana had always called it—was built atop and
around the barbed wire, thereby incorporating the
shorter fence into the larger. The Bison Wall had
been built just within the treeline of the woods,
keeping the small herd within its sheltering
expanse. The wheat was protected from the bison
and, in a fair trade, the bison were given the largest
section of the Richovsky homestead.

It was inside the Bison Wall, among those
Winter-dried and leafless trees, that the warmth of
the land's welcome faded to be slowly overtaken by
a sense of unease.

It was not the simple feeling of being watched
that had Darko slowing defensively and peering
into the depths of every shadow for signs of danger,
it was the feeling of anger that accompanied those
unseen eyes. The feeling of an intense hatred—and
it was directed at him. It was as if these woods—or
something that walked them—despised every fibre
of Darko's being.

Instinctively crouching as he spun a slow circle, eyes sweeping his surroundings, Darko spied a section of broken fence. The wood and branches remained perfectly intact, preserving the fence's function of keeping the bison within its confines, but all three strings of barbed wire and the iron fittings that had once fastened them were torn from their posts and trampled to the ground. The posts that had held them were themselves relatively recently replaced. Darko was able to tell since they bore none of the carvings his father had so meticulously carved into all the others. It was as if a great magnetic force from somewhere deep in the earth had pulled at all that iron, ripping it from its place in the fence and burying it deep in the surrounding snows.

Or, Darko mused worriedly as that baleful presence seemed to draw nearer, *something pushed it down.*

A light, steady wind moaned its way through the woods, rattling branches and rustling dead leaves. The wind's whisper crescendoed directly overhead as that hostile presence descended for Darko. Wind and anger rushed at him, the bitter chill paining his ears, the sound impossibly loud for a wind so light.

He fought the wind's voice with his own. Drawing in as much breath as his frightened, spasming lungs could manage, Darko stood tall, deepened his voice in imitation of his father's and, as Danylo had done in these woods countless times before, he summoned the Richovsky bison.

'*De moji bizony?*' His call briefly silenced the wind, its whispers skittering away, weaving through the trees with a speed only the wind could manage and the hateful presence staggered. Darko began running toward the centre of the closer of the two valleys, the designated meeting place of the bison since first Darko's father had trained their ears for human tongues.

Recovering, the presence and its whispering winds gave chase. It surrounded him, buffeted him with its anger. Dark thoughts slammed into Darko's consciousness as he ran. Suddenly the surroundings he looked on as he ran were overpowered by horrifying mental images.

A house ablaze, black smoke roaring skyward. Children coughing, a mother screaming. Dogs outside, helpless, their barking quieting to soft whines even as the flames swallowed all.

'*De moji bizony?!!*' Darko leapt over a fallen tree, he could see the ridge marking the top of the valley ahead. He tried to concentrate on that ridge, tried to shake off the dark thoughts. The scene of the fire wavered, but only for a moment before that feeble concentration vanished and a new image broke through, filling his mind.

A car on a quiet road, two men in front, three children behind. They approached an intersection with a major highway with alarming speed. As the driver slammed his foot repeatedly, desperately, down on the unresponsive breaks, he turned his panicked expression to face his partner. The other man understood all in that gaze. He gave a sad smile back and squeezed the driver's shoulder. As the car sped toward the intersection, collision with the approaching tractor-trailer imminent, the driver made a final, instinctive decision to save his family. He slammed the wheel as far left as it would go, as fast and as hard as he could manage. Too fast, too hard. Instead of swerving, the car rolled, tumbling directly into the path of the semi where it exploded on impact, metal shearing metal in deafening horror.

'*DE MOJI BIZONY?!!*' This time the shout banished the images completely.

Darko was surprised to find himself standing in the valley, tears rolling down his cheeks. As the echoes of his call faded, the gentle trickling of the diverted river could be heard below. He descended the slope for that stream, the waters growing louder as the winds above faded. And from the crest of the valley's opposite bank, bison appeared.

The woodland bison descended the valley at a slow trot, uninhibited by the steepness of the bank. The rich brown of their hair was dusted with snow, giving the bison an almost ghostly appearance. Darko awaited them at the river's edge. The water was deep enough and flowed quickly enough to keep all but the banks from freezing. And even there, the banks were covered only by a thin layer of brittle, translucent ice.

Darko could feel the presence above, feel its weight slowly descending to the valley's centre where even now the front hooves of half a dozen bison punched through the thin bank-ice, the beasts wading toward Darko across the cold stream.

The first few bison to splash their way to Darko's side immediately grew uneasy upon sensing the hostile presence. They shifted nervously, huffing and sniffing, tossing their heads in the air. The small herd had grown in size since last Darko had seen them, and soon he was surrounded by thirteen bison in a defensive ring, only himself and a yearling within.

The wind above moaned louder and the presence pushed at those in the valley. Darko could feel the vile bitterness edging its way into his own thoughts and feelings. The rattling of wind-whipped branches and the sighing of the gusty winds was like a voice expressing that bitterness. But the meaning of those words remained just beyond Darko's understanding. Like a language he had once known but could no longer recognize.

There seemed to be safety in numbers, for this time as the dark thoughts descended they were weaker, coming in flashes witnessed rather than lived.

A house in the stream of a great and violent flow of floodwaters. The water level reached to just beneath the roof and the family huddled safely atop its tin slope, grandparents, parents, children, grandchildren, a crowd of eleven scared souls waiting for rescue.

Fighting back against the images, Darko searched for a source of strength. He wrapped his fingers around the nearest bison's thick and rough hair.

From upstream there flowed a great tree. No—a plane! Eleven voices cried out as their doom flowed toward them. Their squat home had withstood the mighty force of the flood, but the waters had taken their toll, soaking through every timber, washing out the foundations. The plane's metal hull tore into the water-logged house, collapsing it. Eleven cries were replaced by bubbling, gurgling gasps for air. All were forced down into the water, trapped under the weight and bulk of the roof and plane.

The presence of the bison helped, protecting Darko from the severeness of the despair accompanying the images, but it was not enough to turn away whatever malevolent being floated overhead.

Of course, the river. 'I am Darko Richovsky, this is my land, and here rivers will rise!' He took a single, laboured step toward the stream.

The grandfather, seeing his grandson floating down in the floodwater's currents, dove deeper in a desperate attempt at rescue. By the time he had wrapped his arms around the boy, there was a gap of sunlight above. Lungs burning, he clawed for it desperately.

Darko took another step. There were only three paces now between him and the edges of that stream.

The grandfather broke the surface, gasping for air. The plane and the house rode the surface downstream and the man knew, he could feel it in his heart, that the others would drown beneath all that debris.

Another step.

Miraculously the grandson seemed unharmed. Though he coughed and sputtered briefly, his breathing returned to normal within moments, and the toddler smiled at the old man. Heart breaking and mending all in the same moment, the grandfather found a new strength in the boy's smile and began swimming diagonally for the edge of the floodwaters.

One. More. Step.

Though he neared exhaustion, the grandfather knew he could make it, knew he had to make it. Even if he died, he would deliver the boy to safety.

Darko faltered as one of the bison barrelled into him. The beasts were fighting their own battles of will and their stressed tossing and shifting sent Darko to the ground. He wondered briefly if the bison could understand his intentions, for the collision had knocked him significantly closer to the stream. He clawed his way to cover the short distance remaining, a ragged shout of defiance tearing its way from his throat.

Something slammed into the grandfather, some invisible force that woke old injuries with fresh agony. His hold on the boy was growing weak. The thing slammed into him again and again, but he would not be stopped. He had resigned himself to this swim as his final act and he would not have that final act be a failure. Never before had the man felt such pain, but what is pain to a man about to die? The more he resisted, the angrier the invisible force grew, hitting harder and harder until suddenly it retreated, going someplace deep into the waters below.

Darko understood now. This hateful presence wasn't showing these images to demoralize him and crush his spirit. *The bastard's bragging!* His hands had reached the bank-ice of the stream and he clawed at it weakly, trying to punch a hole through that brittle ice with his cold fingers.

From far below, lifted by a combination of a sizeable air pocket and some malevolent spirit, a car, of all things, rushed for the surface of the floodwaters. The automobile took the grandfather in his old and brittle legs, shattering the bones. It ascended with such force that grandfather and grandson were knocked into the air. The boy flew from the grandfather's hands to be swallowed by a wave. Tossed higher than the toddler, the grandfather landed on the floating car, his back breaking with the impact. There he was stuck unable to move as wave after wave of horrible pain washed over him.

At last Darko's finger tips had pushed through the brittle ice. His fingertips touching water was all the strength he needed. *I don't need to see how your murder ends.* With only the tips of his fingers, now given strength by the flowing water beneath them, Darko was able to pull himself head-first into the stream.

The water was faster, colder, deeper than he had thought, and Darko floundered beneath the surface before managing to dig in his feet, brace himself against the current, and rise in defiance to face the evil spirit above. Though most of the bison had crossed the stream in a single leap, Darko stood thigh-deep in the waters, a full arm span from either bank. As he reoriented himself, water dripping off him so rapidly that it reversed the stream's flow for the briefest of moments, Darko's attention was gripped by the whispering wind.

This time, there were words in those whispers. The voice was harsh, vile as a poison.

'End them. End them as they ended me. They showed no care for me. ME! Me who cared for naught but them. Well, they had their chance to reciprocate. Now it is I who has reason for remuneration and I intend to treat them all with the same wickedness and apathy they showed in forgetting me. And I shan't stop until it is *them* who are forgotten! Gone and forgotten, every one of them, their bones and memories left to rot unto oblivion alongside mine!'

Darko stood in the river looking to the centre of where he felt the presence. Ever so faintly, almost as if it were not there at all, he saw a figure. Dark hair bobbed on her head and, though her spectre floated closer to him, her attention seemed to be elsewhere.

'Begone!' Darko shouted, and she turned to face him then. He could feel the water surging beneath the surface, gathering around his legs, holding them fast against the current.

The spectre glared at Darko menacingly. Then her eyes flashed down to the water swirling about

Darko's legs and suddenly the winds gasped. The bitter anger shifted to desperation. And fear.

Her spectre was suddenly launching away, out of the valley and out of sight. And as her retreat took the winds with it, Darko heard her pleading frantically, 'No, no, not the waters. Not again. No, no, not the waters, no! Not the waters…'

Once she was gone, Darko carefully picked his way up and out of the stream, fully expecting to begin shivering immediately as he fought off the clawing onset of hypothermia. But, to his surprise as dry shoes crunched on crystalline snow, he was completely dry. And warm.

The bison around him began to relax as well. One of the older males nuzzled its solid head with a surprising tenderness against Darko's body. He scratched the tops of the beast's shoulders, wondering for a moment if it was Staryk, the first and oldest of the Richovsky herd, one his father had never been able to butcher.

Before he could search for old scars amidst that thick hair, as one the heads of the bison turned easteard. They froze, listening to some sound Darko could hear no trace of. Then they began leaving, their shambling climb taking them away from that unheard sound.

Darko pulled out his phone to check the time only to find that the battery was dead.

Yep. Seems about right. Talking winds, evil spectres, dreams within dreams of families dying horribly, I'll be waking shortly on my couch. And as bizarre as this all has been, I'm sure it won't be the strangest dream I recall upon waking.

A little surprised that the realization he had been dreaming was not enough to wake him, Darko shrugged his shoulders and set off for the Richovsky home, Demir's house, unsure if his journey would take him to that house, or to wakefulness.

Demir sat at the table with Joel, his neighbour, his friend, struggling to find the right words. *Struggling to find any words,* he admitted. *You could have died!* That seemed the only thought his numbed mind was capable of and the words repeated in his head over, and over, and relentlessly over again.

How long has it been? Five minutes? Ten? An hour? He sipped at his tea. It was still his first cup, and it was still scalding. *Fine then,* he asked himself again sarcastically, *how many seconds?*

He was relieved when Alexander toddled into the kitchen calling for him, putting an end to the uneasy silence punctuated only by the occasional sipping of tea.

'*Tato, tato, tato. Tato, tato, taatoo.*' Demir was still deciphering whether Alex was actually calling him or simply singing, when the boy tugged at his shirt.

'Dad?' Alex asked again, as if offended that Demir had been unable to tell.

'Yes, Alex?'

'Come see what I built!' He demanded excitedly, all trace of being offended vanished.

Like your mother answering the phone during an argument, Demir mused humorously. His private joke brought only sadness in place of mirth as Morgan's drug-slackened smile filled his mind, followed by images of those bloody stitches at the end of her tongue.

'Sure, buddy. What did you make?' He did his best to emulate little Alex, to keep worry from his tone. He succeeded only insofar as sounding utterly exhausted instead.

He turned to Joel, 'You don't mind do you?'

'What?' The man gave a shocked smile. 'Of course not, go see to your son,' he chuckled.

All things considered, you're reacting a whole lot better toward this triple homicide thing than I am. Or the police for that matter… All that time with those dogs is addling your brain, Joel. That shit-eating grin might as well be a wagging tail.

With a grunt of effort, Demir rose and followed his son down the hall to his office where Alexander stood over his work proudly.

'Holy—' Demir could not hide his shock. Beneath Alex's proud stance was displayed a replica of his house, made entirely of the blocks the boy and Klara had been playing with that morning. Alex had included every room, had captured every angle, and it even looked to be the proper scale—at least as much as the blocks had allowed.

Demir bent down and hugged his son. 'That's great, buddy! That's damned good! *Molodets!*' Alex's cheeks turned red and he tried to squirm out of the hug and the compliment. He then sat down and demolished his creation.

Demir wanted to say something, wanted to reassure his son that it was okay to be praised from time to time, as long as a man did not let that praise affect the way he perceived and treated others. He sighed and slumped in his office chair instead.

That is what my father taught me, so why does the lesson ever seem lost on my own son? Why does he refuse to accept a compliment, why is he deferent instead of humble, subservient in place of helpful? Where is your self-esteem, Alex? Where is your spine?

Demir sighed again deeply, stretching in his chair and only realizing as a great yawn accompanied that stretch just how exhausted he was. He knew better than to try saying something to Alex, every attempt in the past had simply made things worse, caused the boy to retreat even farther into that cave he had built for himself. Demir conceded that the whole thing was his fault. Morgan had said on multiple occasions that he was too hard on his son, expected too much of him., that he needed to praise the boy more. *But whenever I do, this happens.*

I'm doing my best here. Fuck, it's not like I can turn to my own dad for advice. And whenever I ask Papa Nate, he insists he cannot give fatherly advice to his grandchild, only grandfatherly advice.

Demir tried to distract himself—he had another fourteen or so years to fuck up Alex's life—so he turned in his desk chair to face his computer and, grabbing the mouse, shook it from sleep mode.

The screen was as he had left it, with the email from his office cancelling the Valentine's Friendship team-building exercise on behalf of a violent altercation. He shook his head incredulously, exactly as he had upon first reading the message that morning. *How are people so foul? How are they so internally broken, that they get into fights over an activity based on friendship?!* He noticed there was an attachment to the message which had auto-loaded, and scrolled down to see it.

Recognition set in immediately. It was the original memo that had contained all the details for the team-building activity. It explained how those in each department were to be given *virtues* and had to secretly find the person whose virtue matched their own. The winner would get to be the boss of the loser for a year. *No wonder there was violence. People will do anything for power, even imagined power in closed systems like an office.* Demir's thoughts dripped with a bitter cynicism toward his fellow man. *Even the lure of getting to send some lesserling for a pen fills people with such a repulsive, jittering thrill, that they're willing to beat the crap out of one another for the fucking privilege.*

Demir sighed again, and this time it was a sigh of relief. Relief that he knew his craft well enough to be permitted to work from home. Relief that he had somehow, miraculously found a handful of the all-too-few decent individuals in this world to surround himself with. His friends, his family. He knew it was unfair, knew he was gifted beyond belief to have such people in his life. He knew that no matter what good he might do in his lifetime, it would never make up for the imbalance of it. He wasn't simply humbled by the thought, he was broken by it.

He made to delete the email, but as his cursor hovered over the command, he noted something in the bottom corner of the memo. Something familiar.

The symbol! In the lower-left corner of the memo attachment there was a copyright symbol next to a nine-pointed star surrounded by a ring. *Or, maybe it's a wheel?* He shoved his chair back from his desk at the shock of it. He then nearly fell out of that chair upon seeing, beneath his desk, that same symbol constructed out of his children's blocks.

Demir stood up hurriedly, one hand reaching for the phone on his desk, the other pointing accusingly at the symbol on the floor. 'Where did you see that?' He demanded of Alex, his words slow, an edge of danger in his tone.

Alex read the worry on his father's face stood up from his blocks. 'I don't know,' he answered. 'Uncle Darko made that.'

'You mean Uncle Joel, Uncle Darko won't be here till supper' Demir corrected, and if Alex had an answer to that, it was cut off by Demir turning around. He began dialling.

Oh Joel, he sighed. *Not the happy dog after all. Beneath those masking smiles, you're broken aren't you? Have you connected the murders in your mind? Do you, even now, connect all the negativity in your life to some great evil? Or worse, to some minor sin you committed in your past?*

The phone was ringing. Demir raised his voice and called for his friend. *I'll sort this all out.* 'Joel! I need you in here please!' He heard a chair scuff against the kitchen floor and the slow approach of footsteps when someone picked up on the other line.

Demir had his boss, David Mokre on speed dial, and it wasn't until he heard the man's characteristic 'Yellow!' in answering the phone that he realized he probably should have called the police first. He hesitated, prompting a slightly-more serious, "Hey" from his boss.

'Uhh, hey David, it's Demir here—'

'I know, man, it's this great thing called Caller ID. You're really going to have to pull your farmer ass into this century one of these days, you know that, don't you?'

'Ha ha. Yeah. Thing is, I'm wondering about that Valentine's activity thing. The one that was cancelled. Where'd you get the idea for that?'

'Oh God, man! Don't rub it in, we've got two people pressing charges for assault. I'm seriously thinking of shutting this whole office down, kicking everyone out, and we can all work like a bunch of hermits from the safety of our own homes. No offence.'

'No, it's not that kind of call…' Joel had arrived, crowding the doorway and looking to Demir curiously. Behind the vet, another form shadowed the hallway, whoever it was stood just around the corner enough to hide his or her identity.

'Sorry, I don't have time to joke around, I'll call back later and explain. I just need to know, did you draft the thing yourself, you find it on Instagram or something like that?'

'Instagram?! Look who just stepped into the modern era—well, more 2015, but still—congratulations!'

'David, I don't have time.' The shadow in the hallway shifted. *Is that Morgan? Why isn't she sleeping?*

'Okay, okay. I was just having a bit of fun. The real icing on the cake of this whole thing is that the activity was given to us by Finster and Gable Inc. those fat cats from downtown who didn't think it was important to pay us for our work. I sent an email about them defaulting on their payments this morning. Those pricks are—'

'Yeah, I got the email. Is their contact info still on file?'

'Sure is, it's tagged on the server under "Scumbag Clients."'

The shadow in the hallway stepped forward and for the briefest of moments, still shadowed as it was, Demir thought he was looking at his father. The illusion was shattered with the man's next step as Darko stepped fully into the light, his dishevelled hair dispelling the thought that he might be mistaken for anyone who looked even remotely stately.

'That's great, David. Thanks so much. Listen, I've really got to go now. Call you back later?' The phone was in the cradle before an answer came.

Demir took a deep breath and turned to his younger brother. *You look like a corpse, Darko. The blue bags under your eyes could be holding oceans. Is that... bison hair on your shirt?*

'Which one of you built this?' he demanded.

'I did. Sorry I didn't say hi, you were with Morgan when I got here.' Darko's voice was weak, raw, as if he had just been shouting.

Any concern Demir had for his brother's wellbeing was overshadowed by the fact that Darko had recreated a symbol associated with a murder. *If you've fallen in with some cult at that university, I swear on Dad that I'll kill you myself.*

'Well...?' Demir demanded. *Come on, brother. You've got some explaining to do.*

CHAPTER TEN: Opposing Virtues

Wednesday, 17 February 2021

'Forlorn and forsaken.' Steven Yung, Honesty, was twisted in his seat, stopping overlong at the intersection to regard his companions and ensure the weight of his words would sink in.

'That is how they answered the door,' he continued. 'But did you see those smiles as we drove away? *Smiles!* Waves, smiles, calls to visit again, and the gentle dabbing of tears with Grace's own kerchief.' He turned his focus to the woman in the passenger seat. 'Nice touch on that one, you're learning quickly.'

'Those parting tears were not of sorrow, not of the abject helplessness that Nessie's family has felt the past few days, but tears of hope!'

He turned to take in both of his companions once more, but all he received for his speech was silence. Fort already had his eyes locked on Grace's side-mirror, tugging away at his ear and Grace's attention was likewise absent, her mouth moving delicately with unvoiced thoughts, her eyes somewhere on the road up ahead.

Eh, good enough, he thought with a half-shrug, twisting around once more to hit the gas.

'Drop you and Fort off at the usual spot?'

'Sounds fine.' Grace did not even turn with her answer, her attention distant.

Honesty thought to stop again, or to say a few more words emphasizing the importance and success of what they had done today. *We changed three lives. We saved them! We turned anger, sadness, confused desperation back into something human. We restored hope today. And in so doing, we returned love to three hardened and bleeding hearts.*

And is that not the true teaching of the Friend? To make this world, so cruel and cold, just a little bit warmer? A kinder world where love triumphs over greed, empathy over selfishness? A world where humanity becomes humane and learns to feel *again?*

Yes, our wheel of a constellation turns overhead, hidden by the light of day, and beneath its bulk we shall continue to crush all that is cold in this world, and replace it with the fire of Friendship.

He looked to Grace then, her mouth still silently mumbling some hidden thoughts. *Perhaps she too reflects as I do. In her own, silent way. And who am I to claim inattentiveness or misunderstanding in interruption of her deepest, most intimate faiths. No, I've said enough. My Minor Virtues are capable enough. I must have faith in them just as they have in me.*

Fort's ear was beginning to hurt from all the tugging, but he couldn't stop now. His eyes were locked on the reflection of Grace's face in the side-mirror, visually caressing the curves of her little nose, peering into the depths of those tiny, dark nostrils. Everything was as it had been before, on their drive to Vanessa's parents' house, but something felt off. Grace looked the same, Fort's ear-pulling was the same, the car, the mirror, nothing had changed. The change was inside him. And it was frightening.

His thoughts flowed freely, abstractly, as he reflected on the accomplishments of the so-called Virtues in this little car. He clenched his jaw, feeling the comforting pressure of teeth grinding on teeth so that no secrets might slip out.

Our little car. Our little famous car. One of the last. Final Five-hundred Aurora, that beautiful "dark cherry metallic" limited edition paint job. That chrome number emblazoned: a resplendent 261 for all the world to see. The celebration of death.

Is all life sacrifice? Vanessa's final hours were a celebration. A romantic date with Honesty, a walk, a picnic beneath the stars—fake stars in an auditorium, but still stars—and surely one final kiss before he killed her, the smearing of a "dark cherry metallic" lipstick across two sets of lips. And these

173

last five-hundred models of the Aurora were a
celebratory sacrifice of their own.

His jaw was aching from the clenching of teeth
and he could taste blood where his single emergent
wisdom tooth was pushing down on bare gums. He
opened his mouth in a loud gasp, somewhat from
the pain, somewhat from the relief of pressure, but
mostly out of a revelation.

This time he could not contain his thoughts. He
felt his mouth moving and clicking from stiffness,
heard the vibration of his own voice in his skull,
but he could not stop it, could not prevent the
secrets from spilling out.

'This is our celebration! Honesty had his final
date, first with Vanessa, then her family. And we're
a part of it. He brought us with him. This
celebration of restoring love to three broken hearts.
And how full we felt, how happy, how fulfilled.
You fucking bastard, you did this to us! Don't you
see, we're going to die?!'

Forthrightness stopped tugging at his ear and
moved to writhing against the seatbelt instead.
Ignoring the concerned questions of his
companions, he slammed his body into the door of
the sacrificial car. He made no effort to actually
leave the vehicle, but every muscle and bone
strained to free itself from the confines of his body.

'It's not dark fucking cherry metallic! It's
blood, it's blood, it's all blood! Free me, kill me,

free me! We're going to die! We're going to die!
WE'RE GOING TO DIE!'

Grace had gotten into the car bitter and
confused. *How could he be right? How can acting
independently of our faith community be justified?
How can disobedience and betrayal of our brothers
and sisters serve them better? This shouldn't be
happening! But I can feel that it's right. My heart
is bursting with an indescribable warmth. The very
touch of the Friend grips me and comforts me for
our work today. Our ugly, traitorous work.*
It was difficult to reconcile her emotions. On
the one hand, Grace felt a satisfying fulfilment
unlike anything ever experienced in her life. It
slowed her heart, warmed her insides, and gave her
head a buzzing weightlessness. But in the midst of
such pleasantness, she was being torn apart by
doubts. *Has Honesty been right all along? How
can I have faith in my god, but not in the very
institution that is devoted to the Friend, to giving
the Friend power? The very institution that
introduced me to my faith? How does Honesty
justify his actions?*
Grace was so deeply entrenched within her own
mind and heart, that it took violent shouting and
banging from the backseat to bring her mind into
the present. The entire car rocked with Fort's

twisting and flopping. Grace spun in her seat in a panic.

'WE'RE GOING TO DIE!'

'What are you talking about, Fort? Calm down. Calm down and look at me, talk to me.' Honesty's eyes bounced between the road and the rear-view mirror. In that soft, appeasing tone, Grace was reminded once again how very young Fort was.

Though the two were only five years apart, the fact that Fort was not yet twenty, made the distance in age seem twice as great. She made an effort to soften her voice and likewise tried to calm the boy.

'Fort, look at me. No, stop with that and look at me. Tell me what's wrong, why are we going to die?'

But it was no use, nothing seemed able to reach Forthrightness. He continued struggling in his seat and shouting of death. He tore his shirt off and began yanking at his belt. And it was only then that Grace realized it was not fear nor panic that marked his tone, but an excited yearning, a gleeful expectancy.

'I am ready, Friend! We are ready! Free us, kill us, free us! WE'RE GONNA DIE!!'

Ljuba Kowalchuk, Lust, had to admit to herself that she had actually enjoyed her afternoon with Fidelity. What had started as an artificial pleasantness had been gently massaged into a genuine, budding friendship. Gently, sensually massaged...

Lust and Fidelity sat in the front of Ljuba's car, unbuckled and turned toward each other. They were enjoying a bit of fast food parked in the snow-covered grass just off the road beneath the Koo-Koo-Sint overpass, patiently awaiting the arrival of their quarry. Lust had kicked off her shoe and was gently caressing her smooth leg with her bare toes. Her eyes were locked on Fidelity's lips. She drank in their gentle parting and aggressive reunification over a mouthful of burger.

What an extraordinarily humble beauty. A truly unique creature. One hand picking at fries, Ljuba's other reached behind her seat to retrieve her purse. She brought the bag around and set it between her legs, the gun-weighted bulk of it on her skirt baring more skin. She noted, mildly amused, that Fidelity had stopped eating. Instead she stared, mouth agape, at Lust's legs, no doubt thinking Lust would dismiss that hungry gaze for interest in the leather purse. *Hmm, I think I've settled on dessert.*

'Mind if I have a taste?' Though Lust's eyes were on Fidelity's burger, the question was charged with a seductive edge.

Lust knew the power her sexuality had over others, knew its limits, and she equally knew that Fidelity's fierce independence made for a

177

potentially dangerous target of that power. Lust glanced nervously at the clock on the dashboard even as Fidelity wordlessly extended a half-eaten burger her way. *I have time,* she reassured herself. *I can do this. Oh, Friend, we're going to do this!*

Lust reached past the burger, grabbing Fidelity's small hands instead, enveloping them in her own. She gently pulled the burger to her mouth, taking a slow bite, just above Fidelity's fingers. She let her mouth linger for a moment, hot breath cascading over the other woman's hand. As she bit down, she gently took one of those fingers between her lips, running her tongue over it with only the slightest of pressure before letting it slip away as she pulled back with her bite.

It was a measured move, timed to the millisecond, and Lust knew she had been exact. The contact had been just quick enough, just soft enough to be mistaken for an awkward accident. Unless—of course—Fidelity was equally interested. *And look at the burning in her eyes. Oh, how she hungers!* Lust waited, confident in her precision.

She enjoyed the other woman's rapt attention, basked in it. Teasing her, Lust chewed slowly. She glanced at the clock once more, just to be sure. She knew Honesty would be driving by to his death sometime within the next ten minutes, but it was not her job to watch for him, it was only her job to clean up the mess if Generosity, Cooperation, and Devotion should fail.

Lust moaned softly, *as if any burger could be that good,* and leaned back in her seat, casually opening the window. When next she turned to her companion, there was a fire in Lust's eyes to match Fidelity's own. Without any words, Lust grabbed what was left of both their meals, threw it out the open window, kicked off her other shoe, and stretched across the centre console to take Fidelity's face in both her hands.

And when Lust planted that first kiss, burning with passion and desire, the quiet gasps and grunts of satisfaction escaping unbidden from Fidelity almost had Lust wondering if it was not somehow Fidelity who had seduced her. Almost.

Cooperation had always thought Devotion to be aptly named. Cooperation and devotion, brothers in faith, business partners, best of friends. Cooperation and Devotion, Tyrell Finster and Edward Gable, had been among the founding members of what they called Friendship: worship of the Friend. A perfectly innocuous name for a guiding faith that was, at times, quite the opposite.

Tyrell Finster's best friend was as devoted to his companions as he was to his faith. Together, Finster and Gable had prepared and executed the very first sacrifice in the name of Friendship.

Together, it was their spark of genius, of disseminating Friendship literature to the masses, that was ever bringing more people into the faith. And, now that their website was finally up and running, Finster and Gable would be bringing in a dozen new followers a day.

Cooperation had to fight the urge to look across at his best friend then. They were each of them, Cooperation, Devotion, and Generosity, standing watch at the edge of the overpass, fighting a shiver in the cold, eyes glued on the approaching traffic. Even with the Winter sun already setting, Honesty's car would be impossible to miss. Not many people drove Oldsmobile Auroras since they had been discontinued, and only five hundred had ever been made in that commemorative dark cherry metallic. But, excited and nervous as Cooperation was, he felt his heartbeat speeding up, hands going clammy, with every vehicle approaching that was even remotely red. He had been there, teetered at the railing, struggling with the weight of the block of reinforced concrete held between his body and the rails of the overpass, for nearly fifteen minutes now.

His only comfort was in having Devotion and Generosity there at his side, each with their own hulking chunks of concrete. He was confident that, together, the three of them would have no trouble accomplishing their task. Committing their murder.

He had been unconvinced that it was the proper course of action at first. How could fewer followers ever be more effective than a great host of them? *And so what if Honesty sacrificed someone and didn't tell us about it until later? Gable and I still haven't told anyone about that Friendship activity we've been distributing throughout the province. Nor of our webpage. Not that we'd ever tell anyone now, of course, or we'll be the next victims.*

But all his lingering doubts were driven off by the comforting constancy of his fellows standing there at his side. He had confidence that theirs was the proper course of action by simple virtue of cooperation being necessary to enact it.

So it was with a smile of anticipation, in place of trepidation, that Cooperation's eyes fixed on the approaching car. Visible from around the bend, the dark metallic cherry and low frame were unmistakable. *Unless, of course, some unlucky bastard who happens to be among the four-hundred ninety-nine others with this exact car happens to be driving through Acton...*

Cooperation hesitated, for just a moment, in hefting his chunk of reinforced concrete, his murder weapon. He entertained the possibility that some supremely unlucky soul had found himself on the wrong road, in the wrong car, at the worst possible time. But to his left, his companions already had their hulks of stone hoisted overhead, so, borrowing from their confidence, Cooperation lifted his own, took a step toward the overpass's edge, and waited for the car's imminent arrival.

Lust's right hand was still on Fidelity's cheek as her left began to slip down, from the woman's chest to her belly. There, she hesitated a moment, before rapping that left hand around Fidelity's waste. Lust's eyes were closed and her body began to rock slowly, rhythmically, through the kisses the two women shared.

There is a music to lovemaking, a rhythm and melody, but it is no pop love-song. Not even close. It's a full orchestral symphony, fluting highs overtaking tromboning lows, a row of timpanis stomping the plodding gate of horses through a field of flowers even as cymbals crash with the diving of winged doves high above. And adjacent to the musicians is a troupe of the finest dancers, their feet a flurry of imperceptible movement as they glide across the stage. And all that is a painting too, colours splashed in evocation of a deep memory, subtle and textured, written across the canvas. And it is a poem, and the sculpting of ice, and a cheetah's last hunt through a sun-baked savannah, and a gazelle's heart attack-inducing flight, and, and...

And it overwhelmed Lust, just as it had every time before, and would every time again. She knew she would have to kill Fidelity as soon as they were done, but she was determined to enjoy this moment as deeply as possible, for as long as possible. While Lust's left hand slowly slipped from Fidelity's waist down to the front of her jeans, Fidelity's hands were also moving. Fidelity's one hand was wrapped tight around Lust's head, holding their faces close together. Though Lust usually hated the feeling of being trapped by a lover, something about Fidelity's particular way of doing it made Lust enjoy it, made her want Fidelity to press harder still. Fidelity's other hand moved now from gripping Lust's thigh and found itself between her legs.

Fidelity opened the purse that was resting there, and reached deep within. *Oh, no, don't tease me, my love. Push harder, harder!*

Instead of pushing harder, the pressure suddenly released and Fidelity pulled back. Lust chased after her, lips grabbing blindly at the air until a firm push back from Fidelity made Lust open her eyes for the first time since they had started kissing.

Oh, thank you Friend! Look how beautiful she is! Lust's eyes slowly tracked downward from Fidelity's dishevelled hair—somehow more beautiful now than before—to those passion-burning eyes, to those delicious lips which had pulled back into a most satisfied smile, down to those full breasts, those muscular arms and dainty hands, and—

Lust suddenly jumped back. In her small, slender fingers, Fidelity held Lust's gun. Ljuba worked her mouth, fighting through the sudden, paralyzing decent of terror to find some life-saving words.

Fidelity said nothing. She just smiled that smug smile, and pulled the trigger.

'Talk to me, Fort, you're scaring me!' Honesty's voice was fraught with worry. Fort's shouting of death had quieted to a soft singing until now. Now, as they rounded a bend in the road, Fort went silent. He looked more aware than he had ever been: he sat straight in his seat, hands folded in his lap, posture perfect, and his eyes were closed. He would respond to neither Honesty nor Grace, their concerned questions falling on uninterested ears.

Honesty had already made up his mind. He would not leave Fort at the normal bus stop with Grace. After Grace was gone, he would take Fort directly home, he would talk with the boy's parents, enduring whatever awkward questions they would ask, weathering whatever vicious accusations they might make, and he would see to Fort's wellbeing.

How can we truly claim to serve the Friend if we cannot even treat each other with a true sense of friendship? How can I live with myself, claiming to be a Major Virtue, if I cannot even be virtuous to a fellow member of the faithful? I will not abandon you to your condition, Fort. This is why we serve the Friend. The Friend will make this a better world where those like you can always count on their fellow Man to lend a hand, to help and to serve, so that healing can take place. Aspergers is a trait you possess, it is not who you are.

'I promise you, Fort, I'll take care of you. We'll see this through together.'

Attention stolen by the image of his silent passenger in the rear-view mirror, Steven Yung failed to notice the figures in the distance crowding the edge of the overpass. And, nearer still, he saw not the car parked off the road, nor the bloom of red that suddenly darkened its windows.

Fidelity spilled out of the car, wiping the blood from her eyes and letting it fall from her open mouth. It all looked black in the twilight-darkened snows. Though she felt like retching from the filth, her disgust was dwarfed by a sense of victory.

I can't believe that worked! That bitch has nothing but sex on her mind. Lust indeed. She was so, extraordinarily self-possessed that she couldn't even fathom that I might've had perfidious plans of

185

my own. And now she's dead for it. Fate sure is fickle, Lust. The Friend is fickle.

You thought that since I was named Fidelity, I was bound in obeisance to the other Major Virtues? It is not a virtue of my personal character towards others, Fidelity is the virtue of my faith for the Friend. I would shoot all eight of you for the Friend if it was in her interest. You thought to kill Honesty for what, for taking initiative in his devotion? It just so happens that little independent sacrifice of his was single the most powerful act of devotion any of us have expressed. Well... until now.

Fidelity leaned forward, peering into the open door of the car, just to make sure Lust was truly dead, and immediately reeled from the scene. Despite most of her head being collapsed and covered in gore, the body of Lust was still twitching, still settling in the front seat. A sense of anxiety washed over Fidelity, threatening to overwhelm her. *Friend, have mercy! What if her gun hadn't been in her purse? Would she have known what I was trying to do? How close was Lust to pulling away and killing me?* Fidelity fought down the rising panic, forced her breathing to slow, and reminded herself that none of those possibilities had occurred. *I'm alive and Lust is dead, and that's all there is to it.*

It was not her hollow words that allowed for Fidelity's impossibly fast recovery from the anxiety attack, it was the death of Lust. As life finally left Lust's body, a surge of power rushed through Fidelity. It was as if every tendon, muscle, and bone was thrumming with energy, as if her very soul was glowing with a blinding incandescence. Worry, unease, these were sensations unknown to her. It was not as powerful as the feeling after Honesty's intimate sacrifice. Not quite. But it was close enough to give Fidelity the sudden feeling that she was unstoppable.

She turned to face the overpass, still struggling to blink bits of Lust out of her eyes. *Who knew there was so much...* uck *inside a person?!* She had seen death up close before, but never like this, never physically *on* her, in her mouth and in her hair.

She was not sure how long she had until Honesty would come driving by to his death, but she was not about to find out. She levelled her gun at those on the overpass, and waited. Like Lust, she was only here to clean up if things should go wrong. Like Lust, she had her own plan for the three men on the overpass.

Patience and Courage, brother and sister and Minor Virtues attached to Fidelity, drove across the overpass for the second time.

'Oh, gosh, we've done it again!' Patience lamented.

'I'm so sorry, I don't know this part of the city.' Courage had taken them first, across the wrong side of the overpass and, now, across in the wrong lane. In a situation as important as this, she would normally have been willing to break the overpass's very strict no lane-changing policy, but with Patience, her little brother in the car, she was not about to set a bad example.

But… isn't that exactly what I'll be doing when I run down those three Major Virtues?

'Don't be sorry, I'm the one who's supposed to be navigating.' Patience had a map of the city sprawled across his lap, his finger proudly marking the tiny intersection that represented where the Koo-Koo-Sint Highway overpassed the road below. He hadn't quite figured out yet that the map was over a decade old and was actually showing what had once been an ordinary intersection.

Courage was barely listening to her brother. She had not, until this very moment, considered just what she had promised. *There's a difference between cleaning the sacrificed body of some anonymous drug-addict off an altar and actually murdering someone you know. Someone whose voice you've heard, whose eyes you've looked into. I can't kill them. I can't do this!*

'Hang on, I'm going to loop around the long way, then we should be in the proper lane.'

'Sure thing, sister! I'll keep my eyes on the map.'

And when I completely miss the overpass this time and suggest we just go home, I'm sure you'll be as patient as you always are with me.

Not that the two kids had any idea of what was going on, but in that moment the life left Lust's body and the surge of power that the Friend blessed each of the devout with skipped over them completely. If they would forsake the Friend, then the Friend would forsake them right back.

Honesty's blood suddenly grew hot and he knew something big had happened. He exchanged a worried glance with Grace, trying not to let the rush of power and energy distract him. He began internally guessing at the possibilities when, from behind, Fort broke his silence in a whisper.

'There goes the first. Do you feel that? It is beginning.'

Though the sun was behind them, and though they were still a full car's length from the overpass, a shadow descended on the car.

Fidelity possessed nothing of the traits her two Minor Virtues embodied. She was cowardly and antsy and when she was with those two charming kids, she often felt more of a surrogate child than anything resembling a mother figure. *Those two need no mother, they have each other. Whatever husk of a bitch calls herself their mother while she sleeps on the couch all day and watches TV all night has no idea of the two marvels living in her house. Of course, if she did, she'd probably take credit for it, treating them more like trophies than children. They love her in spite of her emotional abandonment. Their love is a true love, an unconditional love. It is a love I shall miss seeing.*

Fidelity was not sure if the bond had always been there, or if it was only manifested in this new power gained from Lust's death, she was not even sure if she had been able to feel it at all. She was sure of one thing, however, she felt it when the bond broke. The siblings had come to some agreement on their own and abandoned the faith, abandoned the Friend, abandoned her. *Is there a lesson in that? When two people who know real love reject the teachings of the very deity we claim embodies love?*

She had no time to think on that, for suddenly a blur of dark cherry metallic was speeding by, unmistakable even in the growing darkness. Arm growing tired with the suspended weight in her hand, Fidelity concentrated on those occupying the overpass above and opened fire with a long, anguished cry.

Devotion was the first to throw his weapon off the overpass, hurling it outward with a heavy grunt at the approaching car. Though it appeared that his trajectory was perfect, Cooperation and Generosity were close behind in readying their own projectiles. They would ensure that Lust had no need to finish what they started. It was then, more out of reflex than an actual interest, that Cooperation looked to Lust's car parked off the road. Outside of that car stood Fidelity, not Lust, with a gun pointed straight at them. A gunshot rang out, followed by several more.

Frightened by that first bang, Generosity jumped as he swung his projectile down toward Honesty's car. The shock caused an involuntary contraction of muscles and Generosity was suddenly pulled over the overpass's railing, hands still tight on the piece of reinforced concrete.

Cooperation likewise jumped at the bang. With his own weapon still overhead, Cooperation's reaction was to jump back. Simultaneous with that self-preservative instinct, the bullet hit the rail before him, ricocheted upward and embedded itself into the piece of reinforced concrete he was holding aloft.

The deflected bullet did not strike particularly hard, but the force was unexpected enough for it to drive the weapon out of Cooperation's hands. It tumbled, more than fell, and its path took it directly into the head of Devotion, still recovering from his throw. The stone knocked Devotion onto his back, sandwiching the poor man's head between itself and the sidewalk, one of the reinforcing iron bars driving through the man's eye and into his brain.

It all happened too fast for Cooperation to follow. He had no way of knowing whether it was the second, third, or fourth, but one of the next few bullets to go whizzing by took him in the chest, driving through cotton, flesh, and bone into his heart. As he tumbled backward, he impaled his thigh on a bar of iron protruding from the concrete that still lay atop Devotion's head. Cooperation's momentum tore his leg free, shredding his femoral artery and most of that leg with it.

All three were dead before Fidelity's shout ended in gasping sobs below.

Grace screamed, high and loud as the roof of the car hammered down. She was short enough that its sudden depression missed her head by millimetres. She ducked down instinctively as the car swerved its way into the darkness beneath the overpass. Another vehicle clipped them from the side, sending the Aurora into a spin where it careened into the sloped wall of the overpass, riding it to the very top where the hood collapsed against concrete pillars and the car came to a sudden stop, jarring Grace's neck. Before she could recover, before she realized that the shrill screaming was her own, the car rolled back down that sloped wall, to slam into an SUV attempting to speed through the scene of the accident. That second impact rocketed Grace's head into her own knees as the seatbelt's auto-lock failed, silencing her screams.

She knew she was in shock and, as she sat there surprised that simple recognition of the symptoms wasn't enough for them to go away, Grace listened for sounds of her companions. She was afraid to move. The jarring in her neck had produced the sensation of hot liquid flowing along the base of her skull and she feared broken bones, paralysis, permanent brain damage. Despite the heat she had felt within, despite the layer of sweat soaking her clothes, Grace felt cold. She sat immobile, every muscle tensed to straining, helplessly unsure of what to do until a new rush of power washed over her.

With its onrushing, her tensed muscles relaxed, her hunched form straightened, and her raw throat suddenly felt warm and soothed. She was reminded with that gift of power that she was not merely Grace. She was a sister of the faith, a daughter of the Friend, and her friends needed her.

Her seatbelt was jammed, so she began biting at it, even as she turned to survey the damage.

The initial hit to the roof had warped the entire car, making it difficult to see beyond where she sat. Grace had to lower her head nearly to her knees to peer at Honesty's face. Whatever had struck the roof of their car had done so with enough force to knock Honesty's head into the steering wheel. His face was bleeding, the windshield which had broken without splintering was folded in on him, one edge dangerously close to his jugular. He was clearly unconscious, but Grace could see his body rising and falling softly with laboured breathing.

Thank the Friend! Honesty, how I've misjudged you. You are the purest among us, the most honest —to yourself and to the faith—the most devoted. What are Major and Minor Virtues but titles, what is Grace but a word attributed to me? They don't even make sense! Devotion is a Major Virtue, but Independence a Minor one? How can Grace and Justice both be virtues of love and friendship? What of Remuneration? Is a true love not unconditional?

We are, all of us, first and foremost children of the Friend. The titles and symbols that accompany our faith are meaningless. They're just symbols. That is what you tried to show us with your secretive sacrifice. A sacrifice in truth, for it was only you who lost something. You who gave something to the Friend.

Grace felt like weeping. She could not imagine the pain that came with murdering a fiancée. The pain Honesty had endured freely for the sake of his faith. And despite the scorn and disapproval of the others, he had taken her and Fort along, he had shown them what it all meant. He was no longer Honesty in her eyes, he was each of the Major Virtues, each of the Minor ones, he was love itself, he was the Friend's most loyal and clearest-seeing disciple, and she knew now that she would give her life for his vision.

Unable to turn farther to see what state Fort was in, Grace growled in frustration. She had seen once on TV a man bite clear through his seatbelt to escape a burning car, but either her technique or her teeth seemed unequal to the task. She tried to open the glove compartment, to find some tool to help her. Jammed. She had to slam the thing off its hinges to open it. Other than instruction manuals and insurance information, there was only a blue pen.

Fuck you, Aurora. Grace growled, low and dangerous, and set about using the pen to pierce the fabric of her seatbelt in a straight line where she had been biting. Stab, tear. Stab, tear.

It felt like ages, the initial rush of power—likely from some unknown sacrifice—had subsided to a dull, numbing sense of focus and inner strength, but she managed to tear herself free. She tried the door. It would not budge.

Suddenly feeling crushingly closed in, Grace began to whimper softly. She would not give herself to tears. Not now. She twisted and writhed, the pain in her neck searing, trying to get a look at Fort. When she finally managed to twist around enough to lay eyes on him, she wished that she hadn't.

The roof of the car behind her seat was torn completely open, Fort's midriff ending in a gruesome mix of torn metal and reinforced concrete, some debris of which lay crumbled across the back seat. *Sad as it is, I don't think I'll miss you all that much, creep.* Seeing the shafts of light lancing through the opening in the car's rooftop, Grace thought of a way out of the car, and cursed herself for it.

With grunts of effort, fresh pain in her neck, and the straining of seemingly every muscle in her body, Grace managed to contort herself enough to get into the back seat. She knew some emergency response unit would be there before too long, that she could just wait for their arrival, but the knowledge she was trapped was horrifying enough that it made her yearn to be free with every fibre of her being.

She twisted herself up beneath that hole in the car's roof, peeling back the torn steel with difficulty, and began to squeeze her way through that opening, arms first. She had not realized just how dark it was in the car until she squeezed her head and slender shoulders through that hole. There, emerging into the shadow of the overpass, she blinked away the dust in the air, waiting for her eyes to adjust. as a set of warm and wet hands grabbed her by the forearms and helped to pull her free.

Her eyes finally adjusted to reveal the blood-soaked form of Fidelity just as her hips wiggled free. Sitting on the edge of the car's demolished roof, uncaring of the gore or the cold, or of the fact that she barely knew the other woman, Grace hugged Fidelity tightly, sobbed into her shoulder, and did not move from that spot, did not let go until an ambulance arrived to take them all away.

CHAPTER ELEVEN:
Unwelcome Guests at the Table
Wednesday, 17 February 2021

Milana pulled into the Richovsky driveway at exactly 5:45. Despite Milana's notorious lateness and Ana's chronic tendency to arrive anywhere half an hour early, they somehow messed each other up just enough to arrive precisely on time.

Ana's first thought as they pulled in was one of triumph. *We beat Darko!* That excitement, however, quickly slipped into a growing concern. *Where is he? His last class was at 3:00 today. He should have been here by now.*

That brewing concern, like a dark cloud extending from the back of her mind to the fore, deepened as she left the car to see a spattering of blood in the snow. The drops shone bright red, still appearing wet against their snowy backdrop, except on one side where a pool of it had melted the surrounding snow to create a depression right through to the brown grass where it had darkened to black.

Ana suppressed the urge to look at it more closely. *It's a farm. There are a hundred reasons why there might be blood there. What's wrong with me that I automatically presume someone is hurt?*

She followed Milana to the door, not mentioning what she had seen. Ana knocked once and walked in. It might be Demir's house now, but it would always be the Richovsky home. She had knocked out of courtesy, but entered out of an innate welcome she felt whenever here, a deeply-rooted sense of belonging.

It was home.

Standing in the threshold, kicking off her shoes, Ana was assaulted by scenes of chaos in every direction. Directly in front of her, down the hall, Morgan was emerging from her bedroom in some kind of stupor. She turned to see Ana and Milana in the doorway and pulled a bloody cloth from her mouth to flash a drooling smile. Past Morgan, farther down the hall, she could see Dr. Johnson, the Richovsky vet and neighbour, arms spread, voicing soothing words in an attempt to calm the raised and tense voices of Demir and Darko that spilled from Demir's office.

Out from that room, a room that had been Demir's own when he was a kid, Alexander came running. He shoved his way between Dr. Johnson's legs, gasping with excitement as he made for Ana and Milana with his unsteady run.

Off to Ana's left, Papa Nate appeared. *Now that's a pleasant surprise.* He was holding baby Klara as he walked for the door, but there was a peculiarly strained expression painted across his face.

Time seemed to freeze for Ana as she backed on this strange mix of scenes, for just a moment, before each of them exploded.

Ahead of her, laughter erupted, pouring from Demir's office to roar richly down the hall. It was followed by Darko and Demir spilling out into the hallway, arms on each other's shoulders, to plough into Dr. Johnson with a powerful embrace. *Hmph, boys!*

Between them and Ana, little Alexander stopped dead in his tracks, looked up at his mother's vacant smile, and started bawling. Cries of "Mama! Mama!" drowned out Dr. Johnson's surprised protests as he fought off the hug from Demir and Darko.

To her left, Papa Nate stumbled, his careful grip on Klara relaxing, then going slack. Before Ana could even react, Milana was somehow there, miraculously scooping up Klara in one arm, and holding up a collapsing Papa Nate with the other.

Ana's only response was to stare, wondrously, at her best friend—and accusingly at her grandfather. There she stayed for nearly ten seconds, slightly hunched, mouth agape, and still struggling to get that second shoe off.

It all became so much clearer with supper. Every revelation clarified something in her mind and sapped the hunger from her belly. If the warm stew and fresh buns were meant to soften those blows, they fell laughably short. Ana sat back in her chair now, partially-eaten bun on her plate, spoon firmly planted in her half-empty bowl where it would stay.

Bad news has no place at the supper table. It is a most unwelcome guest.

Milana had stepped outside with the final piece of news, Papa Nate's terminal cancer, claiming to have left her phone in her car. Ana knew she was just trying to give them a moment alone together if they needed it. *Problem is, we don't know what to do with it.*

Look at Darko, slurping over his spoon as if the news had been expected. Or worse, as if it meant nothing to him. There's a fine line between stoicism and apathy, brother. And it's a line you tread far too closely.

And Demir, sitting with his mouth agape, waiting for a response from... who, exactly? Do you expect us to give a speech right back in response to yours? I bet you spent so much time debating how you would tell us this news, that you didn't once consider how we'd react to it. Is that truth finally setting in? Is that why you close your

201

mouth now? Why you avoid my gaze and turn to the comforting sight of your wife.

Ah, Morgan, you poor woman. Even in your painkiller-induced drunkenness, you place a supportive hand on his arm, an instinct by now reflexive more than conscious. And what about your *news? Something about the way Demir told that story doesn't add up. He said Kurgan bowled you over, but he also said that as soon as he opened the door, all three dogs went sprinting concernedly after you. So if Kurgan was actually inside with Demir, then what the hell tackled you hard enough for you to lose part of your tongue?*

Ana knew she was thinking of everything but the actual problem. She forced herself to confront her feelings. Three people and a dog had been brutally murdered, her grandfather was dying. She knew she was being insensitive, knew she was missing the importance of the facts Demir and Dr. Johnson had just laid out for them, knew she was running out of time to make some appropriate comforting comment for the sake of Papa Nate. Despite knowing all that, once she finally confronted that news, Ana could not help but to deliberate which was worse.

Papa Nate and I are so close. Though he always insists he's our grandfather rather than a replacement for dad, he has been, in many ways, a second father to us. I don't even know those people

who died. But they were young, and that's not
supposed to happen. People aren't supposed to be
murdered.

And Papa Nate... well that's the way things go,
isn't it? Old people are supposed to die. it's that
nearness to death that makes us appreciate them
more. Is that a heartless thought? Why is it that
death forcibly caused by a person, no matter the
age of the victim, is more jarring than a cancerous
death? Is it even the death that we react to, then,
or the wickedness of the thing responsible?

She could not help herself. It was as if she
needed to rank the tragedies to determine how she
felt about each one. She knew she would be stuck
in this ponderous loop, this endless spiral of morbid
reflection, until someone said something. The
problem was, she knew Darko would not voice his
thoughts, and she knew both Demir and Papa Nate
would be too concerned over interrupting each
person's internal processing to speak. She looked
across to Morgan who appeared to be asleep in her
hand propped up by an elbow, a stream of drool
slowly making its way to the table. *Not much*
chance there. That leaves you, Dr. Johnson. She
looked to the vet to see him staring at Papa Nate.
Huh, guess this was a shock for you, too.

Fortunately the ringing of Demir's cellphone
broke the silence.

'Hello?' He wouldn't have answered, not at a time like this, except that it was Constable Woods calling, and Demir had to speak with him.

'Hey, Demir, it's Derek Woods calling, it's about the Dr. Johnson case. Listen, man, you should take this somewhere private.'

Demir didn't inquire after an explanation, he'd rather not report that he had potential knowledge of a murderer in front of Papa Nate. He retreated to the living room. Klara was sleeping in her playpen and Alexander was watching some cartoon, he didn't even look up as Demir walked in the room. *Perfect.*

'What is it, Derek?'

'We messed up, man. We should've removed ourselves from the case the second we knew who it was we were dealing with. Problem is, everyone on the force knows Joel, so it would've been a conflict of interest no matter who was involved. We tracked down that missing nurse and she's got a real solid alibi... she's dead.

'She was found in one of Johnson's work vehicles. One of the SUVs he uses for hauling dogs around. He didn't even mention it was missing.'

There was a heavy sigh through the line before Derek continued. 'Dr. Joel Johnson is now our prime suspect. We're on our way over. This call is a complete violation of procedure by the way, but Donald and I figured you got a right to protect your own. I doubt he'll try anything—hell, we don't even know if he's guilty—but I wanted you to get the heads up.'

There was a finality to that last sentence, and Demir had to shake off the shock of Derek's news to remind himself that he had his own important information to share.

'Derek, hold up!'

'What is it? I've gotta go, we're five minutes out and we've got two cruisers coming in with us.'

'It's about that symbol—'

'Listen Demir, we'll get it worked out, don't worry. It's probably just some teens mixed up in a cult or something. You've got enough on your plate at the moment. Seemed like Morgan really did herself in with that whole tongue thing.'

'No, Derek, listen. I know what it is! There's a company called Finster and Gable Inc. They've distributed some Valentine's Day team-building thing to a bunch of offices in town. The symbol is their logo.'

Silence on the other end. Then, 'shit.'

Demir used the opportunity to move closer to the kitchen. He leaned casually in the doorframe, eyes on the window just behind Joel. He would stand in between that man and his kids until the police came, whether he was innocent or not.

Demir heard muffled voices as Derek and Donald quickly came to some kind of a decision on the other end of the line.

'Demir, this is Donald. You're on speaker so we can both hear you. Finster and Gable, what do you know about them?'

'Not much. They contracted us for a webpage, defaulted on payments so our work stopped. It might just be rumours, but I hear they didn't pay the graphic design guy. Maybe the symbol comes from the company, maybe from the designer.'

'Derek again. Demir, this… activity. Did it involve anything with virtues of friendship or love or anything like that?'

'I really didn't read it very well. I've got the email if you want to have a look at it, but yeah, something along those lines. The reward had something to do with supervising the person you beat. It was all sickly competitive.'

Though it was not meant for him, Demir heard Derek give an affirmative, "that's the one" quietly. Then there was a crackling voice, *likely dispatch in the cruiser*, Demir thought, and when next Derek spoke there was an edge of annoyed urgency to his voice.

'Listen Demir, we've gotta go. There's apparently some idiot throwing rocks at cars from an overpass. Two cruisers will be there in a couple minutes, just act normal till then. And thanks for the info. That was good intel, man.'

'See you later, buddy,' Donald threw in before there was a click and the call was cut off.

Demir turned his attention back to that window, pretending to look for stars out in the early February night, all the while eyeing Joel's every movement. And there he stood, until two police cruisers pulled into the driveway, burst through the opened front door, and dragged Joel away.

To his credit, Joel was quite calm and understanding about the whole thing. Demir couldn't decide if that was his dog-like optimism again, or the reaction of a sociopath.

Across the Richovsky field, bison drank at a stream, an artificial, winding runoff of the Clearwater. Upriver, the currents cut through several more farms, through woodland, under bridges, and into the great valley at the centre of Acton. Its source was someplace high in the Rockies, but this evening the banks of the Clearwater swelled of their own accord. There was a great power coalescing somewhere in Acton and every fae-touched man, beast, and spirit felt it.

Not far from the rising waters of that river, in the basement of a house owned by a dead man—his last generous act—Empathy laid upon the altar, commanding once again, that the Minor Virtues open her throat.

And again, they would not. They dared not.

They could, each of them in that room, feel as wave after successive wave of power crashed over them. Empathy felt it so deeply she could identify the source of each one. Lust, sacrificed in the burgeoning of passion. So raw that wave of power, it was caustic. Next came three in quick succession, like a set of rollers in the ocean: Generosity giving his own life, Devotion, then Cooperation. *What a team they made.*

More than the power she felt within herself, Empathy was opened to the feelings of those all around her. The hearts of Fourteen Minor Virtues beat loudly in her ears, their every emotion felt deep within herself.

Then came a new sensation. It started as gleeful elation, then slipped into a longing, an aching need. It was so powerful that it overcame Empathy's own emotions, and only then did she recognize it. *That mix of mercy, pity, hunger, and unmatchable potency... She is here.*

'The Friend is come. Quickly now, brothers and sisters, she needs a body. Give her mine, tear my throat open. She needs it, aches for it. Free the Friend to free yourselves!'

This time they listened, for they could feel it too. A god was arriving in the basement, and it needed a place to anchor its power. It was Forgiveness who at last took the ceremonial knife and, with a surprising sensitivity, slit Empathy's throat.

Empathy's life began pouring out onto that altar, soaking her shirt and staining her neck. Around her the Minor Virtues began chanting, 'Friend. Friend. Friend. Friend.' Then, too soon, the bleeding stopped and the wide wound began to mend.

Empathy felt herself come back from some far off place. She felt she had been gone for hundreds of years, but she could tell by the scene around her that it had been less than a minute. There was a new presence in her body, one that dwarfed her consciousness. *The Friend.*

I am delivered! Praise your graciousness, oh, great force of love. I am ever devoted to You, Friend.

That presence seemed surprised by Empathy's sentience. It slammed down around her, trying to force her out. Empathy fought back desperately, feebly, futilely. Utterly crushed, Empathy's consciousness disappeared once more. On the table, the body which had begun to writhe softly went slack, and drool seeped from the slightly-parted lips.

The Minor Virtues were unperturbed by the body's changes, they continued their chant, now walking circles around that altar—'Friend. Friend. Friend.'—until that body sat up. Then an absolute silence descended on the room. And they knelt before their god.

After the police had gone and Milana had once more returned to the table, and with her—Demir noted—a spark of hope in Ana's otherwise surrendering eyes, Demir made a decision. He waited until Frederic came and took Papa Nate home, putting Morgan and the kids to bed in the meantime, then he sat his siblings—and Milana—at the table once more, and told them everything. He told them about the phone call, about the symbol, he told them all the grisly details of the vet office murder that Dr. Johnson had spared them. And when he had said all he had to say, exhaustion pulling at his eyelids and scratching at his overused throat, he was shocked when Darko said he wanted to add something.

The Richovsky children, with Milana more the other half of Ana than a separate individual, listened patiently to each other and shared their own experiences over the past few days, their memories of Papa Nate and their parents. It was well after 2:00AM when they finally said their goodnights. And, though each now felt better about

Papa Nate's impending death, they had agreed that their father had introduced them long ago to a world that was a part of their own. What they had assumed to be myths and folklore were real things, and something related to these ideas, something big, was unfolding in Acton. Deciding it was too late to drive, and taking comfort in the company of others, Darko, Ana, and Milana decided to stay at the Richovsky farm that night, in a house that had a part of each of them in its walls.

And from without those walls, a woman called Jane was watching. Though a *bean nighe* and a *wechuge* had both come poking around the house, stirring the dogs into defensive barking, Jane had banished them both with a newfound power, sending them running to prey elsewhere.

She too had felt the very moment the Newcomer arrived. And in that swirling storm of power releasing into this world at the moment that the Newcomer's own heart started beating, Jane had felt a magnetic pull toward some place deep in the earth. She had gone to the source of that invitation with all haste and had emerged moments later in a physical body of her own. The body was young, beautiful—it looked more continental than English, but that would have to do. It was also rotted in decomposition, the bits of skin still intact horribly disfigured by the fire that had killed the girl.

As her spirit poured into that body, bones were repaired, flesh mended, and blood restored. So much blood. Jane felt plump with it, as if a single prick would send her deflating as a torrent of it poured out. But it was a body, and it was hers. She had not had a body in centuries. This one might have belonged to someone else at one time, might have been burnt unrecognizable in its moment of death, but now it was restored to scarless beauty. Now it belonged only to Jane.

She raised her arms for the fiftieth time since inhabiting the body and admired her fair skin once again. It was flushed with blood-filled capillaries, the red of it detracting from a truly flawless beauty.

Jane only shrugged with a smile, 'I guess I'm rather sanguine about all of this. Aha ahahahaha….'

PART II: Up Come The Dead

Awaken, awaken now!
And shake dust from bones
Shrug off sleep's leaden weight,
Strike a sentinel's fire
And stand, stand fast!
Stand through the aching,
Dismiss the call of bedcovers.
Rise to the day:
Swing high sleep-soft hands
And beat!

Beat, Beat hard!
Strike drums in chest
Let stretched skin shudder
Shaking the soul's own tattoo
And spit, spit fire!
Spit through teeth clenched,
Curse through lips pursed.
Rise to the day:
Let fly fury's fervour
And Rage!

Rage, rage now!
Protest with lung-borne thunder
Against ashen films on eyes

Against yellowed marrow thinning
And stride, stride for dawn!
Stride past treacherous doubt,
Wade through clawing fatigue.
Rise to the day:
Walk woken with wariness
And tread!

Tread, tread hard!
Cross the meagre fields
Follow rotted fencelines,
Feel the land calling
And hail, hail your home!
Hail every senescent flaw,
Halloo its mirror in yourself.
Rise to the day:
Sing the scop's sanative songs
And stand!

Stand, stand fast!
Bleed into thirsting soil
Bleed as did your fathers
Feed land with your own spirit
And stand, stand awakened!
Stand defiant of every failing,
Straighten proud with success.
Rise to the day:

March mad against another malefic morn
And awaken!

Morning Cycle
- Roman Kalichka

CHAPTER TWELVE: Rising Rivers
Thursday, 18 February 2021

Steven Yung knew he was asleep. He also knew he was alive, and he was not yet sure if this second realization was a comfort or a curse. He was reliving the last few moments of Fort's life over and over again, his mind stuck in that agonizing, self-blaming cycle.

There was nothing I could have done, he sobbed over and over in response to his own attributions of guilt. No matter how emphatic his thoughts, the greater part of his mind knew that he was indeed responsible.

I am the Friend's most trusted servant, and I lost one of her Minor Virtues. I lost my own friend. How could I not have suspected the others would want me dead after killing Vanessa? I should have known they'd be jealous of my accomplishments, I should have not only doubted their faith, but also their loyalty to the cause.

My carelessness cost the life of my friend, a man so young he was practically a child. It has earned me my injuries and this frozen state of unconsciousness. I deserve to relive this cycle of guilt, from now to eternity.

YOU DESERVE NOTHING BUT A PLACE BY MY SIDE, MORTAL. The voice that spoke now in Steven's mind was not his own and he could feel with its arrival a presence so powerful it threatened to break his sense of self. As if a lifetime of development and experiences was no more than a handful of brittle twigs. It was a woman's voice, soft, but unyielding, like a layer of silk draped over a sword's edge. He shivered internally.

BE NOT AFRAID, FOR I AM HERE NOW. HERE, WITH YOU, IN THIS CITY. YOUR DEEDS HAVE AWOKEN ME ONCE MORE INTO A PHYSICAL FORM. YOU AND YOUR FELLOWS WERE SUCCESSFUL. THOSE OF YOU WHO STILL LIVE ARE MAJOR VIRTUES NO LONGER. INSTEAD, I NAME YOU COMPANIONS, FOR I WOULD BREAK BREAD WITH YOU IN THAT OLDEST OF TRADITIONS.

Wait, what do you mean once more? Have you —

STEVEN YUNG, HONESTY, COMPANION. FOR YOUR LOYALTY I SHALL TAKE THESE WOUNDS FROM YOU. I SHALL GRANT YOU THE POWERS YOUR SELFISH BROTHERS AND SISTERS COVETED SO FIERCELY. THEY HAVE DISHONOURED THE FAITH SO I HAVE DISHONOURED THEM IN DEATH. THOSE OF YOU WHO SURVIVE SHALL ALONE BE THE FIRST I PLACE MY TRUST IN, FOR NO OTHERS HAVE YET PROVEN WORTHY.

Please, don't. Use your power to bring Fort back instead. I can feel his absence as clearly as I feel Grace's closeness. Please, bring him back.

YOU KNOW I CANNOT. HIS BLOOD GAVE ME LIFE, ALONG WITH THE BLOOD OF ALL THE OTHERS. I AM A MERCIFUL GOD, COMPANION, YOU KNOW THIS TO BE TRUE. BUT I AM ALSO A THIRSTY GOD, AND THE SACRIFICE OF FORTHRIGHTNESS WAS MOST QUENCHING.

Please! Your words bring such pain. Were I awake, I'd be weeping.

GOODBYE, COMPANION. WHEN NEXT YOU WAKE YOUR INJURIES WILL BE GONE, AND I SHALL BE WAITING IN THE TEMPLE FOR YOUR RETURN.

Just wait—

But she was already gone. Steven Yung was at a loss. So many questions. Her arrival into his world, into a physical body that could be seen and felt, brought as many new doubts as it did reassurances.

In spite of his efforts, Steven's mind went back into that cycle of the catastrophe at the Koo-Koo-Sint overpass, but this time, he stood outside the car and watched it all unfold.

He saw Fidelity in a car with Lust, saw a dark power in Fidelity's eyes as she ended Lust's life. He saw her exit the car, wipe blood from her face, and wheel toward the men on the overpass. Again, a dark power shone in her eyes as she opened fire.

And above, at the edge of the overpass, that same power flashed in Devotion's eyes as he threw a hulking mass of reinforced concrete out into the air, hurtling toward Steven's own vehicle. And all of it, the slight wind changing the trajectory of that concrete, the microscopic flaws in the marrying of metals giving strength to the bullet, the way it sheared and split upon hitting the overpass railing, none of this was luck.

Standing outside it all, witnessing it fully, Honesty grasped the true power of his god, she had guided the very sacrifices that gave her strength. And though he shunned the thought immediately, dismissing it before the doubts had time to find purchase, for the briefest of moments in the darkest reaches of Steven's mind, he wondered if it had been his decision to sacrifice his fiancée at all.

Steven's turbulent mind was calming with a newfound respect for the supreme power of his god. And as that sense of calm was being restored, his mind went blank and he entered the oblivion of a true, deep sleep once more.

It had been a long and perilous night. Through the course the moon's rise and fall, Jane came to see why every wooden fencepost around the Richovsky farm had been marked with sigils of warding, protective marking that she had punched a hole through.

Normally the cold iron of the barbed wire would have been enough to keep out any ghost, but with the power she had gained in the days before the Newcomer's arrival, Jane had found a section of fence without the warding symbols and had been able to bury that iron beneath the snow. Her own personal gate. A gate that countless creatures had sought to pass through during the night.

Power attracts power. It has ever been so. And revenant Jane bleeds power enough to drown my old ghostly form. Not all those creatures sought my destruction, surely. Doubtless some were merely curious, the proverbial mice poking about the clock. Except I needed not strike a single one to send them all scurrying back to their holes. All it took was standing without the walls of this house, a visible presence of power and beauty.

All it took was the threat of destruction.

When, at long last, the dark of Winter's night gave way to the cold sunrise, Jane went back into the house contentedly. And, for the first time in centuries, she had walked through the front door.

Despite the difference in appearance, Morgan had recognized Jane right away. Her physical presence was still accompanied by that same mental presence that had filled Morgan's head when she lay unconscious out in the snows. There was no mistaking it: no matter what lies of relation the young woman's body told, this was Morgan's ancestor, her flesh and blood—well, figuratively speaking.

Gone was Jane's peculiar speech, her timbre, her accent. Gone too that matronly smile, in its stead a youthful one, lips a vivid and unsettlingly red even without any kind of cosmetic augmentation.

Whatever hastily-explained arrival of power had given Jane a corporeal presence had not apparently given her the ability to mend clothing. Her unexpected arrival at the front door in no more than tattered rags smelling of dirt would not have been so easily explained to Demir. Fortunately, Demir had been in the shower, and his siblings still asleep, giving Morgan just enough time to get Jane properly dressed and seated comfortably in the kitchen.

In those frantic seconds spent changing in the dark of Morgan's closet, Jane had whispered fiercely of the threats facing Morgan's family. Of wicked, stalking creatures and broken wards. Morgan had understood hardly a word of it all, but whatever nature of evil Jane spoke of was accompanied by her reassurances that she would protect Morgan and her family. Strangely, Morgan found the whole exchange to be rather comforting.

221

My mind hurts too much, my head spins too violently, to deal with all these monsters you're warning me about. But so long as you're going to look out for us, then welcome home! My own personal ancestral guardian. Take a seat, my mother's mother's mother's mother's... oh why bother, you might be from my father's side for all I know. Take a seat, let me get you some tea.

Demir and his siblings were adorably timid around new people, even—apparently—family. They had listened respectfully to Morgan's lies about Jane being a visiting cousin who had decided to drop by unexpectedly, then left at the first opportunity. The three siblings took Alex and Klara and decided that a walk and some chores outside were preferable company to this newcomer in their lives.

Morgan had been left in the kitchen to make breakfast alone with only Jane for company. Apparently, centuries without having someone to talk to had made Jane a poor partner in conversation. After several attempts to delve into what life had been like in Jane's day, Morgan had given up, cooking in silence as the ghost-with-a-body stood motionless to the side of the counter, mouthing some silent thoughts to herself as she watched.

It's blood-chilling the way you're just standing there. For all the liveliness and youth in your new body, you might as well still be a corpse.

Eventually, mercifully, the doorbell rang.

The door swung open before Jane reached it and Frederic, Nathaniel Bennet's in-home nurse, filled the doorway with his broad shoulders as he backed the wheelchair of his charge up over the lintel.

'Sorry miss,' he offered sheepishly, seeing Morgan's disapproving look, 'Mr. Bennett told me to just go in.'

'Call me Nathaniel!' Papa Nate growled for what was obviously not the first time. Frederic spun the wheelchair so Nate could face Morgan.

'The man's hopeless,' Nate sighed, adding belatedly, 'good morning, dear. How are you?'

'Fine. Glad to have you over again. Please, take a seat at the table, you can keep me company while I work.' Though the pain in Morgan's head still ached dully beneath the suppression of her painkillers, her tongue did not hurt at all. Pain or not, however, with the tip of her tongue now missing and stitched over, Morgan's words came out with a slight impediment, sounding malformed and alien to her own ears.

Frederic helped Nathaniel out of the wheelchair and they followed Morgan into the kitchen. Papa Nate was still able to walk without assistance. He had assured them all the day before that the wheelchair was "just in case."

Though the man did not wince nor limp as he walked, though he breathed not a single word of complaint, Morgan could tell he was in terrible, terrible pain. And lest she strip his sense of pride, that very thing giving him the strength to make the long, agonizing walk to the table, she could not offer a single word of comfort. She turned back to the counter, ashamed that her own cowardice was as profound as Nate's bravery.

Where has your smile gone, Nathaniel? Where's the gentle teasing? You can keep silent those words of frustration and pain, but you cannot hide that sheen of determined sweat on your brow. It must be taking every measure of your being not to cry out in agony.

By the time they reached the table, Morgan was cowering over the vegetables she had already finished chopping, eyes filling with tears. *Why such a violent end for such a gentle soul? Has his generosity, his selflessness in life been for nothing? Is there no justice in death?*

Morgan wiped at the tears before they could fall, forced down those dark thoughts, and turned to introduce Jane. Watching Morgan's movements unceasingly, Jane turned with her ancestor only to visibly reel at the sight of Frederic and Nathan.

Jane, so still only moments ago, was suddenly fidgeting nervously. 'Hil'mJaneMorgan'scousin. CanItalktoyouintheotherroomplease? The words flew so fast from the woman's lips that Morgan might not have understood but for the presence in her mind linking them. Frederic and Nathaniel looked to each other, confusion plain on their faces as they tried to piece together that rambling string of syllables.

Morgan motioned for Jane to lead them into the living room and, as the woman fled, belated calls of "hello, Jane" and "nice to meet you" followed her out of the kitchen.

'Uhh...Sorry.' Morgan offered, cringing at the way she could not quite enunciate the word properly. 'Sit tight, I'll be back in a second to fix you some coffee or tea, so best decide which you want now.'

The moment she rounded the doorway into the living room, Jane had her by the shoulders with a strength that seemed impossible for her thin body. She forced Morgan down into a seat on the couch and only when it was clear Morgan would not stand again did she let go.

'I've told you I am here to protect you. That man, the one with your grandfather. He's no danger to you, but he is... He can...' Jane's fierce whispering faltered. 'Is there any way you can ask him to leave?'

Morgan was frightened. Jane had spoken of more than a dozen monsters she had seen during the night with mild amusement but now, talking of a man who she claimed was no danger, the ghost was afraid. The dull pain of Jane's gripping fingers lingered like a bad memory on Morgan's shoulders.

'Frederic?' she asked incredulous. 'Why? This isn't a… is this… is it a race thing?' Morgan did not know much about Frederic, except that he had been born in Germany. But even in Canada, the darkness of the man's skin would send some into frenzied prying, seeking the man's deepest, darkest roots.

My grandmother was an awful racist, and that was only a couple generations ago. I can't imagine the bigotry in you.

Jane lingered on that thought for a moment, as if perhaps racism really was the issue.

'What does it matter anyway?' Morgan pressed. 'You said yourself he's no danger. Can't you just ignore him? I'm sure he'll ignore you right back.'

Jane just stared in response.

'Well, what choice do you have? Papa Nate needs him here and I'm not about to ask Papa Nate to leave.' Morgan stood back up, meeting Jane's gaze.

'Fine.' Jane sighed, her old ghostly self all too present in that breathy expression.

Though they whispered and a thick, insulated wall separated their voices from his ears, Frederic focused in on the hushed conversation of Morgan and her curious *cousin.* He had only locked eyes on her for a moment, but it was long enough to see that this Jane was some manner of undead, her existence a slight he took personally.

"Is it a race thing?" Ha ha, exactly. More so than you realize, child.

As an angel of death, Frederic came to souls in the last days of their mortal lives and witnessed the separation of soul and body, often easing the pain in the process. He then escorted those souls to Heaven, the most noble profession of any angel. Creatures of undeath were symbols of failure, not his own failure—for the taint on the soul of this Jane woman was older than Frederic's promotion to his current position—but the failure of a brother or sister. He longed to destroy that abomination, ached for its annihilation. She was no mere lingering spirit, but a wholly revenant being.

Alas, he knew he could not interfere. That was not his place. Besides, the revenant had some kind of relationship with his own charge's granddaughter-in-law and he had no business judging and destroying friendships.

Frederic helped to tuck Nathaniel's chair closer to the table and grabbed one of his own, sliding smoothly into his seat. Each of his charges had been a lesson in humility, a lesson in the dire need for him and those like him. Nathaniel was no different. Even now, just after struggling to move a chair, the old man had exhausted his strength and pain wracked his limbs, but aside from a frown of discomfort, Nathaniel betrayed none of it.

More so than most, Frederic's current charge bore the struggles of death with an admirable resolve. Frederic smiled down at the man then looked up quickly as he heard the conversation of the two ladies coming to an abrupt end.

By the time Nathaniel had wrestled free a chair with Frederic's help and slumped down into it triumphantly, he was already exhausted.

How could it all come so quickly? This time last month I didn't suspect a thing, and now I have a cancer that's killing me. It's as if identifying the weakness in my bones was all it took. As if, in giving it name, I also gave it strength.

Nathaniel was breathing heavily, hands pushing feebly against his numb legs.

'At least it's not as painful as everyone says,' he wheezed cheerfully.

'You said just this morning—and these are your own words—"it hurts like the bite of a rabid bitch."' Frederic countered.

'Well, yeah. It did, it does. It hurts like heck! But it's bearable. Through gritted teeth and clenched fists, I can live with this.'

The weight of what he had just said sunk in. He looked over to Frederic, a half-grin cocked. Frederic looked back, his expression identical, and the two burst into laughter just as Morgan and Jane came back into the room.

Something about Morgan was different. She was acting erratically, almost frantically. She returned to her cooking with a frenzied abandon, forgetting all about the hot drinks she had promised to make for them.

Oh dear. Head injuries are nothing to take lightly. I'll have to tell Demir to make sure you're getting more rest.

The cousin, Jane, was no better. She stood in the doorway to the living room, committing to neither the carpet nor linoleum side of that divide, and eyed Frederic with what seemed a mixture of fanatic curiosity and abject terror.

To Nathaniel's surprise, his nurse seemed just as irked by the woman. Though his head was turned to Morgan—not making the tea—his dark irises crowded the corners of his eyes, glued on Jane. If Nate were to describe the man's expression, he could only have said it was part indignation, part indigestion.

Aww, the poor fools are smitten! Good for them.

'So, Morgan, did you listen to the news this morning?' If she would not remember on her own, perhaps he could distract her out of her frenetic cooking. *Straight out of anxiousness and right into making tea. Failing that, maybe she'll just make some to shut me up.*

'Sorry, *grandpa,* not all of us listen to the radio every morning.

Ah, at least your tongue's still sharp—even if your mind's been dulled by the knock on your head. He smiled to himself, proud with the joke.

'Well you didn't miss much. It's all a mess anyway. It always is these days. More of those Valentine's Massacres—that's what they're calling them now. More occult symbols written in blood and other grisly things.'

'Shame.' Jane shook her head from the safety of the doorway, eyes downcast.

Hmm, Nate thought amused, *definitely from out of town, haven't heard anyone around here talk like that in a while.*

'If that's not bad enough, one of the sites might be destroyed soon, all the evidence gone. The river is flash-flooding again. Worst its been in more than ten years. It's so bad that they had to close the bridge. The water's so high on the supports, they don't know if it'll still hold.'

'Shame,' Jane added again, much more emphatically. 'That's horrible. That can't happen! What are the officers doing about it?'

'Huh. Well… lots I guess. They must have their hands full with all of it.'

Odd girl, that one. More concerned with rising water than the rising murder rate. I'd judge you on the peculiarities of your relatives, Morgan, if not for my own daughter's choice in husband. The way Danylo used to go one and on about these river systems, he'd have probably laughed after hearing about the floods.

'Morgan?' *Enough of this coy business, old man, she's ignoring you anyway. If I keep to this road, we'll all end up talking about the weather! We kind of are now, come to think of it. Jesus, just ask for the tea!*

'Can you ma—eauurg…' Nate's words were stolen by some fresh and fierce pain under his left shoulder. he tried to lift his hand from his knee but it wouldn't move.

His pained vocalization cut off in a gurgle and he blinked hard to suppress the rising tears. He needed someone—anyone. Even if they could offer no more than a hand on the shoulder. Foam formed in his mouth as he forced his breath and spit through gritted teeth. He *needed* it.

To his right, Frederic's eyes were still glued to Jane, who herself had half-retreated round the door jamb and was staring now at the nurse in open alarm. Not even Morgan, normally so caring and impossibly attentive in that way that only mothers could be, noticed to offer anything. Her cellphone had started ringing and, in between stirring the potatoes on the stove and checking on whatever was in the oven, she answered it with a perfectly collected "hello."

Nate shut his eyes tight, slowly lowered his forehead to rest on the cool wood of the table, and tried not to cry.

Frederic refused to look away from the revenant. *Witness this, creature of undeath, and know fear. All this pain he suffers, all this pain we suffer together, and I am unflinching.*

He watched Jane shrink under that gaze with a proud satisfaction. *It is not my place to be your undoing, but sure as every mighty wave on the seas comes crashing down, so too will you fall.*

Despite his bravado, both toward Jane and toward himself, Frederic was in agony. He could not fathom how Nathaniel was still conscious. Even taking most of the physical pain coursing through the mortal's body, Frederic was upon his threshold.

The power of the Lord above is unimaginable, revenant. You may have found a body to taxi your tainted soul, but you will never find such bravery, such faith, such strength of spirit as can be found in the Lord.

He continued internally voicing his challenges toward the undead woman, using the emotion to distract him from the pain. But beneath the table, the angel of death winced, closing a single, tight, and shaking fist around his other hand.

Demir left the dogs outside and went into the house with the others. He arrived just as Morgan was hanging up her cellphone with a "thank you, Officer Woods." She looked exhausted and she was running cold water over what looked to be a burnt hand.

He should not have left her alone. Not with that head injury. He should have at least come back the moment Papa Nate and Frederic arrived. But it had been so long since he had gone walking in the fields with his siblings. It had almost felt like they were kids again, like there were no serious cares to be had, like mom and dad were waiting at home for them.

It was a painful sort of nostalgia, the kind that leaves your chest hurting and mouth filling with bile. The kind that makes you want to vomit out your guts, then curl into the fetal position on the floor and weep as you wait for death to come. But it was also beautiful in its own small way. And that tiny note of beauty made all the pain worth it.

He mouthed a *sorry* to Morgan as he kicked off his shoes in the doorway and, despite the clearly difficult morning she had been having, his wife simply shook her head and smiled.

What an angel, thought Demir. *What a beautifully perfect angel!*

CHAPTER THIRTEEN:
February Blues
Thursday, 18 February, 2021

'You get through, Woods?' Donald Philips returned to their shared office, a fresh cup of coffee in either hand, just as Derek returned the phone to the cradle. Donald handed off one of the cups to his partner.

'Thanks,' Derek paused to take a deep breath over the steaming cup. 'Demir was out, I guess, but I caught the Mrs. on her cell. The poor woman's a wreck with her head injury.'

'Oh yeah, it sounded bad. Could you tell just from talking to her on the phone?' Donald returned to his seat at his desk on the opposite side of the room and swivelled in his chair to keep facing his partner.

'Could I ever. Airy as a damn cloud, poor thing! She said they'd get the graphic artist's address tomorrow. I told her that'd be fine.'

'Yeah, that's all right. Sad to say, but that's not exactly a priority right now.' Donald sipped at his coffee contentedly. He hesitated a moment, the bout of conversation was clearly over, but he was reluctant to return to return to the research at his desk just yet.

Donald jerked upright as a new topic of conversation came to him, nearly spilling his coffee. 'Hey, guess who I saw out in the hall?'

'Who?' Though Derek engaged, he turned back to his computer and began typing once more. Unlike Donald who lived for the action of personal interrogations, Derek much preferred conducting research from the safety and comfort of his own desk.

'The Kalichka girl.'

'Who?'

'Maria.'

'Who?'

'You know, that little Crimestopper who's always coming by asking questions about some crime or another.'

'Oh, right.' Derek exclaimed, recognition finally settling in. 'Demir's little brother's friend. What did she want?'

Donald cocked his head, confused, as if Derek had just asked the most unexpected question imaginable. 'Huh… Not a clue. She was bothering the Captain… probably about some crime or another! Ha ha!'

As if summoned, Captain Florence Fremont stepped into their office, causing Donald's half-sincere laughter to double.

'Wo-ho!' Derek joined in, spinning in his chair to face the woman. 'Speak of the devil, eh, Cap?'

Captain Fremont glared down at both of them, unamused. 'You two are awful chipper for this disaster of a morning.' She hefted the bulky folder she held in one hand. 'Let's see if we can't lower you to everyone else's level.'

Twin groans came from the partners. Donald stood up in protest. 'Another case? Captain we've already got—'

'It's not another case, Philips.' Her rueful grin was chilling. 'It's four.'

Both men groaned again, louder this time. The captain just talked over them. 'You're already working most of the Valentine's Massacre cases. They're all clearly related, so here's the rest of them. Yes, you will be working *all* of them. I have the two of you on all the murders, and Constables Dale Anderson and Guy Laforce on the assaults and attempted murders we think to be connected. Those two are, for the purposes of any and all of these cases, yours to direct. Together I want results from the four of you.'

She seemed about to just turn around and leave —she had a tendency of doing that after delivering bad news to her officers—but instead she walked over to Donald's desk. 'Today!' she added for emphasis before taking a minute to peer at Donald's computer screen.

He had pulled up a news article about the river's drastic rise overnight. The article outlined the fact that a professor in Edmonton had actually predicted the series of apparent meteorological events leading to the flash flood and had been trying to warn people for weeks.

'What is this?' the captain demanded. 'God help me, if you're doing personal reading right now, I'm gonna put you on the phones. And fair warning, most of the people calling in this morning are telling me that the flooding river is some kind of terrorist plot. A few are even touting the whole "gay agenda" thing still, and believe it or not those ones are the least crazy!' She shoved her face closer to the screen. 'God, I hate this town,' she added in a mumble.

As much as Donald respected her as a leader, he always thought she was too much of a micromanager. *Sure I goof off from time to time. Who doesn't in this line of work? But I get results, Cap! Isn't that enough?*

With a sigh, Donald knew his quiet moment of conversation over coffee had come to an end. He turned back to face his computer. 'Well, Captain Fremont, we've all been saying these murders are connected to the occult, right? And groups like that usually have some kind of natural connections: reading stars, talks of earthquakes, plagues, floods, you name it. And there's this guy, up in Edmonton right, who apparently knew this flood was gonna happen. And all these murders happened on the eve of the flood. I was just thinking there might be some kind of connection there.'

Across the room, Derek was staring with a gaping jaw. Among the two of them it was unanimously understood that he was the better at research, but he was clearly impressed by Donald's line of thinking.

The captain straightened, slapped her folder of cases down on Donald's desk, crossed her arms and frowned down at him. She watched him squirm under her stern gaze for a moment as she ran through dozens of possibilities in her mind.

After a full minute, her gaze finally softened. 'Great work, Philips. It might lead to nothing, but it might be everything. This professor might have no clue who these people are, but they clearly know him and his work. I want you and Woods to head up there and interview him today.' She turned to leave the room before adding, 'I'll tell Anderson and Laforce, they'll take over for you here. You better get on the road now, guys.'

Constable Connie Martin watched her Captain leave the office of Woods and Philips back into the hall stuffed with desks set two-by-two. *I should be in one of those desks, working.* Instead she sat in a stool—a perp's seat—next to one of the desks, exhausted and awaiting her fate.

At least the captain's smiling. She usually is when she leaves that office. I guess there's a reason Woods and Philips are the only ones who've never lost their office to an outperforming team. Friend help me, why could I never get a partner like one of them!

Florence Fremont seemed like she was trying to avoid her, but from across the room Connie caught the Captain's eyes. It was a silent challenge and the Captain was no coward, she immediately set a course for Connie and marched over. Anyone in her path was smart enough to make way.

All these damned uniforms. Constable Martin had never felt like such an outsider in her own place of work. She was a white tank and black jeans surrounded by a sea of blue. No sentence had been passed yet—none would be for weeks—but she already felt like a criminal.

The sad smile the captain offered on her arrival just made it worse.

'Aww, fuck off, Captain' she moaned. 'Don't give me that pity, just tell me what'll happen.'

Fremont stiffened.

Shit! Forgot she hates cursing. Whatever, too late now.

'I'm not in a position to say. This is a matter for Internal Affairs. You know the protocol, though: immediate suspension, daily check-ins, weekly psych visits, they'll come to a decision eventually.'

'Isn't there anything you can do, Captain? C'mon, we're the only women in this place, you know I can handle as much shi— as much crap as the next guy! Please?'

The captain responded with her characteristic frown and crossed her arms, thinking silently for a minute. Connie waited patiently. It was what the captain did, long silences, angry stares, and eventually a sentencing. And if that sentencing was good or bad depended entirely on how much of her respect you had personally earned or lost over the entire course of whatever relationship you might have with the woman.

'Constable Martin. Connie. I've only ever heard you ask for my help once before: the day you came looking for a job. Most people who apply here do so because they want to be cops, you did so because you didn't want to be something else. I almost turned you away because of it, but something about you made me change my mind. You have a faithfulness to this job, a determination to stay the course, a… a… what's the word I'm looking for?'

'Fidelity?' Martin offered.

'That's it. A fidelity! To the force, to everyone you work with, to the people of this city. I knew you were running from something in your past, but I didn't care. And you've proven again and again that I made the right choice in hiring you. Heck, aside from Woods and Philips, you've got the record of holding an office the longest. That might as well be a statement of employee of the year for what it means in here. I respect you as an officer, Connie, as a person, but you made some horrible decisions last night.'

'Captain I—'

Fremont kept talking over her and it was clear Connie wouldn't get a word in, so she just sat back and listened. The captain picked up the file from the desk next to Connie, flipped to the woman's statement, and began summarizing.

'You arrived on-scene, off-duty and out of uniform, to see an illegally-parked car off the side of the road—a possible case of lost control on the Winter roads based on its location. You stopped upon noticing an occupant in the vehicle, concerned for that person's safety. You arrived to a suicide in progress, witnessed subject Ljuba Kowalchuk shoot herself once in the head. You heard a crashing sound from down the road and witnessed three males throwing large stones from the Koo-Koo-Sint Overpass. You witnessed one car being hit and crashing, you made an instinctive decision, took Kowalchuk's gun and opened fire—from one-hundred-fifty metres!—at the men on the overpass. After subduing them, you saw to the scene of the accident and saved two lives.'

She fixed Connie with that sad smile again. 'Four dead, two saved, you do the math, Connie.'

She was tired of this. And that sense of exhaustion was enough to keep her anxiety at bay, far off in some forgotten place. The captain was now the fourth senior official to read her statement in that same condescending tone. Connie sat up straight and met Fremont's intimidating gaze.

'With respect, Captain, *you* do the math. How many would have died if I didn't subdue those on the overpass?'

The captain reeled, more from the woman's tone than her words. But it was enough to wake her up to some kind of defence for her officer, for that sad smile went back to a frown. Connie had never been happier to see such a sour face. After another minute under that silent, frowning stare, the captain spoke again, her voice softer.

'Alright Connie, it's completely unofficial, and it might not mean a thing, but there is a place in investigations like this one for your commanding officer to give a personal recommendation towards a solution. You know I'm not one to shy on the mental health requirements and, truthfully, I'll demand more than the required number of psych sessions, but for what its worth, I will recommend reinstatement.'

'I don't know what to say, Captain. Thank you.'

'Ah, save it.' All softness left the captain's tone again, leaving her hard and bitter once more. 'I've got phone calls to take and idiots to appease.'

Derek Woods slipped into his coat and tossed Donald's towards him. 'I know we've both been avoiding the subject, but I think Joel's innocent.' Derek had just finished flipping through their case files and had a binder full of them tucked under one arm. He would read them more carefully on the road.

Donald put on the his coat and checked the pocket for his keys. 'We shouldn't be on his case. Cap's excuse was we all know the guy, but c'mon, we're clearly better friends with him than anyone else here. We shouldn't make any kind of statements like that yet. Even if they are just between us.' He grabbed his hat, the coffee he had poured into a travel mug, and opened the office door for his partner to walk through.

'I know, I know. But look, Donald!' The two left their office for the hall and began to make their way through the rows of paired desks toward the exit. 'All the other potential suspects—including the one confession—are practically brainwashed!

He's got nothing of this cult-fanatic mindset. Some of the witness statements from these new cases are chilling, man. These people are freaking out about love and friendship being the motive to their actions. Joel's nothing like that.'

Donald stopped his partner to fix him with a sombre look. 'Listen, it sounds good, buddy. I want to believe it, I can tell you want to believe it, but we can't be saying stuff like this yet. We've got to do this properly…' he directed Derek's gaze to where Officer Martin sat in a staring match with the captain. 'Now more than ever.'

'I don't care what anyone says, it's a damn good thing she was there. Imagine how many other people could have been hurt if she hadn't stopped those guys on the overpass.'

'Derek!' Donald glared at his partner, lowering his voice to a whisper. 'Not with the Captain around' he chastised. 'Do you want to lose the office?'

Derek started walking again with a sigh. 'Well, good thing we've got this long drive ahead of us. We can talk *all* about it then, ha ha.'

'I hate you,' Donald groaned.

As they closed the final distance to the station's front doors, a small waste bin came hurtling by to slam agains the wall next to them, sending papers flying everywhere. The turned to see a rough-looking homeless man being pinned against a desk. He was shouting something about Rufus needing to be found.

The two officers looked to one another and shrugged. 'Lost dog?' Derek offered.

'Poor guy.' Donald opened the door and gestured Derek through. They didn't have time for distractions like this. There was a possible cult of mass murderers in Acton and, today of all days, they were being sent away from the action to Edmonton.

CHAPTER FOURTEEN: Keep an Eye on the Sky
Thursday, 18 February, 2021

Mal left the police station for the second time in two days. The only officer who seemed to have shown any interest in his case was now suspended. *And for what? For saving the lives of innocent people on the road? This is bullshit! She might be the only decent cop in this town, and they suspend her. Ridiculous!*

Mal had relied on the police more times than he could count. Being homeless through Canadian winters was no easy feat, and on more than one occasion, he'd been picked up by a sympathetic cop and put in holding overnight. A warm bed—the stainless steel bench in that room was more of a bed than he often had—coffee in the morning, sometimes even a muffin or a doughnut on the way out: it made the winters bearable. In a city where most people hated the homeless, it was nice to know there was a place he could go where they had to—by law—look out for him. But now he was beginning to see just how shallow that care was.

His best friend had been missing since Tuesday and the cops had refused to take his case seriously. The indifference with which they had dismissed

Rufus still pulled at something behind Mal's eyes, making the anger rise again. Their dismissive words still rang in his ears.

'Your friend has no fixed address, where exactly are you suggesting he's missing from? He probably just moved to another part of the city, or maybe he got on a bus to try his luck elsewhere. Hate to break it to you, but Acton's homeless registry has about a sixty percent turnover every year. You ain't the first friend to be left behind.'

He repeated his own reply in his head. *He's lived at Two Stone Camp for three years, just because it's a squatter's home in the river valley doesn't make it any less permanent. I know he's missing because he's my best friend. Do you have any idea how hard it is to trust someone when you're homeless? We trust each other enough to share a tent, to share our stashes. It's been us against the bitter cold of the world's indifference since 2016. If a clean-shaven man had come in here and told you the same about his friend you would have cared, you would have launched a search. And the only difference between us is that both the people in that scenario are lucky enough to have a real place to live!'* And if throwing that trash can hadn't driven home Mal's point, then nothing could have.

'Steady, Mal.' Mal fought to calm himself, using the words Rufus normally would to suppress the building rage. It was that rage that led him to throwing the garbage can. *And maybe that rage is part of why they're not looking for Rufus right now, Stupid!*

'No, no! Easy, Mal. Respect self, respect the world: that's the order it's gotta be.' He hugged himself tight, nearly sobbing the words he used to hear from Rufus almost every day. *Respect self, respect the world.* Nobody understood the world like Rufus. Nobody understood Mal like Rufus. Nobody else had ever cared enough to try. Not even Mal's ex-fiancée, not even the psychologist she had sent him to for his rage.

That man had coldly taken thousands of dollars professing to help Mal manage his anger. Not once had the shrink ever gone deeper, to try and root out the cause of that rage. It was all breathing exercises and thinking about consequences. *It was all bullshit. Rufus did more for me in two weeks of knowing him than that shrink did in months of paid sessions!*

Mal had not really been aware of where he was headed, preoccupied as he was with controlling the rising anger, the grief over Rufus's absence and the sense of abject helplessness that lingered just beneath the surface. That dreaded state of darkness was held at bay by a pitiful, sputtering flame, and right now it was only the imagined presence of Rufus at his side that kept it from going out.

In that state of unawareness, Mal's feet took him a few blocks from the station, down a wooden staircase and into some kind of partially-wooded park. There was a man-made pond in the centre with a trampled-snow walking path encircling it. Mal supposed the pond must be some kind of drainage system for the city, for a steady current across the centre of its surface had kept a channel unfrozen. He figured an underground channel took that water straight into the river—no doubt contributing to its swollen banks.

Mal made for a bench near the small section of woods that started at the top of the stairs and extended right to the pond path's edge. It was not until he got closer that Mal saw the bench was occupied. Another homeless man was curled in the fetal position, wearing one coat with another wrapped tightly round him like a blanket. Though this morning was relatively warm—hovering around negative five Celsius—Mal supposed spending all night out here could not have been.

He would have made for another bench out of a well-learned sense of caution, but the man sat up and looked right at Mal before moving to the bench's edge, evidently making room to share. Mal gave the man a smile before sitting down. He could not help but feel a little nervous, and he spent a moment determining whether the man might be dangerous.

Grey in the hair: Middle aged. Looks stronger than me. Harder. He's probably been homeless longer. Two coats, warm toque, gloves—damn those are nice! Mal noticed only now that the man had been sleeping on a thick quilt to prevent the cold gripping him from under the bench. Though the stranger pulled himself to one side, he left the quilt rolled out over the length of the bench and gestured for Mal to take a seat atop its warmth.

The man's hawkish features stabbed out from under his toque and hood like the billed face of a bird amid heavy winter plumage. Mal paused in front of the bench, gesturing toward the open seat to be sure. As the man nodded, birdlike head bobbing, Mal noticed the outer lining of the man's jacket was not fur, but fine, white feathers.

Winglike, he spread his arms wide, smiled, and gave a little seated bow, 'Welcome to Littlepond Park.' The gestures, his features, and that high voice combined to reinforce the man's avian presence and Mal blinked hard to dispel the image of this bird-man lest it bring laughter.

'Creative name, I know,' the man continued sardonically, 'but then, isn't there something to be said for descriptive names? I mean, my friends call me Per—not for the Scandinavian variant of Peter —but short for Peregrine Falcon. It is because, though I don't see it, I have been told I possess the features of that bird.'

The smile was genuine. It was warmer than the quilt Mal now sat down on—softer too. It drew him in and for a moment the imagined presence of Rufus once more at his side was nearly tangible enough to reach out and touch.

'He's told you his name, it would be rude not to share yours,' Mal spoke for Rufus. Per reeled in surprise, no doubt thinking Mal was crazy or maybe high—not that Mal blamed him. Per just didn't understand how important his friendship with Rufus was. *And until Rufus is found, this pretend Rufus can't leave my side, or...* He sniffed involuntarily. *Or I just might die.*

'You're right, Rufus.' Mal talking to himself elicited no reaction from Per this time. Mal found that comforting, so he continued.

'Well Per, my friends call me Mal.'

Per gave a smile, his small, thin mouth and tiny teeth looking like a serrated beak in the shadow of that mountainous nose. 'I confess, Mal, that I already know your name. I hear it the last Friday of every month at the Koo-Koo-Sint Shelter when people gather for their welfare cheques. I hear it every time a new woman comes to the Mountain Flower Shelter. Though not many recognize your face, your reputation has spread across Acton. You are the man who first spoke the words "Big cheque or little, we're all payed beneath the same sky." That simple phrase is why you're famous.'

Mal turned to Rufus, confused. 'What is he—?' but Per kept talking over him.

'Let's leave Rufus out of this, for now. This is just you and me, Mal. Or would you like a reminder of your real name? Terrence Rumbolt of the O'Chiese Nation.' Per's tone grew hard and the high pitch of his voice was no longer comical, but intimidating. It was only then that Mal noticed the cast of the man's skin. What he had mistaken for a shadow beneath the hood was actually a dark tone nearly a match for his own.

Is this man an Elder? A family member? How do you know me?

Per continued, not noticing, or perhaps ignoring, Mal's growing unease. 'All you had to do was say it once. A defiant remark as you kissed your first welfare cheque. And it stuck. I know you're no longer on benefits, but if you were to go by the Koo-Koo-Sint Shelter on a cheque day, you'd hear that line on every pair of lips. It has been ritualized. Those words are posted on the wall, they are spoken, prayer-like, as every man and woman reaches across the counter for his or her cheque, for that small, measured token of salvation.'

'I am famous for that?! I quote poems in three languages. My name—Mal—is an earned name: Baudelaire's *Les Fleurs du mal,* my most cherished collection, it is the poetry I most often speak of.

You're telling me that none of those world-famous lines stuck with anyone? That my own half-hearted quip about sharing a sky is something that people latched onto?

He returned to his imagined image of his friend, 'Rufus, what is—?'

'Don't ask Rufus!' Per's interrupting shout was stern, absolute. 'Ask me.'

'What are you talking about? Who are you? How do you know me?'

'I am talking about you, Terrence. And I could turn that next question right back on you: who are *you*? Do you know anymore? Do you know the consequences of that little ritual you've started? Men and women will grab their cheques and say the words. It might be for show or for laughs in the shelter, but outside, on their own, they really believe. They believe! More now than in over a hundred years, men and women will look into the sky and give thanks. They give thanks that no matter what happens in this world, no matter how much they lose or how much they need take from others, we all share the same, unchanging sky. This one thing cannot be taken from anyone. You did that, Terrence. Not some other poet you admire, not some celebrated icon of wealth and fame, you. So my question to you is, do *you* believe?'

'Rufus, you know I—'

'NOT TO RUFUS! TO ME!'

Mal did not shrink from the shout this time, he sat up straighter, defending himself. 'I give thanks to the sky, to the Creator, I have not lost so much as you might think since I left O'Chiese.' Mal felt backed into a corner and there was a dangerous edge of defiance in his tone now. *What right do you have to ask anyway? What does O'Chiese care what I do with my life? What is it you believe, Old Man?*

'Answer the question I am asking, don't tell me what you think I want to hear. I'm not from your reserve. I'm not some caring Elder come to track you down. Revel or despair in this statement, but know it to be the truth: *nobody cares you're gone.* So quit trying to assuage me, just answer me. Do *you* believe?'

'Do I believe those words: "big cheque or little, we're all payed beneath the same sky?" No! Not anymore. It's not a shared sky anymore. It might still be shared by me, but not by others. I've seen people looking nowhere but down all day. The world has beaten the hope out of them, the world has cast down their eyes.

'And what of Rufus who you'd have me ignore? Where is the sky for him? Where is Rufus?!' Mal was not sure when, but somewhere in the midst of those words, he had stood up. He stared down at Per, defiance and anger twin flames behind his

255

eyes. They flashed threateningly, but Per looked unaffected, and he smiled his little beak smile once more.

In spite of the cold expression, his answering voice was soft, 'There is no sky for Rufus anymore. There is nothing. The man is gone, his soul devoured. Listen carefully, Terrence for I shall only once make you this offer. The beasts that obliterated Rufus's soul have done the same to six others and they will continue to devour the souls of the living until they are themselves destroyed.

'Your soul is aglow, Terrence. I see it behind your eyes. Though that glow was dim when first you sat down, it burns now like a sun within you. It is that glow that first spread the words to the homeless of Acton that the sky belongs to all. Go forth, Terrence, remind your brothers and sisters of those words and of the fire within each of us. They will follow you. Take as many as you can to the Clearwater footbridge. There you will meet the beasts who consumed the soul of Rufus. And there you will destroy them together with the fire you possess.'

Tears ran down Mal's face and he did not wipe at them. His eyes were locked on the water-blurred image of Per before him. There was only Per and Mal. With the stranger's words, Rufus had gone. Utterly gone. Even the imagined presence that had been so sharp only minutes before was now absent, and Mal knew it would never return. He could not bring back Rufus, could no longer share the sky with his friend. But he could damn well take the sky from those responsible, and he knew now that he would. He had to.

Per stood now as well, a full head and shoulders shorter than Mal. He placed a hand on Mal's shoulder that could barely be felt, so soft was the weight of that hand. Mal shivered beneath the gentle touch.

'Start with the Koo-Koo-Sint Shelter. Remind the people there of its namesake: David Thompson, the Stargazer. He was blind in one eye, but his gaze never wavered. He spent a lifetime looking upwards and mapped more of the Northwest than any soul in history. He knew ours was a shared sky. He looked to the sky above Acton and found salvation. Now it is your turn: look to the sky and see what you find.'

Per then collected his quilt and walked casually into the small section of woods behind the bench. By the time Mal realized he was leaving and went after him, there was no trace of the strange man among the trees. Had he thought to look skyward in that moment, however, Mal might have seen a single peregrine falcon wheeling overhead.

It was a quiet day, an empty day. The kind of day where you sit around doing nothing at all.

It was perfect.

Darko spent the day with his family. He didn't worry about school and didn't worry about his sick grandfather—even now sleeping in the next room. Darko himself had enjoyed a full night's restful sleep for once, as if nothing more than being back in his old bed had been needed. So his insomnia was added to the list of things he need not concern himself over today. And if Darko had taken the time to go through that full list, he would have found hundreds of little worries not plaguing him— but to go through that list would be to worry about them, and today Darko could ignore it all.

The suppression of that many worries was no easy feat, and Darko kept looking up to where Demir stood at the counter, hovering over an electric kettle that seemed to be taking hours to boil. *A little tea, and I can get right back on track not worrying about anything.*

Breathe, man, focus on your day.

Cards, playing with my niece and nephew, a walk outside here and there, the occasional chore to occupy my mind and keep me feeling useful: this is the life I want. This is the life I need.

It's a wretched shame that today is so far removed from reality.

Though he was certainly more relaxed than normal, Darko knew that today would eventually come to an end and, come tomorrow, he'd be back to his classes, and back to fighting all the regular worries he fought so hard not to worry about.

'Got any fives?' he asked Alexander, only realizing after the question that he himself had no fives in his own hand.

He didn't care. It wasn't winning he sought after, it was playing. Playing all day. Playing forever. He needed this, he needed his family close; if not, he was pretty sure his mind would break and someone would find him days later, a stream of saliva dripping from mouth to lap as he sat staring at a blank wall somewhere.

'*Ni. Lovysh rybu!*' the boy responded with his own made-up response in Ukrainian. Darko was pretty sure he had just been told to 'catch a fish,' but he had lost so much Ukrainian in the last few years that he was no longer certain.

He drew another card with a sigh. *Why can't life be like this moment forever?*

He handed off a seven to Ana who jumped on her turn as if she had been waiting an eternity.

Just focus, he commanded himself. *Ignore tomorrow for today. Focus on this moment and enjoy it.*

He looked up from his cards to the quietly whispering kettle on the counter. *Would you boil already?!*

Just go already, go! Ana pressed her handful of cards, now one seven lighter, against her lower lip where several minutes of doing so had imprinted a thin, white crease. She waited for Papa Nate's in-home nurse, Frederic, to take his turn. Then she'd be waiting for Darko, and then she'd be waiting for Alex, again, and again, and again. She stared at Frederic a little harder. *The toddler's more present in this game than you and Darko!*

The day had been perfectly uncomplicated. A late morning, a large breakfast, a bit of a walk outside, some chatting with Morgan and her odd cousin, and now some cards. And in the six or so hours since Papa Nate had arrived, he had been awake for collectively fewer than a forty minutes. As nice a distraction as this game was, Ana could not shake that thought from her mind. *He's dying!*

Yet for all the day's evident simplicity, it was treacherously difficult to get through. Every few minutes there would be some fresh thought that threatened to send her running into her old room, diving beneath her bed, and weeping in that dark space as she had done for weeks after her dad died.

For all Milana's compassionate text messages, Ana had not been able to respond to a single one. *What would I say? "My grandfather's dying and I'm sad?" What do I even want her response to be?*

'Go fish!' Ana snapped, far too aggressively, when Frederic finally spoke up to ask if she had any fives. *Darko just asked Alex if he had any, moron.*

Without Milana here at her side, it was like going through the day blindfolded, as if she had been deprived of the sense she most strongly relied on. For all these conversations and games, and insignificant, hollow interactions, nothing could effectively pull Ana's mind from thoughts of her dying grandfather and the fact that her best friend was not here at her side to help her get through it.

They had spent days apart before, countless days apart. But lately, Ana was finding herself more and more reliant on Milana's presence, not for any purpose or action, but simply for having Milana at there her side. She felt unwell without Milana around: sick, empty, like a leafless tree in the midst of Summer's bloom or a spider with half its legs ripped off, twitching helplessly on the floor. *And she's only been gone six hours.*

Just play the game, Ana cooed to herself gently, *play the game for now, go see Milana tomorrow, and enjoy this day with your family. When Papa Nate wakes, we'll have a nice talk before he has to go home and I'll tell him how much I love him and appreciate all he's done. I'll tell him—*

Ana forced her thoughts back to the game to banish the water that had began welling in her eyes.

She blinked away the tears before anyone would notice and sniffed at the sharp tingling in her sinuses.

For heaven's sake, when is this kettle gonna boil?!

Demir turned his gaze from the slowly-heating kettle and smiled as Ana drew another card. *What a gift! What a gift to be able to play away our day like this with such a grave tomorrow suspended overhead like some mythical king's sword. Strange shadow-beasts and hungry wechuge stalk the streets of Acton, and might have sated their appetites on Darko if not for rusalky of all things! Comically-overdressed thugs pad through Darko's neighbourhood, giving chase to young women. Where is the light in this world?*

Demir remembered enough from his younger days to know that those so-called thugs were likely the same impa shilup that had attacked Darko. His father had taught him that many creatures unused to human states of dress often failed in effectively disguising themselves by wearing too many clothes.

He recalled Darko's first encounter with the impa shilup. *Or too few...*

Demir struggled to recall more of his father's teachings. He found his mind going back to those lessons a lot these past couple days, with little success. Nothing had seemed like a lesson at the time, they were all words and stories that poured as naturally from his father as water runs downhill. Demir had trouble even recognizing which tales were real and which mere flights of fancy.

'They all sound fucking fanciful!' he growled under his breath.

Only Alexander had heard Demir's outburst and, looking up at his father from over his cards, eyes wide with concern, Demir casually waved his son away and turned back to preparing the mugs for tea.

He knew all his father's tales of riverspawn and how the Richovsky family had earned its name. And he knew also of Outsiders, all manner of beings from other realms that often preyed on the likes of humans when they found themselves here, in the realm of mankind. *My realm.* He did not know for certain how his father had died—the narrative of a sudden sickness had been explanation enough for Darko and Ana, but Demir had never really bought it.

The truth of that death had never seemed that important to Demir. *Dad's gone and Darko and Ana need taking care of. That's all that had ever mattered to me—all that ever should have mattered. What did it matter, at that time, what the cause of death had been? But now...*

But now with wicked things stalking the world outside his home, Demir was strongly beginning to suspect his father had been killed fighting one of those evil beings.

'Demir!' Ana shouted. Would you stop that?' Ana, Darko, Frederic, and Alexander were all staring at him from above their card game.

Demir looked up, surprised. He realized that he had begun pacing and went back now to his spot along the counter where he waited for the water to boil.

Just then, Morgan and her cousin Jane entered the kitchen from the living room. Jane seemed to glide more than walk to join the card players at the kitchen table. Morgan, for all her animated conversing with Jane in the next room, looked dazed enough to fall over. A rather concerning thought, considering she was carrying Klara. Demir began pacing again.

'If steps could make water boil faster, we'd all have drunk our fill by now.' Jane's joke was met with laughter from all but Frederic and Demir. Those two fixed Jane with dark scowls, but Demir's flash of anger disappeared with a peck on the cheek from Morgan.

Can you blame me for pacing? Weeks, possibly only days left to live, and Papa Nate is sleeping in the next room. This was supposed to be a day spent with him! But all he has the strength for is short spells of conversation between hours-long bouts of rest.

As Morgan walked past Demir to put Klara in her playpen, he looked accusingly toward his siblings. *I know I've always been the worrier among the three of us, but neither of you seem particularly concerned that our grandfather is dying in the next room! It's great that you can relax and play in a time of crisis like this, but after Mom and Dad died, this man raised us. We wouldn't have had food on the table, we wouldn't be on the family farm now, if not for him!*

I promise you, if none of you were here right now, I'd be curled up in Morgan's arms, bawling like a fucking baby.

He turned that accusing gaze to the stove. *How long does it take for a kettle to boil?!*

CHAPTER FIFTEEN:
Questioning Authority
Thursday, 18 February 2021

'Look, Professor Loepel,' Donald Philips began again, this time unable to keep the frustration from his tone, 'we know you had nothing to do with these murders. You've given us your alibi four times now, you've called in two of your fellow faculty members—without our prompting—to support your claims. That's not what we were asking for when we came in here twenty minutes ago, and it's not what we're asking for now! So, once again, were you, at *any* point, in *any* sort of contact, with *anyone*, about *any* of your flood-related findings, *anywhere* in the vicinity of Acton.'

'Oh, no, Constable, I haven't been to Acton. I assure you, I've been in Edmonton for the past three weeks!'

The professor was the very archetype of nervous wreck. He had begun sweating the second he saw the blue uniforms and his dress shirt was now soaked through, nipples peering out on either side of the tie like two weeping eyes. Donald wanted to join in that weeping.

He inhaled deeply, not sure yet if the next words out of his own mouth would be shouted or whispered threateningly. Fortunately, for the sake of his sanity, his partner took over.

'Oh yes, we know *all* about your whereabouts, Professor. You've been very helpful in that regard, thank you. What about any communication at all? Not in person. Something on social media, phone calls, emails, you name it.'

'Well, now that you mention it, Constable, I was in an email chain for a few days with someone about my findings. And—hey!—come to think of it, she did say she was from Acton. She was a graduate student, I believe, Faculty of Astronomy, but with wide interests.' Professor Loepel's gaze went to the ceiling wistfully, completely forgetting for a moment the circumstances that had led his thoughts to whatever far away place they had retreated to.

'Ahem.' Donald brought the man back to reality curtly. 'And would you happen to have any contact information of this woman? A phone number, email address, a *name…*'

'Certainly. It would have been a little difficult to communicate effectively through email without a corresponding address, ha ha ha.'

There was a moment of silence again as Donald looked hopelessly at the Professor, then turned desperately to his partner.

'Oh. Would you like me to get it for you?' Professor Loepel finally offered.

'YES!' the other two shouted in unison.

'Right now, or…?'

Donald's answering cry of frustration sent the man running for his computer.

A half hour later, the two officers left the province's capital in much the same way they had entered it: a bad cup of coffee in each cupholder, and a mutual feeling of futility hanging between them like some dark storm cloud.

'What a useless day!' Donald lamented. It was already quarter past four and they had only a single, likely dead-end lead to show for their efforts.

'Not completely, Philips. We learnt it's possible to sweat about a litre out of the human body and stay standing!'

Derek's joke was met with no more than a small smile. Donald just wasn't in the mood. Truth be told, he found himself empathizing with the awkward professor they had interviewed. After all, there was a man—a brilliant man, and expert in his field—and he couldn't give a stranger the time of day without crippling himself with his own anxieties. *His life must be anguishing.*

Donald really wanted no more than to slowly sip his coffee, wallow for the long drive back to Acton, and turn in early. *Tomorrow's a new day. We'll start fresh and early, we'll chase what leads we've got, we'll convene with Anderson and Laforce, and we'll get these guys.*

Today was a write-off, but tomorrow doesn't have to be. Some cases progress by the hour, others by the day. We'll be in the office by six, out chasing clues by nine. We'll put a stop to whatever group is doing this to the people of their own city...

He dwelt on that thought for a while. Unlike other officers, Donald Philips refused to put a face to a criminal before they were behind bars. But faceless or not, that formless silhouette of a guilty party did have some definite defining qualities.

Dammit, Derek's right. There's no way Joel can be a part of this group...

It was then, just as Donald was descending into the formative stages of his wallowing, that he was distracted by his partner's silence. Derek had not gone quiet due to a lack of conversation, but out of a newfound concentration.

Derek suddenly reached for the cruiser's built-in computer system, extended the monitor on its guiding arm to mere inches from his nose, and cranked out the detachable keyboard. A furious clacking ensued as Derek's eager fingers descended on those keys.

Donald couldn't see a thing. The only way the system would operate with the vehicle in drive was if the monitor was safely on the passenger's side, out of distracting-distance of the average driver. Surrendering to his curiosity, Donald decided his wallowing could wait.

'What's got you so worked up, Woods?'

But the man didn't answer, he was too busy caught up in whatever new idea had stolen his entire attention away.

With a sigh, Donald flicked on the radio, turned down the volume so as not to disturb his partner too much, and settled deep into his seat for the long drive. The moment of wallowing had passed, and Donald knew that when Derek got like this, it could be two minutes or two hours before he would come out of his working frenzy long enough to share whatever train of thought had taken him for a speeding ride away from his immediate surroundings.

Sure enough, not even a single song had played before Derek slammed the monitor back into its recess on the dash, leaned forward to cut the radio, and snapped his cellphone to his ear.

He was curt on the phone. All constabulary, no conversation.

'Yeah. It's me. You got it…? What do you mean third?' Derek sipped at his coffee and grimaced. It was not good.

'What? What?!' he asked again with increasing intensity. 'WHAT?! And now ours? Prof's introverted fan, that's the one. Tell the Captain, would you? Thanks. You too.'

Donald looked over expectantly as his partner hung up the phone, but Derek was not quite done. Without a word, he switched back on the radio and turned it up a little. As The Loved Ones were wrapping a tune about feeling like they lost some fight—*fitting,* Donald mused—Derek began tearing through the folder-turned-binder of case files, jotting down notes here and there.

Eric Bachmann followed The Loved Ones, somewhat soothing Donald's impatience and making this period of suspenseful waiting much more tolerable. Donald had been through this process with Derek over and over. No amount of encouraging, chastising, or even threatening had improved communication much. It was something Derek had done since they were teens working on school projects together. He knew the only thing he could do was to wait it out.

A few songs later, Derek's pen slowed. Then, after a few radio advertisements, it stopped completely. At last Derek closed the last of the files with a sigh and twisted in his seat to face his partner.

'Sorry. I know you hate it when I do that. I'm just afraid of losing my train of—'

'No need to apologize. Just tell me what you've got.'

'Right. I was looking up Professor Loepel's lead on the off-chance a stuffy academic might be in the system. Well, she had an entry all right: brand new, only the most basic biometrics added so far. It was only in noticing that her page was still tagged as an open entry that I realized the name was familiar: Vanessa Herald.

Donald looked from the road to Derek. It really wasn't familiar to him at all.

Reading his partner's blank stare, Derek elaborated. 'Vanessa Herald—your entry too, I'm just gonna point out—was the first victim of the Valentines Massacre. The one killed at the university.'

Donald swore under his breath. *Should've caught that one.* He sat a little straighter.

Derek continued. 'Since her entry was still so bare—that's on us man, we've got a shitload of paperwork to do! Anyway, file was bare, like I said, so I called the office. Anderson's on phones by the way, must have pissed off the captain, ha ha. I sent my logs through before I called, so he had the page pulled up, and he mentions this is the third time he's seen the woman's file.'

'Third?'

'Third. The first was the murder, third right now. The second? Koo-Koo-Sint Overpass. Turns out that this woman's fiancé was the driver of the vehicle hit. Steven Yung, a man that we interviewed.'

He paused to let the connection sink in. Both took a sip of their coffees.

'Here's what I'm thinking. I know we're never supposed to say it till the investigation's all wrapped up with a bow on top, but that Yung guy was as innocent as anyone I've ever met. Hell, Joel Johnson is more suspicious than he was—and Joel's a friend!'

Somehow, Donald already knew he wouldn't like what was coming next.

'His fiancée, his truest love in this world, was interested in this whole flood business—flood business that's probably connected to the murders. She gets murdered, brutally mutilated, carved up with cultic symbols. Then, less that a week later, someone tries to kill him! Not in any kind of way to connect it to the cult thing—not cut up and marked—but quick and expedient. The kind of murder meant to keep someone quiet.'

Finally reaching the main part of the highway, Donald accelerated to 110. As if spurred on by the vehicle's speed, Derek managed to twist a little farther in his seat, squaring his upper body to face Donald directly.

And then the hand gestures began. And Donald knew that this was about to be a very, very long drive.

'So, what if this Vanessa was the leader of some kind of cult, right? She does the research, sets up beliefs based on scientific fact, establishes whatever it is they believe in. She's probably the leader—or at least the brains behind the leader. Then, at some point, someone decides there's too much logic, too much sense in this cult, and there's a splintering. Some people don't like her much and they off her, use her murder as some kind of sick sacrificing ritual to kick off the hell they're unleashing across the city. Then, realizing she had a fiancé and worried about what she might have told the guy, they go after him!'

It ain't bad, Woods. It's a start, and that's more than we had half an hour ago, but God dammit, it's unrefined. We'll work it out yet, but forgive me if I don't jump to the same conclusions you do. At least not quite yet. I mean, this is all based on one woman with no connections to most of the other victims. How important could she really be?

'…Vanessa Herald,' the Friend was saying, 'a most memorable sacrifice. A most delicious one. Perhaps even *the* most delicious one, for we all felt its intensity. That was, until your brave display of… fidelity, my daughter. You shall be a Major Virtue no longer, but a Companion. It was your closeness to me that gave me this form…' her penetrating gaze somehow deepened, making Fidelity feel for a moment like the god was inside her very soul—and perhaps she was— 'and this power,' she finished meaningfully.

Fidelity stood in her place, too frightened to speak until the Friend dismissed her with a casual wave. 'Thank you for your words, most honoured…' Fidelity trailed off once it became clear the Friend was no longer listening to her response.

The god—in Emotion's body—sat in some kind of library chair that had been brought to the basement from who-knew-where, looking out upon the gathered Minor Virtues and…*others*, and asked them questions.

She had apparently been doing so all day. In between the introduction, adoption, and indoctrination of these Others—mostly beings from inhuman realms come to swear fealty—the Friend took every spare moment to return to her seat and resume her questioning.

How many questions can one being have? Hundreds? To believe Comfort and Gratitude, it must be in the tens of thousands! Well, not Comfort and Gratitude any longer. Lisa and Carl now. Companions like me. And the most common answer from the Friend's disciples in response to her endless questions: "We don't know."

Foreign words, places, people, most of them unheard of. And to every answer, no matter how empty and shallow or packed with meaning, never anything more than a simple nod in response.

You are truly a god, then. Enigmatic and mystical—not to mention terrifyingly powerful—the kind of being that leaves us all wondering after your great plan for us. If plan you have at all.

Just what have we unleashed?

The basement no longer felt like a home to Connie. Not that it ever had—not really—but it had felt like the kind of place that might one day feel like a home. Had.

Since the day she decided to make the most of her dual-citizenship and ditch Mississippi for good, there had been two defining moments in the life of Connie Martin: the day she became Constable Connie Martin, and the day she became Fidelity.

And on a single day, both these defining parts of who she now was became strained. It was a crisis of identity. The sustaining of one could very well be at the expense of the other. The god that had given meaning to her life was finally before her, but its arrival had not been accompanied by some great revelation like she had hoped. Only by more questions.

Who and what are you, Friend? You wear the face of Empathy but exhibit none of that sweet girl's compassion. None of her caring or understanding. I know it might have only been a job for her, her role to show empathy. She might have been callously indifferent internally, but she performed her duties admirably.

So what does that make you? A god who offers only a token thanks for her existence before casually waving away the most faithful of her followers? A god who asks a thousand questions about a world we thought Her fit to rule? A world we counted on Her making better! A god who now profanes Her own temple with a dozen strangers. Some, unknown citizens of Acton. Others, denizens of far-off and alien places.

And some not so alien.

Connie Martin's stepfather had been a Choctaw headman and she'd be lying if she said his constant references to all things spiritual hadn't been one of the driving forces pushing her out of Mississippi. But less than an hour ago, after a lifetime of insisting her stepfather's beliefs were foolish and without proof, she had been passed by a handful of impa shilup on her way into the house.

Oh, I'll bet you're laughing in your grave now. Choking out an "I told you so" round a mouthful of earth. Actual impa shilup, all the way up here in Acton. Hell, if you didn't have so little ambition in life, I'd suspect were among them, hissing and clicking about being back with bigger better gifts for the Friend.

What brings such monsters here, to the home of our faith? The seductive draw of power. And our god confers blessings on each of these monsters who already have it in terrifying qualities but gives the humans among us no more than mouse's measure of that same power.

And what of Your Companions who have already brought so much, Friend. We brought you life. What happened to your once Major Virtues, the fiercest supporters of your cause? Most are dead, one hospitalized, and the rest wander your basement temple feeling ignored...

Fidelity—and no matter what her god said, she had earned the right to call herself Fidelity—turned away from the Friend's continuing questions and the crowd of Minor Virtues, strangers, and unknown creatures. Fidelity's eyes fell on the closed door next to the stairs. There was a smear of dried blood above the handle and—though silent now—Fidelity had heard muffled crying from within when first she came down the stairs.

Deciding she'd rather not know what was going on behind that door, Fidelity kept her eyes moving till they fell on the stairs themselves. They were old, grey-carpeted things, with the occasional stain here and there. Fidelity had once stared, arms crossed and frowning disapprovingly, as her two Minor Virtues slid down those stairs, giggling with every thump of their backsides on the steps. She had only reacted so harshly out of respect for the sanctity of this place.

Now she wanted to cry picturing that memory. *Those two sweet souls, too innocent for the price needed to bring a god into this world. And now they're gone, our connection severed. And for all my faith, I find myself missing them, envying their innocence, wondering if theirs was not the better choice.*

Fidelity suddenly found herself longing to reconnect with the few faith-based connections she had left. The Major Virtues were no more, but the Companions were now the Friend's greatest supporters. No matter how she felt now, Fidelity knew she was not alone.

In spite of the Friend's outward indifference towards them, She owed her manifestation to those Companions. Perhaps it was time the Companions reunited and discussed what they could do, now that the Friend had arrived, to serve Her. And—perhaps somewhat tangentially—what they could do to best continue serving *their* cause, regardless of the Friend's place therein.

Within five minutes, Fidelity was back in her car, this time with Lisa Kim and Carl Fischer. Together they would meet with the Honesty—a man whose true name she had yet to learn—and so reunite the Companions.

CHAPTER SIXTEEN: Short Winter Days
Thursday. 18 February 2021

Old prejudices die hard, but they can still be killed.

If someone had suggested to Nathaniel Bennett ten or so years ago that he would one day place his life in the hands of a black man, his exact words would have likely been "kill me now."

Now he shook his head in shame at the mere thought of that. His self-professed wisdom that there were good and bad eggs in every basket had slowly revealed itself to him over the years as no better than a veiled racism. No matter how progressive he thought the little quip was, it had always been followed by anecdotes of how any basket of eggs off-white or darker tended to have more bad than good.

It had taken the open minds of younger generations to chip away at that wall of obstinacy. His own daughter's husband had a darker cast to his skin, and to Nathaniel it spelled an ancestry of aggressiveness, of orientals invading and raping. He had never said a word to his daughter, he respected her too much for that, but he feared for her and her children, fully expecting they would arrive one tragic night covered in bruises and begging for a place to stay.

But every kind act of Danylo Richovsky, every endearing smile flashed at him from his wife and children, had brought a slow realization to Nathaniel that his was an outdated way of thinking —*if it had ever been an acceptable way of thinking at all.* And though his grandkids shared that same somewhat-darker-than-white skin tone, Demir darker than the others, Nathaniel had never once questioned their goodness.

It is a new world. A world of crumbling barriers and soaring revelations. It is a world that's left me behind.

He winced at a flash of pain as he shifted in his seat.

And not a moment too soon.

He had been staring at Frederic's broad back for several minutes now, reflecting. Appreciating.

More than his fatalistic doctor—and the slough of second-opinion givers that followed—more than Nathaniel's own instincts of self-preservation, more than even his own stubborn family, it was Frederic who had best looked after Nathaniel in these last few days.

The man's a paragon! The very picture of caregiver. My companion in my final days…

Not quite so pretty as Leah, he laughed to himself. *But could be a whole lot worse.*

The very day his wife had died, Nathaniel had known that his would be a lonely death. Hers had been too, in a way. *A brain aneurism while I slept next to her, oblivious.* As sad a thought as it was, this diagnosis had filled Nathaniel's last few days with more outings and visits from family and friends than he would normally have in several months.

Nothing to make you feel alive like dying.

Nathaniel did not fear the actual dying part of his inevitable death. He had been raised in the Anglican Church and no matter what life and the media had thrown at him, his faith was unwavering. He had always found a way to reconcile his beliefs.

He was a firm believer in the Earth's ancient age, a supporter of contraceptives, evolution, and the legality of abortion, but he also believed in the eternal life of the soul, Heaven and... lesser Heaven—he had never learnt quite enough about Hell to understand its cosmic role, much less believe in its existence. But for all his beliefs and anxieties, Nathaniel could rest confidently that, when his mortal body finally let go and his immortal soul left this world, it would find a place of peace in the embrace of God.

What Nathaniel did fear, however, was the time between then and now.

He had spent only part of the day with his family—most of it asleep—and it had taken the full extent of his physical capabilities. He was probably healthier today than he ever would be again, and already he was becoming a burden on those he cherished most. He could feel the heightened tensions when he was in the room, the anxiety of those that wanted to be there for him, to take his pain, but could offer no more than a sympathetic smile. It was a different kind of agony entirely on its own.

Images of his three smiling grandchildren filled his mind.

It was unjust, plain and simple, losing your parents so young. I did what I could for you: money, food, clothes. But I could never bring myself to parent you the way I did my own children. And no matter how much I tried to give you, I could never take away that loss, could never give you back your childhood.

He sighed in his chair, heavy enough to cause Frederic to look up from his paperwork and start making his way over.

I will not be a burden to you in death, children. I owe you that much at least, he silently vowed, *owe it to your father's memory. To your mother.*

'How's the pain, Mr. Bennett?' Frederic checked his watch. 'You're okay for another dose now if you need.'

Nate thought for a moment. He was not in any considerable pain at the moment: nothing more than the general discomfort and achiness of old age. He had not—mercifully—had another of those attacking fits of agony since returning home —not that the medication could do anything for those fits anyway—but even that dull and constant pain was beginning to pulse a little more severely.

'Okay then,' he said. 'Best to stay on top of it.'

He watched Frederic disappear over a shoulder toward the kitchen to fetch a single pill of the most potent medication he had ever experienced. Frederic warned Nate with every dose about the dangers of taking more than the designated amount in each six-hour period.

I'm a burden on you too, Frederic, but it seems like this is your calling, your passionately-pursued purpose in life, so... perhaps I don't need to feel quite so guilty for relying on you.

Nate was beginning to think of Frederic as a sort of pseudo-son. Not that he felt he lacked anything in his relationship with his biological son. It was just a role he had always fell into naturally. *Or maybe forced others into.*

Ahh, Joseph doesn't deserve that. Poor boy was as robbed of a parent as his niece and nephews. From the moment Theresa died, I couldn't stand the thought of losing him too. I abandoned him as much as I abandoned those kids—right up until their father died too. And now, Joseph, you have to watch a father die, except I was never there for you the way Danylo was for his little ones. And I'm sure you feel as guilty as me about the whole thing, and that's what hurts the most, because you were only a victim. Jesus Christ! I couldn't even find it in me to make it to your wedding.

He sighed again, but this time no one was around to hear it. He would have cried too, he was sure, if he wasn't just so damn tired.

He was not quite sure why, but the fact that he could sigh audibly and have it go unheard seemed preferable to him somehow.

He sighed again, loud and long, just to feel it one more time.

It happened exactly as Per said it would. A simple mention of the words he was famous for, occasionally further proof that he was indeed Mal by way of some badly-quoted Baudelaire, and people were willing to follow. "Big cheque or little, we're all payed under the same sky." People loved those words, sang them out with laughter and latched onto Mal like their personal saviour.

The magic of the phrase was far from universal. Some had no idea what Mal spoke of, most simply ignored him, pretending he wasn't there. One man had spat in his face and thrown a poorly-aimed punch before Mal managed to skitter away. But slowly, inspiringly, more and more began to follow.

When Mal returned to Two Stone Camp that evening, he opened his and Rufus's tents to his new companions. New tents were erected around the site and that night, instead of a single soul, cold and alone, the small camp was bursting with fourteen.

Above those fourteen souls, aglow with the slow and steady smouldering of companionship, and above their small camp nestled in the river valley, a peregrine falcon wheeled, catching an updraft and letting it take him higher into the skies above Acton. His skies. Long had the people below looked up at his domain in awe. Their sacrifices— mostly of time and thought, but occassionally of prayer—had given him power. He turned on a new current, banking for the north side of the river and his rendezvous point.

Not bad, Terrence. Not bad at all. Still, I was hoping you'd head to the bridge today. But the winds of fate blow where they will.

Perhaps this delay is for the best. Let the bridge go unprotected this evening. Let the creatures of shadow have one more night in this realm. One more night beneath my skies.

Per was no god. He was no more than an empowered spirit. The spirit of Acton's skies. Though he was not without power—and that power had grown considerably with the Newcomer's arrival—it was a passive kind of might he wielded. A push here, a gentle guiding there. His own path was as fickle as the winds blowing through his skies, and even less predictable. In so many ways his kind of power seemed directly opposed by the aggressive potency manifested in this Newcomer.

Yes, you are nothing like the spirits of this land. There is no passiveness, no enigmatic wisdom in the ways you interact with mortals. Your power is a storm and you the very charges of lightning that would strike out and destroy. You are a being of direct action, of aggression. Even in your newfound body, that power is barely contained. Everything even remotely connected to the spirituality of our collective existence was touched by your arrival. Even I, so very much your counterpoint and opposed to your coming, have been made stronger.

It is a strength I reject. It is an uninvited strength, an unwanted strength. A strength that does not guide, but forces. And even before your arrival, you began forcing all manner of wicked beings into your open arms. Your presence here is unwelcome, Newcomer, and it must be answered.

Per wheeled once, catching a shadow below as a line darted through the tall grasses at the river's edge—a mouse. He dove for it, impossibly fast. The earth here was covered by no snows, but by little orange flowers in full bloom, some strain of iris, and healthy grasses that looked months into growth. The air bore the smell of summer.

A mere metre and a half above his quarry, Per snapped his wings wide. They filled with air, arresting his descent. The audible snap of his wings catching the air was enough to startle the little mouse, who turned in a panic, black eyes growing to fill its small face. A startled squeak was forced out of the rodent as the air pushed by Per's wings sent the frail creature tumbling through the grasses.

Per landed softly, chittering with laughter.

'It's not like you to arrive on time, Per,' the mouse squeaked after righting itself.

Sun sets so early these days I thought I was already late.

'Nor like you to let a hungry bird catch you by surprise,' Per answered, preening at one wing. 'I did not think you would come. Don't you have something more important to do: like hiding in a buffalo's skull somewhere?'

The mouse *tsked,* a clear indication that he saw no humour in Per's words, only immaturity. 'You're too caught up in the past, Per. Winds of change are blowing. You had best ride with them. The arrival of the Newcomer will change life in Acton, so let's look not behind, but forward this night.'

Creator's wisdom! It was only a joke, Mouse!

The two creatures stood in silence then, one in the other's shadow, staring at the river expectantly. With its swollen banks there was no rocky beach or earthen cliff, the water was higher than either bank remembered. Quiet waves levelled out amid the whispering grasses before them. it would have been serene but for all the potential horror it portended.

Per did not know much about rusalky. Refusing even to acknowledge the term, he preferred to identify those they waited for as a single, collective river spirit. And in some ways they were—just not in the ways he wished. He did know, however, that in even the most romanticized tales of rusalky, they always caused some horror for some group among mankind.

He was in no particular rush for them to arrive.

But arrive they did. A life came to the waters at length, an energy, and the surface of the river broke as the three young women emerged, their floral dresses already dry as they stepped to the water's edge. Tiny ripples lapped at their bare feet. With the Newcomer's manifestation, and the arrival of all that power, Per wondered for a moment if the three were now able to leave the waters of their river completely.

He quickly dismissed the question as a stupid one. *They are as much a part of this river as I am of the sky. They are no more a single wave or ripple than I am this one bird. If our little rodent friend here were to die, his kind would still number comfortably in the millions. There is an ebb and flow to life, a rising and falling of its currents. And we are bound to that cycle each within our own realms. No matter the power I might possess, I could never be aught but a spirit of Acton's skies. And these river sisters are equally bound to their own domain.*

As if hearing Per's thoughts and laughing at them, the rusalky continued out of the water, placing him and Mouse between themselves and the river. *Then again,* Per thought, chagrined, *I've been wrong before.*

The rusalky and the mouse must have been equally lost in their own thoughts or, perhaps, they were simply content with the silence, for it was several minutes before anyone spoke.

Mouse was the first to break the silence with a rather unhelpful, 'Well…'

Fine. I shall be the one to begin this. Already the winds pull at me, guiding me away from this place.

'There is a new presence in these lands,' Per began, 'and we must—'

'She is called the Friend,' Mouse interrupted. 'No spirit like you, nor mortal like me, she is a god.

291

A minor one, at the moment, but power attracts power, and even the most insignificant of gods tends to grow mighty.'

'The Friend… The—' Per struggled to recall the path of his thoughts. He swept a wing over his face and began again. 'She may be a transient presence here, or she might become a fixture. Though I might despise some of the beings she attracts, the Friend herself is unknown to us. What kind of being is she? Can she be trusted? Her name alone is answer to that, but whether simply or sardonically so remains to be seen. How do we react?'

It was Maritsa, one of the river sisters, who spoke next. 'We did tell you this was coming. We've warned of Her arrival for months.'

'Of her danger,' Omelja added.

'So perhaps you'll heed us now when we say She must be opposed. If she is not opposed…' the third, Rosalia, seemed content to leave her warning at that, her sisters nodding emphatically.

'What? If she is not opposed, what? Quit being so *spirity!*' Mouse squeaked in annoyance.

'Well,' Rosalia continued, 'If she is not opposed, all that is Acton will be destroyed.

Mouse gave a thoughtful *hmmm* in answer, quieting the reflexive response that had been rising to Per's beak. He supposed it was for the best, as whatever he had been about to say would not have been particularly well thought out.

'Hmmm...' Mouse said again. 'Acton is not ours to preserve. Yours is only the sky above the city,' Mouse turned from pointing his little paw at Per to pointing it towards the sisters, 'And yours is only this river running through it. And mine...' he looked again to Per with a wink, 'Well mine is in the skull of buffalo, is it not?'

Per gave Mouse a sour look in response. Mouse simply continued, ignoring Per as if he really were no more than the bird standing in the grasses.

'My point is, the city of Acton has its own spirit. And that spirit is the people who make Acton what it is. If they decide the Friend has a place in their city, then we have no business opposing Her. Simple as that.'

Per stretched his wings and cocked his head. *You make a good point, Mouse. Something I had not considered. Acton's skies sometimes give sun, other times rain, and it is only those below who decide the worth of each. To one, the rains are a gift; to another, a curse. And it is the right of every soul to feel the way he or she will. I withhold neither sun nor rain, I simply am. The skies simply are. And those of Acton simply are as well: each in his or her own way.*

Per was about to speak in agreement of Mouse when Rosalia spoke first. Her voice was quiet, calm, like the ripples at the river's edge. But there was a depth to them, a depth that threatened the same swift undercurrents found in the mightiest parts of the Clearwater. Per shivered.

'Your words are hollow, Rodent. As in the tales of the beginning, when your so-called Napi gave you dominion over all, you abandoned it for the sake of your own convenience, casting onto humankind a burden rightfully your own. The mice of this world will ever place convenience above all else. In the beginning you condemned humans to a fate of your earning for the sake of a simple and easy life and now, though the dangers are not of your making, you would seek abandonment once again.'

'You forget,' Omelja continued, her tone a match for her sister's, 'the three of us were once citizens of Acton, once a part of its spirit, as you claim. There are those within Acton who would, if they knew the danger She poses, pray to every god and spirit they know, for salvation from the impending destruction the Friend will bring.'

Maritsa spoke with a finality to conclude what her sisters had begun. 'The Friend's arrival threatens to seduce. Even we three nearly succumbed to the promised power. If I had not found the riverspawn, even now we might have been in service to Her instead.'

There was an abrupt change in tone then, and Maritsa's sisters reeled in unison, looking to Maritsa as if she had just sprung a second head. 'Found him?' Omelja asked, incredulous. 'You tried to seduce him!' Rosalia began laughing with such animation that Per nearly missed Omelja's next words.

'Don't pretend it was anything more than a fateful accident. You weren't looking for a riverspawn, you were looking for a husband!'

CHAPTER SEVENTEEN:
Long Winter Nights
Thursday, 18 February 2021

Her day had passed like a ghost. She had floated, unnoticed, from class to empty class, her interactions with other students rare and meaningless besides. It was as if a veil had been draped over her soul, preventing her from truly feeling the world around her. It dulled the senses and numbed the mind.

Even at home, in the comforting presence of her family, everything and everyone seemed impossibly distant. There was engagement— conversation, playful banter, a shared meal—but no connection.

Since her parents had moved into Acton to be closer to their jobs, Milana normally stayed with her aunt in Oak Creek during the week. Ana had practically moved in with them as well, since the Richovsky farm was a decent drive from town and Ana had no vehicle. Her mother had never approved of the arrangement and that evening, with the whole extended family gathered for a dinner, she had made that known.

'Now I'm not suggesting you kick her out, that's your aunt's call' and she had fixed her sister with a look that said it was anything but. 'But you can't keep taking on the pain of others, Milana. Be your own person. Live your own life. Who is Milana without Ana? You two have grown so codependent you can't even go one normal day without her at your side. You won't be friends forever, no matter what you think now. The sooner you figure out who you are on your own, the better it will be for both of you.'

Her mother hadn't meant to be vicious with her words, Milana knew, but a mother's words were supposed to support, to comfort. Her mother's words had crippled her, had cut away the mountain on which she had stood most of her life. And now Milana fell from that height, waiting to hit bottom. Again and again, those words rang in her mind, each time cutting deeper than before. It was perhaps the truth of them that hurt the most.

I know we realistically won't have each other forever, but why cheapen today with fears of tomorrow? You don't know what will happen, Mom. Yeah, maybe, realistically we'll drift apart, find our own paths staying in touch only nominally until the day contact fades away. But why are you counting on that being the fate of our friendship? Maybe instead we'll be friends forever. Maybe we'll be in the same classes next year, maybe we'll go into business together as veterinarians. We've only been planning all this for the past three years.

As harsh as reality glares, I think what Ana and I shine brighter.

But for all her indignation, for every defiant, fist-shaking word spoken in her head, Milana had been outwardly cowed. She had nodded along to her mother's chastising, had given a tight-lipped smile at the reassurance that her mother's words had been harsh "for her own good" and, when her mother insisted she go to judo alone tonight, "the beginning of a more independent Milana," she had done exactly as she was told.

Now, in the judo studio's parking lot, waiting for one of her favourite songs to end, she let go of the bitterness still pooled in her chest. She knew it wasn't right to be mad at her mom, knew that the woman was only looking out for her in the best way she knew how.

Milana cut the engine as the final, sustained note of the song faded out. She checked her phone again. Still no response from Ana. She quickly typed out a new message: **Hey, how'd the day go? Think you'll make it to school tomorrow? Here if you want to talk.**

She stared down at the words, thumb hovering over the send button, for nearly a full minute. *You'd think for best friends, finding the right words wouldn't be so damn hard. Would Ana find this message reassuring? Am I even sending it for her reassurance?*

...Or for mine?

Dammit, Mom!

With a deep breath, Milana shoved her phone into her purse, decision still unmade, and tore off the seatbelt. *I need a break. No more analyzing messages, or friendships, or feelings. No more inner arguments and self-pity. I'm going to get in that studio, judo-toss the crap out of some people in sparring, wear myself to exhaustion, and sleep this whole thing away till tomorrow.*

'Good plan,' she sighed, stepping out of the car.

To her right, a young couple had just arrived as well. Though they had exited the car, they hovered over the opened trunk, seemingly on the verge of either arguing or making out. Milana had seen them before, though they did not attend the class very often. Neither was particularly talented, nor particularly driven enough to improve. *I won't be sparring with the two of you. I need a partner who can really kick my ass. And whose ass I can kick right back.*

Her mind catalogued potential sparring partners as she crossed the dark parking lot for the studio doors. The single street lamp above cast everything in a yellow glow, dimmed by the row of thick spruces obscuring its true radiance. The upstairs lights were on in the studio, bright and white, darkened silhouettes visible already warming up. Someone would be down to lock the studio doors in a couple minutes. Anyone more than five minutes late would have to head back home.

Milana was just reaching the last row of parking spots between her car and the studio when she heard a shrill scream from behind. It was immediately recognizable as the young woman from the couple.

Seriously? Now? Breaking up in a parking lot over a class neither of you really seem to care about? But a second scream, this time from the man, had Milana cursing her own coldness. Guiltily, she turned back the way she had come, phone already in her hand with 911 dialled, her thumb poised over the call button.

A third scream came, again from the man, "HEEELLL—" It was cut short by a heavy *clunk*. Milana rushed for that sound, blood rising. She suddenly grew violently defensive over these two strangers. This was *her* judo class, *her* parking lot, and *her* classmates. And if anyone thought to ruin any of that for her, they would receive a swift education in everything Milana had learnt in that studio behind her.

I had a hell of a day, I've never needed to fight someone more than I do right now, and if whoever's harassing this couple is gonna stop me from kicking asses inside, then I'll do it right out here!

She rounded a truck to see several shapes in the shadow of a dark van. Inside the van, darker forms of black marked the driver and front passenger, and both seemed to be looking at her. Though she could hear the van running, not a single light was on, inside or out. On the side of the van, three shadowed forms, looking barely human, were forcing the two smaller—and comparatively brighter—forms into the van. The woman sobbed quietly, acquiescing to the animated gestures of her captors and the man had been knocked unconscious, bleeding from a cut above his eye even as he was tossed roughly to the floor of the van.

What shocked Milana most about the scene before her was that she recognized the five dark forms. She had never seen them before—if she could even call witnessing the bleeding shadows of their true forms *seeing* them now—but she could *feel* their familiarity. The three outside the van turned to regard her with what she imagined were smiles on their vaguely-humanlike faces. Unsettlingly charming, one of the smiling forms stepped toward Milana, out of the shadow of the van and into the full glow of the streetlight.

Despite being fully lit now, nothing about the form changed. It was still a giant, hulking shadow, nearly seven feet tall, an invisible smile welcoming her to come closer. She knew these five creatures to be the same men who had chased her and Ana to Darko's door two nights before.

'Oh, where's your little friend, girl?' the close one sneered.

'Don't matter.' the passenger of the van poked his shadowed face out the window, thicker shadows dripped like saliva from where its mouth should have been. 'She was the more appetizing of the two.'

'Oh yes,' returned the first gleefully, 'a meal as full as a thousand meals! An entire city's worth of souls in one. A nation's!'

'A plane's,' the passenger countered, 'technically speaking, that is.'

'Yes, a plane's' seethed the first hungrily. 'She will make the greatest gift to the Newcomer. A gift to be paid back in POWER!'

As he shouted the word, he was suddenly upon her. Shadowy arms as strong as steel bars embraced Milana, lifted her from the ground and deposited her promptly in the van. Before she could even spit foul words of defiance at the beast, the van door slammed shut behind her. Outside, the three forms seemed to melt into the surrounding shadows of the night and the driver put the van in gear and began driving off.

Milana had seen too many movies, imagined too many horrid scenarios to simply surrender to her fate. *I'm getting out of this van or I'm dying in the attempt.*

Despite the driver's alarming speed and overly-dramatic turns, Milana gained her feet and charged for the wheel. Out of nowhere—or, more correctly, out of some shadow between her and the driver's seat—one of the other shadowy creatures suddenly rose in her path. It was like charging the van itself.

Milana fell to her backside, her head spinning painfully.

Hissing and clicking reached her distantly from the front of the van. The shadowy form still towering over her, seemingly unaffected by the van's constant motion, voiced some hisses and clicks of its own. The sounds were like whispers, there was a tone to them and, after a moment, Milana realized that the beasts were talking to one another.

'Hey! Shut up!' Terullimp commanded from the driver's seat. The little creature's defiance, though initially charming, was quickly becoming a nuisance.

Shiloksa looked to his brother, a little hurt by his rough tone. 'Are you sure we cannot devour her ourselves? The power from her alone would surely be more than the Newcomer can give us.'

Terullimp shook his head and clicked his disappointment. 'Ever shortsighted, Shiloksa. Where is your sense of ambition? Where your planning for the future? Would her soul—souls?—be worth more today or tomorrow than whatever gift the Newcomer gives us? Without question. This may even be the case for the next few weeks, even a year. But what about after that year? The taste of this meal will fade and we shall once again have nothing. Except this time, nothing will be accompanied by the Newcomer's enmity for our spiting Her.

'No, this is the wiser course of action. The more permanent course. Let us selflessly give away this priceless prize and, in so doing, be vested as the most loyal, most powerful of the Friend's servants. Over the years our power will only grow for our loyalty. Our power will be infinite. So we live under the shadow of another, so what? Isn't that what we're used to after all?'

The four other impa shilup in the van erupted in laughter, even the two who hid their true forms in the shadows of the back seats. Terullimp found himself laughing as well. It was an old joke, but well placed.

Shiloksa hissed an ascent to his brother's wise words. 'An ambitious vision indeed. And a delicious one. But what of the short term? She seems harmless enough, but I won't make the mistake of underestimating one of this world's inhabitants again. Isn't that why we attacked the couple instead of attempting to sway them?'

'Wise words yourself,' Terullimp commented. 'You're right. For the short term, I think some gentle shackles will do. Let her continue to voice her complaints, however. Maybe she'll tire herself out.'

With his brother's permission, Shiloksa worked with the others to place binds of shadow around the girl's wrists and ankles, securing her to the van's dark floor.

It served to shut the annoying thing up for all of four seconds, before she channeled all that trapped energy into shouting forth a string of curses that sent Shiloksa fleeing back into the shadows beneath the front seats.

For his own part, Terullimp was not entirely confident with all the idioms she used, but suffice to say within a few seconds he was beginning to doubt not only his ability as a being of immense cunning and power, but even the relationship he had with his dear brothers.

After a minute or two more with no slowing from the creature in the back, Terullimp lifted the suppression he had placed over the van, its lights came back on blindingly and, with a hissed sigh, Terullimp turned on the radio and cranked the volume.

Milana's throat was raw when they at last parked the car and dragged her into the road. The five creatures of shadow kept their distance this time, as did the other girl who had been captured. That other girl, clinging pathetically to her unconscious boyfriend, actually looked more afraid of Milana than of the five brutes who had kidnapped her.

So much for trying to help you. You're kind of the reason I'm here. All I had to do was keep walking to judo and I wouldn't be in this mess. You think you're afraid of me now? Just wait till I get us out of here!

The threatening glow in Milana's eye sent the girl skittering even farther away, but it went unnoticed to Milana. She was busy memorizing every detail of the street. Even as her vision was stolen with some kind of clinging shadow over her eyes, even as she could feel herself being dragged into a house, across a tiled floor, and down into a basement, her mind was only repeating one thing.

Cul-de-sac, ten-minute drive from judo, three blue houses in a row, and a name on stone: Richmond. Richmond, cul-de-sac, three blue houses. Richmond, cul-de-sac...

When at last the supernatural blindfold was removed, her careful recitation halted with the shock of the sight before her. She sat along one wall in a room full of captives like herself. Human waste had collected in a corner opposite and the smell had her on the verge of vomiting. A few of the others in the room were unconscious, one nearer the centre of the room looked to be truly dead, his open eyes staring out of a slightly-blue face straight at her. But the most shocking of all was the girl who was helping guide the knocked-out man from the young couple into a supine position against the wall to Milana's right: Stephanie Horowitz.

The two locked eyes, Milana glaring hatred, Stephanie buffeting the force of that gaze with her own stunned stare before she wheeled and took her own seat across the room where she promptly buried her head in her hands.

Milana leaned her head back against the wall, sighed heavily—even that simple action tugging at the pain in her raw throat—and quietly began to cry.

When Per was once again soaring through the skies, he decided the outcome of the meeting was not overly surprising. He was not happy with the outcome, but he had been expecting it.

Per had eventually come to agree with the river sisters that the Friend must be opposed. Not just the undesirables the Friend's presence had been attracting, but the very god Herself. At every turn in their brief argument, Per had been swayed first one way, then another. First he backed Mouse, then the sisters, then Mouse again. Even his own concerns changed during the course of the argument as freely as the direction of the winds he now rode.

How can we face the Friend? Her power dwarfs ours.

'We will gather allies' had been the response.

Why will you not join us, Mouse? Are we not all inhabitants of the same Earth? Do we not sleep beneath the same skies and drink of the same waters?

Mouse had been unyielding in his point of view. He had only given ground in acknowledging that the true spirit of Acton—her people—were not completely aware of what the Friend's arrival would mean for their city. 'For my own small part, I shall wake them to the potential dangers so they may react as they will.' Even that small gesture had been a huge comfort to Per's misgivings.

Yet, even with allies, only the suggestion of the river sisters that we strike swiftly to catch the Friend off guard truly gives us a chance of victory. The Friend's own immense power blinds her to ours. With allies, careful planning, and the springing of the perfect trap this can work.

A fresh current of cold air descended down and to his right, Per let himself be drawn down with the force of it. His new position gave him a slightly different view of the city below and again his mind shifted.

All those plans sounded good in the moment, made it sound like we might have a real chance. There is not enough power in all of Acton to oppose the Friend on equal ground with hopes of triumph, but by following the cunning of the River Sisters, we just might prevail.

He screeched, long and loud. *I will kill or banish this god, or be destroyed in the attempt. That much is clear to me. Together with the allies we gather, we shall protect the people of Acton from the wicked things the Friend invites to this city. But where is the honour in striking from the shadows to confront the Friend herself? Where is the spirit of courage? Where the humanity?*

This fresh current was carrying Per downward with alarming speed toward a darkened house below. Though the evening was yet young, the skies were already black. Suspiciously, not a single light shone from the house.

It was the site of death, of murder. Per could feel the cold vacuum left by the souls of a family of six sent away to some afterlife in a far off place. *Or perhaps to oblivion.* He was not entirely sure where those souls had gone.

The house across the street from this dark dwelling was the very temple the Friend now called home. *Just as the River Sisters had said, the Friend is a menace to the people of Acton. In effort to expand her infantile church, she sends her faithful to butcher a family, and now uses their home as a waiting room for those beings wishing to treat with her.*

In the attic of the dark house, Per's keen eyes could make out two huge forms through the skylight. They looked much like humans, but were broader in every way. Their necks stretched out horizontally, their shoulders sloped backwards, and where their skin was exposed Per could make out a pattern like scales. They had a peculiar aura about them, something that marked them as Outsiders, beings of some other realm, drawn to Acton by the pull of the Friend's power.

Gods who would make promises to mortals are all too rare these days—in any realm. Gods who would intervene on the processes of everyday life are a magnet for those seeking power over those same processes. Whether their wishes are malevolent or benevolent, such beings are a danger, one and all.

As he drew nearer, Per noted how the edges of the physical forms of these two beings seemed to fade and blend with the surrounding darkness. *Not so distant from those impa shilup, are you? Let's*

*make this for Rufus then, a man who respected the
skies above till his very end. I was the last vision in
his dying eyes, and I will be the last in yours. For
Rufus, it was a vision of hope, but for you…*

Per let out a fearsome shriek as he dove for the
attic skylight. In the last instant before impact with
the glass, Per left the body of the peregrine falcon
—the bird panicked, pulled up short and reeled
away with furious flapping—his incorporeal form
sliding through the molecules making up the
window without damaging it, and dove for the face
of the closer being.

Unlike the Friend, per's only means of physical
manifestation was to temporarily borrow the body
of a creature living in his domain. His true self was
formless, it was a thing of spirituality, not a
creature or force to be seen or felt. It took all his
strength now to gather that formlessness into an
incorporeal manifestation. The result was a weak,
translucent, vaguely-blue, vaguely-winged shape.

Its weakness was childlike. But the beings in
the attic were also not material beings. They were
strangers to this Earth, Outsiders, and like Per they
were weakened in this place.

Unlike Per, however, they had not dwelt around
Acton for centuries. They had not waxed and
waned with the fickle faith of Acton's citizens in
the skies over their heads. These beings had no

connection to this place. So, despite Per's relative frailty, to these Outsiders, he was indomitable.

He collided with the face of the first Outsider, the wavering image of his talons deeply digging into the creature's eyes, and from those talons lightning struck. He flapped his great wings a single time. Hard. Thunder answered the lightning, shaking the house to its concrete footings and shattered every window in the place. As the thunder continued rolling, the lightning arced furiously from Per's talons through the Outsider's eyes, into its brain and down through its body to stop all four hearts before jumping out into the second Outsider where it did the same.

In seconds, the two Outsiders in the attic, and all those on the floors below awaiting the Friend's invitation for an audience, were no more than charred husks of carbon staining the walls and floors.

Yes, let your souls speed away to whatever afterlife you believe in. See my mercy in not devouring souls as your kind do. And fear the strength that is that mercy.

Per winged away, reaching out his senses for a nearby conduit for his being. A whisky jack stirred awake in a tree nearby and took off for the skies and for Two Stone Camp.

Sorry, River Sisters, I know you had designs on surprising the Friend, but that is not my way. Our message has been delivered and the Friend now knows we oppose her. There shall be honour in the battle to come.

CHAPTER EIGHTEEN: A Friendly Goodnight

Friday, 19 February 2021

It was gentle at first, a small, nearly imperceptible tug. Some impulse from the waking world reaching through the veil to disturb her sleeping mind. Like when the sound of distant conversation makes its way into a dream, or when a physical sensation like hunger slowly pulls one awake.

It *had* been gentle…

Now it broke through to all her senses, no gentle probing but the clawed hand of a demon tearing through that barrier of sleep to grab her, full-fisted by the collar, and yank her into wakefulness!

'Ana.' She heard it again, and her eyes snapped open.

'Anaaa!' the voice pleaded with urgency, with desperation.

Every fibre of logical thinking in her argued—railed—that this was all a dream, that the best way of confronting it would be to roll over and try to fall into a deeper sleep. But the heart is not so easily cowed as the mind, and Ana's demanded—quite simply and firmly—that this was no dream. That this voice, so closely connected to that very heart, now needed help. And that Ana would provide it.

'Milana?' she hazarded a whisper into the dark of her room.

Wherever the voice of her friend was coming from, her own seemed unable to reach.

'*ANA!*'

It was not sound, Ana realized, but a kind of emotional presence that reached her. It didn't just fill her ears, it washed over and through her entire body, filling it with a sense of Milana's very being at her side.

It was like hearing her voice, smelling her hair —which, despite the use of identical shampoos always smelled better than Ana's own—feeling her touch, looking upon her, and somehow tasting her presence all at once. But it was only there in those two, short syllables. Then it was gone.

And this time, it did not come back.

Ana sat up in her bed, her mind abuzz with worry.

She darted for her phone, yanked it from the charger in the wall, punched in a call to Milana, and waited.

It rang loudly into the silent night. She pulled it away from her cheek, listening to the ringing, and glanced at the time on her phone: 2:41.

The irrationality of it all struck her. *It must've been a dream… Of course it was a dream!*

She breathed a sigh, hoping it would ease the tension knotting in her stomach—it didn't—and lifted the still ringing phone away from her ear to end the call.

Click. Hissing. A man's voice. '…Hello?'

Another bout of furious hissing from farther away. Then, angrily, 'What are you—? Throw that thing out the window!'

There was a rush of air, a deafening clattering, the fading sound of a passing vehicle, then silence.

Ana was now wide awake. She got out of bed and started pacing.

Calm down, calm down. Maybe someone just stole her phone… The words sounded hollow even to her. She could feel her heart's quick beating against her chest.

No! That was her. I heard her. She needs me!

No! That part was a dream, something you must've put together from not seeing Milana all day. She's probably home in bed right now, sleeping the night away. She's fine. You're just missing her is all, and the stolen phone is just coincidence.

She growled in frustration, the quiet throatiness alarmingly loud in her otherwise silent bedroom. Ana knew she had argued herself into a corner: she didn't believe in coincidences. She knew it was often hard to find connections among those coincident things seemingly unconnected, and she knew that sometimes she never could. But that didn't mean there were no connections to be found. It just meant that, within Ana's limited scope of perception, they remained unseen.

Regardless of how illogical it sounded, Ana was now convinced something was wrong and that Milana was in danger. Whether a dream or not, there was enough weirdness going on to make her genuinely afraid. She flipped through the contacts on her phone for the number of the only other person she knew in her judo class, and hammered out a message: **Hey Dilan, it's Ana from judo. Just wondering if you saw Milana at class tonight.**

She sent it without a thought. *So what if it's nearly three in the morning, I hope it wakes him. I hope he rolls over in annoyance and responds.*

Please let him respond!

At a loss for what else she could do, short of calling Milana's mother and sending the woman into a panic, Ana did the only thing she could. She sat back down at the foot of her bed and waited.

The tears were gone. The fear was gone. There was only a grim determination. The kind of incontestable will that causes forest fires to leap the widest of rivers. The kind of tenacity that allows thousand year-old lichen to cling to the faces of mountains weathering season after storm-wracked season. The kind of unyielding grit that allows one best friend to access a deeply internal strength, reach out with it, and grasp the other best friend.

It worked! It actually freaking worked!

Had the circumstances of the achievement been different, Milana would be jumping with elation. But, still locked in a room in a stranger's basement as she was, Milana allowed herself only the smallest of fist pumps, followed by a cold smile.

She had gotten through. She could do so again. She was somewhat surprised not to let herself be overtaken by some ridiculous flight of fancy following the success. Telepathy was the stuff of comic books and the sorts of novels that Demir read. Surely any ordinary person discovering the ability to communicate to others wholly in his or her mind would logically wonder what other sorts of miraculous abilities they possessed. But not Milana.

To Milana—though exhilarating—getting through to Ana was only a mild surprise. They were better best friends than most best friends; the establishment of a telepathic link between them seemed somehow natural, like the deepening of an already unfathomable friendship. If anything, it was vindicating, a confirmation of how extraordinary their friendship truly was.

Milana inhaled deeply—at least, as deeply as she could in the stench of the room. It had only gotten worse since her arrival. The sharpness of blood—enough to hurt her nostrils—and human waste. The combination had caused another of the captives to empty her stomach onto herself, contributing to the vileness in the air. The dead body near the centre of the room still stared at her, its lifeless gaze somehow judgemental, accusatory.

With an effort, she stood up. It was the first time she had risen to her feet in what must have been hours, and her knees creaked and groaned through the ascent. She stretched out slowly, feeling the blood return to her stiff limbs. As it rushed from her skull she became lightheaded and reached a hand out against the filthy wall to steady herself. She weathered the dizziness with closed eyes until it passed.

For the first time since her arrival, she took in her surroundings more critically. Where once a window had rested in the upper part of the wall there was now only a solid layer of brick, making the locked door the only means of egress. There were eight others in the room—excluding the unmoving body. Eight people to save. The young couple from judo sat in a corner quietly whispering to one another, three others were asleep along one of the walls, two others sat staring blankly ahead exactly as she had been doing before making the effort to reach out to Ana. That left only Stephanie. Poor, benighted Stephanie, head buried in her hands as she mumbled in grief about never *really* wanting to hurt anyone.

Part of Milana wanted to go sit next to her, ask her what had happened and console her. But she suspected Stephanie really *had* hurt someone, and sympathy was far from her heart in that moment. She also knew that no real, practical help could be delivered while they were locked in this basement.

She stretched out one last time, long and slow, and sat back down, wriggling until finding a position that could pass for comfortable given the circumstances, knees folded to chest, back straight against the wall. She closed her eyes and once more pictured her best friend.

'Ana!'

She jolted awake from her half-seated position, nearly falling off the foot of the bed where exhaustion had crept up on her. Her phone was still clutched in her fist and, almost as a reflex, she turned it on. No new messages. Time: 3:02. *What the hell is happening?*

She was still debating whether or not she was asleep when the voice rang out again. It was not something to be heard, more something to be felt. Not the sound of her name being called so much as the feeling she would get after hearing it. The snapping of attention, the faint flutter of her heart, a reflexive smile being suppressed by worry.

'Milana?' She felt back rather than speaking.

'Finally! You always were a slow learner.'

'What the hell is going on? Your phone—'

'It's messed up, I know. I was kidnapped. You have to help me. I'm about a ten-minute drive from the judo studio, I saw a sign that said "Richmond," and three blue houses in a row when I got here before they blindfolded me.'

'And…?' Ana prompted.

'That's all I have. I…' A sense of panic entered their conversation, like a misting ran: cold and smelling of dust, it slowly soaked into Ana's being.

'Milana?! What's going on?' There was no response, and a moment later Ana felt their connection severed, taking with it Milana's sense of panic but leaving Ana's own.'

'Do you know who I am?' A woman stood in the doorway looking down on Milana. Despite the woman's stern, almost matronly voice, she looked quite young, the softness of her face friendly and inviting. It took a moment for Milana's brain to accept that the figure before her was indeed the one speaking.

Milana slowly shook her head "no," but the woman was already talking again. If she hadn't already known the answer to her own question, it was clear she did not care what it was.

'I am Empathy. I am Compassion. I am Love. I have had more names than you've had years and more years than you have names in your head. Here, I am called the Friend.'

The woman waited expectantly.

'Okay… Friend.…'

'Good. And your name?' The Friend took a step into the room, shutting the door behind her. It was only then that Milana noticed the crowd of men, women, and… *other beings* behind the Friend. She only caught a glimpse before the door was closed. It was enough for a new wave of fear to course through her. *What are they going to do to me?*

'I am Milana' She fought to keep her voice calm and level. *They aren't going to do a damn thing. I'm going to get out of here, and I'm taking these other prisoners with me. Even snivelling, pretending-not-to-watch Stephanie!*

'Hmm' The Friend seemed unconvinced, as if Milana had given a fake name, or somehow messed up its pronunciation. 'For now, perhaps.'

She crossed her arms across her body and continued forward until she towered over Milana. Milana wanted to stand, to rise and look her in the eyes with defiance. But as that gaze continued to bear down on her, she found that she lacked the strength.

'Well, Milana,' the woman began matter of factly, 'I am a god, and you have been brought here as an offering to me. As a sacrifice.'

Milana swallowed hard, finding it difficult now even to speak, so heavy was the woman's gaze.

'But fear not, my child, for what did I name myself to you?'

The woman's gaze seemed to shift slightly, and Milana found herself able to answer weakly. 'Friend?'

'Friend. There are many forms of sacrifice, Child, and your death would serve but a finite purpose in an infinite life. I would much rather have you provide a different sort of sacrifice to me.'

The Friend hesitated, then seemed to visibly relax, and began casually pacing the room. She kicked dismissively at the dead body. The impacted leg swung upward before falling back down and settling into the exact same position. The Friend took in the whole of the room, sneering in disgust at the corner stained with human waste, then smiling and winking as she moved past Stephanie whose head was buried in her arms in a pretend sleep. *Coward!* At last, the Friend completed her circuit and turned back to Milana.

'I could feel it, you know, your secret little *reaching out.* I know not what you did with that power, nor who or what you might have been reaching for. There is far too much going on around here for any kind of precision in sensing these things.' She gestured broadly as if the whole of the neighbourhood was somehow to blame. 'But I know you possess power. And rather than kill you, I would work with you. Or—rather—have you work with me.'

Milana found the strength to stand then. She did not know who or what this so-called god was— *goddess of arrogance maybe*—did not know what it wanted—*beyond a general wickedness*—but Milana sure as hell wasn't about to let anyone strong-arm her into anything. She managed to rise about halfway before the Friend spoke again, her words almost mocking beneath that amused smile.

'In any case, I hardly expect to win you over in a single night.' She added under her breath: 'there's a house across the street that needs my attention anyway…' Turning her heavy gaze back to Milana, she grabbed her by the shoulders and slowly guided her back to a seated position. 'For now, Child, rest.'

An unnatural exhaustion suddenly weighed Milana's eyelids, pulling them shut. It tugged at her limbs, pulling her back to the ground even without the help of the Friend's pushing. It sank into her bones and seeped into her brain. Milana was asleep in seconds.

'Hmm.' The Friend said, crossing her arms pensively. 'A resilient spirit.' She had been working to put Milana asleep from the moment she had entered the room.

The Friend walked back for the door, still a little weak from the exertion. She had hardly expected to use that much of her power—*much less being required to lay hands on the girl just to put her to sleep!* She steadied herself against the door jamb, waiting a moment to recover her strength. How could she possibly hope to lead her selfless followers in the creation of a better world if they could not trust in her absolute might.

After a couple minutes, she inhaled deeply, grimaced at the assaulting stench, and left the room.

CHAPTER NINETEEN: A Less Friendly Good Morning

Friday, 19 February 2021

Darko was once again in his apartment building: Greybrick House. He sat at a table not his own, in an apartment not his own, staring into the eyes of a cat—again—not his own. The table looked to have been burnt almost to the point of collapsing, but there was enough stability in it yet to support the weight of both Darko's planted elbows and the unmoving cat. It was the oldest, most grizzled feline he had ever seen. Its fur was bluish-black, matted down in some places, marked by scars in others. The tip of one ear was missing, seemingly bitten off ages ago, and the entirety of the other ear had been discoloured and disfigured from frostbite. Despite the rest of its disposition, the eyes staring across at Darko were filled with kindness, an almost human gentleness brimming in those icy blue pools.

That's when he noticed it. Round pupils, not vertical. The eyes of a human, out of place in this feline skull. Darko sat up straighter at the table, only now recognizing the rest of his surroundings. The entire place seemed shelled out by a fire. The charred table where he and the cat sat seemed about the only piece of furniture still standing. The room was nearly pitch black. Thin shafts of light broke through cracks along the boarded windows, the rest of the place lit by that sourceless, muted glow one only sees in dreams.

It was the room above his own, almost exactly as he had seen it in his dreams two nights before. The rocking chair he had seen the old, white-haired man in was sitting in the corner exactly as last time. The only difference was that this time, the room's inhabitant was feline.

Somehow, Darko had taken in his entire surroundings without breaking his stare from the cat and, in that same mysterious way, he now saw the room's smoke-scarred door begin to shake as the boards sealing the room from the hallway-side were disturbed.

The cat arched its back, its hackles rising with enough force to disturb the suspended ash in the air, sending a cloud of it toward the ceiling. The commotion at the door continued and the cat broke its gaze from Darko, wheeling to face the source of the noise. Darko leaned back, unsure where to look now that the target of his attention had moved. He too looked to the door.

At its base was a mound of settled ashes and, as the boards on the other side of the door were fully torn away with a great cracking and the telltale squeak of nails being pulled from wood, that mound rushed forth in a growing cloud. Darko reflexively turned away, shielding his eyes and mouth.

When the cloud had passed, he looked back toward the door. It was brighter now, light coming through the spots in that portal where the fire had chewed through the wood. Darko could see only a single set of legs on the other side, but whoever they belonged to was no friend of the cat. The cat stood at the edge of the table, crouched and ready to pounce. A low, continuous growl rumbling from its body. That rumble was more akin to a roar of thunder than the roar of a cat.

Seeing the cat so dismayed, a trembling terror gripped Darko. He stood and took a step away from the table nervously, leaving it and its feline occupant between him and the door. He looked around for something, anything to use in his defence. The chair he had been sitting in seconds ago was gone, and there was nothing else in the room but debris. Even the piles of rubble marking the once-counter and cupboards seemed made wholly of ash.

Out of time.

The door swung open, light shot in from the hallway, blinding Darko to the face of the silhouetted figure who made to enter the room. The cat's growl rose in pitch, becoming a hissing shriek and the creature leapt, claws leading, in attack. Darko bolted in the other direction.

He turned over in bed and his eyes rolled open, cutting off whatever dream he had been dreaming. *Must've been something pleasant,* he mused with a sleepy smile. *It's always the best ones that escape memory. Too good for the cold and dark of the world and all of that...*

He closed his eyes again, trying desperately to catch one last glimpse of whatever retreating images had been there moments ago.

Only black. He opened his eyes with a shrug, grateful, at least, to have awoken with a smile.

He couldn't recall what time he had gone to bed the night before, he didn't know the time now, and he realized that in either case, he really didn't care. For the second night in a row, Darko had slept fully, soundly. It was a strangle feeling, a feeling of completeness. It made him feel like smiling.

Without any of the usual groaning and eye-rubbing, Darko slipped out of his bed, pulled a shirt on, and made for the door, his grin brightly leading the way.

Ana stared into the woodgrain of the kitchen table, tracing the patterns with her gaze. A gaze that might have set the wood afire were it made of lesser stuff.

There was a glass of water next to her. It had stood untouched since she set it down. She had wanted tea, but feared waking the rest of the house with the kettle's loud whistle and roar. She had not been able to return to sleep after Milana left in a panic. She'd been unable to do much of anything but worry since then. Worry, and plan.

She had had enough sense to know a call to the police without more information would be fruitless. If anything, it was more likely to land her in trouble than any suspected phone-thieving kidnappers.

Her laptop was still at Milana's aunt's house and Morgan's cousin Jane was sleeping in Demir's office, so Ana had been stuck with her phone instead of a computer. It had taken much longer on the small device, but she had googled "Richmond," pulled up online maps of the city trying to find a street name, community developments, anything. She had even found an online phone directory and looked up the address of every family under the surname "Richmond." None were anywhere near the judo studio, the closest one being nearer to a twenty minute drive away than ten. It was entirely possible that Milana had misjudged the time it took to make it to wherever she was being held, or that differences in traffic had made the journey shorter, but short of going into Acton and driving around to each address herself, she was doubtful she'd be able to find anything.

Which is why she needed a car—Darko's car.

From down the hall, the sound of a door opening told Ana someone else was awake. She looked up from the table toward the hall expectantly. After their father died, Ana had spent long hours in her room thinking about life and death, hope and hopelessness. She had been able to tell the footsteps of every member of her family, even through a firmly closed door marked with an angry sign bidding others not to enter. The soft, scuffing steps that approached were Darko's.

Sure enough, the younger of her brother's rounded the corner into the kitchen. He froze, evidently surprised to see Ana already awake— though she could have sworn he was looking more at the table than at her—then, shaking off the surprise, he pulled out a chair and sat across from her.

What is with you? There was a gaping smile in Darko's face, wide enough for a bird to land in. Flashing garishly in the dark of winter morn, the stupid grin made Ana embarrassed for him. It was ill-suited to his face, giving him the image of a grotesque along the roofline of some old church. Ana resisted the urge to outwardly cringe. Or laugh.

'Morning, Darko. Slept well?'

'Beautifully! Feels almost like rising from the grave!'

She frowned at that. *Kind of an insensitive analogy given Papa Nate's situation, don't you think?* She was not one for dissembling, especially among family, but she needed Darko's help and disparaging comments would not be the path to getting it. *How do I approach this tactfully?*

'Car.' She blurted out. *Not like that!* 'Umm… Can I borrow your car today?' she tried again.

Darko's sickeningly sweet smile deepened. 'Don't worry, Snizhana! I'll drive you!'

She could feel her hatred for the name deep in the pit of her stomach. It was no easy accomplishment, resisting her reflex to snap at him. But if civility was required to help Milana, then she could be Snizhana. She would only have to stomach his giddiness temporarily.

It's only Darko anyway, she reminded herself. *Now if it had been someone like Stephanie…*

'It's just that… I'm not exactly planning on taking the car to school. I was thinking of picking up Milana and skipping to spend the day out with her. You know, considering everything that's happened.'

Darko seemed taken aback, as if he had somehow forgotten his grandfather was dying. His smile disappeared. Though he still sounded cheery enough, that gleam that had been in his eyes accompanying the smile did not return. Ana was almost sad to see it go. Almost.

'Well, sure then. Can you just drop me off at my place first? I want to grab stuff for my classes. You can keep the car after—I'm not sure if the road bridge is open anyway considering the flooding. I'll just walk to campus.'

Ana's sigh of relief was so pronounced that she feared her brother would begin prying, asking questions she wasn't ready to answer. But whatever deep thoughts were causing his face to scrunch up into what was a far more natural expression for him than that smile had been, Ana was not among them.

Out of the kitchen and down the hall, from behind the closed door of Demir's old bedroom-turned-office-turned-guest bedroom, Jane listened to Darko and Ana making plans about leaving the house, and she breathed a sigh of relief. She had been forced to avoid that boy as much as Frederic, lest he somehow recognize her.

She would be alone with only her descendants and a single outsider. And, for all his physical strength, Jane did not think of Demir as a threat. Husband or not, she was already so close to Morgan that the woman had been willing to lie to him about who Jane was.

Jane allowed her creativity to run wild as she ruminated on all the vast possibilities of how they could spend the day alone together. She smiled broadly.

The body she now inhabited as her own had been one often ready to smile in life, and the jaws and cheeks and lips all fell with a natural ease into that practiced position. But if the soul that had once called the body home could have read Jane's thoughts then, the young woman would not have smiled, but screamed.

Demir ended the call on his cell and slid down from sitting against the headboard to curl back under the covers with his wife.

Feeling her husband's cold skin against her warm body, Morgan groaned in protest. But as those cold arms wrapped tight around her, that groan turned into a soft sound of appreciation. There was probably no better place in the world, she decided, than in the arms of a loved one.

Morgan had yet to open her eyes, and she wasn't about to. The blood pounded forcefully in her skull, raging like a stormy sea against a frail harbour wall.

'So they'll come?' she asked, eyes still locked tight.

'Yes. Uncle Jo and Aunt Caroline will be here in a few hours' Demir said reassuringly. Morgan had always loved the way his voice sounded in the morning. Deeper, somehow fuller, she snuggled closer to him.

'So what's the plan, my man?' *Anything to keep hearing that voice.*

'Well, I suppose Darko and Ana will want to go back to school today or do something on their own, but, if not, they're always welcome to come along. We can have a quiet morning here. The Bennetts said they'll be here for elevenish. Then they'll stay and watch the kids and we can go get that graphic designer's info. from the office. And then... Maybe do lunch out?

She could tell from the change in tone that his eyes were now on her. She smiled softly and nodded, careful not to jar her head too much.

'So... lunch out, that's settled. Then maybe take you to a doctor, ha ha. Then we can pop by Papa Nate's for the afternoon before heading home. How does that sound?'

Morgan feared the quiet conversation was drawing to a close. That all too soon she'd have to get up, get dressed, and face the day. She groaned again.

'I like the sound of everything except a visit to a doctor. What are they going to do, give me more pills?' She had decided to stop taking the prescribed pain meds that morning. They drowned her mind, making thoughts flounder about, slow and just out of reach. That still-stinging burn on her hand was a reminder of just how drastic her change under the medication was.

'What do you want to do for lunch?' It was another attempt to keep Demir talking, to keep their bodies close. *Just stay with me five more minutes. Please.*

'Whatever you want, dear. We can talk about it during the day.' He smacked her bottom. 'C'mon! Time to get up!'

Moment over. She knew that whenever he used "dear" in a conversation, his interest was already elsewhere. It was his term of verbal appeasement. Morgan groaned a third time, this one half a roar with all the frustration she poured into it, rolled over reluctantly, and opened her eyes.

Her eyelids fluttered. A flood of light, a flash of pain. The twin incandescent bulbs overhead droned loudly into the otherwise silent room. They glowered down at her with all the arrogant weight of the Friend's own gaze. Milana lifted a hand to shield her eyes.

The room was different. The dead body had been removed and sunshine-yellow towels laid out to cover the carpet in its place. Their brightness was a mockery of whatever dark stains the body had left in the carpet beneath. The corner of the room soiled by human waste had been scrubbed clean, no trace that it had ever been more or less than an ordinary corner. A stout tripod now occupied the corner. Hot, red-glowing stones filled a shelf on that tripod beneath the shallow cauldron it held. And, in that dish: rose petals floated on the surface of the almost-boiling water.

The smell of the place no longer made Milana grimace. It made her feel like vomiting. It bore a sweet smell the way that mould bears a sweet smell. It stunk of roses—cloyingly so—it filled not just her nostrils, but began crowding her sense of taste as well.

The others in the room were all fast asleep and, memory coming back to her belatedly, Milana realized that the Friend must have used some kind of power on them all. She immediately reached out for Ana, and was met with a wall of silence.

She realized then that she had been utterly silent. She heard no rustle of clothing when raising a hand to shield her eyes, heard not the gentle clicking of her teeth as she thought—a dentist-hated habit she hadn't quite kicked—she couldn't even hear her own breathing. From without the door too there was no longer the quiet hum of conversation, broken by the occasional bout of chanting, there was only silence.

She looked to her right, at the young couple asleep in each other's arms. Not a grunt of snoring nor so much as the whisper of breath. And yet she could still hear the sharp droning of the lights in the ceiling. With a silent gasp, she clapped her hands hard. Nothing. She tried to shout, to scream and, though she could feel the rawness in her throat, she could hear not a sound.

She leapt to her feet and charged the door, throwing shoulder checks and kicking near the handle as she had seen in the movies. Though the portal rattled in its place, it would not yield, and what felt like thunderous thumping produced no noise.

Disappointed, Milana reached out for the handle. Maybe if she could tear or kick the thing off, she'd have a better chance of breaking through. Or, at the very least, she'd be able to peer through the hole into the room beyond.

Flesh touched brass. Agony.

Milana did hear sound then, the sizzling of her flesh on the doorknob, now glowing hot as the stones in the tripod, and her own shrieking cry of pain. She had to use her other hand to tear the first away. As soon as contact was broken, her cries became silent once more. She spat on her hand, hoping it would alleviate the burning. Overcoming the fear of examining the injury, she looked down at her hand. She immediately began to cry.

The sight of the wound was as worrisome as the pain itself. Her seared flesh was mottled with pinks, reds, and whites. In one spot she could see exposed bone. The first degree burns produced almost no pain, nerves burnt clean away, but surrounding them were second and third degree burns that had her whimpering silently as she slowly backed away from the door.

The glowing of the handle faded once Milana's hand was gone revealing, etched into the metal of the knob, nine lines emanating from a single point with a perfect circle around it. She did not recognize the symbol, but she knew from her initial scan of the room that it had not been there the whole time, only put there once the Friend's prisoners were put to sleep.

Well, Friend, if you're the goddess of arrogance, then I'm the goddess of stubbornness. You insisted on calling me "Child" in our brief talk and you were right, in a way. I was the kind of child who touched every hot surface I had been warned away from. I was the child who thought that maybe this time, for some reason, it wouldn't hurt so bad. It'll take a lot more than a few scratches in a doorknob to keep me as your prisoner.

So, you have made me silent, have made the others in this room silent, and probably made

everything outside the room silent to us as well.
But you could not take away sound entirely. The
lights still hum and if the water on that tripod was
boiling I'm sure I'd hear its bubbles. And your
little symbol on the doorknob—maybe the cause of
silencing us—does allow sound to get through. I'll
find a way out of this.

Milana returned to her seat along the wall, shut
her eyes once more, and tried to concentrate harder.

PART III: And Down Go the Living

In giants' passing are craters left
Deep as the sea and wide as the plains.
How sublime are such perilous places,
Where wandering will leave you lost,
Where to idle would be to sink and drown,
To descend into disaster!
So walk soft when thunderous footsteps
approach.
Tread not too near the crater's edge.
Just pull the covers high and pray,
Pray that this giant won't walk too close.

"I want to die with lipstick on"
Was my mother's dying wish.
She applied it herself with shaking, scarred
hands.
And she smiled, red and broad,
Deep as the sea and wide as the plains.
Then her breathing drew short and her eyes
drew shut.
So I pulled the covers high and prayed,
Prayed that this giant would not pass too close.

But I had been brought up on this giant's broad back
And I fell into that crater as she passed away.

All My Living Days
- Roman Kalichka

CHAPTER TWENTY:
Ghosted Footsteps
Friday, 19 February 2021

Demir wasn't feeling particularly talkative. The morning had passed far too quickly, his siblings leaving even before Uncle Jo and Aunt Caroline arrived. His parting words to them of "if you need anything at all, please call" had been accepted with smiles and nods, but Demir knew Darko and Ana too well for that. Darko was too stubborn to admit when he had a problem that required his own attention, much less someone else's. And something unusual was bothering Ana today—but then again, wasn't it always something whenever Milana was not around—and he thought she was even less likely to reach out if she needed something. *So was the offer for their benefit? Or my own?*

The brief spell after breakfast where nothing needed doing, where Demir had been able to play with Alex and Klara, had been cut painfully short by the arrival of his aunt and uncle.

Now that the kids were being looked after and he was in the car on the way out of the driveway, he just wanted to get the errands out of the way as quickly as possible, enjoy a nice lunch out with his wife, and then spend the afternoon with his grandfather. He longed for a simple day like the day before, but knew it was likely well out of reach now. He also knew he probably would not enjoy his lunch. *Not with Jane tagging along.*

That is, if she ever gets her ass in the car so we can leave!

Jane had not done anything to arouse concern, nor said anything particularly out of place—in both cases anything untoward could be explained away by the woman's apparent social anxiety, the kind that had made her so far incapable of saying a word to either Darko or Frederic. Yet, despite the lack of rationality, Demir was just was not comfortable with the notion of leaving her alone with his children, even with Uncle Jo and Aunt Caroline there. *It might be unnecessary caution*, he was willing to admit to himself, but he did not care either way. He did not even trust any of their three dogs alone in a room with Klara. *All it takes is one oversight. And it doesn't matter if Jane's family or not!*

That had been a difficult conversation with Morgan. As much as he didn't want to use it as an excuse—mostly because she would not accept it as one—Morgan was *still* doped up from those pain meds and not thinking clearly.

For all Jane's initial elation that she would be included in this outing, Demir and Morgan sat alone in the front seat of the family van still waiting for the woman to join them. There was no conversation and the silence lingering in its absence was far from the usual, comfortable kind. It was a stuttered, awkward thing.

He looked to Morgan with a closed-mouth smile. She mirrored the gesture.

Ah, we'll be fine. Let's just take this one step at a time. Who knows, maybe we'll even enjoy this little family outing.

He checked the time on the dash, rolled down his window and stuck his head out into the cool winter air.

'Jane! Are you nearly ready?' came the call from the idling van behind her.

She had spilled out of the van in a hurry, feigning interest in the opened gate at the edge of the driveway. In reality it was not interest, but fright that had sparked her actions. her concern was for wards that might be in place, like those carved on each of the fence posts forming what had been—until she had come along—an unbreakable barrier around the Richovsky farm.

Sure enough, she could feel something beneath the dirt driveway, right here where the gate would swing shut. It did not matter that the iron gate was open wide, this hidden thing formed a rigid barrier.

It was likely some buried artifact of protection, unreachable by her powers even if she did not have an audience in the van behind her. To be near it was to bring a sharp pain to the ears. To step into its protective circle very well might mean death in truth. Or, at the very least, a complete eradication from her current body.

Jane waved dismissively at Demir and gingerly skirted the edges of the protected area which spanned the full width of the road. There was a narrow gap less than a metre wide between the barrier and the nearest gatepost where she managed to squeeze through, grimacing at the sharp ringing in her ears.

'Whew!' She exclaimed, once past the danger before turning back to face Demir. 'Well. Won't you pick a lady up?'

Demir smiled, nodded, rolled up his window and made a comment to his wife before driving over to retrieve Jane.

To ordinary ears, Demir's quip would have been imperceptible from this distance, but, as she far from ordinary, Jane heard every word: 'If I see one, I'll go get her.'

Jane did not blame Morgan for not laughing.

Donald Philips wiped at his eyes and yawned loudly as he put the cruiser in park.

'I told you to stop that!' Derek barked, stifling a yawn of his own. 'Or you'll get me started.'

Neither had been able to sleep very well, their minds ablaze with theories on the murderous cult plaguing their city. Philips had given up on those short, fitful spells of sleep by 5:30. Knowing his partner would also be up—and deciding if he wasn't, then he ought to be—Donald had called Derek, and the two were in the office by six, hammering away at their coffee cups and sipping away at their keyboards. Or... had it been the other way around?

Woods shook his head, hoping some of the sleep might come cascading off with the pinch of dandruff he watched drift down. *Bad day to skip a shower. Jesus, I'm too tired to think.*

Just gotta work. Put foot two in front of foot one and walk. Connect clue one with clue two and solve this mess.

Philips slapped the sides of the steering wheel with both hands. 'We're here! Out we get!'

The two tumbled from the cruiser.

It has *been a productive morning,* Woods reassured himself as they made their way slowly across the parking lot. *We're completely caught up on whatever paperwork and filing there is to get caught up on at this point, we made a few phone calls, talked over our findings with Anderson and*

Laforce, discussed strategy with them, made a game plan for the day. All in all, not a bad morning. Not at all.

It's not even noon yet and we're already making our fist call. Efficiency itself. 'Get ready, perp, here we come!'

Philips looked askance at his partner. 'Shouldn't that be "get ready, perk?" Ha ha!' He held the door open for Derek to go first.

There was no line. Derek went straight to the counter. 'Two lattes, an extra shot in each. Please.'

'Right away, Sir.

'Oh no, put that away. We need you guys now more than ever. It's on the house.'

Well it might not be worth a damn in dissuading a murderous cult of fanatics from setting up shop in town, but at least the APS on my coat carries enough weight for a couple free coffees.

Frida who had been Courage a mere two days before, whistled softly to herself, chair reclined, feet up on the desk that said RECEPTION, as she worked at the crossword puzzle in the back of her magazine. The theme was "Mythology and Lore."

I started the Trojan War. *Helen? Paris? Hmm… Nine letters. None of the usual suspects, I see.*

Frida was the only one who had come into work today. With the eponymous owners of the firm, Finster and Gable, dead, most employees had taken time off out of grief. *Or perhaps,* the more cynical part of her mused, *out of fear they won't be compensated for their time.*

Courage had gotten this job as a secretary from her father, a one-time colleague of Mr. Gable, and she was not about to disappoint her dad by not showing up for work, no matter if neither of her bosses would ever return or not! So, even though there had not been a single caller all morning, on the phone or at the door, she was still here, ready to do her job. She had let herself in this morning, she would work a full eight hours and not a minute less, and she would lock up on her way home. She had to be a good role model for her brother after all.

Hmm… fifth letter's an **O**. *What was the name of that Greek king? Agamemnon? No. That doesn't fit.*

There came a buzzing from the intercom. Frida ignored it. There were five other businesses in the complex and people had a habit of pushing the buzzer at the top before reading that there were individual ones for each of the businesses.

Bzzzt! Bzzzt!

She continued whistling.

Bzz-bzz-bzz-bzz-bzz-bzz-bzzzzzzzzzt!

'Woah, woah! All right, all right! Sue a girl!'

She put down her crossword and looked over at the monitor. Two men hovered at the door, one holding some kind of paper toward the camera, the other with a small file folder tucked under one arm and holding two coffees. She punched the intercom.

'Welcome to Finster and Gable, do you have an appointment?' she sang more than said.

'We have a warrant' came an equally musical reply. It was only then that Frida noticed the police uniforms.

Huh. Good enough, I guess. 'Come on in, Constables. Suite one-o-one.'

She held down the little key icon until they were inside. When she let it go the screen flashed to black before the screensaver flicked back on. Finster and Gable had a thing for Italian Renaissance paintings—*talk about a stereotype for men of wealth*—and the screensaver was a steady stream of them. She had most memorized by now.

Uccello's The Presentation of the Virgin: Gable always described it as an experiment with perspective and lighting. St. Sebastian by Mantegna: I never liked this one. Faith or not, who surrenders to a bow-and-arrow firing squad? Wouldn't you fight tooth and nail to escape that.

*I'd rather die in an escape attempt, then let myself
get tied to a pillar and peppered with arrows.*

*Ahh, here's a classic. Sandro Botticelli—all
those Italian painters have names like fancy
cheeses—The Birth of Venus. She's gorgeous.
She's just looking so...*

Frida gasped with delight. 'That's it!
Aphrodite!' *Of course! It was her promising
Helen to Paris that kicked the whole thing off.* She
stood up quickly, scratched down the goddess's
name, tossed the crossword back on top of the
reception desk, and rushed to the door to meet the
policemen.

She panicked for a second, as their footsteps
approached down the hall. *What's the most not-
guilty pose I can stand in? Not that I am not-guilty
—not entirely—but they're probably here for
Finster and Gable. They were the big guys, not me.
And besides, I'm out now. Completely out!*

In the end, she decided that folding her hands on
the side of her hip was the most natural pose to
take.

Woods and Philips were met at the door to the
law office by a young woman standing in the most
awkward position Donald had ever seen. She was
smiling broadly, forcefully, with her hands folded
over the lower part of her stomach and slightly off

to one side. *You look like the victim of a damn knife wound!*

'Here.' Donald said gruffly, handing the woman the search warrant as they entered. *What was it Anderson had said this morning? "Never approach a law office without a warrant." Just take a look at this place, how nervous this woman is: a damn post worker could search this place for all her fear of a uniform!* Derek strode past the woman and set his folder and their coffees down on her desk to free up his hands.

The woman took the warrant as if it were on fire, transferring it from Philips's hands next to her open magazine on the desk with no more than a glance at the words on the paper. She stammered out something like a thank-you, swallowed hard, and offered, 'Welcome to Finster and Gable! How may I help you today?'

The two constables had a bad habit of "prey-stalking," as Captain Fremont liked to phrase it in her reprimands, of wandering around the person they talked to like wolves sizing up a meal, sussing out weaknesses and marking morsels for the post-hunt feast. In this moment, the secretary of Finster and Gable appeared to be their next victim.

Donald stalked to the woman's left, leading her in a slow spin away from Derek who slunk behind her, idly picking up things on the desk and setting them back down after a quick examination: folders, a stapler, a monitor... He skimmed the woman's magazine before turning it back to the crossword where he marked something with a finger and *hmm*-ed at it. With a smoothness that was almost rehearsed, they then swapped places, with Donald taking to rummaging behind the woman's back as Derek held her attention with more questions.

'So, Miss... never got your name, did we?'

'I'm Frida.'

'So, Frida, what is it you do here?'

'Secretarial things, mostly. Reception, office supply, occasional assistant work. Greeting, answering phones, making appointments, filing, ...' She couldn't think of anything else, breaking off the sentence hanging on that last word.

'I see. And in your filing, ...' Derek mimicked, 'did you ever come across the kind of thing that might make you think Mr. Finster or Mr. Gable were anything less than perfect, law-abiding citizens? *Outside of their usual crookery as lawyers,* he wanted to add. But he had far more tact than that.

'Aside from being lawyers, ha ha!' Donald added from behind the woman. Derek just shut his eyes in a tired kind of way, ignoring the comment.

'No, nothing like that,' Frida responded. She had taken an oath of secrecy after all—even if that oath had been made as Courage.

Derek kept towing her attention in a slow circle, he kept an eye on Donald, preparing to switch roles once again.

Donald swept in front of the woman as Derek slipped behind. 'Well then,' Donald began, 'Miss F —'

Frida stopped spinning and raised her hands to either side of her head. 'Stop that! If you want to talk to me, do it face to face. I'm not some Maypole for you to dance about all merry and gay!'

Derek looked across at his partner and raised his eyebrows. Donald's response was an open-mouthed grin. *Yeah, yeah, you like her already. Get your ass over here.*

As if reading Derek's thoughts, Donald joined him directly in front of, and a respectful distance away from, Frida. What their captain didn't understand was that their prey-stalking—which was actually a rather appropriate term—was a method of getting the measure of a person. *Push until they push back, then you know the line. If they don't push back at all, then you've got the run of them.*

Donald gripped his belt, took a half-step forward and took over the questioning. 'Sorry about that, Miss Frida, procedure and all that.'

'I'll bet.' Was her flat response.

'Is there any kind of computer database we can access, or…'

'Sorry, I don't have access to that kind of stuff. And those who do didn't come in today. There is a room filled with physical case files though, if that —'

'Thank God!' Donald couldn't keep his professional composure. He had spent nearly ten hours in the last two days in front of a computer screen. The chance to sift through physical sheets of paper was making him giddy.

Derek was far less thrilled, though he had the presence of mind to make his frustrated groan an internal one. *Control-F, keyword. As simple as that, Philips. How many times do I have to remind you of that? But physical files? We'll be here for hours!*

'That would be great, thanks.' Derek was sure he was nearly successful in his attempt to sound genuine. 'Lead the way.'

Demir sat at the desk of his boss, a humble nameplate staking the territory as belonging to David Mokre. He was attempting to navigate the maze that was Sightliner's shared drive.

The place was completely closed down. David had given everyone a week to "sort yourselves out!" as the frustrated email had put it. Demir was pretty sure his boss was simply hoping the trouble makers would not return. The charges of assault had been upgraded to attempted murder after some exotic poisons were found in the break-room. An email had been sent with instructions to contact the police should anyone know the whereabouts of the woman responsible. She was some young girl Demir knew only by reputation: hired out of a buffet line in the Fall—*because Sightliner's so modern that apparently we don't even do resumés anymore. All this violence over some stupid game and stupid office politics. And people still ask what's so great about working from home.*

Morgan sat next to him, fiddling idly on her phone and spinning slowly on a swivel chair she had brought in from one of the cubicles outside David's office. She was like a kid on the thing. Even Jane had watched in amused silence as Morgan went round and round, and round and round for minutes before growing bored and leaving. Jane had not returned since. Demir did not know where she had gone off to. He didn't care enough to find out either, just happy to not have her hovering over his shoulder making little comments every few seconds as she had been doing on the drive.

Squeak. Round went the chair. *Squeak.* Again.

The entry for Finster and Gable was neither under "F" nor "G" so, scrolling to the top of all the recently-edited accounts, Demir read every folder title going down the long list. As. *Squeak.* Bs, Cs. *Squeak.* Ds, Es. *Squeak.* F—

'That can't be good for your head, dear.'

'Ugh! Don't *dear* me! You said this wouldn't take long. Let me help at least.' The severity of her words was cut by the peculiarity of her tongue-injured pronunciation. Demir knew that to laugh would be a most dangerous response. He kept his eyes glued on the screen in front of him to mitigate that risk.

'I'd like to, but this is the only computer I have access to.'

'Fine. But I can still do something else. I've got my phone, an internet connection, what's the name of this company? Maybe they give credit to the graphic designer on the site itself?'

'They're called Finster and Gable Inc. But they probably won't have much of a website. We stopped development as soon as they defaulted on their payments.'

'Aha! Right here: "Finster and Gable Inc. Law Offices and Legal Advice." Some of the title links are broken, but there's actually quite a bit here.'

'Okay, but if they wouldn't pay their graphic designer, do you really think they'd give the guy credit on their website?'

'Probably not, *DEAR,* but at least I feel like I'm contributing now. Maybe I'll find something else that's useful. You said these guys are probably connected to the murders after all.' She bent over her phone and resumed spinning. *Squeak. Squeak. Squeak…*

Demir had kept skimming as they talked and was now all the way at the Ts when a particular name caught his eye: "Toomanyteeth.'"

He remembered a client from three years before, when Sightliner was just David, his roommate, and Demir. The man's real name had been Dr. Oonis and the website had been to attract patients to the new practice the man was opening in Calgary. The man had carried the unfortunate trait of having three teeth in the centre of his smile in place of the ordinary two.

Demir opened the file, navigated a couple more nested within, launched the webpage and, sure enough: **Dr. Oonis: A Doctor for the Whole Family**.

So, David's giving everyone little nicknames, eh? I wonder what mine is…

'These guys made that weird Valentine's activity, right?' Morgan asked.

'Yeah, something about friendship or getting along? Along those lines.' *I can probably search backward from the names of files I've created.*

'Sounds about right. They have a little activity set up here on their website about "the search for Friendship—" Capital "F" Friendship. It starts at their office which is downtown-ish and leads somewhere else. To "the heart of all Friendship" as they call it.'

'What?' Demir rolled away from the desk to look at his wife's phone. Sure enough, there was a kind of scavenger hunt based on a map of Acton. It was polished, complete with mobile support. Demir wasn't abuzz of everything going on at work, being based as he was at home, but he was certain he would have heard about something like this being commissioned for a law office.

'Either David's been hiring some mixed up staff, or Finster and Gable have some weird priorities.'

'Had,' his wife corrected.

Demir looked to her in confusion.

'Oh. Maybe I forgot to tell you. When Derek and Donald called yesterday, they said they had to follow up with the graphic designer after the Overpass incident. Finster and Gable were apparently among the dead who had been hurling stones at passing vehicles. I'm sure I mentioned it...' She looked around doubtfully, the way a drowning woman might look to a waterlogged piece of flotsam too small to support her weight.

And I'm sure you didn't.

Damn, it hurts to see you like this. As soon as we're done here, we'll get lunch, then straight to the Doctor's. I'm not putting this off.

He wheeled back to David's computer with a renewed determination. He opened one of his old files, followed the cataloguing information, and found the parent folder with his own nickname. *The Lone Wolf, huh? Not half bad.* He smiled to himself.

And that smile deepened as a realization struck him. *What was that David had said on the phone? "They're tagged under scumbag clients?" Guess it wasn't a joke.* He searched the file name. There it was.

'This is actually pretty fun,' Morgan admitted almost guiltily from behind him. The scavenger hunt held her attention so firmly now that even the spinning had stopped.

'Help me with this clue. It's a place in Acton. "Where the path of the Stargazer passes over another." I mean, that could be anything. It's too —'

'Koo-Koo-Sint Overpass.' Demir did not look up.

'How do you figure that?'

'Mix of a good memory and Grade Seven Social Studies. It used to be called the David Thompson Highway, back before the overpass was built. Koo-

Koo-Sint, comes from one of the Salishian languages, means something roughly equivalent to Stargazer.'

'Well aren't you just so smart.' Demir was startled by her hot breath in his ear. 'You do the honours.' She had moved the map on the phone over the Koo-Koo-Sint Overpass. He pressed the location, causing little celebratory stars to shoot out and a new clue to pop up.

Morgan retreated with a kiss before he could read it. 'Can't let you get all the fun,' she said coyly.

Jane stood on the other side of the office's solid wall, listening closely until she was sure they were in the clear. In the closeness of their connection, Jane had accidentally passed some direct knowledge on to Morgan, giving the poor, injury-addled girl the names of the dead not yet released to the public.

Even after she was sure Demir was not pressing the issue, Jane stayed there, tight up against the wall, feeling its solidity. For centuries she had passed through such walls, no substance to her or the barrier. Now, however, they were both substantial enough to stop each other. She knew she could destroy the wall with a single, powerful blow. She knew she could sunder it apart and walk right through the smouldering hole into the office beyond, but it wasn't the same as walking through it. Just a veiled, insubstantial being crossing through veiled, insubstantial environments. She almost missed it. Now she was part of that environment and her actions had physical consequences. She felt bold, felt that she had to be bold. She could create, she could destroy, and there was plenty of both on her agenda.

Jane had murdered time exploring the offices of Sightliner, now she waited over its wilting corpse, leaning against the office wall in expectation of Morgan and Demir's eventual emergence. The closest thing to excitement or entertainment she had experienced was a trip to the break-room where the alleged attempted murder had taken place. It had been scrubbed clean, the masking stench of bleach still hovering in the air. But Jane's senses were more acute now than they had ever been in life, and the metallic tang of blood was only covered over, not gone. She could taste the violence that had taken place in the room, the slashing kitchen knife, the bodies thrown in self-defence. The stony smell of the pain, the sweet iron taste of blood, it was delicious.

She licked her lips from her spot along the wall as she continued listening to Morgan and her husband with boredom. Jane longed to be away from this place, back to the Richovsky farm with no inconvenient visitors, no river-controlling brother-in-law, no indomitable angel standing guard over an old man, just Morgan—her descendent—and those she had birthed. Jane yearned for that family. Hungered for them.

Demir opened the folder and scrolled through all the related files until he found one marked Bad-omens-should-have-heeded. *How do you ever find anything with these names?!*

The graphic designer was apparently a one-man company named Neo Designs. *How original.* He scrolled down the contact form. *Phone number, address. Perfect.*

'Got it,' he informed Morgan as he pulled out his phone. He scrolled through his contacts for Donald's cell number. Before he found it, the phone was ringing. **Snizhana Richovsky.**

He looked to Morgan with a mix of concern and confusion. 'It's Ana. Why would she—'

'Just answer it, Demir! You told them to call if they needed anything, didn't you?'

'Demir?' Ana sounded out of breath. 'Demir are you there?'

'I'm here Ana.'

'I need a favour.'

CHAPTER TWENTY-ONE:
Disapproving Rodents
Friday, 19 February 2021

Darko had known from the moment he had woken up that today was different. It was a good day, but more than that, it was a special day. The air seemed just a bit clearer, the colours of his surroundings just a bit sharper, and, though grey clouds filled its vault high above, the sky seemed somehow just a bit bigger.

He and Ana had not talked overmuch. A bit at the kitchen table waiting for the others to get up, a bit on their walk to his car, then some more on the drive until she had dropped him off at Greybrick House. But what talking they had done felt closer, deeper, than it had in months.

He could tell her had been was elsewhere the entire morning. Not that he blamed her of course. *You were the youngest when mom and dad died, Papa Nate was the closest thing you ever got to a real parent and I'm sure it's torturing you to know that he is dying now too.* But even across that distance between Darko and Ana, there had been a few real, wholesome connections spaced out across the morning. Connections where it felt Darko was not simply talking to Ana, the closed-off teenager, but to Snizhana Richovsky, his sister. Chief among these close moments had been Darko's realization that Ana was lying.

He knew she wasn't going to any mall, no matter how many precise details she added to convince him. It was not the overly detailed account which gave her away. In fact, in the moment, those details had nearly sold the story to Darko. No, it was nothing so logical, so coldly rational. It was but a simple, heartfelt thing. It was the way she brushed off mention of Milana.

Ana and Milana had only been best friends for three years, only a fifth of the time Darko had known and loved his friends, Randy and Maria, but those friendships had never been comparable—not by any measure. It was as if, in each other, Ana and Milana had found that perfect best-friendship that most people experience only vicariously through movies or television. Ana was far closer to Milana than she had ever been with any of her family. *And who can blame her when, one-by-one, members of this family abandon her in death.* Even when she and Milana fought, they did so within the unbreakable bonds of their friendship, impervious to outside manipulation.

It was because of the strength of that friendship that Darko knew in avoiding mention of Milana, Ana's concerns involved her directly. He realized too that this, more so than Papa Nate's impending death, was the cause for Ana's distance. He could not fathom what could possibly make his sister clam up about her closest friend, but Darko knew it was not his business. If Ana wanted to include him she would, and consequently, frustratingly, she did not.

When Ana dropped him off, Darko had been able to offer no more than a weak "if you need anything, just call me." He had hoped it did not sound as hollow as Demir's identical offer earlier that morning.

Now, nearly two hours later, he still had to force himself to stop focussing on that final interaction and start focussing on his present surroundings.

On the topic of best friends, your lack of attentiveness to Randy's story isn't exactly the mark of a good friend. His self-chastisement was only effective in pushing concerns over Ana away, not in eradicating them completely. They joined that mountain of other concerns, its peak stabbing sharply behind his eyes and threatening tears when he let his guard down. He turned to focus on Randy and his story.

'…and I figured, I don't start classes till noon tomorrow, might as well stay.' Randy paused to take a swig from his water bottle. 'And I want to reiterate again, she was single, and really, really, really, really good looking! So I stayed, lost track of time, probably drank more than I should have, and the next thing I know, it's two in the morning and I'm outside without a jacket 'cause it was so blessedly hot in her apartment that I needed some air.'

They were in their favourite spot in the Student Union Building, ensconced in the upholstered chairs around a table cluttered with laptops and books. Randy was becoming increasingly animated as his story progressed, edging closer and closer to the table. He set his water bottle down, freeing his hands for more expansive gestures.

Darko's concentration was beginning to slip once more. *I wish my car had GPS. I'd be a whole lot more comfortable if I just knew where she was.*

'...a fully. Naked. Man. And he tells me that he dropped his car keys in a parking lot at the end of the street and says how he feels like an ass, bending over, trying to find them in the dark. And I laugh at his choice of words and he's laughing that I might as well be in the same boat, out in the cold with only a t-shirt and jeans. So, I do the human thing, and I offer to give him a hand without asking too many questions of how he got into this embarrassing little predicament.

'You did not!' Maria interjected.

'You bet his bare ass I did! I followed him right to the end of the street, into the edge of some shadowy parking lot, and if things hadn't been weird enough up to that point, I see this mouse in

367

front of me.' He was so close to the edge of his chair now, that he was practically standing.

Even Darko, with his mind so ready to be elsewhere, found himself leaning in, listening intently.

'Now I must have had more to drink than I thought, because this was no ordinary mouse to me. This thing was so animate in its movements, I felt like I recognized it. To me, this creature was centuries-old, millennia maybe, and it looked at me with the saddest, deepest disappointment.'

Darko stifled a laugh.

'It's not funny, man! Like more disappointed than when my mom found out I only dropped my Native Studies course because I was failing it.

'Now, you know me and my mom are Blackfoot, and that was always something I was interested in because it was something we had just for us. It made me different, special, compared to my half-brothers. Well, as sad as it is to say, there's not a whole lot you can do if that's something you're interested in. What was once known was taken from us, as was any means of going back, of relearning any of it. And we never had a chance to adjust to the modernization of life: global communication, interaction. So now, even if there is some rare thing you're sure you know because your mom was sure of it, and her dad was sure of it, and his dad too, all the way back seven generations or more. Even if that's the case, there'll be some guy from the next band over all too quick to tell you you're wrong, and it's actually like this. Or, in some cases, a guy with a doctorate on the subject flunking you because what your mom told you is different from what his folks taught him!'

'Randy?' Maria offered softly, not wanting him to bring up the whole Native Studies thing again. They had all heard his frustrations with the course a dozen times or more.

'Sorry, there's a point to all this, I'm not just complaining. One of these things that I know for sure is the story of how mankind came to be the dominant species. And maybe dominant's not the right word, more like the *chief* species. It started with, Napi, Creator, showing a game to all creation.

'Many creatures wanted to be chief, Beaver and Bear were among the loudest in their arguments, and every night they would sit in a council and debate. A decision could not be reached amongst themselves so they turned to Napi. Rather than simply appointing a chief, Napi took a knucklebone from his pouch, put it in his right hand, then moved his hands back and forth in plain view, passing the bone from palm to palm.' Randy stopped to mime the gestures in the game.

'He sang a gambling song as he performed and then he held his two hands out, closed, with their backs to the sky. Since Bear had been the first to declare his wish to be chief, Napi let him guess the hand. Bear had last seen the knucklebone passed into Napi's right hand so that was the hand he chose, but when Napi opened it, it was empty.

'He taught each of them the game and for days they played, King's Court style. Bear had the bone until he was beaten by Beaver, then Beaver was beaten by Buffalo, and so on, until the bone made its way to the tiny hands of Mouse, and Mouse could not be bested as he was the quickest and cleverest of all people. They had all agreed to the game and so Mouse People were declared to be the dominant species. But, in a lesson of eternal humility, Mouse decided he would rather stay in the safety of his bison-skull home and give the title to another—us.

'Now you'll fully understand what I mean when I say this little mouse in the parking lot was looking at me with severe disappointment. I felt this gift of prominence given to humankind was something I was an insult to. What have I ever done for this earth in my position of greatness? Probably more harm than good.'

He stopped to take a few deep breaths and waited for the gravity of his words to sink in. The others sat back, equally humbled by the experience Randy shared.

'So there I am, standing in a dark parking lot at two in the morning, re-thinking every decision in my life that led me down this road—not to mention freezing my ass off. And it was only then that it occurred to me how unnatural it was for some ass-naked guy to come asking for help finding keys at this hour and then dragging me off to a dark parking lot where—again, only then did I notice—the only vehicle around is some dark van with dark shapes moving in the front seat.

'All this sank in, and I high-tailed it out of there. I called a cab and went home. I didn't even go back up to say goodbye to her or get my coat.'

Sensing that his story was coming to a close, Maria leaned in and reached out a hand slowly, lovingly, in the sort of way that only a truly close friend could, to cuff Randy sharply on the side of his head.

'Ouch!'

'Ouch. Yeah, ouch. Do you realize how dangerous what you did was?'

'Yeah, I do now! I called my mom this morning, told her I'm never drinking again. She took that seriously too, said she wouldn't hear it unless I was willing to swear. I gave my word and that's that. And life's already looking up.'

Randy held up his winter coat with a proud smile.

'I thought you said…' Darko began.

'Went back for it just this morning. She gave it back with a peck on the cheek and a wink. And I went through the pockets a little later on and look what else she left me.'

Randy grinned from ear to ear holding up a piece of paper with the girl's number on it.

Ana felt very much the fearful child she thought she had left behind. There was just so much happening so quickly. An unstoppable momentum, one that would have her tumbling headlong off a cliff's edge onto field of jagged rocks with a single misstep.

And so she knew she could not misstep. Not by a single toenail. To falter would be to fail and, for the sake of Milana, she would not fail.

Ana had made a list in her phone of every address in the city she could find with any kind of connection to "Richmond." She had started with those closest to the judo studio and slowly spiralled outward from there. She was on her fourth or fifth stop—she was too frantic to keep an accurate count —and even as she drove towards it, the path seemed different, as if she had travelled this way before.

It was the same feeling she got when approaching home from a new direction: she might not have ever seen these particular trees or that cluster of buildings before, but there was a sense, deep within her, that she was approaching home. Except it was no mere farmstead in this case. It was Milana, her dearest friend. She knew even as she was pulling into the cul-de-sac that this was the place.

Sure enough, ahead on her right: three blue houses. She parked down the street from them to observe from afar. The middle house of the three had a large boulder out front near the street with the name "Richmond" carved deeply into its face. Ana took the keys out of the ignition and inhaled deeply, shakily.

Okay. How do I do this? Call the police, wait five minutes, then charge in? That should give me enough time to find Milana, or at least to find some way of proving she's in there. Then the police can arrest those responsible when they arrive. And if I'm wrong, ...

Well I just better not be wrong.

She decided she would call Demir to have him pick up the car, just in case things should turn bad, whether that meant her arrest or worse. *For Darko's sake. A bad outcome of all this for me shouldn't be one for Darko too. He's having such a good day.*

She smiled, a twinge of sadness marring the expression. She had felt much closer to Darko today than in years. *Who knew all it would take for people to connect with you is a smile and a mind not half-dead out of exhaustion.* She sniffed hard and wiped at her eyes even though they were still dry. There could be no risk of tears with so much at stake.

'Demir?' Ana tried not to let any of the panic she was feeling touch her tone. 'Demir are you there?' She doubted she was very successful.

'I'm here Ana.' *Thank God!*

'I need a favour. I need you to come pick up Darko's car for him. He said he'll walk home, so you don't need to take it all the way to the university, just to his apartment.'

'Of course, anything you need…' *Oh, bless you, Demir!* '…but why don't you just hang on to it if he doesn't need it till later? That way you still have the vehicle if you need it.'

Okay. That's fair. I didn't really think that excuse through. But don't you get all helpful now!

'Uh… I'm going to spend the night at a friend's house.' *It's not totally a lie. If we get through all this together, I won't be leaving Milana's side for a week!* 'I'm here right now actually.'

'Oh, okay, anything you need.' *Why do you sound afraid of me?* 'Which friend? Where should I go to pick up the car?'

Ana was more cautious with her lies this time around. She could not very well claim it was

374

Milana. Though that would arouse the least suspicion with the name itself, Demir knew Milana's address—and the addresses of most of her family as well. Ana filed quickly through a list of not-friends and almost-friends in her mind. There was really no one in the world quite like Milana, no one she could claim to be willing to overnight with without choking on the thought. It had to be a name Demir had heard before to sound more believable. Though it was hardly believable to herself, one name came to mind.

'Oh, it's just Stephanie. You know, the one who started working for the same company as you in the Fall?'

There was a sharp intake of breath from Demir, followed by a whispered 'What the hell?'

'Okay gotta run! I'll text you the address. The sooner you can make it, the better. Thanks again!' She hung up before he could respond. She was not sure what had aroused his apparent suspicion there, but she didn't have the time to dwell on it.

She fired off the address of the middle blue house to Demir. Once he took Darko's car away, it would be time for action: she would call the police, make up some story about escalating domestic violence or an impending suicide—whichever she decided would elicit a faster response—then she would storm the house. Ana did not know how much time she had until Demir came, but she would use what time there was to reach out to Milana.

Making sure the doors were locked, Ana reclined her seat until she was out of sight and tried to focus on her friend. She thought of all those sensations she had felt when last they spoke in person. The effects on all five senses, that comfort in her head, the closeness in her heart.

BUZZ! BUZZ!

Concentration shattered, Ana decided she might as well look at the text message. It was from Demir: **Got it. We will be there in ten minutes.**

Not very much time at all then.

Darko had been all ears from the mention of an oddly-placed naked man and, when Randy finished his story, Darko decided to follow in Ana's example by treating his friends as actual friends. *Trust someone for once. What's the worst that could happen?* He put his trust in them then, telling Maria and Randy all that he had talked about with his family: the impa shilup at the river, the wechuge in the streets, Finster and Gable's friendship activity seemingly being behind the murder spree, all of it. He left out the part about Papa Nate though. He knew they would feel sorrow on his behalf and he couldn't justify being the cause of that. *Why make them worry more?*

Darko fully expected Randy to act with the usual caution and unease, as he did when confronting even the least confrontational of problems. He was also prepared for Maria to chastise him for not sharing sooner before diving into an impassioned attempt to solve these crimes with this new information. And yet, expectations are but ghostly projections and—if his single encounter at the Richovsky farm could be taken as patterned behaviour—Darko was no good with ghosts.

Though certainly on the right track, Darko had dramatically underestimated the reactions of his friends. Like magnetically repellent forces, the two reacted each in their own strong ways. Randy leapt from his seat, launching into a tirade on moral responsibilities. He claimed the most morally appropriate action in this case would be inaction, to let the authorities carry out their authorized mandate. Maria, on the other hand, skipped the chastising altogether, lunging for Darko's laptop on the table. Her fingers attacked the keyboard in a case-cracking clattering.

Darko stood from his chair to crowd over Maria's shoulder. She had already opened three tabs on his browser, three separate searches already loading: "Finster and Gable, friendship source; Finster and Gable Inc., graphic designer; Finster and Gable Inc., official website."

'You guys aren't listening!' Randy insisted. 'Stop whatever you're doing, Maria. Let's just leave this alone. Please?'

'Did you not hear Darko?' Maria didn't even bother looking up from the laptop, already skimming Finster and Gable's official website. 'These are killers. We're not getting involved for any kind of personal pride or reward, we're doing it to help people!'

Darko squinted at the page Maria had just opened: **Scavenger Hunt: Find the Heart of all Friendship.** She scrolled down to reveal a map of Acton and a text box with some kind of question written within. Before Darko had even read it, Maria clicked somewhere on the map and the question was replaced by a new one. *This isn't exactly what you'd expect on a lawyer's website.*

'Besides,' Maria lowered her voice to a whisper, 'he was attacked by those things, he lifted water out of the river! Darko's already knee-deep in this. We can either abandon him and stay out of it, or we can be decent friends and decent human beings and help where we can. So, you still think ignoring all this is the right thing to do?'

'Jeez, Maria, I would've come around eventually. No need for all the guilt. I just thought we should weigh our options.' Randy sat back down defeated.

'Weighed, measured, and purchased.' She turned the laptop so Darko and Randy could see it better. There were confetti animations around the edges of the screen and and over the map were nine lines in white emanating from a single source in the centre marked by a heart of deep red. It was a perfect representation of the symbol that had been associated with the cultic murders. Here, it apparently marked a map to the Heart of all Friendship. Beneath the symbol the actual street address was written. Maria took a picture of it with her phone. 'Hope you're both done classes for the day, because we've got ourselves a suspicious residence to investigate.'

Darko was still reeling from the speed with which Maria had come up with a plan, still trying to figure out what he was looking at. Randy began groaning and packing his books into his backpack. Maria was somehow already prepared to leave

'We'll take the footbridge across the river. With the main road bridge closed, buses are delayed by an hour at this point. You said your sister's gonna drop off your car at your apartment?'

'Uhh…'

'Good. We can stop there first and continue on after.'

Darko and Randy were already outside and on their way into the river valley before they fully registered exactly what was happening.

'Jane!' Demir called out again.

He stood at the main doors of Sightliner with Morgan ready to head out. Demir had been terrified on the phone. he could tell something must be terribly wrong with Ana. She was the kind of person to sort out even the toughest of problems on her own—to a fault. The simple act of her asking someone else for help was sign enough that things were very bad indeed. He had wanted to press her for information, but he feared Ana would retreat from such scrutiny, simply ending the call with some excuse that she wouldn't actually need his help after all.

He had been forced to hold it in on the phone, to mask his trepidation and offer help without question. He only hoped she was lying about who she was meeting, because Stephanie was the Sightliner employee wanted on charges of attempted murder. Once he reached her, he could confront Ana for more details. There, in person, Ana would have nowhere to retreat.

Of course, he would have to get to her first.

'Jane!' he called for a fourth time. 'We're in a hurry here!' *Where is that woman?*

Jane threw down the book with a growl. *All right, all right, I'm coming!*

She was rummaging through an office labelled **VP Marketing - S. Horowitz**. Overcome with boredom, Jane had followed the scent of all that violence in the break room to this spot. The air in here was thick with it, filling her senses and dulling them to other stimuli. The book she had been holding was in itself of no consequence, but from the hands that held those pages there had been left behind that fingerprint of a fanatic. Of a murderer. *Or, in this case, only an attempted murderer. Just couldn't take the final step could you?*

With the book back where she had found it— more or less, and who would really notice if it was out of place anyway—Jane finally turned to go. She paused in the doorway, took one last deep inhalation of the heady air, and marched off to put an end to Demir's beckoning.

'What took you so long?' was all the gratitude he offered on her arrival.

'If you must know, I was… relieving myself.' *Hah! At least you have the courtesy to appear embarrassed.*

Demir held the door opened for Morgan and Jane to go first. Morgan, eyes and mind clearly elsewhere, passed by with a mumbled thanks, but Jane stood her ground in the doorway and glared at Demir until he went first.

Good boy.

There was not a word between the three of them as they walked around the building to the back where they had parked the van. Morgan was a good ten or fifteen paces ahead of Demir, and Demir a couple in front of Jane. She did not mind the silence, though she did wonder if the couple were not planning something in those quiet little heads of theirs. She would have to take care of that.

Not three steps into the parking lot, Demir suddenly froze, going rigid. His path was blocked by the most insignificant creature—a mouse. He stood in place for a moment, looking ahead to an unaware Morgan and then back to the mouse. Jane nearly laughed out loud then. *How cliché. A masculine, muscular farmboy afraid of a mouse.*

Demir diverted his path, giving the creature a wide berth as he went by, not taking his suspicious eyes from the rodent until he was past. Once behind the rodent, he scurried after his wife in exhibition of traits belonging to the very creature he avoided. Morgan was already shutting the van's passenger door and settling in.

Jane would not be forced aside by any mere rodent. She walked right up to the creature and fixed it with the same glare she had used on Demir. The creature's tail and whiskers twitched, its body shook up and down with its furious heartbeat, but those beady eyes did not break their stare, and the mouse did not back down a single step.

Jane glanced up toward the van to ensure no eyes were on her. No human eyes.

Seeing Demir and Morgan distracted by their own conversation in the van, Jane crouched down low to the mouse, sticking her face as close to the rodent's as she could without sullying her clothes. Then she hissed.

Without so much as a squeak, the mouse turned and pattered away, far too slowly for Jane's satisfaction. But then, she didn't have all day to go chasing down every insufferable creature that looked at her funny, now did she.

As Jane settled into the backseat of the van, feeling again somewhat subdued by being cast into the back seat like a child, she lifted her fingers to her nose and breathed in. She was hoping for some remnants of the smell from that book, some vestige of violence to settle her mind. All she smelled was burnt flesh, remnants of this body's own violent memories.

Despite the snows drifted up between the roads and the sidewalks, despite the dashboard's thermometer displaying an external temperature of negative sixteen, the afternoon sun was warm enough through the windshield to bake Morgan gently in her seat. It was close enough to evening on this February afternoon to make the distinction between the two a matter of outlook or disposition more so than one of accuracy. As it was, in this moment, regardless of the time of day, Morgan was best disposed to take a nap.

She fought hard against the gentle head-nodding, the vehicle's quiet rocking, tried shedding the comforting warmth of her coat, but none of it was having any success in pushing away the drowsiness. Even that constant ache in her head, now spread to her neck and shoulders, seemed somehow to contribute to that urge to fall asleep.

With a yawn wide enough to swallow a good-sized rodent, Morgan sat up straighter in her seat. Demir's warm hand, so gentle in its grip she had forgotten it was holding hers, pulled away. Before she could voice a protest, he was putting his phone in her hand instead.

'Can you go to that last text I got from Ana and read off the address? I know it was eighty-something street, but I forgot which something that something was.'

Morgan took the phone without a word, punched in the correct password after the second, fatigue-clumsied attempt, and found the message in question. She tried to keep from yawning again as she read off the address.

'Fifty-twenty-nine, eighty…'

'Fifty-twenty-nine, eighty what?' Demir prompted.

'Fifty-twenty-nine, eighty-second A street. Just wait though.' Morgan managed to shred her sleepiness with an effort then, finding it replaced by a mounting dread.

She hurriedly fished her own phone out of her jacket pocket. It was still opened to the page where she had completed the scavenger hunt activity. There was an address below the red heart and a congratulatory message welcoming her to come down to the heart of all friendship: **5035 82nd A Street.**

'Fifty-thirty-five, eighty-second A street.' she breathed out in amazement.

'What?'

'That's the address given when you win this Friendship activity. Its right across the street from the address Ana sent you.'

'Shit.' The van came to a stop at a red light and Demir looked to Morgan now, a kind of desperation in his eyes. It hurt her more to see that pleading, lost look than all the pain in her head, neck, and shoulders combined. And it hurt even more to know that there was really nothing she could do to help him. She reached for his hand.

He pulled it away just before their fingers met. 'Shit!' he repeated, angrily this time. 'I never called Donald!'

Their vehicle was the first one moving as soon as the light changed to green. A bit of that desperation in Demir's eyes had been replaced by determination. He kept his eyes on the road ahead as he spelled out a plan. As much, Morgan knew, for his benefit as for her own.

'Okay. Can you call Donald, let him and Derek know that I have the graphic designer's address now and I will send it to them when I get a chance. Then tell them how you got this address to come up on the website, and tell him Ana's in that area and she's being weird about what she's doing there. Ask them if they can meet us there.'

From the back seat Jane leaned forward, a word of encouragement or comfort, Morgan was sure, ready on the woman's lips.

'Well isn't this exciting?!'

Not quite what I had in mind.

CHAPTER TWENTY-TWO:
Courage and the Closet
Friday, 19 February 2021

Frida had decided she rather liked these two policemen. Maybe it was the way they didn't take themselves too seriously, or maybe it was the fact that they and her crossword were likely the only things to drag her out of the day's state of perpetual boredom, but whatever it was, she decided she was grateful for it.

Not idly had Frida been given the title of Courage as a Minor Virtue of Friendship. None of the disciples had been idly named. Though Frida had never been one to think of herself as courageous in her younger days, all it had taken was her younger brother's insistence that this was chief among her qualities for Frida to make a conscious effort to embody courageousness in all she did, every single day.

Frida loved her parents, not in the you're-my-parents-so-I-have-to kind of way that most people seemed to, but she truly thought they were the very best parents in the entire world. They seemed to know so much. Not about facts or trivia, but about the important stuff, about life itself. So when they had told her it was her duty, as an elder sister, to be the absolute best role model that a younger brother could dream of, it was a duty she took to boldly, courageously.

Yet, for all her courage and all her wishes to help these nice policemen as a good role model should, Frida had sworn vows of secrecy, and could not exactly tell the men that Finster and Gable had been among the nine founding members of a cult of friendship that had gone around sacrificing Acton's undesirables—to be fair, most of whom were not that far from death to begin with—and had then gone on to incite several of their god's lesser followers into committing acts of gross violence, including real, terrible, gruesome murder. But neither could she do nothing.

Derek Woods had left her and Donald in the file vault, giving up for the time being with the paper documents and claiming that he would have a better chance getting something off of Frida's computer than in that sea of poorly-organized paper. *Hey! I organized that,* had been her first thought, but Derek seemed like a rather linear thinker, so her next thought had been rather more pragmatic. *Perhaps I can lead you gentlemen in stumbling onto something.*

As these things tend to, one thought had led to another, and within the span of a single minute, Frida had a grand plan forming in her mind. She had found, in her devotion to the Friend, that she was possessed of certain gifts. A kind of subconscious sense for things. It was nothing so dramatic as a full-blown sixth sense. It was far more subtle than that, and far less universal. It was in the same realm as those peculiar affinities that lets one wake up at exactly the time they wished, or that ability after being blinded and spun round and round of being able to point in the direction of home. Or, in this case, a sense that Donald would likely reach for that file perched precariously on the shelf's edge there.

Frida approached Donald, masking her intentions by making some comment about going after Derek to provide some assistance. Donald didn't look up from the file his nose was buried in. The man seemed to possess a hunger for pouring over these files, his coffee sat on one of the shelves, untouched since Frida had led them into this room. Frida took that cup, still half-full or more, and placed it just slightly on the edge of the precariously-perched file.

Finding it difficult to mask her sudden triumphant smile, Frida turned away and left the room, preparing to make good on her promise to help Derek.

Derek had left the file vault behind. The fluorescent lighting, the windowless enclosure, the smell of enough manila to ruin the taste of his coffee, he simply could not handle it anymore. He had slumped in Frida's chair at the receptionist desk, neatly laid out the case files they had brought with them across the desktop, and fiddled around in the computer's hard drive for all of three minutes before realizing what an utter dead end it was.

With a guilty look over one shoulder to make sure Donald hadn't come forth from his file cave, Derek picked up Frida's crossword puzzle and began skimming the clues.

The sudden sound of his phone ringing startled Derek right up out of the chair. He returned the crossword quickly with another guilty glance back down the hall and answered his phone.

'Detective Derek Woods, APS.'

'Derek, it's Morgan Richovsky. Is everything alright? I couldn't get through to Donald?'

'Oh I've been saying that for years, ha ha! No, everything's fine, just working. You have that address for us?'

'Umm...' she sounded unsure. Derek instinctively sat back down and started to repack the case files he had lain out. 'Demir has it yes, we'll email it in a bit here. But there's something else right now. That Finster and Gable company.' with mention of the company's name, Derek stopped packing up. He waited.

'That Finster and Gable company,' Morgan repeated, 'the one that made that Friendship activity, I was on their website and found a different activity. It's a kind of scavenger hunt laid out over a map of Acton. At the end of this is an invitation to go to the "Heart of all Friendship." It leads to a house in Acton, the address is fifty-thirty-five, eighty-second A street. That might not be anything, but Ana, Demir's sister just texted that she is at a house practically across the street and she needs help. Demir says something's off with the whole picture.'

Derek jotted down the address as Morgan said it, by the time she finished explaining the situation, he was shutting the fully-repacked case files. *Sounds like we're needed.*

'Demir's probably right about that. He's always had a gut for these kinds of things. Would've made a fine cop. What can we do, Morgan? Do you want us to meet you there?

'Please.'

'We're on our way two minutes ago.' Derek rose with alacrity. He hung up and turned to march back to the file vault and explain the situation to Donald, but was greeted, quite surprisingly, by Frida standing directly in his path.

'Whoah! Scared me a little there, ha ha. I didn't hear you come up the hall. Look, thanks for all your help, we'll have to come back, something's come up.'

'Did you mention you needed an address?' Frida asked, ignoring the sense of urgency in his tone—if she heard it at all. Her eyes were not on Derek as she spoke, but on the side of the folder containing his case files, right where he had hastily scrawled the address given by Morgan.

'Oh yeah, that was another thing we had to see to,' Derek played off, not really sure what Frida was poking at here. 'We were actually looking for the address of the graphic designers your bosses used for their company logo.'

Frida did look Derek in the eyes then, and her smile was so full and genuine that the rising lump in Derek's throat, and rising suspicion in his mind, disappeared simultaneously. 'Well, we do have that information actually, if you still need it.'

'What? Why would Finster and Gable keep that if they didn't even pay the guy?'

'Well it's a business contact, isn't it? And what are you talking about? They didn't pay her money, sure, but they paid her in a fancy supper invitation instead. The woman agreed to it.' Frida leaned past Derek to get at her computer's keyboard. A few quick keystrokes and double-clicks later and she had pulled up a contact card. 'And... print.'

Derek walked to the nearby printer and retrieved the emerging paper. 'Well, thanks again. This is a huge help. Like I said, we'll probably be back in the next few days here to—'

'Uh oh.' Frida interrupted. 'Looks like it was a fake address.' She had pulled up the address from the contact card on the browser to reveal the location of a large grocery store. 'The number looks real enough though, let's give that a call!'

'No— Wait. What are you—?' Frida handed her phone to Derek, mouthing out 'It's ringing' with a finger to her lips. 'I'll go get Donald,' she whispered, scurrying up the hallway and leaving a very confused Derek behind.

Figments. Puffs of smoke with no flame below. Just solid, binding statements built atop the crumbled and incomplete foundation that are the laws of this country. No wonder most people think of lawyers as crooks. These jerks literally interpret a law one way, to suit their case one time, and a completely opposing way to support a different case the next!

Donald closed the folder he had been buried in and tucked it back into the shelf. He looked around for his next victim. *The problem with these files is that they're too client-focussed. There's not enough about Finster and Gable themselves to spell out any kind of wickedness or criminal involvement—*

393

not that they'd be stupid enough to implicate themselves, I would assume.

Ah, what were you all about again? Donald's eyes came to rest on the folder he had set aside some time ago. *Something about friendship in this one right? A good-faith clause of some kind or other.* He reached for it, still wracking his brain as to what exactly had caught his eye within. He noted as he pulled at the corner of the folder that he had set his coffee down on the folder's edge. Reacting to the fear of the cup falling more than the actual risk of it doing so, Donald quickly shoved the folder back the other way.

Too hard, too late. The force knocked the cup clean off the shelf. Painfully slowly, Donald watched it tumble to the ground below where the lid popped off and a large puddle of coffee splashed out over the tiled floor.

'Oh dear!' Frida called from the doorway where she had just reentered the room. 'You'd best clean that up before the smell sets in.' Donald looked up to see her frowning down at him disappointedly from across the room, hands on her hips. He opened his mouth to make a sheepish apology but was cut off. 'Well, best get started with it then. There's a mop in the closet at the end there.' She pointed to the opposite end of the room.

Cursing himself for his clumsiness, Donald picked his way over the puddle and made for the closet door set in the room's back wall. He had thought the wall there let out onto the street, but he was only realizing now as he approached it that there was not a single window in its length across the room. *That can't be up to code for a street-facing wall. Can it?*

He understood why there were no windows the second he opened the closet door. He didn't bother shouting down the hall, didn't bother reaching for his cellphone, he went straight for his radio and gun.

'Dispatch, this is Phips,' he gave his radio signature. 'We're gonna need backup on our location.'

He turned to face Frida once more, but kept the gun pointed into the closet. 'Did you know this was here, Frida?'

'What? A mop?'

Milana had made little progress, which was not to say none at all, but what progress had been made was small and insignificant. She had discovered that when concentrating as hard as possible, when truly straining to reach out to Ana, the markings on the doorknob glowed anew and the burn on her hand reached new terrifying levels of agony. She still could not hear a sound—aside from the lights droning overhead—which was even more

395

unnerving now that a few of the room's other occupants had woken and were moving around, their panic clear indication that they were suffering the same experience.

With the absence of that sense for what seemed like an eternity, it was a disorienting moment when the door swung open and the world's sounds returned to Milana with all the crushing force of a landslide. She curled into a protective ball, shielding her ears from the assault. A troupe of people entered, men and women, young and old. They wore casual, everyday clothes, but they might as well have been in long black robes for all the dark seriousness and ceremony in their actions.

Once Milana's brain finally identified the torrent of sounds bearing down on her, she realized the room was filled with loud chanting emanating from the main room beyond the opened door. She peered over her protectively-shielding arms at the group that had entered. Some were bearing torches, some mediaeval-looking shackles, all looking around the room hungrily. One of them pointed at her, then looked to the doorway for something like permission.

In walked the Friend herself. She bore the same arrogant kind of authority as when Milana had first seen her, but something was off this time. There was an edge of franticness in her eyes, like the first cracks of pressure on something about to explode into shattering ruination. Milana did not want to find out whether it would be the Friend destroyed in such such an outburst, or everyone around her.

'No not her. And not the sweet couple in each other's arms, or the brothers, they are too valuable. Someone who is alone, just those who are alone. Start with that one over there, she had a chance to follow the faith but rejected it.'

Milana followed the Friend's pointing finger to Stephanie. *No, no, no.* Four of the men rushed forward and dragged Stephanie to her feet. The girl started kicking and screaming, lashing out with her hands for the eyes of those nearest, but her strength was pitiful in comparison, and without even needing the chains, they pinned her arms down and began carrying her from the room. 'Help, please! You can't do this! I won't tell anyone, just let me go!' Her head continued thrashing around looking pleadingly, helplessly at the others in the room, prisoners, captors, any who might find some mercy within. As if afraid to acknowledge her situation to someone who knew her personally, that gaze swung right past Milana, not even settling on her for a moment.

No matter her personal relationship with Stephanie, Milana had made a promise to herself. With what strength she had, she would be the protector of those in this room, a champion of the imprisoned and afraid. With a shallow, shaking breath, Milana rose to her feet and charged at the men carrying Stephanie.

As if she had anticipated that very action, the Friend took a casual step to one side, reached out and embraced Milana as she made to dart by. The woman's arms might as well have been made from steel. Milana was pinned in place by that embrace, unable to do more than shout futilely in protest.

'You can't—' she cut herself off as a new sensation entered her mind. Or, perhaps it had been there since the door opened, merely drowned out by all the other things going on around her.

'Watch us,' the Friend gloated. 'Everyone out, take her to the altar. Do not worry about this one.'

Milana! Ana's presence filled her mind. *What's happening? You're in pain!*

'My my, you two are persistent.' As the last of her followers left, the Friend gave Milana an abrupt shove and made for the door. 'I can feel her now, the one you talk to. Sorry for the disturbance, how about some peace and quiet?' She slammed the door, shutting out Ana and all sound once again.

No one else in the room seemed to have moved. They cowered against the walls, some crying silently. The smell of urine reached Milana briefly before being overpowered by rose petals once again. She did not return to her place along the wall. Instead, she strode toward the door.

Ana had no idea what was going on. She had felt fear, distress, and pain. And it had been enough to make her own hand hurt. But then it had all been cut off abruptly, alarmingly so. She decided she could not wait for Demir to take the vehicle, could not make her carefully-timed phone call to the police, she had to move now. She texted the address of the blue house to 911 with the message **HELP ME!** before exiting the car and sprinted up the sidewalk for the blue house.

The second she arrived she knew something was wrong. There was no glass in the fanlight. Ana took a step back from the door, her arm still half-poised to strike in furious knocking. Though there was no breeze to make the drawn curtains to her left so much as stir, their colours were a little too bright to be behind glass. Something glinted in the evening sun near the edge of the nearest glassless window.

Ana stepped down from the sidewalk, approaching the window cautiously. There, at the edge of the frame, a small shard of glass. If there had been more, they had been cleaned away. Not bothering for the door, Ana stood on her toes and reached in to pull the curtain aside. The thick fabric billowed out as she pulled at it, blocking her view of the room within for a moment longer, and when she drew it away enough to see clearly, Ana almost wished she hadn't.

She was looking into the living room of the house, where the bodies of a family of four were neatly arrayed in a row across the floor. Thousands of bits of glass from their shattered television and family photos blanketed them. To their side, on the couch in the room, were two more corpses, charred and burnt in what looked like a lightning pattern in several places. Toward what Ana assumed was the hallway lay another body, also charred. What it was, she had no idea. It roughly resembled a human, but seemed to have too few ribs and too long a torso.

The thought of going in there to find Milana made her shiver.

Derek was thanking the graphic designer—a rather reasonable woman by the name of Grace—when he heard Donald's radio call. He hung up the phone and went sprinting down the hallway after his partner. He had his handcuffs out before he even reached Frida.

'What? A mop?' she was asking Donald.

'What's going on, Philips,' Derek asked urgently, approaching Frida with the raised cuffs in one hand, his second hand resting on his holster. Donald's gaze kept sweeping back and forth between Frida and what looked to be am opened closet.

'Ah, don't bother with those, Woods, just keep an eye on her would you? I think it's empty.'

'What is? The closet?' Derek asked, confused.

Donald's response bit with a frustrated sarcasm. 'Yeah, the closet.'

'There's a mop in the closet' Donald mimicked in his head. *You knew. You knew your employers were up to something. Maybe you never had the guts to look in here yourself, but you knew more or less what was back here.*

Donald's mind flashed back to that moment when Frida had stated she was leaving the room to check on Derek. In the memory, he could just make out Frida at the edge of his vision: her arms moving, the temporary scent of coffee over that of manila. Coffee he had not smelled for over an hour. *Because the cup sat still for more than an hour. You set that whole damn thing up didn't you?*

His gaze swung back to Frida once more—this time impressed—before he entered the closet.

Within the closet there was a mop, sure enough, and a broom and dustpan, a small, battery-powered vacuum, a plethora of cleaning products, the whole works. There was also no back wall. In its place were red beads hanging down.

Donald pushed them aside, his gun leading his way into the room. It was roughly twice the size of the file room, likely more than half of the entire office space owned by Finster and Gable Inc. The walls were painted red, giving the place the look of some kind of garish sex dungeon. And the black, leather-walled altar at the centre of the room certainly didn't help get away from that image.

The room was empty of occupants, Donald was relieved to see, but here and there dark, questionable stains marred the room's red carpeting. There was a bookshelf in one corner filled with not just books, but file folders too. *That's likely what we need.* The far wall of the room was indeed the one nearest the street and its six windows had been covered in a translucent, red film. In the centre of each window was the nine-pointed star symbol.

Donald was on his second surveying lap around the room, gun comfortably away back in its holster when Derek came in, one hand on Frida's arm.

'Look, Donald, this find is something else, and we will definitely be back, but right before you radioed out, I got a call from Morgan. Sounds like Demir's sister's in some kind of trouble, which means Demir's about to be in some kind of trouble. Now I know we can't exactly leave this—and her' he eyed Frida with a kind of frustrated annoyance that somehow only made Donald more impressed by her '—but the second reinforcements get here and we fill them in, we better hit the road.'

Rivers will rise.

Zealously, Maria fell into a position of leading Randy and Darko through the river valley. There were only two problems with this. Firstly, she actually had no idea where she was going, and just sort of assumed Darko would correct her if she took a wrong turn. The second problem was that Darko's mind was not on the path beneath him, but rather, on where it had led in the past. In other words, Darko's mind was locked on the image of not-Volkhova and her musical voice prophesying the rising of rivers. *And, indeed,* he pondered, *they have risen.*

So it was with great surprise and no small amount of alarm, that Maria took the three of them around a switchback in the path and straight into the broadside of a veritable hoard of Acton's homeless on some kind of biblical exodus through —and, she hoped, out of—the river valley. Maria waited until they had completely passed her, forty people or more, and continued on in their wake.

Had Darko been paying attention, he might have remarked that the path Maria was taking was not the fastest or most efficient path toward the footbridge. But, lost inwardly as he was, Darko barely even registered the presence of others on the path. He just walked on silently, eyes on something far, far away, and mouth silently mumbling that same portent of flooding.

Anderson and Laforce had apparently been sent on some call, so it was Captain Florence Fremont herself who came leading a small investigative team. She had demanded Donald tell her everything they had discovered and how they had come to discover it, so Derek had been left alone, all packed up and standing impatiently between the reception desk and the door. Frida, who Donald had insisted need not be arrested, sat at the desk, and attempted, for the second time, to draw Derek into conversation.

'Hey, do you know of any fruits associated with Aphrodite? I was thinking maybe it was kind of an on-the-nose thing. Like maybe it's one of her kids? Cupid. That was one right? What was his Greek equivalent again?'

Derek had been content with waiting impatiently, debating whether or not he should ask to use a bathroom before they left, but now he sighed heavily. He knew she would keep this up until he engaged. *I give up.* 'You're worrying about the wrong things. It's a bad crossword to begin with: whoever wrote it is mixing up Greek and Roman names all over the place. There's even a clue I saw in there which I'm fairly certain was a reference to Gilgamesh. Not exactly a Greco-Roman figure.'

Derek left his spot leaning against the wall and approached the desk. 'What else do you have? What's the actual wording of the clue? How many letters?'

'Uhh, five. Could be Cupid, I guess. The full clue is "the fruit given by number thirty-five." And thirty-five is Aphrodite—she started the Trojan War.'

Derek stopped three steps from the desk. He had just seen Donald emerge from the file vault down the hall. Though the Captain still had him pinned in conversation at the end of the corridor, it looked like Donald was about to make good his escape.

'Yeah, I saw that one,' he answered distantly, attention still down the hall. 'To help you out in the order of your questions, it's an apple. *Tei kallistei* ring any bells? Your number thirty-five is wrong. It's not Aphrodite, it's Discordia.'

Donald came rushing up the hallway, gesturing for Derek to get a move on. If they didn't leave now, they would be here for hours. Frida did not look up to watch them go. She was staring unblinkingly at her crossword puzzle, a sense of shocked realization settling in. She did not notice when her pencil fell from her slackened grip, nor did she notice the police captain return it to her desk with a smile.

She was finally beginning to understand why there seemed to be so much strife in the faith of Friendship and why the followers were so obsessed with that one star, Epsilon Boötis, Pulcherrima. The Friend was not nearly so friendly as Frida had thought.

Tei kallistei: to the most beautiful.

Discordia may have left it out for the three goddesses to fight over, but it was her *apple.*

CHAPTER TWENTY-THREE:
A Friend at the Door
Friday, 19 February 2021

Having been awake and staring at the dotted ceiling overhead for several minutes, Honesty sat up in his hospital bed and slapped himself hard.

'Nothing like a heavy hand to turn a boy into a man.' Just like dad used to say. Of course, it hurt a lot more then, and maybe it was the pain itself that had done the man-making. The stinging pain, the hot needles of shame. Now I feel nothing. The Friend's strength has taken all pain and injury from me. She has made me more than mere man.

And not once did she strike me, Dad.

But I know it was your heavy-handed guidance that led me down the road to the Friend in the first place, so I am grateful for that. And you always did say those strikes caused you more pain than me. Having conducted a sacrifice or two myself, I believe it. So I'm sorry for that. For all the pain I've caused you. And I hope in your final days, your only company an empty hospital room like this one, you did not relive too much of that pain.

I only wish Mom's sensitivity hadn't convinced you away from treating your other son with that same dedication, the same tradition, that you raised me with. I wish you would've shown the same strength and resilience. The same discipline. If you had, I feel it may have saved him.

Not once was poor Daniel ever given that heavy hand of guidance, and perhaps that's why he never truly learnt what it was to be a man. He was a kid, a selfish brat and an idiot to the very end. They only life he cared for was his own—and even then, maybe not that much.

Driving drunk, killing that poor family.

Steven Yung wiped the gathering water from his eyes and barked a gruff laugh. *Guess I can still feel pain. At least where it counts*

Danny, you never gave me a choice, little brother. You broke the laws of nature, of humanity. I had to balance those lives you took. I had to take yours.

The tears flowed freely now, and this time he did not bother to wipe them away.

My first sacrifice, though I did not know it at the time. I didn't feel the Friend's presence until after the deed was done. Not until I stood over your unmoving body, blood dripping from the knife still in my hand.

He did wipe at his tears then, with a sniffle. *I didn't slap myself to drag all these memories up. I did it to feel my new power, to feel the Friend's gifts. I survived while Fort did not. I was healed.*

I am more than Steven Yung now, more than Honesty. I am a Companion of the Friend herself!

He thought back to the lessons the Friend had taught him long ago, to the words she had spoken in his mind after the death of his brother: 'The difficult moments of this world are always, and will always be, countered by the truly wondrous. Sure there is strife, but there is harmony also; discord and accord together, locked in a beauteous, weaving dance until the end of time. And even that dance is not immune to the balance, it is marked both by the occasional misstep and the rare moment of truly transcendental grace.'

With those final thoughts, Steven rose out of the hospital bed, gathered his hospital gown about himself for the sake of modesty, and made to find Grace. He could feel her here in the hospital, somewhere off on this same level. The same way he could feel the Friend's presence, like a warm light, to the west and nearer the river, at Generosity's house.

Milana took several deep breaths, extended her already-burnt hand, and grasped the doorknob.

Red flooded her vision. An incinerating pain shot through her palm and up her arm, and the noise of her surroundings slammed in on her once more. The smell of her own burning flesh eradicated the rose-stink of the room. Milana clenched her teeth hard and reached out beyond the pain, beyond the incessant chanting without the room, She reached beyond the building itself and found Ana. She was close.

'*I need you.*'

A new jolting sensation shook her arm and Milana looked down to see the doorknob smoking, disintegrating in her hand. There was a flash of white and what was left of the doorknob exploded, violently taking the entire lower half of her hand with it.

She tucked her horribly disfigured and burnt hand tight to her chest, afraid to look at the damage done. What she had seen was black, white, red, and bronze, burnt flesh, blistered flesh, bone, and chunks of the exploded doorknob fused into it all. Her pinky and ring finger, and a good portion of her palm, were simply gone. The fresh flood of pain washing over Milana rocked her back on her heels, threatening to unbalance her. She rode it out valiantly, and the wave that next followed was not one of agony, but of anger.

Door ruined, Milana yanked it open by its tattered boards and charged into the room beyond.

Ana had just worked up the courage to push the unlocked door open and take her first, tentative steps into the blue house when Milana's presence came slamming back into her mind.

I need you.

And like a shining beacon, Ana suddenly knew where her friend was. *I'm in the wrong house!*

The pain and distress she had felt from Milana the last time they made contact had increased a hundredfold. Something terrible was happening.

Ana wheeled and sprinted out of the house, down the walkway, out into the street without bothering to check for traffic, and was brought to an abrupt and painful halt by a solid arm wrapping around her midsection, knocking the air from her lungs.

She gulped breath after breath, unable to exhale, eyes growing wide and wet. She turned to see the face of Demir looking down on her. She shook her head furiously, fought feebly against his grip, anything to communicate that he had to let her go.

He offered the opposite. 'You're not going anywhere until you tell me what the hell is going on! Do you have any idea what's in that house you're so eagerly running toward? Do you?!' Ana had not heard Demir yell in years. It was terrifying.

From behind Demir, Ana saw Jane silently glide into view. She was pulling Morgan by the hand. Morgan looked like she had taken too many pain pills the way she was practically asleep on her feet. She let Jane pull her along without protest.

Steven opened the door of his room to the shocking sight of another Major Virtue, another—he could tell—Companion of the Friend. Fidelity seemed surprised to see the door opening, and it was not until after she had begun talking that she noticed her hand still upraised in preparation for knocking and lowered it.

'Grace claimed you had woken up.' she said. 'I admit I was skeptical. I guess I forgot what that connection felt like.' She looked away, something like embarrassment on her face.

When Fidelity turned to face him again, there was a grave determination in her eyes, a sense of urgency. I guess by now you've had some kind of contact with the Friend? You always were favoured above the rest of us.'

Steven gave no response, but Connie Martin didn't need police training to know the answer. It was made as clear in Steven's silence as it could have been in words.

'Good.' She continued. 'So you know what I've gone through to get us here. And I know what you've gone through. I know how... sacrificial your sacrifices have been. That puts us—the two of us out of the Friend's four surviving Major

Virtues—on a level playing field. One we've been on since before Her arrival. Let's forget the other two for now, they're waiting with Grace. I'm sure that, like me, your unique form of faith has not changed because of the Friend's arrival.'

'You said Grace sent you?' Steven did not address what Fidelity was getting at right away. *This can be a teaching moment, so long as I treat it with the care and patience it deserves.* He motioned for Fidelity to lead the way. He could only sense the direction and distance to Grace, but was left blind to the winding ways of the hospital's corridors.

Once they were underway and Steven had time to think of all the weight in what Fidelity was *not* saying—which was at least equal in weight to the words she actually did say—he addressed what the woman was getting at.

'We are Major Virtues no longer, but Companions. I'm sure you already know, but my true name is Steven and I would very much like to learn yours.'

'Connie.'

'Well, Connie,' he seemed surprised with the name, as if it was not quite a match for the woman before him, 'We are Companions now. And because we are now all Companions in the eyes of the Friend, and in the eyes of each other, the four of us are all on even footing after all. There is no need to form secret subgroups anymore. It did not work out so well for Lust, did it?

'I'd like to think we're past all that now. But no matter what our official titles are, our personalities have not changed. The Friend did not name me Honesty out of luck, nor you Fidelity out of fondness for the word. These are ideas—no, inherent qualities—that can be separated from us no more easily than a limb.'

Ah, quite a perfect response I think. Not that I feel pride in it, but I do hope you feel pride through me, Friend.

They arrived at a short, dead-end wing of the hall and, feeling Grace in the room on the right, Steven slipped ahead of Connie. *The four Companions, the sharers of bread shall be united, and we shall go as one to the Friend, and break bread with her.*

Had Steven not been so filled in that moment with the promise of a brighter tomorrow, had he not been riding the high of this new strength and energy bestowed upon him by his god, he might have been suspicious as to why Connie, who had been not a half-step behind as they made the turn into this short wing, was now hanging back. But Steven was none of these things, so he walked into Grace's room full of bliss, not realizing for more than a minute, that Connie had gone.

Not quite past all that after all.

Milana took quick stock of her surroundings. The way upstairs was behind her and to the left, immediately neighbouring the door she had just came out of. The other prisoners in the room were already crowding behind her and looking for a way out. The path to to the stairs, to freedom, was unblocked, but Stephanie was at the far end of the room, at the far end of escape. Two men had her pinned to the wall as a woman carved shallow cuts into Stephanie's palms.

So unexpected, so miraculous was Milana's escape from the room that few of the Friend's followers were able to react for several moments. Even the Friend herself stood—looking statuesque and stupid—at the head of what looked to Milana like some kind of sacrificial altar in stunned silence. Those among the Friend's helpers who did react were sluggish and inept in their reactions.

Milana ran at the nearest chanting, torch-bearing, fanatic idiot, ripped the torch from her hands, and set it at the base of one of the basement's walls. The paint darkened from white, to brown, to black, and in seconds the wall was aflame. But Milana had not stayed to watch, she ducked past the a weakly-reaching disciple of the Friend, and charged at those holding Stephanie.

They had not taken Milana's shoes after her capture. Being considerate followers of the Friend, not a single individual among the faithful had worn their shoes down into this basement, which gave Milana another advantage over all of them. Her sprint across the room took her shoed, stomping steps over several unprotected feet and, upon reaching Stephanie, a single solid kick at the nearest man's crotch set Stephanie free as the others hurried backwards. Milana grabbed Stephanie's arm and swung her in the direction of the stairs. The girl ran without further encouragement.

It was only then that a real effort of resistance began. The Friend turned to the woman who had been carving the symbols of Friendship into their first victim's hands and wrenched the sacrificial knife from her grip. She then turned to the stairs where the other prisoners were rushing away.

'Stop them! None leave this basement alive! They will know what it is to cross me!'

Stephanie reached the first stair and began her ascent just as a group of the Friend's supporters closed in around the base of the steps, blocking Milana who was close behind. Milana did not slow her charge, causing the group to move away in fear of the impending impact. All except one.

He was a large man, much bigger than Milana, and he stopped her momentum entirely as he grabbed her. He put his full weight into pulling her to the side, ready to throw her to the ground. And that was his mistake.

Milana thought back to the judo class she had been robbed from attending. *Guess I get to beat the crap out of someone after all.* With his full weight being put into his movements, it was not difficult for Milana to redirect the entirety of that force first to one side, then, once she had a solid grip on his neck with her good hand, right over her back. She threw him to the basement floor with such force that his skull could be heard cracking against the cement underlaying the thin carpet.

There were others around her now, ready to strike but hesitant, fearful. Milana charged the two steps to the nearest one—another torch bearer—and relieved the man of his burden. She turned to the next closest, another intimidatingly large man, lifted the bottom of his shirt, and shoved the torch up there. The cotton of his shirt, or maybe the bright blue dye, ignited before Milana even pulled her hand away.

There was only a single woman between her and the stairs now. She shoved the large, burning man away, into an oncoming group of others and ran for the final woman. She darted to her left then, just when the woman lunged for her, Milana reversed directions, spinning around the woman's other side.

As that spin took Milana round again to face the stairs, her eyes widened to see the Friend now blocking what had been a clear path. She found herself unable to move and that surprised expression turned to one of confusion before, belatedly, she felt something like a pinch in her chest.

Milana looked down to see the Friend's hand wrapped tightly around the hilt of the sacrificial knife, its blade buried in Milana's chest, between two ribs and straight into her heart. There was surprisingly little pain, or perhaps it simply felt insignificant next to the pain in Milana's hand, or maybe she was simply out of pain to feel, past the limit of her brain's ability to process. What she did feel was a rushing warmth spreading through her chest. For some strange reason, as that warmth spread it left a chill in its wake.

Milana shivered and something like a squeak came from her lips. It sounded alien even to her.

The Friend had not taken her eyes off of Milana and as Milana looked back up at her murderer, their eyes met. There was a surprising gentleness in the Friend's expression. Something almost like sympathy.

'I never wanted it to come to this. Go in peace.' The Friend then reached forth her other hand to grip Milana's shoulder. There was a feeling of total numbness now and, though Milana knew the hand was there, she could not feel its weight. With a grunt, the Friend twisted the knife sharply. There was a horrible sound as flesh tore and ribs cracked and Milana's world went dark.

She knew something was off as she slipped away from a state of awareness. She had no concept really of where she was or why she was there, and her brain kept repeating that distracting cracking sound. Falling into unconsciousness, she decided it sounded rather like an applause. She smiled, proud of whatever achievement had earned that expression of praise. And passed out.

Stephanie watched from the top of the stairs, mouth agape. She felt like throwing up watching her classmate and friend being stabbed with an impossible strength. Then, in another display of that godly might, the goddess twisted the knife, shattering bone. As she drew the knife free there was another cracking sound, and the Friend's hand emerged holding only a broken hilt. the knife's blade had lodged deep into one of Milana's ribs and snapped.

A fighter till the very end.

The spreading fires below cast the scene in a flickering glow. Smoke was already beginning to climb the stairs out of the basement. Stephanie knew it would be only moments before every last one of the basement's occupants came tearing up the stairs in pursuit.

Stephanie closed the door at the top of the stairs, locked it, and ran into the house's kitchen where the other prisoners all stood waiting.

'Why are you all standing here? We have to leave now!' She picked a path at random and ran through the curiously bare house until she found a door. She took the group through it into the house's backyard, out the back gate, and ran up the bike path there for the nearest major road.

'LOOK!' Ana wheezed, finally able to speak. Demir turned in the direction of Ana's pointing hand to see his wife being pulled toward the house by Jane.

'Morgan. Jane. What are you doing?'

'So this is where it all comes from, yeah?' Jane's voice sounded strange, almost giddy. 'The heart of all Friendship? Well let's get a closer look, shall we?'

'Jane, stop!' Demir commanded to no avail. 'Come on,' he growled, changing tactics. He grabbed Ana by the hand and pulled her along after Jane. Jane was just reaching the front door when Ana suddenly tore free of her brother's grip, collapsing to the ground with the rawest, most despairing cry of human emotion Demir had ever heard.

It was like claws of rusted iron had hooked their way into Ana's heart and then torn it out of her chest, snapping every rib along the way. The line connecting her and Milana was burning, incinerating to nothing. Ana could do nothing but fall to the ground in the fetal position and bawl like a helpless child, the knowledge of what was happening overwhelming.

She's dying!

Unable to pull Ana to her feet, but more urgently concerned with what Jane was doing to his wife, Demir let go of his sister and ran after Jane who was just now reaching for the doorknob.

'Jane don't!'

The Friend had been beaten, she knew that now. That stubborn girl had killed one of her followers, knocked another unconscious, and had compromised their place of worship.

The Friend had commanded the impa shilup to serve as sentries around her temple-house, but their inability to stop the prisoners escaping told her they had abandoned their duties. With so much power from so many entities in this area, it was impossible to tell who was the source of which. *Well, slightly easier now,* she mused, as one of those lights of power was winking out.

She was still annoyed with herself for breaking her knife, the only conventional weapon—*somehow!*—among all her followers. The basement was aflame, there could be no saving it now. So, like so many times in her past, the goddess led her faithful followers away from disaster and toward a new home. Up the stairs, smashing through the locked door with ease, through the kitchen, down the hall, and out the front door.

To freedom. To new beginnings. To—
A revenant?

Demir thought his warning might have worked, for Jane hesitated then. But the door swung open from the inside and out stepped a woman, a veritable army of men and women crowded behind her. One of the woman's arms was covered in blood, still wet and dripping, from fingertips to elbow, and in that hand was the broken and blood-soaked handle of a knife.

CHAPTER TWENTY-FOUR:
Fire and Water
Friday, 19 February 2021

'Should have gone at that law office. Should have definitely gone then.' Derek was no longer being shy about it. He really needed to pee and he let Donald know it.

'Hey you're driving. Do something about it.'

'You told me to get in the drivers seat! And I can't do anything now, we've got to get to the house Morgan told us about!'

'I only said that because you got to the car first. I thought it would be faster. Guess I just forgot how slowly you drive.'

'A defensive driver always stays five kilometres per hour under the speed limit' Derek recited.

'That's not true at all. And you're a cop. It's scary that you don't know that.'

'Whatever, I can't think right now. I have to pee! Hey, do you think maybe the owners of the house we're going to will let me use their bathroom?'

'Ha ha! Twenty dollars says they won't.'

Grace knew she was entirely devoted to him now. Only two days ago, if she had known there was a conspiracy to kill Honesty, she very well may have joined its ranks. So much clarity had come to her in so little time. It was staggering. Now she knew Honesty was truly a gift to the faith. More than that, she knew he was a gift to the human race itself.

When your mortal comrades want you dead, but your immortal god keeps playing favourites, the path is pretty clear. I only hope when I meet you in person, Friend, that you won't judge my doubts too harshly.

Silent prayer over, Grace turned to Steven again, and again an unbidden grin beamed forth. 'Lisa and Carl said as soon as she left the room to get you, that Fidelity was not coming back. "Fidelity's fidelity is over." Do you think so too, Honesty? Even after she saved our lives?'

'Her path is her own, Grace. Though, I do not think it will stray far from the Friend, no. And remember, she may not have saved us, not directly. Even though Lust and the others tried to kill us, it was in sacrifice that they sought to do so, an effort to bring themselves closer to the Friend. And in saving us, Fidelity simply made a different sacrifice, different offerings on the same altar, so to speak. We can only hope that they all found the Friend in death.'

Grace said nothing for a time, simply marvelling at Steven's wisdoms. He seemed to know so much more now that he had been near death. It made her happy knowing Fort must be someplace better now too. It made her happy she wouldn't have to deal with that twerp anymore too, but he had been young and mentally afflicted, and so she knew that was something she was not supposed to say.

'I think it's about time we go back, now that you're ready, Steven,' Carl said, 'and take audience with the Friend as her full contingent of faithful Companions.'

There were a few pointed emphases on certain words there, and Grace could not help but feel Carl was contradicting Steven. She looked to Steven, ready to back his word, to defend him from the lesser believers. She would be *his* grace and, in so doing, she would be the grace for all humanity.

But if veiled contradictions had been intended, then veiled they remained. Steven simply nodded, accepted the pile of fresh clothes Lisa had for him, and went into the bathroom to change.

They pulled to a stop at a red light—the longest red light Derek had ever seen. He waited, and waited, and waited, and still the light remained red.

'Aaagghh, why won't it change?!' Derek knew they were close. He could see a bike path to the right, past the next exit off the main thoroughfare, and he had a hunch that path led directly to the residential neighbourhood he was heading toward. There was a crowd, where that path met the road, in frantic conversation with a couple pulled-over vehicles. If the situation had not been so desperate, Derek would have insisted in checking on them first.

Though Derek was the one who needed to find a bathroom, Donald was becoming dangerously close to peeing himself in laughter. He had been laughing uncontrollably for most of the drive.

'Just turn on the siren,' Donald suggested, 'get through the red then you can slow down to your precious five kilometres under the limit again.'

The look Derek gave to him then was one of shocked abhorrence. 'I have never done that in my life. Not once. My integrity as a constable of the law would be shattered by an action like that!

'Never, ever, will I use the sirens or lights for my own personal comfort or ease. They are only for emergencies.' He glared at his laughing partner indignantly.

'Never!'

Connie Martin had tried talking to Lisa Kim and Carl Fischer, appealing to them both as the Major Virtues of Comfort and Gratitude and as

Companions, she had tried gently broaching the subject with Honesty, but they were all of them nothing but blind fanatics. *Every last one of them!*

Do you believe in our vision anymore? In our mission? In that faith we had in capital-F Friendship before She came along? Or do you only believe now in that thing *you created out of your own selfish and lost needs for a true leader? And what a leader she makes. All she does is sit around asking questions!*

Well not me! If there are two things I value most in this world, it's my faith and my profession. In that order. But both are predicated on helping this world—saving it from itself—and in that my faith has failed.

I'll take a lesson from lesser virtues on this one, I'll make the patient choice, the courageous choice, and bid you all a fond farewell. But me? I'm done with all of this.

'Goodbye, Steven, Lisa, Carl. Goodbye, Grace, and all those other Minor Virtues in Generosity's basement. And farewell to you, Friend. I am no longer a part of this.'

With that, Connie gave her keys a turn in the ignition, set her hands to the wheel with a sigh, took one last calming breath, and reached for the gearshift.

She hesitated.

From her spot in visitor parking, she had a clear view of the main road running alongside the hospital. At the stoplight there before her was an APS squad car, designation 261: Constables Woods and Philips. Grace had mentioned when Connie first arrived that a constable had called to ask about her graphic design work for Finster and Gable Inc. It was in being hired to draw up that logo that Grace had been introduced to the faith.

Damn! Cooperation and Devotion, you promised there would be no trail!

Connie knew she had an important decision before her. She could warn the Friend, or warn the constables—she was not sure who would be in the most danger if a meeting should occur. But to do so might lead her right back into the Friend's false promises, or to losing her job permanently. Or even worse, perhaps the Friend would somehow sense her desire to leave and devise some wicked punishment of godly proportions.

But she also knew that to simply depart, to ignore it all and leave, would have consequences of its own. To abandon the god she had helped bring into this world, and to abandon police colleagues she had worked with for nearly a decade to a confrontation with each other would be cold and uncaring. She would be actively reinforcing the kind of world she had fought so hard to destroy.

Suddenly the sirens on the squad car flicked on, blazing a trail the vehicle then followed through the red light.

Growling in frustration, Connie slammed the gearshift and peeled out of her parking spot. None of her possible options felt particularly courageous or patient at the moment.

Upon seeing the woman, Jane shoved Morgan behind her protectively. Demir lunged for his wife and took her up in a protective hug. She was practically unconscious on her feet now, but seemed to regain the slightest alertness upon contact with her husband. He looked back to Jane, to help her, maybe protect her from these cultists, but Jane needed no help.

Jane stood her ground in the doorway, matching iron stares with the bloody-handed woman in silence. Distant sirens cut the air and, remarkably, it was the stranger who then backed down.

'Fine. I don't have time for this.' The woman stepped down off the walkway. 'They're all yours, Revenant.' She then led twenty or more people out of the house. Rather than making for the road, they went through the house's back yard, and down into the woods beyond.

Kallista, Pulcherrima, the most beautiful, Epsilon Boötis had become something of an unofficial mascot for the Friend, a celestial body to which the followers of Friendship turned their eyes and prayers. It was talked about casually among most of Her followers, but some took the relationship of their god and that star far more literally than others. Among those who took to the literal belief that this star *was* their god, they pointed out that it looked dimmer now that the Friend had a physical manifestation here on Earth, a major part of that star's power pulled away, diverted to where it was needed most.

Those who had been more scientifically inclined in their view of this relationship knew that Epsilon Boötis was in fact two stars, and looked no dimmer today than last week—barring the clarity of the skies overhead. In fact, regardless of any believer's earthly and fallible perceptions, the brighter of the two celestial entities making up Epsilon Boötis had long ago exhausted its hydrogen core, expanding as its writhing fires continued to swallow all. It was now a late-stage star with more than four times the mass of the Sun, expanded to more than thirty-three times the Sun's radius, and outshining that same Sun more than fivehundredfold.

It was with a fire of comparably staggering proportions that Ana's grief and tears were abruptly burned up in a raging fury, a grim bitterness the only ashes left behind. She rose to her feet, walked past her brother and his wife, past Jane, and into the smoke-spewing house.

That she had never been here before was irrelevant. She could feel her way past every room and twisting hallway. She could feel Milana down in the basement where the smoke was thicker. Ana knelt then, at the base of the stairs, over her best friend's bloodied body. That sense of Milana that she felt deep within her flared brightly and close for just the briefest of moments as Ana touched Milana's non-burnt hand—and in that moment, Ana could have sworn that the smile gracing her friend's face deepened—but then it was gone. It was all gone, that connection to Milana severed completely, like some star shining more than five-hundred times brighter than the Sun burnt its last, and winking out.

Three vehicles made the turn into the cul-de-sac within the span of only a single minute, none of those arriving taking note of anyone who came after.

Constables Woods and Philips peeled onto the scene and the two men raced from the car in opposite directions. Just as they had been about to make the turn-off from the main thoroughfare, Dispatch had reached out about a text message sent to 911. Derek raced for the blue house in the middle of a set of three, hand on his buttoned holster as he went through the already-open door. Donald dashed the other way, across the street for his friend Demir, clearly suffering some distress seated on the sidewalk and cradling his wife in his arms outside of a smoking house.

The next vehicle to arrive was Connie Martin's. Not wanting to draw the attention of her colleagues —spiritual or occupational—she parked her car near the mouth of the cul-de-sac. From there she took in the smoking house of worship and the police arrival. Seeking a better view, Connie left her car, jogging around to the back of the house of Friendship and peered through the windows. Smoke obscured the scene, but she managed to make out a mostly-empty basement, its only occupants four bodies. *Is that one moving?*

Connie flung herself backward as one of the ceremonial braziers came flying through the window, followed shortly after by a young girl who Connie was certain was not among the Friend's congregation. Connie watched, concerned as this young and angry woman, taking no note of Connie sprawled on the snow next to the window, marched with purpose into the woods below the house. Connie debated a moment, cursed, then followed the girl on foot into those woods.

The Companions were the last to arrive, Steven lamenting the loss of his beautiful Aurora—*another*

432

sacrifice, in a way—and being forced to ride along in Gary's van. Grace was similarly displeased, twitching in the backseat the whole ride, nervous to be in a vehicle again so soon after their attempted murder. Steven watched Connie making for the charnel house's backyard—he still refused to think of the profane place as a temple—then watched as she emerged into view shortly after, evidently chasing another woman into the woods below the house. He could feel the Friend was down in that direction as well. *A reunion for you then, Connie,* he gloated. *I knew your path would not take you far from the Friend.*

They all got out of the van together and Steven sent the other two Companions in pursuit of the Friend with promises to be along shortly. Once Lisa and Gary had gone, Steven said privately to Grace, 'Just because our immediate calling, to bring the Friend into the world, has been successful, does not mean we can forget our larger mission. Look how lovingly that couple is embracing there on the sidewalk, at the edge of disaster, staving off despair with nothing more than the comfort they find in one another. Let us see to them. Perhaps, given their present circumstances, they will be open to receiving the Friend's light.

With that, Steven led Grace toward to couple. He assumed they were a from the neighbourhood and feared the fire might spread. Or perhaps they were relatives of the hapless elderly couple who had owned the blue house across the street before the Friend's impending arrival started attracting new followers and they had… *expanded* their real estate. But as Steven neared, he realized that neither was the case, for neither scenario could have justified why the man then left the woman with the newly-arrived police officer, and entered the burning house.

'Stay with the girl, Grace, see if you can't offer some of the Friend's love. My new strength will protect me from the flames.'

'Whatever you say.' *My, she's been far more agreeable today. Miss me in my coma, did you, Grace?*

Steven walked past the crowd at the house's entrance, careful not to make eye contact with the officer who he recognized from his interrogation after Vanessa's death, and followed the man into the burning house.

Steven did a quick jog through the main floor before deciding that the man must have descended into the burning basement. Even with his new god-given strength, Steven's throat and eyes began stinging with the acrid smoke, and it hung so thickly in the stairway that Steven had to go down several steps before making out the silhouette of the man at the bottom.

As Steven reached the bottom of the steps himself, he nearly went back up, for the fire had spread beyond stopping now and, other than the man he had followed down, there was nothing in the basement worth saving. Three bodies were sprawled on the ground here and there: one, dead or unconscious along the far wall; one, blackened and still burning nearish the stairs; and the final one, a young girl with her torso soaked in blood, lying face-up, a smile on her face.

The man stood over that body, looking down on her with no tears, nothing but a kind of grim stoicism, as if in this corpse was all the evil of the world and that this unjust death was a simple reality. Like he had seen and would see often again this most constant companion of life: death.

The perfect state of mind for sharing the Friend's light. So why do I get the feeling that you would be less than gracious to hear an invitation into our circle?

Demir had no words. He stood silently, shoulders heaving with every smoke-choked breath as he seethed, angry, indignant. There was also a modicum of relief, for when first seeing the body of a young girl, Demir had feared it might be Ana. Now where that relief had been, shame was quickly gaining ground.

Oh no, not Ana, let's rejoice. It's only her best friend instead. Only the single living being who seemed able to get through to Ana after our parents died. The only living being to return a smile to a child who had forgotten what smiling was. The only living—

Oh gods, not living anymore…

'Umm… Pardon the intrusion, but I think we had better go. We can't do anything for them.'

Demir had neither heard nor seen the man approaching, but there was no gasp of surprise, no reflexive jump of fear. It was as if even his most primal instincts were wholly overcome, wearied by the sight before him.

'I'm not here for them.' The steadiness of Demir's voice surprised even himself. 'I'm here for my sister.'

When the man spoke, Steven might have shivered if not for the encroaching heat of the now-uncomfortably-close flames. The man's voice was somehow even more grim than his expression, more fear-inducing than that dark cast of his features, that stoic stand wreathed in the fire-lit smoke all around him.

With mention of the man's sister, Steven suddenly had a pretty good idea of who the girl was he had seen Connie chasing after. *If I could somehow convince him that she's not here without raising his suspicions, maybe—*

Oh what does it matter? This is a man's life!

'Before coming in, I saw two women rush out from the backyard, I'll bet one was your sister.'

There was no response from the man, no movement, no change of expression at all. Steven was beginning to suspect the man's grim implacability was in fact a lack of mental acuity. He was about to reach out for the man's arm when a section of the drywall near the far end of the basement came crashing down in a fresh flaring of the flames. Even by the stairs and partially shielded by the man's wide stance, the blast of heat that came forth had Steven cowering beneath his futilely-raised arms.

'That may be so,' the man finally spoke, 'but I cannot leave her here.' For the first time since Steven's arrival, the man looked up and made eye contact. 'Will you help me lift her out of here?' There was the faintest display of helplessness in the request, enough to make Steven's heart ache. He knew he had no choice but to help, but as he looked down on the body in preparation to move it, he froze.

Steven's eyes were locked on that smile, that genuine, heart-warming smile. That familiar smile. *Now where did I...* Realization struck Steven with such a weight that, if the house had come collapsing down in that moment to crush him, it would have felt like a snowflake on the shoulder.

You're the girl, the janitor, from the night with Vanessa. You and your friend were so full of friendship, so inspiring!

What has happened in my absence?

Demir saw some change overtake the man as he looked down at the girl, and he began muttering to himself furiously. When he looked up again at Demir, there was a deep grief in his eyes.

'There has been a terrible, terrible mistake. I can make this right!' he added desperately. 'She will help me make this right!' The man dropped to his knees and launched himself into CPR. Demir had already checked the body for vitals and aside from the lack of pulse, the knife-blade still embedded in her heart told Demir there was nothing he could do. But as the man began pumping away at Milana's chest, something in the way Milana's legs moved, made him drop to his knees and check again.

A pulse! A heartbeat!

Demir knew survival was unlikely with a knifewound to the heart, especially considering Milana was still not breathing on her own, but he also knew there were already police on the scene, paramedics and firefighters would be close behind, and the nearest hospital was practically around the corner. *If we can just get her there, she might have a chance.*

It was then that, with a thunderous crash, the section of ceiling above the stairs collapsed, taking half of the adjacent room with it, and cutting off the way out of the basement, cutting off any means of help reaching Milana.

Demir looked around frantically, feeling trapped. He could no longer see more than a couple metres in front of him with all the smoke. Smoke that should have been painfully filling his lungs and reaching in like sandpaper fingers behind his eyes. Strangely, however, he felt nothing: Discomfort over the smells of burning flesh and melting plastics—which, for some reason were cut a little milder with the scent of roses—and a growing sense of panic over the intensifying heat, but relatively, remarkably, Demir felt the spreading reassurance of calmness.

He then recognized the invisible pocket of moistened air around his head, swirling in tight, imperceptible pulses that kept the smoke out of his eyes and out of the air he breathed. It was something he had not done since his teenage years, since before his father died. With the death of Danylo Richovsky, Demir had let go of that gift being passed on to him.

Memory of those lessons had been a pure thing: irrigating the Winter's runoff for the best benefit of their crops, keeping those streams unfrozen in the coldest months to water the bison, even making use of the hot spring to keep, deep within the woods of their farm, a pocket of healthy vegetation through the Winter. These were memories Demir had buried with his father, having not the heart to carry on the lessons without him. Yet now, with this instinctive act of self preservation, every moment of every lesson seemed at the forefront of his mind, poised to be brought to bear.

Demir looked back from the collapsed section of ceiling to the man performing CPR, his arms now covered in blood to the elbows. *He knows what he's doing. Just keep the fire away, find a path for the paramedics.*

Demir drew deeply from that clean air around his head, widened his stance as his father had shown him a thousand times before, a thousand dead memories ago, and reached out. He extended heart and head, every sense he possessed, seeking any and every trace of that lifeblood of all things: water. He did not have to reach far.

There, beneath the house, next to the house, in the house. It was everywhere, housed in pipes of copper or iron, frozen in the cracks of the concrete foundation beneath him, in the city's line to the cul-de-sac's only fire hydrant two doors down, and it was all within reach. Demir grasped for it, as if his mind and heart had a hand of their own, a hand able to grasp, to mould, and to command water.

Demir pulled up water from the earth beneath them, the pressure of its movement melting ice and frost and adding it to the flood he carried. Decades of frost weathering had covered the house's foundations in hairline fractures like some great spidered tapestry. Demir brought the water into each and every one of those imperceptibly thin cracks, and pushed.

There was a moment of silence as the pressure built up. It was a heavy silence, full, pregnant with a force unimaginable. The other man looked up in alarm, breaking the rhythm of his chest compressions.

'Keep going!' Demir commanded. 'I'll take care of the fire.'

It was almost a gentle process, the way the gravel, sand, and slag aggregate pulled away from the binding cement, allowing the water to slide through. Water which was now several degrees warmer from the pressure of its journey. But any trace of that gentleness was eradicated as the water found—*forced*—its path, surging up through the basement's floor and sawing through the thin layer of carpet to leap upon the nearest flames.

Letting the pressure of its movement syphon more of the water from below, Demir reached out for those other sources. He wielded them like weapons. There was a lancing through the iron joins of piping like they were paper and, in the bathroom upstairs, a leak sprung through the wall. The city's line to the hydrant was solid, the space confined, but the hydrant itself used a clapper valve. Demir pulled the water away from the hydrant, the vacuum drawing the valve open, he then slid a line of water over that valve and held it there, keeping the valve open, and tore the rest of it up and out of the hydrant in a serpent stream to come crashing through the streetside basement window.

Steven watched in wonderment as this man seemed to somehow conjure water up through the very floor of the basement to soak the fires. He brought more in to fight them: down from the stairs and crashing through a window to pounce upon the nearest flames. And through it all, Steven remained dry, the girl beneath him remained dry, and the oppressive heat finally began to abate.

Steven was growing worried. Even with all this progress, even with all his goddess-given strength, he could feel the girl's life force hanging on a precipice between returning stably or slipping away for good. Steven's own strength had already begun to fade. He had cut his palm deeply against the edge of the broken knife blade with his first chest compression, and it continued to bleed freely. It was his own blood as much as the girl's that now covered both arms to the elbows, soaked his shirt, and caked and matted where it splattered up onto his face and hair.

He blinked to find that he had passed out—or zoned out, maybe, as the compressions had not broken rhythm—and looked down to the girl's smiling face. He could not meet that smile evenly. His was an apologetic look, a pleading look.

I don't think I can save you.

The admission was a painful one. As painful as the knowledge that his peers, fellow followers of the god he treasured and adored, had done this.

We are fighting for a world where the kind of rare friendship you displayed with your companion is the norm. We must make sacrifices from within our own ranks, not prey on those without them.

I am truly, deeply sorry, my dear. This never should have happened.

Jane was alarmed by that first display of power. A follower of the very goddess she had come face-to-face with—*and damn my curiosity for nearly being the death of me! ...again!*—using the power of that goddess not to kill, as the goddess Herself had done, but to restore life. *A duel with death itself, you brave mortal. Foolish mortal, for not all are as resilient as I.*

She was even more shocked when the man she had completely dismissed as the smallest of obstacles, a mere crack in the surface of the road she floated over, displayed an immense power of his own, wielded it in terrifying efficiency. She was beginning to think this family would prove more troublesome than anticipated. *At least until he is out of the way. And perhaps our little goddess is just the one to help with that.*

Jane looked on as the fire hydrant tore itself apart, feeding a steady stream of water out from what was now a hole in the earth, arcing gently over a snowbank, and in through the basement window. And she shivered as these two men, each blessed with a titanic might, continued exerting that strength to the point of exhaustion and beyond against the most primal of enemies: one against fire, the other against death itself.

Only one was successful.

CHAPTER TWENTY-FIVE:
Shadow and Water
Friday, 19 February 2021

Ana stumbled and nearly fell when, like a drumming in her own chest, she felt Milana's heart flutter back to life. Or, at least, something like life. Ana had seen the body, seen the broken blade of a knife lodged in her friend's heart and ribs. It was not in some naive dream that Ana worked toward her goals of opening a veterinary practice, whenever she and Milana had the chance, they studied—anatomy, medicine, healthcare in general—and she could recognize fatal injury when she saw it. She knew that Milana's lungs had been flooded, drowned in blood. She knew that, even if her friend's heart began beating again, as it was now, the knife's stuck position would further shred that precious organ with every stuttering beat.

Though Ana could feel life returning faintly to her friend, the girl herself, the *Milana* of her, did not return. And for that Ana was grateful. *You have suffered enough, go in peace.*

She regained her footing, steadying herself against a thick tree trunk, and trudged on through the woods, what had been a run now slowed to a kind of leaping jog in the deep and soft snows here among the trees.

He shoved his hands deeper in his pockets and shivered. With the risen waters of the river, it was much, much colder down in the deep of the valley than it had been on the campus above. Darko moved a little closer to Randy again, hoping they might find warmth in their proximity.

The three friends had continued following the gang of homeless for a few minutes before, impatient with their lack of speed, Maria had cut down a side path to go around them toward the bridge. They were nowhere in sight now, but Darko still found himself looking about nervously for them. He remembered all too well his last encounter with a homeless man on these trails. *If that man had been an omen for my meeting with the impa shilup, what could a whole group of them mean?*

But for every nervous glance, and for every shiver with the cold, the chief occupier of Darko's mind was far more pleasant. He could see their faces quite clearly in his head: three rusalky singing his name and prophesying this flood. Each of the women was beautiful in her own way, but central in Darko's mind, nearest his heart, was not Volkova.

'There's the bridge,' Randy breathed with relief. 'Whoah! Look at the water!'

Darko could not help but look, he stared in awe and a healthy measure of fear. The river had risen indeed. The waters of the Clearwater lapped at the edges of the bridge's platform, the occasional bit of turbulence cresting the steel trim there and soaking the stone surface of the bridge.

'It's lower that the main road bridge,' Maria began, 'I was expecting the water would be high. But not like this! Is it even safe to cross?'

'Well it looks pretty sturdy now, I can't see the three of us making a significant difference,' Randy offered.

With a shrug, Darko slipped past Randy and Maria and led the way to the bridge, eager for the possibility that the three rusalky might show themselves. He had his doubts, there were no telltale flowers along the river's flooded banks, he experienced no lightheadedness, no visions, but as he got closer to the bridge he thought he might have seen the barest shifting of a shadow behind one of the trees on the river's opposite bank, and so hope outshone all his reasoned thinking.

Randy and Maria fell in step behind him, but the three of them had not made it more than ten steps collectively onto the footbridge before a voice began shouting from behind.

'STOP!' it commanded. 'Not one step farther!'

It had been the first night at two Stone Camp not shadowed by loneliness since Rufus's disappearance and, because of that, Mal had looked up to the sky that morning, and given thanks. Then he had set eyes and feet to the earth and gone about following Per's directions, collecting the lost and discarded, and adding them to his family.

Forty-eight they now numbered, and like ghosts the forty-eight of them had set out at long last, weaving through the trees and between the snowdrifts in the river valley toward the footbridge. Mal was not sure what fate awaited them, but he knew that whoever, or whatever, they met at the bridge would pay for what had been done to Rufus.

Despite his best efforts to avoid prejudice, Mal was indeed surprised by the nature of these beasts. *They're just kids.*

Though they were forty-eight individuals with forty-eight life stories, forty-eight reasons for being here in this moment, and at least forty-eight doubts over these same reasons, they were as one. So while Mal dealt with the shock of these three students being the bane of Rufus, it was another from the mob behind who gave the command for them to halt.

On the footbridge. Right where Per said you would be. Like some kind of broken machine his mind took in the vast stimuli all about him, processed it, and in place of reason, in place of a thoughtful course of action, spat out angst and scraps of Baudelaire. It was not for nothing, that people had taken to calling him Mal.

"Lorsque, par un décret des puissances suprêmes, le Poète apparaît en ce monde ennuyé…" *Now why would that, of all the pieces that might have come to mind? Am I the Poet? Are these three?*

He could feel the rage bubbling up, aggravated by the seemingly random recollection of this poem as much as it was by the three individuals before him.

What evil things are you to hide in such innocent-looking bodies? Perhaps it is fear of a miscarriage of justice that makes me unable to move.

'Rufus, how should I—'

He stopped himself from going down that road again. *No. Rufus is gone now. That is why I am here. That is why we are all here. For you, Rufus. And for justice.*

Though he knew the others were fully capable, that simply to look at them in a meaningful way would spur them to action, and though bile, sour and afraid, rose in his throat, Mal took it upon himself to approach the three wicked beings.

'Uhh…hi,' the nearest one offered with Mal's approach. *No doubt you hope that silver tongue might allow you to escape judgement.*

'Hello,' Mal responded flatly. *No need to be rude in the execution of justice. It is in manners that we might keep our humanity.* 'We have come to make you answer for Rufus.'

The confused looks the three exchanged did not deter Mal, not now that he had taken these first steps toward his mandate, toward justice and vengeance. Surely they had rehearsed this reaction many times over. Still, it would not be very meaningful if those responsible did not at least admit to their evil ways. He prompted further.

'I am not surprised by your response, heartless ones. Surely a homeless man meant little to you. Barely batted an eye, probably, before you killed him. It was somewhere in this very valley, this home for all those without, that you destroyed him!'

Mal felt the anger break through his weak hold and he took a half-step forward menacingly. This time he did not seek to quell it, did not think to mask the shaking that took him next. His only thought to the belated arrival of this rage that he would use to destroy those who had destroyed his friend was, *took you long enough!*

At mention of a homeless man being killed in this valley, the farthest of the three, the mop-haired one, betrayed recognition in his glistening eyes.

Gotcha!

Maritsa hung back with her sisters, watching in mild amusement as the scene of a classic mix-up unfolded before them. They had not bothered climbing to land just yet, limited as they were out of the water.

This was too good to interrupt. She would stop it, of course, if things got out of hand… probably.

Leave it to that flighty sky-spirit to agree with us, then ruin any element of surprise in a unilateral attack—though a devastating one to be fair— against the Friend's agents, and then mistakenly turn his gaggle of misfit followers against his own allies! At least, she hoped it was a mistakenly.

Dammit! I wouldn't even put it past you to turn on us now, you unpredictable vulture!

As if reading her sister's thoughts, or perhaps reasoning roughly the same on her own, Rosalia slid closer to the bridge protectively. Her movements did not even disturb the surface above them by so much as a ripple. Not that anyone would have noticed a ripple, given the Clearwater's turbulent state.

Instinctively, Maritsa followed in that nearly-invisible wake under the water, and Omelja was close behind. If one were to enter the fray, they would all do so. No matter how faithful Per's little gang, the three rusalky would have no trouble tearing them apart if it came to that. All forty-eight of them.

Shiloksa shivered involuntarily, and he could feel the derisive whispered hiss of laughter from one of his brothers.

'Gonna piss yourself with all the excitement, Shiloksa, like some of the humans we've taken?' Terullimp asked.

'I can't help it.' Shiloksa was not even embarrassed. 'Since the Friend's blessing, I feel... filled. Full of power, and I'm anxious to unleash it. What's that word the human's use?'

The soft clicking and hissing from the others told Shiloksa they did not know.

'Pregnant!' The word finally came to him. 'I feel pregnant! Ready to give birth to my power!'

'I think that's something else.' Terullimp offered hesitantly. 'I think that's more closely related to our spawning cycles.'

'Gross! And it doesn't matter.' He shook his head, a habit he had picked up from a few of their victims in this world. 'All I'm trying to say is that I'm ready to use these new gifts of the Friend's power.'

He peeked out from the tree's shadow once more, eyes on their quarry. How perfect that what had become their favoured hunting grounds would lead them straight into an opportunity to exact revenge against that pesky riverspawn.

He could feel power emanating from the bridge they watched below. All beings had experienced a deepening of power with the Friend's arrival, even those naive souls who thought themselves powerless. Mere proximity to the god made this section of the world—this world—a little more translucent, bringing all manner of otherworldly powers closer. But what boons the riverspawn might have received with the Friend's coming would be pale, almost invisible, in comparison to an actual blessing from the goddess herself.

Shiloksa knew the impa shilup could win this fight. Even if the two people with their prey happened to also be riverspawn, even if that entire horde approaching the boy aided him in his fight, Shiloksa and his brothers would prove the superiority of shadow.

We are probably strong enough to take on the Friend Herself already!

...Which is a comforting thought, considering we betrayed her orders and abandoned our posts for the sake of this hunt. But we did not declare our loyalty to be bossed around, we did so for an alliance, for mutual benefit. Our amazing gift for Her blessing. And that gift is worth at least a few acts of disobedience.

Smug with the thought that they might one day overthrow their new mistress, and that such a day might not be so far off after all, and thirsty for revenge against this wielder of waters, Shiloksa peeked out from behind the tree once more and looked, really looked, at the scene before him.

'No wonder it's taking so long for them to cross. We're not his only enemies it seems.'

'Hey!' Terullimp called, dangerously loud for a whisper, 'what if they get to him before we do?'

The others all peeked out as well, and started hissing and clicking in alarm. They were all talking so loud, Shiloksa feared they might lose the element of surprise.

'Now is the time, brothers!' Terullimp announced. 'Now we claim our prize!'

'Brother, wait—'

'CHARGE!'

Shiloksa took a moment to react before stumbling into a charge, once again, at the very back of the pack.

Darko would not be cowed, not here in his domain. He continued walking backward slowly, palms outward to appease this horde that would not be appeased. he had tried to explain that he thought he knew who this Rufus was and that he knew the creatures responsible, but his words had fallen on closed ears and closed, fanatical minds.

The leader of this gang had shouted something in French, and his army began closing on the bridge. Darko held his breath, more in anticipation for his own actions than out of a fear of those threatening him, and through puffed cheeks exhaled slowly.

Almost there. Just another step or two…
Nothing.

Or three. And… there! His foot touched water on the surface of the bridge. It was only milimetres deep, puddled in some depression caused by a fault in the stone, but it was deep enough.

He exhaled the rest of his great breath in one great puff as he lifted water from the river around him. Two columns shot skyward in tandem with his furiously gesturing hands. He was not entirely sure if the gestures were needed, but they had helped him thus far, so Darko continued, fearing that to stop might result in soaking himself again.

He twirled his arms, twisting those great columns of water with a dangerous speed. his eyes had been on the water he moved, concentration stealing away awareness of his surroundings, but now he looked before him once more and could not help but grin. The entire, charging horde had stopped dead in their tracks, fear-filled eyes fixed on him!

Fixed on… He tried bobbing his head side-to-side to get a better impression of where in fact they were all looking. *Maria? Behind—?*

Darko spun to see five hulking shadowy shapes descending for the bridge with alarming speed. They had grown since last Darko had seen them and something was indefinably different about the shade of their forms too: not lighter, not darker but somehow, shadowy-er.

Darko did not let fear take hold. He pulled those spouts of water back several metres, coiling them in anticipation to strike.

He never got the chance.

Two of the impa shilup set their first foot on the bridge simultaneously, and before the second fell, a blur rose from the river and leapt over the bridge, the grace of its gentle arc broken only by the act of grabbing the two creatures and dragging them into the river with it.

Though the next two tried to stop upon seeing their fellows disappear, their momentum was too great. As they reached the bridge they too were yanked off of it by blurs of motion, one after the other in quick succession. The last of the impa shilup, farther from the pack and quicker to react, stopped short of the bridge. Even as Darko prepared to unleash his aquatic fury on the creature, a new shadow descended from above.

Unlike the impa shilup, this new beast was wholly of this world. The falcon broke its dive to set its talons deep into the shoulders of the last impa shilup and there was a blinding flash of blue light. When Darko finally managed to blink away the afterimage—an afterimage which showed a great white bird a hundred times the size of the small falcon before him—the last remaining impa shilup was nowhere to be seen.

Perhaps not entirely of this world then.

Maritsa broke the surface again, this time with none of the grace she had shown before. She leapt to the river's flooded bank, standing ankle-deep in the turbulent waters. The snow drift nearest to her began to melt, and the grasses underfoot shook off their Winter brown for Summer's stiff green. She flicked her hand violently, and the last of the greyish shadow—something like the blood of those creatures—dripped free from her fingers. She turned to those on the bridge.

'Put those down, Riverspawn, before you hurt somebody!' She waved her hand to command the water downward, but nothing happened. She masked it as a simple dismissive gesture. It was difficult—and humiliating—to keep in mind that a riverspawn, no matter how raw or unrefined his or her power, had more command over the river than she ever would. She was rusalka, as much a part of the river as the waters. If this riverspawn ever became a riverlord in truth, he would even have command over her.

I'll leave the waters of this river for another before I ever let that happen!

Fortunately, Darko was still far from being a riverlord, and he let the waters fall all around him as commanded. Maritsa noted the subtleties in his actions. Either he had a natural speed for learning, or the Friend's arrival had given him strength unimaginable. He had gone from one who had soaked himself with nothing but a tiny push from one of Maritsa's sisters to one who seemed incapable of relinquishing his control of the waters even if he tried. And as he let the waters fall around him, he let not a single wayward drop find its way onto any of his companions or Per's horde behind him.

When the waters cleared, Darko turned to her saying nothing, simply fixing his eyes on hers with a stupid grin. Rosalia and Omelja rose to her side and they did not have to giggle audibly for Maritsa to know exactly what they were thinking.

One of Darko's companions took a few steps towards them, wonderment on her face. 'You're mermaids!' She gasped.

Maritsa turned her nose up at the girl. 'Does it look like I have a fish tail to you?'

'Well,' this time is was Darko's other companion who spoke, 'it might be hidden under your dress there. I mean, you can't really tell.'

'I will not lift my dress, if that is what you are implying! I am rusalka—river, spirit, woman—no part of me is a fish.'

'Why would you engage them?' Omelja asked annoyed. 'This is a matter of urgency.'

'It is indeed' spoke the the middle-aged man now approaching the bridge where the bird had been, the feather linings of his two coats shimmering lightly in the breeze.

He looked right past those on the bridge toward the crowd of transients. 'I apologize for the wind's changes, Mal, I did not foresee this… efficiency. Though Rufus is avenged, I need your help still. The one that these creatures worked for, to whom they swore their loyalty, is still darkening Acton's skies, still taking lives. Will you stand up for those skies once more?'

'Plonger au fond du gouffre, Enfer ou Ciel, qu'importe?' was his enigmatic answer. Maritsa knew no French, but she knew determination when she saw it, and this man was ready to die for something. She only hoped Per's flightiness would keep them as allies through the fight to come.

'And where do you think you're going?' Maritsa asked. While Per had been speaking, Darko and his companions had slipped past the man and were just starting to make their way up the bank on the bridge's opposite side. 'Surely you do not think your part in this is over?'

'I don't have any idea what *this* is,' Darko countered, 'but we have information about murderers and we have a duty to stop them.' If Darko had tried to sound stern or commanding, he failed completely, the words forming into almost giddy things as they were pushed out through his grinning maw.

Martisa just sighed. Rosalia was far more patient. 'Don't you realize it's all connected? Who do you think they've been performing those murders for? They serve a god they call the Friend. The Friend is, at this moment, approaching the river upstream from here. We would *ask*' and she looked pointedly at Maritsa as she emphasized that word, 'that you would come with us and help restore peace to Acton.

Darko turned back to his friends, not willing to make a decision without consulting them. Fortunately the girl he was with stepped forward in his place.

'Just lead the way!' she offered.

Maritsa liked her already. *Well, aside from the mermaid comment.*

The fire was as good as out by the time the firetruck came peeling into the cul-de-sac only four minutes later. Jane had been able to feel most of what had gone on in the basement, but even for those without an acute sense for power, such as her own, the failed desperate attempt to save the girl's life was written plainly on the faces of Demir and the other man as they emerged from the ruined house.

A minute or two later, after cleared for entry by the firefighters, the paramedics emerged, pants soaked to the knees, bearing the girl's bloody body. Jane watched, curious, as the man that had emerged with Demir did not join them there on the sidewalk, but slowly slunk farther away until, no doubt thinking he was out of sight, the man rushed down the hill behind the house, into the woods after all the others.

Jane looked down to where Demir sat next to Morgan, holding her hands. *Oh not this again! Every time you touch, you start to break her out of my spell! I've about had it with you Demir!*

Morgan was saying something to Demir about his sister, she was still near enough to incoherence that it was no more than mumbled nonsense, 'where… *grbldidred*… Ana?'

Demir looked to his wife for her to repeat her question and, in that moment, Jane made a choice.

Perhaps this goddess can be worked with, after all. Surely a being of such power would relish the chance to defeat a rival like Demir, to consume his soul and all the power within. So it's one fewer victim for me, I still have the three others, mother and children. And as Demir does not share my blood anyway, why should I miss him?

'What's that, dear?' Jane asked as innocently as she could. 'Where is Ana? Well let's go find out.' Jane reached down to grab Morgan by the arm and, in a betrayal of her inhuman strength, yanked the woman to her feet. She set off at a run, dragging Morgan behind her. Morgan could offer no more protest than another quiet, unintelligible mumble.

Though the water had not touched him, Demir felt as though he had walked the floor of an ocean, and he felt an ocean's worth of weight and pressure bearing down on him still. He was sluggish, numbed, his thoughts and feelings far away, beyond reach.

It took Demir several seconds to react. One moment he had been leaning in for a better ear on what his wife was trying to say, the next she was simply gone, being dragged down into the woods behind the house by that vile cousin of hers—and Demir was seriously beginning to doubt they were cousins at all.

When the shock finally wore off enough for him to move, Demir leapt to his feet and turned to Constable Philips, who had not left Morgan's side during this entire ordeal. At least, not until she had up and left his.

'What are you standing around for?! You saw that, didn't you? Unlawful abduction!'

'I thought you said they were cousins?'

'Donald!!'

'Well, go after her, Demir! I can't leave until Derek's back. We'll be right behind you, I promise.'

Stupid police protocol and safety regulations! Demir rose to his feet once more, skirted the flooded section of the yard, crossed the narrow bike path, and descended the rise into the woods. *Gods help me, woman, if you harm her in the slightest, yours will be the next body the EMTs are pulling out of here.*

CHAPTER TWENTY-SIX:
Friend and Water
Friday, 19 February 2021

The Friend had chosen the path toward the river because, after taking a moment to probe for them, she could feel her most powerful servants still living, the five impa shilup brothers on whom she had endowed a potent blessing, in roughly that direction. But as she neared the river, those little lights pinpointing some abstract space in her mental map winked out.

She brought her group to a stop. There was still power off in that direction, but whoever possessed it did not serve her. At least, not yet.

All around they were closing in, from the river below, from her shattered temple above. The Friend felt no fear. She felt excitement, validation, purpose.

Strife. It is who I am. I bring both discord and harmony. I come to this world to shape it, and am cast aside or destroyed when my work is complete. So has it been for thousands of years and so will it be for thousands more.

Not idly had the Friend been spending her hours since her return. She had spent every moment she could spare asking questions, and learning. Each answer, even those hidden behind the vacant stares of a face ignorantly spewing 'I don't know,' brought the Friend closer to learning of the world since she last left and learning of its state now. And she had knowledge unimaginable.

When that time comes once again for me to be ousted, I shall accept my fate with as much grace as my nature allows. But I've only just arrived, my work here is far from finished.

The Friend urged her faithful to action once more. They followed her another hundred or so metres deeper into the valley.

There. Perfectly between them all. Let all come at the same time. Let there be a harmonious meeting to this chaotic encounter. Let them each feel all that I am.

The Friend directed her followers to stand in a rough circle with her as its centre. The snow was shin-deep here, but the Friend barely noticed, her mind was already on the moments to come. Those fateful, charged moments. There she continued to stand, silently, as her followers began to shiver all around her, and waited.

Already too close for the Friend to sense without probing directly, Ana crouched down behind a particularly thick clump of brambles, eyes boring holes into her friend's murderer. She had been intent on accosting this woman, a hound caught the scent of blood, but now that she was this close, she had no idea what to do.

'Hey, you! You killed my friend and I hope you die!' Yeah, real powerful stuff.

She buried her head in her cold hands and wondered what Milana might do were the roles reversed.

The mere thought threatened to overturn the rage with sorrow once more. She would not let it.

The roles aren't reversed. She's dead and I'm here and there's no help in playing hypotheticals, so think, dammit!

Connie Martin lost all sense of the devotee and became every bit of the constable within. She too was crouched and hidden from view. Though she safely chose the deep centre of a copse of thick-trunked trees, Connie was mostly relying on the grey of dusk to hide her presence. She watched the young woman gracelessly bury her head in her hands and was struck with a pang of sympathy so potent it brought with it a physical pain.

She knew she was no longer here to warn the Friend of the police headed this way—surely the Friend would never had needed such a warning to begin with. No, she was here to help this girl. Not to save her, not to give her salvation, nothing so pompous or arrogant. She was simply here to help the girl, whatever that might mean.

She crouched a little lower a moment later as Lisa Kim and Carl Fischer went sprinting by to join their god. *And surely Steven Yung, the Friend's most favoured Companion, is only steps behind you.*

Physical body or not, Jane did not stomp and stumble her way into the valley as the others had before her, she glided down, pulling along her descendent as if Morgan weighed not a thing, just a ghostly burden brought along for the journey.

She was extending her senses to guide herself toward the goddess, true, but she was fairly certain that even without the extended capabilities of her perceptions, she would have spotted the two cowering fools. One was too inwardly focussed to notice much of anything, and the other was too focused on the first to even hear Jane's approach.

There was a third, one that could be felt but not seen, one of power. Jane thought of going after that one. She might not be of Jane's line, but the girl could be used as leverage. However, Jane's very journey into this valley was in the hopes of precluding any conflict with either Demir or the Friend—or, at least her inclusion in any conflict that might take place.

So Jane left the three hiding women to their own devices, started stamping around unnecessarily gracelessly to make her presence known, and approached the Friend.

The Friend felt them before she saw them. *Ha ha, how perfect, how wonderful, how delicious. Now approach, all of you! All of you so desperate to make a mark of significance in your tiny, insignificant lives. You would do better to work in units of several generations rather than single lifespans. Only one of you here sees the value in that, and she's gone so mad, I might just put her down out of pity. So yes, approach, and hear me. For I shall offer the impossible. I shall give you that chance at significance.*

Demir felt her in his head as he was still making his way down the hill. He could not see her yet, but he knew without any doubts who the source of the feeling was. At first it was just a pressure, like a hat bound too tight, but as that pressure grew it also deepened, deepened into full thoughts, voice-like, tracing their way through his mind. His feet stopped moving of their own accord and, exactly one-hundred paces from the Friend, he halted. And listened.

DEMIR RICHOVSKY, YOU, OF ALL THOSE HERE, SURPRISE ME. GIVEN WHAT YOUR FATHER WAS,

GIVEN WHAT YOU MIGHT HAVE BEEN, TO SEE YOU
SUNKEN TO SOMETHING SO LOW IS
HEARTBREAKING. IF ONLY YOUR BELOVED KNEW
WHAT YOU WERE CAPABLE OF; SHE IS A STRONG
WOMAN, AND WOULD NOT SUFFER THIS WEAK
VERSION OF YOU!

Demir had been expecting something along these lines. An effort of whatever this beast of power was to offer something. He had spent four years of university, not to mention most of his childhood, absorbed in the various folklores of the world, and there were maybe a handful of stories across the world's many cultures that included both someone accepting the offer given by a higher power of malevolence and a happy ending. But in the insurmountable majority of those stories, the outcome of such dealings led to a worse fate.

Of course, in the real world, people made those kinds of deals daily. And when they did, in the real world, it was for mutual benefit.

Do not try to tempt me creature, for I shall not be tempted. If you are willing to bargain, than let me save you the trouble by making my demands. I want my family safe. I want them left out of whatever future endeavours you and your followers undertake. I want the police following me to be given the same protection. And, if it is within your power, I want the dead girl, Milana, back.

AN HONEST MAN, A PRINCIPLED MAN. DO NOT
MISTAKE MY ACCUSATIONS AS CRUEL, I SEE MUCH
STRENGTH IN YOU, AND I SEE FULL WELL WHY YOU
HIDE BEHIND THIS CHARADE OF WEAKNESS. IF I
DID NOT KNOW YOU TO BE SO RESOLUTE, I WOULD
SEEK *YOUR* LOYALTY, BUT SINCE YOU WERE CANDID
SO SHALL I BE. EVEN NOW YOUR… COUSIN IS
OFFERING A BETTER DEAL FOR A LESSER PRICE,
BUT OF THE TWO OF YOU, I KNOW YOU WOULD
KEEP YOUR WORD.

LET ME GIVE YOU A COUNTER OFFER—LOOK AT
US, TRADING DEALS LIKE PEDLARS, ONLY OUR COIN
IS BLOOD—I CANNOT GIVE YOU THE GIRL BACK,
SHE IS LONG GONE FROM HERE, BUT I OFFER YOUR
GRANDFATHER, YOUR BELOVED PAPA NATE IN HER
STEAD. I CANNOT GUARANTEE HIS LIFE FOR ANY
SIGNIFICANT AMOUNT OF TIME, BUT I CAN
COMPLETELY, AND SAFELY, REMOVE ALL TRACE OF
CANCER FROM HIM. HE MAY STILL DIE TOMORROW
OF SOME OTHER CAUSE, BUT IT WILL AT LEAST GIVE
HIM A CHANCE. AND IT WILL GIVE YOU ALL THE
TIME TO ADJUST, TO SAY PROPER GOODBYES.

FOR THESE GESTURES OF MY GOOD WILL, I
WOULD ASK YOU TO NOT INCLUDE JANE IN YOUR
REQUEST TO PROTECT YOUR FAMILY. NOT THAT I
FORESEE YOUR PROTESTS TO THIS, BUT HER I
WOULD CLAIM FOR MYSELF.

Demir had been prepared to stand and fight if
this creature did not agree to his exact terms, but

her counter offer was surprisingly generous. True, Morgan might take issue to losing Jane, but for Papa Nate…

Demir took a step forward, closer to the Friend.

Jane was smiling even before the first words reached her mind.

So predictable. You recognize me as revenant, yet forget I've been on this earth for hundreds of years? What gifts would you give to one so generous as I?

So YOU SEEK AN ALLIANCE OF SORTS, DO YOU, REVENANT? WELL I AM HAPPY TO OBLIGE. YOU WOULD GIVE ME THIS RIVERLORD, THIS, DEMIR, AND WHAT WOULD YOU ASK IN RETURN?

Nothing, Goddess. It is an alliance of convenience, yours and mine, and I would not inconvenience you with further demands. You get a powerful soul, and I get the convenience of not having to deal with him on my own. What more could either of us ask for?

AND WHAT OF AFTER THIS NIGHT? AFTER YOU'VE SATED YOUR HUNGER ON THE REST OF THE FULLER LINE HERE IN ACTON, WHAT THEN? SHE HAS PARENTS IN CALGARY. A YOUNGER SISTER TOO. WOULD YOU HUNGER FOR THEM NEXT, OR WILL YOU LEAVE THIS PLACE AS MY DOMAIN.

Consider me gone already, Goddess. It is more satisfying for me to leave some in sorrow. I officially recognize your domain and shall not return once my business here is done. And until then, I shall be as a ghost in the walls. You won't even know I'm here.

The lies came easily to her, her word was as elusive as her ethereal form had been. Jane's next thoughts were for herself alone.

If it were just Morgan's parents I would truly leave. They would hardly be likely to have more children after such a tragedy—and even if they did I could always come back—but to learn of a younger sister, that is something else entirely. I can play the ghost again, I can wait until she marries and has children, stoke the fires of anticipation, whet the appetite, only to strike five, ten years from now. And if this so-called god should come questioning me then, well then our next conversation might be a little more... impassioned.

Darko knew they were close when the first of the rusalky left the water. He knew they could not stay long away from their domain, and so he had looked about more sharply, listened more carefully, for signs of... something. In spite of all his clear expectations of danger, he really had very little idea of what exactly they were walking into. Not that

472

he let it bother him overmuch, of course, standing as he was this close to not-Volkhova.

Maritsa, he sang to himself. She had finally revealed her name, and what a beautiful one it was. *Maritsa.* It was a name he could see himself saying for the rest of his life. Before he knew it, his sharpened senses were once more turned inwards, not searching for signs of danger, but exploring the possibilities of the future.

Can there be a life for a man and a rusalka. Could she even see me in that way? Would she be willing to try such a life? These were the thoughts on Darko's mind when, just starting up from the river's edge, some new sensation slammed into his mind, shattering his present thoughts.

HELLO, DARKO RICHOVSKY. LOVESICK, WORRY-RICH DARKO RICHOVSKY.

Uhh, hello?

...Mom?

NO, MY DEAR, I'M AFRAID NOT. THOUGH, SAD AS IT IS, I'M NOT SURPRISED YOUR MIND WENT THERE. I AM CALLED THE FRIEND, AND YOU ARE ON YOUR WAY TO DO BATTLE WITH ME. BUT I OFFER YOU A DIFFERENT SOLUTION. A SOLUTION OF PEACE.

I DO NOT WISH TO PLACE THE BLAME ON ANY INDIVIDUAL OR GROUP, BUT THERE IS ENOUGH MISUNDERSTANDING IN THIS VALLEY TO DROWN

ALL OF ACTON. I AM NOT EVIL. HAVE YOU EVER
KNOWN ANY BEING WITH A NAME AS INNOCENT AS
THE FRIEND, TO BE ANYTHING BUT BENEVOLENT? I
CAN BRING PEACE TO ACTON AND, DARKO, I CAN
BRING PEACE TO YOU.

He dared say nothing, dared think nothing. He
was not sure what this being was, but if it was in
his mind, nothing would be safe.

I KNOW WHY YOU STRUGGLE TO SLEEP, I KNOW
WHY YOU PUSH AWAY EVERY WORRY, FEAR, AND
PROBLEM IN YOUR LIFE, I KNOW WHY YOU SHOVE
IT ALL DOWN AND TRY TO BURY IT. IF I REMIND
YOU NOW THAT YOUR GRANDFATHER IS DYING,
YOU CANNOT DISGUISE FROM ME THE REFLEX OF
SURPRISE THAT BETRAYS YOU. YOU PUSH IT ALL
DOWN SO DEEPLY YOU WILL NOT EVEN
ACKNOWLEDGE HIS STATE!

Darko was speechless, not that he would have
said anything either way, but it was true, her
mention of it had not incited a remembering, it had
incited a fully new realization. He had indeed
pushed the reality of Papa Nate's condition clean
out of his mind. He wondered if there were other,
worse matters he had repressed so deeply they were
now gone completely.

DO NOT DESPAIR WITH THE REALIZATION,
DARKO. IT IS BUT THE FIRST STEP TO HEALING.
AND IN YOUR CASE THE SOLUTION IS A SIMPLE
ONE. IT'S ONE AS OLD AS TIME ITSELF. AT THE

CORE OF ALL THE REASONS YOU SUPPRESS THESE
FEARS, WORRIES, PROBLEMS, IS THIS: LONELINESS.

YOU ARE LONELY, DARKO, BUT I CAN GIVE YOU
MEANING. I CAN GIVE YOU SOMEONE WHO WILL
LOVE YOU, WHO YOU CAN SHARE ALL THESE
FRIGHTFUL THOUGHTS WITH. EVEN MORE
FULFILLING, IT WILL BE SOMEONE FOR YOU TO
LOVE RIGHT BACK, SOMEONE WHOSE MOUNTAIN OF
WORRIES AND FEARS YOU CAN CLIMB IN RETURN.

I OFFER THIS FREELY, DARKO. LET ME SHOW
YOU JUST HOW GREAT OF A FRIEND I CAN BE.

Darko found himself taking a steady, climbing
step up, away from the river, toward the source of
these grand promises.

They were individuals and yet, through the
Clearwater they were one. Though each had
spoken of going off to new waters one day, they
each knew none could leave while the other two
remained. To do so for any of them would not just
be leaving a friend and sister behind, it would be
leaving a part of herself behind—two parts. One
simply could not sustain such a loss and remain
even one-third whole. So, although Maritsa felt the
Friend only in her own mind, she knew the exact
words and visions were being given to her sisters as
well.

YOU HAVE EVER BEEN SERVANTS TO BEINGS OF GREATER POWER BUT LESSER STRENGTH. IT TAKES A WOMAN TO COMPREHEND THE FULL MEANING OF THAT STATEMENT. EVEN NOW, WITH ACTON'S LITTLE RIVERSPAWNS ALL AROUND ME HERE, YOU WOULD HAVE THEM DO YOUR BIDDING, BUT CANNOT. YOU REMAIN RELIANT ON THEM. AND IF YOUR PLIABLE LITTLE DARKO HERE SHOULD ONE DAY BECOME A RIVERLORD, YOU WOULD HAVE EVEN LESS FREEDOM, AND NEVER MIND THAT IT WAS THE THREE OF YOU TO BRING DARKO INTO SUCH POWER. THAT IS THE SIMPLE REALITY, THE HARSH REALITY OF YOUR WORLD.

I AM THE FRIEND, SOWER OF DISCORD AND BRINGER OF HARMONY. THESE TWO NEED NOT BE, AND RARELY ARE, DOLED OUT IN EQUAL PORTIONS. LET ME SHOW YOU THE LATTER. LET ME FREE YOU. I WOULD NOT ASK YOUR SERVICE IN RETURN, FOR THAT WOULD HARDLY BE A TRUE FREEDOM. I ASK ONLY FOR PEACE, FOR HARMONY IN TRUTH. I ASK THAT YOU REEVALUATE THIS SITUATION YOU HAVE SO GRAVELY MISREAD. ALLOW ME TO BE *YOUR* FRIEND AND MAKE *YOU* TRUE RULERS OF THE CLEARWATER.

As one, the three rusalky strode forward.

Per was already back in his consistently-favourite form, the peregrine falcon. Expecting what was coming, he alighted on a rather comfortable-looking limb of a snow-dusted elm. Unlike most of its neighbours, this tree, and this limb especially, had retained many of its leaves into winter. Those leaves caught on the wind now, bowing the tree gently, taking Per to a distance of exactly one-hundred human-paces from the Friend who stood below. Her presence filled his mind.

I CONFESS, I FIND MYSELF SMILING TO FEEL YOU HERE, SKY SPIRIT. IN ALL MY INCARNATIONS, NEVER HAVE I BEEN CROSSED SO OPENLY, SO HONOURABLY. I MUST ADMIT, I AM OUT OF MY DEPTH IN THE FACE OF SUCH TREATMENT. OF ALL THOSE PRESENT YOU HAVE DONE THE MOST TO WRONG ME, AND YET, IT IS FOR NONE OTHER THAN YOU THAT I FEEL THE STRONGEST RESPECT. IF YOU WOULD HAVE MY PEACE, I SEEK TO GIVE IT.

I WONDER ONLY WHY A SPIRIT COMMANDING SUCH RESPECT IS GIVEN SO LITTLE IN RETURN. YOU NEED A PERMANENT SET OF FOLLOWERS SO YOUR POWER CAN BE CONSTANT. I SHALL RID YOU OF THIS WAXING AND WANING. I SHALL DEDICATE A SUBSET OF MY OWN FAITHFUL TO YOUR WORSHIP AND SERVICE. NO LONGER A PLASTIC BAG, A PIECE OF REFUSE, FLOATING ON THE WIND, YOU WILL BE THE FALCON YOU EMBODY IN TRUTH! YOU HAVE EARNED NO LESS.

Per was not one to make decisions so quickly, nor with such finality. At that moment, the wind strengthened, pushing the branch he occupied onward, closer to the Friend, and in that Per had his answer.

Being too close for the Friend to sense beyond her own aura of power and being visibly hidden from the goddess's eyes, Ana was effectively invisible to the goddess. She was not approached with offers in the same way as so many others and had, in fact, no idea that so many others were indeed approaching in that moment.

Ana's mind had been warring with itself over what to do? To charge senselessly at the wall of the woman's fire-eyed followers? At the woman herself? To throw a rock as hard as possible and hope it would draw blood? There was nothing in Ana's power she could do as suitable answer for what had been done to Milana. And, Ana was beginning to realize, even if she had all the power in the world, there was nothing at all that could suitably answer so terrible an act.

She turned to leave, to slink away, when her eyes caught movement from up the slope, back the way she had come. She saw Jane there, taking a slow, dramatically purposeful step closer. In tow was Morgan, looking drunk or drugged, slack-jawed, dull-eyed, and barely coherent.

Ana had felt the pain of tragedy before. The deaths of both her parents, the family dog, Yurko, her kindergarten teacher, Mrs. Rahn. And with each new death, she had withdrawn further and further within herself and, with the lone exception of Milana, the only people she had been able to turn to were family.

Family really is everything, just like Papa Nate's always saying. And this woman, this thing, *cousin or not, is no family to Morgan. There is no way this is the pain meds or the head injury. Not this bad, and not to Morgan. She was practically as good as new this morning, and she said she was going to stop taking the meds. Who the hell is this bitch?*

They were too far yet for Ana to confront the woman directly, but she would not let anyone mistreat her family in any way. Not ever again. Outside of Milana, Morgan was the closest thing to a sister Ana had ever had, and legally speaking at least they were sisters in truth. Ana tried to reach out for Morgan the same way she had to Milana, to *feel* her sister-in-law as being at her side, speaking with her.

Perhaps it was made easier by her anger, still burning hot and strong beneath a layer of calm resolution, or perhaps it was made so by the fact that she could see Morgan, partially, through the brambles and branches up the slope, whatever the cause, Morgan suddenly stood straight, arresting Jane's momentum completely. She looked down the slope at Ana and despite the distance, there was eye contact there. A deeper connection too.

'*Morgan, wake up! Who is this woman?*'

'*Ana! I can't… It's so slow. Please.*'

Ana was not sure exactly what she did next, she was fantasizing punching Jane in the face, as much over the loss of Milana—which, to be fair, Jane had nothing to do with—as over what seemed to be some kind of drugging of her sister-in-law. She had only imagined the punch, two or three different ways, sure, but watching from her position, Ana reeled to see Jane physically knocked to the ground as if struck in the face.

The moment the woman's hand was wrenched free from Morgan's with the force of the blow, a visible change took hold of Morgan. She turned to her side and called out.

'Demir?!'

It all came crumbling down so quickly. Such a harmonious meeting so callously shattered into chaos by the smallest oversight. *Another riverspawn? What, are you hatched from eggs in a streambed, how many of you are there?!*

I offered an accord, and you have collectively chosen discord. So be it. I am master of both domains.

Though it certainly helped, the Friend needed no sacrificial dagger to inflict harm. She was the goddess of strife and harmony, and what greater cause of strife is there than death. She could, given sufficient effort, deal death itself. She was reaching out for the youngest of the riverspawns with that very intention when the first column of water slammed into her chest with the force of a racing firetruck. Before she could recover enough to focus on the girl again, the Friend was hit by four more streams of slightly lesser force.

Carl Fischer, like all the Major Virtues, had been given a SIG P-something-or-other handgun as a tool to use in their worship. Finster and Gable had covered the costs and the legalities, or illegalities, as he expected, of the whole thing. He had not fired his once and, aside from handling the safety, all he really remembered was that it held ten rounds.

Lisa Kim stood at his side, her pistol also in hand. They had been strictly instructed not to harm anyone about to join them in the valley when they arrived to join the Friend here, but now that water cannons were attacking their god from every direction and a horde of what looked to be mostly angry transients was charging in their direction, Carl presumed this might be an acceptable exception. Connie was probably long gone, having abandoned them. Steven still hadn't arrived, and the Friend only knew where Grace was—not that Carl really cared, the woman was only a Minor Virtue after all—so for now, he and Lisa were alone. Two senior clerics among a mob of lesser, and some brand new, acolytes.

He did some quick math in his head, with twenty rounds between them, at the absolute most, they could stop twenty of the onrushing attackers. That was not exactly a comforting accounting, for it appeared to be fewer than half of those bearing down on them.

Math be damned was about the only cogent thought outside of pants-wetting panic that he managed to get out—alongside only four bullets—before the first of the attackers reached him. She was middle-aged, might have been pretty with more hair or a cleaner face, but as her fist met his skull he decided looks weren't everything. He dropped his gun, curled into the fetal position, and braced his hands over the back of his neck and head protectively.

Mal had led the charge himself. 'Big cheque or little, we're all payed beneath the same sky,' he had reminded his companions shortly before they arrived. They were fitting last words to those who had been his family in his last days. He saw only two guns among their enemy, and only ten or so pairs of eyes with a fighting spirit behind them. For a moment he had felt invincible. He covered forty, fifty, sixty metres as three bullets went whizzing by: a tree somewhere nearby splintering with the impact, the whistle of a bullet going harmlessly past his ear toward the great vault above, the sharp slap of one hitting the river behind them. Alas, the sound of the fourth bullet was far less poetic, it was a solid, tearing, wet thing as the bullet found Mal's heart.

The impact sent him tumbling on the slope so violently he heard a bone snap before his body came to rest, face-up, beneath a tree.

The view made up for that bullet. It was spectacular.

Mal could almost forget the fact that he was dying with the image before him. The cold, winter air gave the darkening sky something of a crisper image. Ocean-deep blues and saint's-robes greys swirled above, telling a most dramatic tale in their travels. He fancied himself up there, among God's own colours, amid this painting by the Creator's own hand.

'Le ciel est triste et beau comme un grand reposoir.'

The man—*the bird?*—called Per had not exactly been forthcoming in his details of what would await them farther along the river, but everything he had said, Darko realized, as enigmatic as it was, had so far proven true.

'You will arrive to a delay.' Check.

'The sky always asks too much.' Well, if by that you mean, you, then yeah, I think sending those people charging into a hail of gunfire was a little excessive, don't you?

'You will offer water to a friend.' Needlessly cryptic, but sure, check.

'The Friend's arrogance will cause her to ignore most attacks, she will only go after the strongest first.' Well, that sounds pretty straightforward, but I guess we'll have to see.

Darko was hurling as much water as he could, with as much force as he could, and still it was almost laughable how easily one of the others took not only his, but all five streams of water, twisting and cavorting them into knots before they each slammed into the Friend from a different direction. He figured it was an effort to disguise who was responsible for that largest, most powerful stream of water, though since it had been the first to hit and from farther up the valley, Darko was not convinced it would be an effective effort.

Given his brief encounters with the rusalky and hazy memories of watching his brother and father out practicing their *irrigation exercises* on the farm,

Darko had a sinking feeling he knew who was responsible for that fifth stream of water. And this was one worry he would not push down, not force out of his mind. Instead he used it, he used all his fear that the Friend, who moved so easily beneath their collective blasting of her body, was even now moving to attack the strongest among them. And so he fought to be that strongest one.

He did not fear the consequences should he succeed, that was an easy fear to keep out of mind, only those should he fail.

Demir was ashamed. Ashamed that he had been considering betraying his principles for a few more years with his grandfather. He knew that, regardless of his intentions in such a bargain, if Papa Nate had ever heard about it, he would have chastised Demir heavily for his lack of conviction. He channeled that shame, his love for Papa Nate, for Morgan and Ana who were rushing toward each other through the snows on the slopes, his love for his kids at home, and for Darko, wherever he may be. He channelled it all into a more violent use of his abilities than he had ever thought possible. Were it not a god in that body, bones would have broken with that first impact of water to chest.

Yet, as strong and violent as the force of his attack was, one of the other beings likewise wielding water against the Friend had both strength and finesse enough to take the water he brought to bear from the snows in the valley above him and twist it amongst the other streams, knotting them around the Friend. It was a humbling strength.

Maritsa launched herself in the wake of the water she pushed, landing upslope from the Friend. She continued hurling her power with all her might while simultaneously suppressing the powers of Darko and Demir. *'The sky always asks too much.' Well, here it is Per. I just hope you're right.*

The Friend had been wrong about one thing. A riverlord, certainly could have dominion over rusalky, but it was not dominion taken by force, it needed to be given willingly. Without the river's cooperation, a riverlord would be lord over no more than a puddle with a current. And in their combined effort, Maritsa and her sisters had no trouble suppressing the powers of the two riverspawn wielding water alongside them.

Maritsa was impressed with Darko though, she had not expected him to have understood Per's cryptic advice. *'The sky always asks too much.'* Yet here he was, weaving their respective attacks to disguise the source of each one. *A brave little gambit, Riverspawn, for it could lead this god into attacking you by mistake.*

The Friend knew she was outmatched when Per, *that squirming, lowly worm,* unleashed something like lightning into the knot of water slamming into her. She could barely think of turning this around on her attackers, using every shred of the power she possessed just to keep this body alive.

Outmatched or not, She knew this group would fall with the simplest push. They needed only to lose a being of power, one who gave them hope, confidence they could win. If the Friend could crush such a being, then the will of the others to continue fighting would likewise be crushed.

She would have gone for Per if she knew where he was in that moment. Instead, she took of the power she was using in shielding herself to probe for him. Despite her efforts, not to mention the pain that her weakened shield allowed to break through, she could not feel a single bird around her, not for a hundred paces in any direction. Without Per as an option, she settled for the second strongest among them, the one who had first attacked her so boldly.

DO NOT TAKE COMFORT THAT YOUR DEATH WILL BE A NOBLE ONE, DEMIR RICHOVSKY, FOR WHEN I AM FINISHED WITH YOU, I SHALL TAKE YOUR SISTER AND I SHALL CORRUPT HER TO MY CAUSE! YOUR WIFE, YOUR BELOVED, STRONG WIFE WOULD RESIST SUCH CORRUPTION, AND SHE HAS NO AILING GRANDFATHER FOR ME TO USE AS LEVERAGE, SO

HER I SHALL USE TO FEED MY POWERS. I SHALL
CONSUME HER SOUL, DEMIR! GIVE UP,
RIVERLORD! SURRENDER, AND I MAY YET FIND
SOME MERCY IN MY HEART.

They were, each of the water-wielding whelps,
so wreathed in the weapon of their wielding, so
wrapped up in spouts of whirling water, that the
Friend could not even see Demir. But sight is the
crutch of lesser beings, and the Friend was certain
it was him from the power of his attacks.

She divided her power then. As much as
possible she kept her defences intact, but with
every other fibre of her being she wrought death
down upon the creature before her.

It was slow at first, and she felt one of her own
ribs crack beneath the pressure of her attackers
before seeing any results. A moment of sustained
effort later, some of the water hitting her sputtered,
then halted completely. There was a great splash as
the figure before her collapsed, and the weight of
the attack on her weakened. She used a bit more of
her strength then to move, rushing to the sight of
her victim's fall. She would look him in the eyes
with his dying breath if she could. And she would
smile cruelly at him.

The Friend covered only half of the distance
before she stopped, feeling the being's life leaving
completely. But even from this distance she could
see, as the splashing water settled, golden hair

flowing out from the head of her victim up the slope.

'LIES!' she hissed.

The attacks did not stop then as she had expected, they redoubled. It was as if the power of her assailants had before been suppressed somehow, but now it hit with full force.

Another rib racked, then a third. Per's lightning-like force attacked again, charring her flesh, and rattling through Her to the bone. The pressure was unbearable.

With an audible *CRACK*, the Friend's spine snapped, and the body she inhabited collapsed, utterly destroying her earthly presence not for the first time. Nor for the last.

Unnoticed by any around, Mouse scurried away from the body of Maritsa. It had been Per's idea, the knotting of the streams of water to confound their sources, and Mouse had agreed. The price was indeed too heavy, though, he supposed, somewhat of an inevitability.

Without Maritsa around, the balance of the forces around Acton would be thrown off, the banks of the Clearwater would not just swell in the coming days, they would rage. But those were the worries of greater beings, not of Mouse. So he scampered along, across the scene of the battle, past the body that had once held the Friend, and into a tiny burrow in the now conveniently-thawed ground.

'Like knucklebones in palms,' he squeaked, before disappearing.

CHAPTER TWENTY-SEVEN:
Blood and Water
Friday, 19 February 2021

Steven Yung had only sought to restore a warmth to the world, to give people back the friendships that mankind had once known. He had known there would be a heavy price: he knew that with his brother, Daniel; with his fiancée, Vanessa; with no fewer than four of his fellow Major Virtues —five if he included Empathy whose body the Friend had needed as her own—but he had never expected the price to be *this*. And in this price, Steven did not know whether it was success or failure he faced.

I brought her here, I was nearly face-to-face with her. She was here on Earth as I envisioned. But for mere days? What consequences can that have had other than these bodies before me and in my wake? Where is the warmer world? Where is the harmony You were to bring with the strife? Have I been the cause of all this?

Despite the shocking display of violence in their attack, and in spite of their losses sustained, the homeless were surprisingly gentle in their subsequent subduing and makeshift-arresting of the Friend's faithful. Honesty walked unsteadily down the valley, now slick with melted snow, toward them, hands outstretched and together, in a sort of 'capture me' gesture.

Grace supposed it was only her zealous pace that had allowed her to arrive before the others, and it was perhaps the specificity of that same zeal that made her hide rather than join the Friend's circle of faithful. She was devoted to this cause, she knew, but she was having an increasingly difficult time reconciling this cause, Honesty's cause, with that of this woman who called herself the Friend. And yet, Grace had grown accustomed to the habit of serving. So she stayed crouched, head buried in her hands, unable to decide.

She might have been lost completely, she might have gone charging in to the defence of those recalcitrant pretenders, had it not been for Fidelity. *Dear, sweet, Fidelity, you have saved me. I should never have doubted you, only the falseness of those who claimed to support the same cause as you, as us.*

Connie Martin had come forward out of her own hiding place to embrace Grace just as she had been about to charge into certain death. But now it was Grace's turn. She barrelled into the side of Steven, pulling him down behind a nearby tree. *I will be your grace as Connie was mine.* He stared up at her in confusion.

'Do not give yourself up to them. This facade of a church, this hypocrite's haven is no more, but we, us, our pure cause is yet whole. Let us get away from this place, from the memory of these sanctimonious sons of bitches and start anew. It is just us now, Grace and Steven and the ever-faithful Connie. She will join us later and we shall talk, but for now we must leave this place.

Steven followed along numbly, not saying a word.

What better way to be reinstated than helping to catch those responsible for the largest murder-spree in Acton's history? Oh yes, Constables Woods and Philips, I followed the clues and here I am! Toss me a pair of those handcuffs, and I'll clap up this one's hands for you. He shot the dead one by the tree over there, I watched it happen.

Connie Martin fell in place without any suspicion. Suspension or not, all hands were needed now. She helped to arrest the Friend's faithful. And they were so faithful, or perhaps just so numbed by the experience, that not a single one of them attempted to accuse her of being among them.

Connie could not help but be a little hurt by that. *I was among you! I was among the best of you! I still am, that's why I'm here handcuffing you, instead of the other way around. Now you better*

493

break that judging gaze before I start breaking fingers!

Once she had finished with the handcuffing and the hesitant, low-key interrogation from Donald and Derek, Connie worked to help the victims. She had decided she could much better serve the cause as a member of the police force. Her first sign of trouble should have been when her faith and job became at odds with one another. She would never let the two clash again. They would be one. *They are one.* When she had a chance to meet with them later, she, Grace, and Steven would have a long talk about just what their cause could accomplish next.

For the number of people involved and the peculiarity of the case, the Richovskys, Randy, and Maria had been allowed to leave surprisingly soon after Woods and Philips had arrived on the scene. The two remaining rusalky had taken Maritsa's body into the river with them shortly after the Friend was defeated, not giving Darko a chance to say goodbye. There was no trace of Jane, and for the better since Morgan was noticeably recovered now that she was gone from her side.

Together, the six of them took Demir's van in silence to the closest place they might find respite, Darko's apartment. Not a single word had been said on the journey. Each of the Richovskys seemed too exhausted to even stand up straight—

Randy had had to drive. But even Randy and Maria were so numbed by the experience, shocked by the violent charge of the homeless against the fanatics, by the bullets hitting trees to either side of them, that they too were without words.

Demir was trying desperately not to think about it, but his mind was relentless in its pursuit of answers. *She was an old spirit for sure, probably a god at one point in her past—she certainly had the arrogance of one. No matter what she might have been claiming, she was no god this evening or, if she was, she was in the weakest, fledgling state possible. Days old in her corporeal manifestation. At the most.*

And which god then? Promises of peace, an affinity for chaos? Could it be Eris, I wonder? There was a faux-cult of Discordianism formed in the '60s. I guess this could be some odd corruption of the same movement?

Though he kept insisting to himself that it was over, that he should be focussing as much as possible on Morgan and forgetting all of this, he already had three books in mind to crack open and rifle through upon his return home.

Demir and Morgan had been in the back of the van together with Ana seated between them, but now that they were out of the van, crossing the street to enter Greybrick House, he and his wife shared a silent, meaningful hug before following after the others.

Maria averted her eyes from the embrace. *That's a private moment between a woman and her husband, not for me to gawk over.* She felt supremely uncomfortable in this company. It wasn't the people—she loved each and every one of them to bits—it was the fact that they had just left a scene of supernatural wonders and grisly murders. And at least one of those murders had been partially at the hands of one of her best friends. She did not doubt that there was a good reason, but it was not a reason she had yet heard, and until she had some real, meaningful answers, she was certain this sickening feeling in the pit of her stomach would persist.

Maria was the first to reach the door after Darko unlocked it, so she held it open and waited for the others to file through. She pulled out her cell phone and called her dad as the others passed.

'*Slukhayu*!'

'Dad?' She really didn't feel like making the effort to speak Ukrainian at the moment, and her father must have heard something along those lines in the tone of her voice.

'Maria, is everything okay?'

'Everything's fine, Dad. I was just wondering if you could maybe give Randy and I a ride home. The busses are all over the place today with the bridge being closed and we don't really want to wait.'

'Sure thing, Sweetie. Are you on campus still? Isn't it a bit late?'

'No, we're at Darko's. You remember where it is, right?'

'Sure do! I actually was just about to leave the office, so I can be there in ten minutes or so. How does that sound?'

'Perfect. Thanks, Dad.'

'*Pa-pa, Serden'ko!*'

Maria breathed a sigh of relief. *At least that's taken care of. Ten minutes here in awkward silence, or maybe some answers if people feel like talking—I won't push Darko until he's ready—then I can forget about all of this, for the night at least.*

Maria was the last to go through the door into the apartment and in a corner, by a closed door at the end of the hall, she saw a very old looking cat. She wanted to rush over and pet it, but she could hear shouting from behind the door it paced in front of, and fear stayed her hand. With a sigh, she turned away and followed the others up the stairs.

Darko felt frayed, like a ragged and weak rope about to snap. When the Friend had spoken to him in his mind, there had been a sort of connection of souls. He had felt all the things she was and, he was sure, she had felt the same in him. He knew she was indeed a creature of wickedness and that, in part, made the fact that he had destroyed her somewhat easier to bear. But he had also felt goodness there. She really did want to make the world a more love-filled place.

Greater love, greater hate, an increased intensity to all things, or less of both? Who's to say which is right or wrong? Who's even to say which is better? It had not been a matter of putting down something evil to him, it had been personal, defensive. Once he had felt Demir there in the valley and known that he would likely be the first the Friend would attack, Darko had seen but one course of action. And yet, he suspected that on some level the Friend had not been destroyed. Defeated sure, but somewhere, somehow, some part of her was left, and so there was no guilt over his actions, just the uncomfortable weight of responsibility.

Darko led the way up the stairs, the others following behind silently. He knew it wasn't fair to Randy and Maria that he had not said a word to them since they had left the valley, he knew that as soon as they were in his apartment he would have a lot of explaining to do, but still, he had not been able to bring himself to speak. Which made it worse, probably, that the first phrase he uttered, as he reached his floor to see his apartment door splintered and slammed open, was a thoroughly drained, 'kill me now.'

The hug they shared outside the van seemed to physically heal her. She poured all the grief of the past few days into that embrace: the fatigue, the frustrations, the injury, the confusion. All of it, she had come to realize, had been caused by Jane. At their first meeting the woman had spoken of seeing entire lines of her descendants being wiped out and Morgan was beginning to fear that Jane might have been the primary agent of, rather than mere witness to, those tragedies. *She claimed to be here to protect me, but if she was around protecting all those others, then how could they have come to meet their ends? I should have seen this sooner!*

It took considerable effort not to disparage herself into a state of self-pity, but she knew that doing so would only be counterproductive. So she told herself that, as a supernatural being, Jane likely had a supernatural ability to fool her. *And who knows, maybe it's even true.*

Thinking so heavily about Jane as she made her way up the stairs in Darko's apartment complex, Morgan did not notice at first, the presence of the woman in the back of her mind. It was not until hearing Darko's outburst and reacting with immediate protective worry, that she recognized that faint sense.

'It's Jane!' she shouted from the stairwell.

At hearing the warning, Ana pushed her way past Randy and Darko and ran for the opened door. Her brothers were exhausted, wiped out, they had avenged Milana, they had brought some semblance of justice back into the world. They had protected her and the memory of her friend. Now it would be her turn. She had attacked Jane before and she would do it again.

'Who's Jane?' she heard Randy ask confusedly from the stairs. 'And where did that cat come from?!'

But she was no longer listening. From the open doorway, she could see Jane standing at the opposite end of the apartment, in front of the table.

'Did you think you could get away so easily? Did you not think I would follow you here?' Jane seemed to be speaking generally, but then she took a step forward and looked directly to Ana. 'You can go, dear. I'll even let your brothers and all your little friends go too. Just let me take my daughter with me. Let me have my Morgan.'

'You won't take anyone!' Ana imagined punching the woman again, harder than the time in the valley, but aside from a little flinch, the woman gave no reaction.

'Oh yes, that was quite surprising out there in the woods, but it will not work again.' Jane continued advancing toward Ana and, swallowing hard, Ana stood her ground. 'I outmatch you, all of you.' Jane's voice crescendoed to shouting. 'Both mentally and physically, I am a giant alongside the likes of you! Stand aside or be crushed underfoot!' Ana fell back half a step in spite of herself and remained frozen there. As Jane reached her, the woman flashed Ana an arrogant smile and pulled back a balled fist in preparation to strike.

The blow never fell. As Jane's arm came swinging forward it was batted aside by another. An old man's arm, covered in wispy hairs of snow white and ash grey met the woman's blow with impossible strength. Surprisingly gently, the man strode by Ana, pushing her aside with his other arm before using that arm to grab Jane by the throat.

'You are not welcome here.' Though his voice was rasping and raw, the tone was gentle, forgiving. 'I shall give you one chance to leave now, I suggest you take it. If not, I shall force you out.

'Unhand me, Hob! I am no mere ghost you can simply cast out, I am a revenant! I shall destroy you, I shall bring this entire dwelling to ruin, if you provoke me.' Jane slammed aside the old man's throat-grabbing hand with one arm, breaking his grip, and with the other she struck violently at his torso.

The old man seemed to somehow bend around the blow. Twisting with the momentum, he came to a stop behind Jane, where he placed an open palm against the back of the woman's head. There was a great sound like a shout, though it seemed to come from that upraised hand rather than the man's mouth, and suddenly Jane's eyes rolled shut, the blood drained from her features, and she collapsed to the floor.

Ana's eyes were glued to that body, it looked nothing like Jane anymore. It was a not a body recently left by the living, it was a years-old corpse, with terrible burns scarring most of the rotted flesh that remained. So enrapt was Ana by the sight that she took no note of the old man stepping casually to the side. Her attention was not stolen away for several moments more, not until her line of sight was broken by a very old cat leaping over the body and rushing out of the room behind her.

Roman Kalichka, known around Oak Creek simply as Pan Kalichka had been Danylo Richovsky's closest friend in Canada. He was called Pan Kalichka at his work here in the city as well, though in this case it was simply because his boss had mistaken the title Pan as his actual name. He saw too little of the Richovskys these days, so after his daughter called, though she sounded rather distressed, he began to look forward to this chance to see Darko again.

Part of the reason he and Danylo had been so close was due to their shared affinity for things most would call folklore. *If it's real, even if it's just under the surface, I think folklore gives the misleading impression that it's all fiction.* He and Danylo had called it the Veiled World, and they had spent more than a decade in a sort of partnership managing it in and around the area of Acton. They had worked well together too, right up until Roman's retirement after losing most of both legs in a bog fire.

The humour was not lost on Roman how, after so much time spent in so many dangerous situations, the one thing that had put him out of commission was something totally ordinary and natural, just under the surface. True, the injuries had been sustained in pursuit of a salamander who had likely lit the thing in the first place, but it was, in itself, an injury entirely of this world.

Despite his retirement since before Danylo's death, the moment Roman left his vehicle, lowering himself into his wheelchair, he knew something was off here. The *veil* of the veiled world was pulled back, the air thick with dissipating power, like smoke lingering over an extinguished flame. He raced his chair into the apartment waved his way through the inner door, not bothering with the buzzer, and wheeled about the main floor, searching for the elevator.

'*Chortivnya!*' He cursed. He had forgotten that Darko's place was not handicap accessible. At least not past the first floor. There was a grizzled cat sitting at the base of the stairs eyeing him and it hissed with his curse.

'*Domovyk,*' he nodded respectfully and apologized, '*Vybachte.*' Seemingly content with the man's actions, the household deity scampered away up the stairs.

He fished his cellphone out of his pocket, and called his daughter.

'I know her!' Maria repeated more emphatically. *What is going on? How is this possible?* She was pacing back and forth in Darko's kitchen, hands tangled up in her hair and tugging roughly. *How, how, how, how, HOW?!*

'Well, quite pacing and tell us how!' Randy demanded.

'There's a picture of her and her sister in my house! Remember the kidnapping I stopped when I was ten? Well this is the sister of the girl I saved. She was kidnapped a weak before and burnt to death by some arsonist. It was around when my dad lost his legs, he was involved in it too. I'm not really sure how, but the police kept coming to our house and asking him questions about it.'

'So you're saying Jane's been dead more than ten years?' Darko asked skeptically.

YES! But before Maria could answer, Demir stepped in.

'The woman said she was a revenant. This was never her body. I believe you are correct, Maria, and I believe our father was also involved in this somehow. I have some vague memories of him talking about a murderous salamander…

'You said he's coming here right? I would very much like to speak with him.'

Just then Maria's cellphone started vibrating in her pocket.

It felt wrong, but they left the body there on the floor in Darko's entryway, and went down all together to meet Pan Kalichka. Demir was the first to speak.

'Good to see you again, Pan Roman. I know you're here to take Maria and Randy home, but I can't let you guys leave just yet. Not till you tell us about your work with our father. Your work with the "Veiled World" as he called it.'

Roman took a deep, steadying breath. 'This has been a conversation more than ten years in the making. Why don't you all come back to my place and we can talk about everything. I'll answer any questions you have and offer everything I can. I have a feeling this may well take all night.'

Frederic could not recall weeping before. Ever. And yet he had broken down with the pain twice earlier this day. He had done all he could for Nathaniel Bennett, both as an in-home care giver and in his capacity as an angel, but the man's time was at an end. Overcome with a fit of supreme weakness, Nate had struggled so hard with the strings on his pants that he soiled himself before finally calling Frederic for help. Frederic had known in that moment, had seen in the man's eyes, that he was done.

The line is in a different place for every individual. For most it's pain, emotional or physical, for others, like Nate, it was pride. Though in Nate's case it was not the act of asking for help he had a problem with, it was being a burden to his family that he could not bear. Frederic had read in the man's eyes, felt in the man's heart the natural, logical path, his thoughts had taken.

I will not *put them through this. They have suffered so much already, I can't be the one to make them go through all of this again. They have each other, they'll be fine. I can make a few innocent changes on my meds calendar to cover up. They never have to know, to know would be a burden in itself, so they won't ever know.*

He had asked Frederic to go out to get them some food and, understanding the impulse to be alone, Frederic had taken the vehicle one street over, out of sight of Nate's house, before returning on foot. He had stood outside the bathroom as, in a rare moment of stubborn strength, Nate shaved his face before swallowing a handful of pills.

Minutes later he stood outside Nate's bedroom, watching in his mind as Nate's body started from its drugged sleep. It went completely rigid, muscles straining, but there was no breath. Locked in that rigid position, suffocating, Nate was dead in a minute, his oxygen-deprived heart slowing to a stop.

There was no evidence of an overdose, and when Frederic called the ambulance and the police came to investigate the in-home death, they would all conclude the cancer had done its work. The Richovskys would, as Nate had known, be fine, maybe even better for lack of the burden. None of this, however, could take the weight from Frederic's shoulders.

He would call for an ambulance in a few minutes, he decided. For now, he slumped down to the floor and, for only the third time in his life, he wept. The first two times earlier that day had been out of the unbearable pain he shared with Nate. This time, however, the pain was his alone.

EPILOGUE: Stubborn Souls

It was more than twenty-four hours before Jane's lingering soul found a new corpse to occupy and was rejuvenated. Though she was whole and in a body once more, and though the body was human-enough to be comfortable, Jane was overcome with anguish. Shortly before her destruction, the cursed hob had banished her from that material plane where all her vile ancestors still lived. All those wicked descendants who had *still* never found her body, who had casually cast aside her memory as just another victim of time and circumstance.

She did not know which world she now inhabited, but she could feel them still on some other plane, her descendants. With a burning hatred, she could still sense those who had sent her here. They felt impossibly far. Like tiny dots marking villages on a map, the existence and position of certain souls were inked in her mind: family, enemies, the number had grown since last she'd found a body. She was eager to find them all. To make all those burning little dots go out...

Though often forgotten by the larger powers of the world, Sri Lanka sits, teaming with life, in the midst of the Indian Ocean. Northeast of her capital, Colombo, is an often-forgotten mountain peak known as Yakdessagala. At the top of this peak stands Kuvanna, an often-forgotten girl.

Though fluent in Sinhalese, Dutch, and English, Kuvanna preferred to speak the often-forgotten Vedda that her parents had taught her. She spoke it now to the night sky.

'*Meeattanne kiriamilaatto kalaapojjen mangaccana kota eeattanne badapojje kakulek randaala indatibaala tibenava.*'

It was a quotation of her people, the context and origins forgotten. '*When our great grandmother was walking in the forest there was a child conceived in her womb.*'

And I've followed shamefully in your footsteps, grandmother. A night of weakness, a lifetime of shame.

The boy she had thought of as her boyfriend had bragged about it online, her parents had found out, her teachers, her friends. She had not gone home after her friend told her, she had run. She had gotten on the first train out of Colombo, and she had run.

There was no child in her case, *guess grandma never heard of a condom,* but there was also no room for mystical forest lovers in the modern day, so here she was.

Kuvanna felt tired, exhausted with the lying, the words of appeasement, all of it. She had been the kind of girl others called a pillar of community, she had been academic, involved, socially conscious, all those things that make a parent smile. But none of that had been her, not really, so she had revelled in her night of freedom, rollicked and rolled in it, and no, she did not regret it. She only regretted her choice of companion.

And though so very many things could be so easily forgotten, Kuvanna knew that this could never be. She knew this was, would be, a permanent stain on her character. Worse than that, it would mark her parents—good, caring, community-minded people—as vile, amoral monsters who had raised this... this *slut* who corrupted such a good, academic and athletic boy. *Yeah, because he's the victim here.*

'Fuck you.'

Kuvanna jumped from the ledge, leaving Yakdessagala behind. She had decided making it quick would be best, so she took the strength from that moment of anger and ran with it—jumped with it.

The Sri Lankan suicide crisis was just another one of those things that was so often forgotten, and when the drama and dust of all this finally settled, her parents would no longer be the shapers of a monster, but the victims of a tragedy. Kuvanna was smiling by the time she hit the ground.

Milana blinked her eyes open and raised an arm to shield them from the light that shone down through the vibrant green overhead.

Pain.

The arm she raised was covered in bruises, dirt, and small cuts, but not a single burn marked it. She sat up and looked at the rest of her body. It was not her body. It was darker, covered in small scrapes and minor injuries. The hair that hung in a mess all around her was of a brown so dark it was nearly black.

From somewhere far away, deep within her mind, a voice groaned as if being forced awake from a particularly good sleep.

NO, NO NO! HOW AM I ALIVE? HOW DID THIS HAPPEN?!

Your time here is not yet done. Milana's words came reflexively rather than consciously, and with them came a flood of memories, of her soul joining the souls of the dying, giving them life, living alongside them or in place of them, of her soul living a hundred lives, a thousand! With this flood of memories came one memory shining brightly above all others, a soul that was a perfect counterpoint of her own, a true best friend if ever such a thing existed. She was overcome with a sense of urgency.

What is your name, girl? She knew she did not need to ask, the girl's mind, her thoughts, feelings, memories, they were all Milana's now. She could push this woman into oblivion for the rest of the time this body lived, she had done so with cruel souls before and could do so again, but this girl seemed nice enough, just confused, so she asked.

I AM KUVANNA.

Well, Kuvanna, it's nice to meet you. My name is Milana, and we're one now, for quite a while likely. I feel your pain and, though I do not condone it—I condemn it in fact—I can understand why you jumped.

I hope you'll come to see that no tragedy, no matter how severe, should ever be answered with suicide.

There was a feeling of embarrassment, it was not Milana's own. She rose to her feet, a bit awkwardly in this new body. It was miraculously unharmed aside from small, superficial injuries. Milana looked up at the mountain Kuvanna had leapt from and nodded.

But that is not to say this tragedy should go unanswered. You have been wronged, Kuvanna. We have been wronged.

She started walking down the slope, weaving through openings in the thick undergrowth of this forest.

Though I hope you'll agree with me that this wrongdoing should be dealt with mercifully, it must first be answered with justice.

Her feet soon found a steady rhythm and, as uncomfortable as it had been at first, Milana was finding Kuvanna's sustained presence reinforcing, as if she now had the strength of two women. And that was a most fortunate thing, she realized as a break in vegetation revealed the expanse before her and just how massive this mountain really was, for they had a very, very long journey ahead.

THE END

Made in the USA
Middletown, DE
16 April 2018